Sperm Soldier

EVETS ORNUM

PAGE PUBLISHING, INC.
New York, NY

First originally published by Page Publishing, Inc. 2019

ISBN 978-1-68456-618-1 (Paperback)
ISBN 978-1-68456-620-4 (Hardcover)
ISBN 978-1-68456-619-8 (Digital)

Printed in the United States of America

Iraq: The Revelation

The bone-wrenching roar of Mad Max's A-10 sent the al-Qaida insurgents diving for cover. Max looked over his shoulder at the ground below. Fire and streaks of rocket smoke filled the streets of Ramadi. With his radio tuned to ground chatter, he could hear the men's concern for locating the mortars.

Max's eyes stayed fixed momentarily on the dusty pink circles below. *How many in that convoy were dead from the massive IED?* he pondered.

His mind flashed to the pink frozen cranberry bogs he used to fly over back home. Sprinklers protecting the berries from frost would make circles of pink ice coating the maroon bushes. The airfield in which Max had learned how to fly was surrounded by these bogs.

It was his fuel alarm that brought him back into the present moment, and just in time. Whether it could be called luck, fortune, or a spiritual gift, that split second he stayed locked on those pink circles took him right over the twin tower mask.

Behind the walls he could see the mortar team scrambling. His Vulcan Minigun read 653. *Thirty seconds of hell,* Max thought as he punched the throttle and went ballistic.

When he hit twenty-five thousand feet, he throttled off and rolled American. Hanging inverted, he decided against the rules of engagement and nosed over, beginning his descent. Knowing the enemy was well within a safe zone, Mad Max switched to thermal.

With his fuel light flashing and heart pounding, he zeroed in. The nose of his A-10 screaming toward the mosque, he let loose a burst of the thirty-millimeter gun. Fiery sparks erupted as he touched off another hundred rounds, and at three thousand feet, he went Winchester. Pulling out, he split the twin towers, once again firing his tail flares, and headed east to Camp Fallujah.

In his wake was a Marine division with seven dead and nine wounded, along with several vehicles that were on fire. It was a well-executed ambush pinning the column in on both ends. The Marines gathered up the body parts of their comrades while Max gathered his thought. They were grateful for his defiance, their radio abuzz with Max's shooting.

Max knew he had violated the rules of engagement. He knew he would be punished, maybe suspended from combat, but he also knew that firing on that mortar team saved lots of soldiers, and he could live with his decision. He tuned in to the Felugia FOB and lowered his radio. He was flying on vapors when he made the call for immediate landing.

Max stood at attention. The base's commanding officer's office was a cool sixty-eight degrees, and the sweat on his neck made his hair bristle.

"At ease, Munro," said the CO.

Max barely moved. The CO kept his eyes trained on the information coming in on his PC.

"Son, you better pray your nose camera shows a mortar team behind that wall," the officer said sternly.

"Absolutely, sir," Max Munro replied.

The CO ordered the hog crew chief to upload the video as soon as possible. The feed was downloading without Max's knowing.

"What time were you over the convoy?"

"I received the call at 11:11 a.m.," Max told the man.

The CO slid the scroll to 11:10. "You roll in hot?" he asked, but before Max could respond, his eyes began to enlarge as he watched the approach from Max's warthog nose camera.

Max was one hundred feet off the deck when he passed the convoy.

"Want to explain the altitude, Major?" again, he asked sternly.

Max didn't hesitate. "Sir, the call was for roof sniper. I wanted to draw fire, sir. They were not on any roof. They were hiding in the upper windows, low and slow in position to rip 'em out, sir, until mortars began raining down."

The CO was glued to his monitor. He witnessed the destruction, the IED craters and fallen Marines, then only sky. He looked up briefly at his major, still at attention, and when he refocused he could see the mosque and courtyard in the center of the screen. As if it were a two-hundred-power zoom enlarging rapidly, three figures crouched behind the east wall appeared and then disappeared in a bloody whirlwind of dust and stone.

The CO stood up and saluted his pilot. "There won't be a request for investigation. I have seen enough."

Suddenly, the phone rang.

"Dismissed!" the commanding officer bellowed.

Max was hardly out the door when he heard his superior loudly ask, "What? Three right legs? What the fuck does that mean?"

There were no words of reassurance from the scientific communities, no medical explanation, no known phenomenon, act of nature, or birthplace screwup. There were three right legs and one soldier whose DNA matched all three!

As he lay in the bed, waiting to hear if his leg could be reattached, the medical team at Johns Hopkins pored over the strands in front of them.

"All have the same father," one doctor remarked. "It's the only possible explanation."

"No," a nurse technician commented. "My sister's husband had dead swimmers. She wanted to give birth instead of adopting, so they found what they considered a match at a sperm bank. She was artificially inseminated."

"So these three Marines, two of whom we can't question, all had impotent fathers? And then they all chose the same sperm donor? Is that what you're telling me?"

US Air Force photo by Master Sgt. Jeffrey Allen

Call sign "Mad Max" inscribed in Italian just beyond
the slanted eye of the sneering A-10

Confession

"I'm going with you." Mark's voice sounded rejuvenated.

Senator Cole paused. "Mark, you don't know what's in store. Best I go alone."

"No chance in hell, Joe. And I'm driving!"

Mark opened the garage door and removed the canvas cover of his prize Chevelle. The triple-black convertible 454-4 speed was a head turner in the seventies. Now? Well, this car was as rare as a Californian condor. A beast and symbol of American performance.

The screen door opened as a slender woman walked onto the porch. "Planning on selling her?" she said sarcastically.

"Nope. Just going to file her up for tomorrow. I'm taking her to see Joe."

The military hearing was set for nine fifteen at Andrews Air Force Joint Base in DC. Former senator Cole had called in to an old general friend and briefed him of the situation after hearing through a doctor about the three-leg case. Immediately the joint chiefs were notified and the best forensics gathered. Lavenger and Cole were going to face the music, an unthinkable, unbelievable muse of the decade orchestrated over fifty years ago. Music for Mark that would finally free his soul.

Lavenger pulled into the Washington Plaza Hotel at 7:39 sharp.

"No surprise here, Joe!" Mark said loudly as he pulled under the overhang, his voice nearly reaching Joe over the rumble of the motor.

"What's that, Mark?" Joe said, holding his hand to his ear, the other gripping his leather case.

"No surprise you're out front and ready, on time, Joe," Mark said, laughing. "Want the top up, or should I leave it down, Joe?"

Joe climbed in slowly as everyone who could notice did. "She sounds good, Mark. You take better care of her than Lisa!" Joe said, smiling.

Mark pumped the gas twice before easing out the clutch, then pumped it again as he eased to a stop. "I figure we take a drive around, stop for coffee."

Joe just clutched his briefcase and nodded.

As they drove around the capital, the two began to feel the pride of their work. The flag still flew red, white, and blue, and to these two old men, that meant a lot.

"Joe, I am going to speak at the hearing today," Mark said as he shifted his machine. "I have thought about it, and I don't want you to worry."

Senator Cole was a master in the political arena. Slowed by age, he was still formidable.

"I need to, Joe," Mark said, looking over at his longtime friend.

Joe said little. "The address on Luke Street, you got it?" he asked

"Yes. There is a garage around the corner. I will drop you in front."

Joe smiled. He knew Mark was looking out for him.

"Nonsense, my friend. We're pulling up front and walking in like we own the place."

Mark pulled up to 110 and shut off his car. The sounds of exhaust cooling were synonyms to the two men easing back into their bucket seats.

Joe grabbed Mark's hand. "Let's go see what they think they know, my friend."

Mark was not the least hesitant, but his age prevented any speed. The two headed in to Luke Street armed with the revealing truth and the willingness to fire.

The Beginning

The polished oak door closed with a clack, breaking the rhythm of her high heels, which were ticking like an amplified clock in the drab hallway. Shadows crawled along the wall, following Emily down to a gleaming corridor. Sunlight poured through glass doors, a blinding glare bleaching the floor.

Emily Strong shielded her eyes with her hand and exited onto a bustling street. Nervously she collected her breath and headed for the station. Thoughts of shame, morality, and uncertainty rumbled through her mind.

"God and country, God and country." The words from Mr. Lavenger were growing louder in her mind, drowning out the busy street. "You'll have time to think on the train," she reminded herself, focusing now on the departures: New Haven.

"Emily Fitzgerald: single mother, torpedo factory worker, lives in Derby, Connecticut, widowed during World War II. Her husband was killed in action on December 8, one day after Pearl Harbor, in the Philippines," Lavenger read aloud into the phone receiver.

"Yes, she seems very confident. I believe she is…patriotic… yes. I showed her the equipment and photo of the sergeant. She has till tomorrow to decide…yes. Under the circumstances, I believe he will…would I? In a New York minute! I take it you were successful with the others? I'll make the necessary arrangements…yes."

The Southern train car was cold and almost vacant. "Harlem to New Haven!" was the conductor's call.

Emily began running scenarios over in her mind. *And to what do you feel you owe your country? You are playing God. It's deceitful. What if he finds out? What if anyone finds out? Women on the assembly line would have sex with a supervisor to get promoted...or even just for a pair of silk stockings. This is different. This is important.*

Thoughts raced through Emily's mind. No wonder the ad was so vague. *They trusted me...why? Because of Matt? Were there others? Could I? Should I? The money, you need the money.*

There were more thoughts in her head than miles of track. At every stop, she had a new revelation.

"Next stop, New Haven!" called the conductor.

Mrs. Tyburski popped into her mind. *No worries there.* Emily sighed in relief. She will help. *She would watch Matty over the weekend. I will be gone three days...three days from Thursday. I will be able to get ahead, move away, start over.*

The bus rolled through scenic Orange, past the Maltby lakes and farms. Fresh autumn air blew through the open windows, lifting Emily's auburn hair as crimson leaves swirled past her window.

Autumn's crisp air brought a chill to her slender neck. Dishonorable thoughts hung in her mind as the bus slowed in front of Saint Michael's Church. Seduction, sex, and deception. *One more stop...the polish bakery. I have to speak to Mrs. Tyburski and then, if successful, go home to pack. I need to call, yes, call.*

"Department of Defense!"

"Mr. Lavenger, please."

"One moment."

"Lavenger! Oh, hello, Mrs. Fitzgerald. You arrived safely home?"

"Yes," replied Emily.

"Did you also arrive at a decision?" Lavenger asked.

"Yes. Yes, sir, I did."

"Good. I will make the necessary arrangements. A car will arrive at 2:00 p.m. tomorrow, and the driver will hand you a small suitcase. In it will be all the necessary information. Remember, Mrs. Fitzgerald, no one—I repeat—tell no one and you will have what you deserve. And our country....our country will never know. But your decision, Mrs. Fitzgerald...we will all benefit from your decision. Goodbye, Mrs. Fitzgerald."

Emily lifted up the picture from the stand and set it quickly upright, shamefully averting her eyes, then covering them as she wept into her hands. It had been two years since she last saw her Matthew alive. She had gazed at that photo a hundred times, wishing, praying to God to help get her through. Emily cried aloud and grabbed Matthew's photo. *It's in my hands now. I have to go! I have to give to our country, to our son! I have to, for me, and for Matty.*

Work in Connecticut was abundant, but hard. Factories lined the Housatonic River from Waterbury down through Shelton, Ansonia, and Derby. Men weren't scarce either, and attracting them was never an issue. Emily was a classic beauty for her day. Her slender, athletic frame could be wrapped in burlap and she would still turn heads. Wavy auburn hair and hazel eyes didn't hurt either. She had her mother's looks and her father's demeanor. "Growed up good," as they say in Ohio.

Strong Is the Gate That
Leads to Her Heart

The Strongs earned their living ferrying goods on the Ohio River. Emily learned responsibility, hard work, and determination were ingredients necessary for success. Her brothers and father worked the steam engines, and Emily would manage the books, collect fares, and sometimes even navigate the muddy water. Mrs. Strong ran their riverfront home and office. Martha Strong directed the flow of goods while raising her youngest child, Maxwell, a feisty young six-year-old.

Martha raised four children on the river, always mindful of the challenges, but it wasn't until Max that she found her resolve being tested, even as a seasoned parent. He had already worn out a path in the lawn to and from the woodshed. "Don't sass me, Maxwell," you would hear just before Max headed out the door for another bundle.

Carrying nearly his body weight in wood, Max grudgingly labored to feed the stove and fire. *He either likes being punished or he likes keeping a warm house!* Martha mused. Either way, Max kept things lively.

How he always seemed to know whenever his father was near could only be described as eerie. Martha would see Max running with York, his black dog, hell-bent for the dock, long before she heard her husband's whistle.

The *Annabell Rose* had a classic steam whistle like most of the ships navigating the burgs (as in newborn, Pittsburg, plats burg, etc). To the human ear, they sounded the same, but York could discern the difference. When she blew at the narrows some three miles downriver, his ears perked and he began to whine. It wasn't until Brandon, her eldest, told her of this that Martha realized how Max knew.

The trip from their home, Marietta, Ohio, to Pittsburg, Pennsylvania, was over 150 miles. Timing that distance was nearly impossible for a child. *I thought he visited with spirits for the longest time,* Martha thought. "I was too frightened to tell anyone in fear they would take him," she told her husband one night after she learned of his fascination.

Passengers Included

Ferrying goods was one thing, but people—that was a world all its own. Transitions for some, business travel for others. A three-day passage to Cincinnati on a riverboat wasn't the only option. There were trains and planes, motorcars, and even horses, but traveling on the river was an unexpected pleasure, even for the veteran traveler-sightseer. The scenery along the river could be considered a foregone conclusion. You passengers could walk around the porch-style decking of the *Annabell*, and the upper level even had a small snack bar complete with a sandwich menu. Commuters had their own cabins, sleeping two or four, and roomy stalls for their horses.

There were entertaining stops along the way, and most traveler folks adored the Strongs' home in Marietta, the favorite overnight stop for family and crew.

Marietta was a full day's ride from the dock at Pleasant Harbor. Once you hit the Ohio River, it was a downhill run cruising 10–12 knots. Passengers had ten to fifteen minutes to leave the ship for either business or pleasure at two of the four stops along the way. Other than that, they stayed on board, moving rhythmically regularly to the paddles' rhythmic chug.

On more than one, there were several occasions where a slick-tongued devil would try to tickle Emily's ear. She was confident and shrewd, and few ever received a reply. She learned how to read more than river currents and saw her share of fools.

Springtime water would swell the banks, making faster trips from Cincinnati up to Pittsburg. The frequency of the traveling vessel caught the eye of a young wharf rat the Strong boys called Fitsy.

The *Annabell* looked like most stern-paddled stern-wheeler ferries, but none had such a crew.

Fitsy's father worked a turnstile, the afternoon shift on the Allegany, and that was how Matthew Fitzgerald knew his way around the docks, well enough to have every schedule memorized. Timing the *Annabell Rose's* arrival was tricky, but Fitsy was the Houdini clairvoyant of Pleasant Wharf. Conveniently, he arrived just in time to catch a line and cleat her bow.

Playing it cool, he befriended Emily's brothers, helping them out when he could. Working hard and keeping track of the *Annabell's* goods, Fitsy earned a few free rides back west to Cincinnati. Brandon and Joseph kept him busy, stoking the burners, keeping up the steam, and tightening shifting cargo. They even, on occasion, had him feeding a few of the horses aboard.

He was a quick study and learned how to seat a valve, synchronize the port and starboard engines, and oil the pistons that powered the wheel. Fitsy made it a point to help out Emily too, not that she needed any, but it was a good excuse to try to win her hand. Emily played along but mostly acted aloof. Matt was just happy to be near her.

Emily and Matt shared more than glances on those long, slow rides. They became close friends, sharing stories, and sometimes even dreams. Matt, as Emily called him, was heading for the naval academy. Like most adventurous young men, he aimed high and hoped to become an aviator.

Emily admired his loyalty and courage in joining the armed forces. She let him go on about it being his duty to help the country's allies. She knew it was more of a "boy's adventure" but also knew of the dangers. Stories of horror and terror filled the papers as Europe was gearing up for war. Things were busy on the river, too, with the factory and mills in full production.

Captain Maxwell Strong was a seasoned navigator. He had experience in the waters from the Saint Lawrence to the Mississippi, where he traveled extensively from his youth till his midthirties, gathering a world of knowledge along the way.

Captain Strong wanted a family and a business, knowing he needed to be present to be both a husband and father. He harvested the knowledge of the rivers, selected a point of origin for commerce, and with the support of his wife, Martha, purchased the home in Marietta, Ohio.

The Strong Family

Max Strong worked for a company out of Wheeling, West Virginia, pushing a barge down the Muskegon River. Not an ideal job, but Strong had a plan. He would earn enough to pick up a salvage boat. If he found one that needed great repairs, he could store her in his yard and work on her in his spare time. His plan might have taken more time than was available initially, but things began happening to speed his dream along.

Bootlegging was becoming the number one way to earn on the river. Strong was offered big money by a number of different individuals tempting him to deliver "fragile freight." They had ships but no captains. Risk versus reward, a common dilemma, but Strong was cautious.

He sometimes worked the double shift, as they called it, smuggling booze in the coal barge. *Double shift* meant your pay was doubled! Strong wrestled with the idiocy of his risk—he could go to jail for double his pay! Not wanting the stress but needing the money, he, too, had to decide. If running booze could land him in jail, better quit while he was ahead.

Bootleggers and gamblers ran amok more often as time went on, having their cargo, and sometimes even their vessel, seized. It didn't take long to fill areas of impound, and auctions soon followed. River captains were increasing in demand. Offers were pouring in. Max wasn't about to become a bootlegger; he steered clear of that sort of trouble, not even allowing himself to indulge in hard liquor.

One afternoon, while he was working on the river, Max Strong's life was about to change. The *Annabell Rose*, a classic steamboat, was heading up to Zanesville, Ohio, pushing hard with a deep keel. She was loaded with eight tons of Tennessee brew. Her destination was Mock's Packaging Warehouse.

Strong slowed the coal barge at Fisher's Lock just south of Zanesville, a custom to onlookers. He noticed more men in suits than jeans, an odd sight for a normal day. Some in uniform. He knew it was a bust!

Don't sweat it, be cool, they don't even notice me, he thought. *Yeah, right.* "Backing down" and yelling at the tender. *Just a glimpse from that one guy...great, he went back to his paperwork.* Fisher's Lock was the only lock between Philo and Marietta.

"Hurry this guy along," an officer said to the locksman.

"She fills when she fills" was his reply. "Get! Hi-ya!" And the horses took their places.

Strong looked out the doghouse of the steam-powered barge at his two-man crew tending the lines. *Come on, come on! One foot of water—how long does that take?* Two teams of horses began to pull the cantilever, one on each side of the lock. The flag dropped, and Strong powered up steam.

The three-knot barge was fast for her day, but an eight-pound walleye couldn't have left Fisher's Lock faster. *Double shift! Double shit!* he thought. *Close one!*

Strong had stopped at Mock's for a pickup. He had the boys wrap the cargo in canvas and bury it evenly in the stern of the barge, keeping a natural grade on the coal. Strong's crew took care in burying the cases of booze deep and even.

"See, fellas?" Strong yelled out the pilothouse. "Took a bit of work, but it was well worth it!" Two sooty smiles of acknowledgment looked back, the gleam of their triumph cutting through their filthy faces.

"We're not home yet," Strong emphasized. "Just glad you boys didn't run!"

"Double pay, Captain Strong, double pay!"

So they weren't there for me... As soon as he got it out, twin steam stacks appeared on the horizon. *She's moving,* Strong thought. Black-and-white smoke billowed above the rigid tree line. *Someone is coming hard,* Strong mused. *He's who they're after.*

Strong had to yield at the curve in hopes of not running aground and giving way to the center channel. The *Annabell Rose* rounded the river bend and powered starboard. Strong folded one corner of a distress flag, signaling the steamboat captain, which was a common warning signal for that time. She was on a collision course with Ohio Valley Law Enforcement, who were patiently waiting three miles upriver.

The *Annabell* passed port to port. Impressed with her lines and powerful stern drive, Strong watched as she turned 180 degrees and powered back upriver, the trees along the bank vanishing behind her smoke. *What a boat!* Strong thought. *She was about to be impounded!*

It was late afternoon when Strong delivered the coal up the river to Vienna. Navigating home in his pram, he noticed a riverboat tied to the bank. Wooden planks extended past a sandbar into the forested shoreline, forming a crude but effective road. *Clever idea,* thought Strong, but he erased it from his mind as soon as it entered.

The man at the helm recognized Strong's hat and woolen jacket and blew a short whistle. Strong reluctantly turned toward her bow. Facing his boat upriver, he eased over within earshot from the enthusiastic captain.

"You saved my ass, pal!" shouted the captain, grinning from ear to ear. "I owe you one."

"Yeah," Strong said with a smile. "How about giving me the *Annabell* and we'll call it even?"

"Hey, not a bad idea. Maybe we can work something out!"

"Well, I'm heading home to Marietta. The white house past marker three, if you want to stop for dinner."

"I'll be finished here in three. Catch up to you at the Narrows," the man replied.

Strong was not naïve; he figured this guy was hot and was just looking for a place to lie low, but he did owe him a favor.

Martha Strong was preparing dinner when she heard a peculiar whistle. Looking out over the kitchen windowsill, she saw Max tying up his pram, and following behind him was a stunning riverboat. Strong, using his incredible foresight, had already begun expanding the dock at his riverfront home, accommodating such a vessel.

The river flowed west to east, and she eased along the dock starboard side. "Just the bow and spring line, friend!" shouted the captain. "I've gotta shut her down." He disappeared from the bridge, emerging moments after releasing steam.

"The name's Strong, Max Strong."

"Nice to meet you, Max." Wiping his hand on a rag, he shook it with vigor. "Bailey, Jon Bailey. Can't thank you enough."

"You were heavy in the water. Surprised you made it this far," Strong said.

"Luck of the Irish," Bailey replied, "and lucky you tipped me off."

Martha watched the men extend pleasantries and began to set another plate.

The walk up to the house usually only took a few minutes, but Max wanted to get a good feel for Riverboat Bailey before inviting him into his home. He showed him around his property, filling him in on the local trade.

Bailey was way ahead of him. "Max, I'm looking to get out. Today was my last run! My ship is a bit warm, but I own the paper on her and I'm looking to deal. Do you talk business at your table, Max, or should we continue out here?"

Max paused. "We will talk over dessert."

Brandon, Emily, and Driscol sat wide-eyed at the table. Captain Bailey was quite a spokesman. With his strong Boston accent, they hung on every word. He spoke of the island of Martha's Vineyard, where his family grew cranberries. How people would pay a local to take them bass-fishing in places named Cuttyhunk and Cleveland's Ledge. "A boat a lot like your father's pram could earn you a nice living out where I'm from," Bailey told them, padding his hand before dessert.

Martha was an elegant host, proper and respectful. Jon Bailey thanked her earnestly. "Why don't you let the children explore the *Annabell*, Max? Just keep them away from the steam."

"Martha, can you take them? Bailey and I were about to make a trade," Max said in a serious tone.

The Strong children raced down the hill and onto the dock. Emily was first to jump on board. They were ecstatic and scattered like mice, with Martha close behind.

Max was eager to hear Jon's proposition, leery still, but intensely curious. Jon kept it brief. "Max, I made a load of cash in the past few months. I bought this boat from an impound in Virginia. I have a buyer for her in Philly," he stated as he showed Max the papers. "I was going to head east after I unloaded and finalized the deal, but you really saved my ass, so now I have to make a choice. See, I just wanted to get my hands on some land back home before I take up again with a merchant ship crossing the Atlantic. I want to make sure I leave something tangible behind, in case I find myself at the bottom of the deep blue!"

He paused.

"Max, I will ask you for this. Your boat and $200 a month deposited into a bank of your choice, in an account in both of our names. Pay this for five years, and the *Annabell Rose* is yours."

Max did the math quickly. "Ah, $12,000? I could have bought her at auction in a month if I let you pass for half that!"

"Good point," Bailey replied. "How's $125 a month, same term?"

"You have all the papers on board?" asked Strong.

"Come on, Max, I'll show you around your new boat."

To San Francisco, Our First Soldier

The gray sedan eased to a stop with a squeak, sending a chill up Emily's spine. She quickly descended the porch steps and entered the rear door that the driver, leaning over the seat, had opened. *Such a gentleman,* Emily began to think sarcastically but embarrassedly stopped. *Who am I to judge any more? What if he knows?*

"Here, miss. Mr. Lavenger said you will have everything you need in here."

Emily pulled the briefcase over the seat.

"Just relax, miss. We have a two-hour ride to the airport. Sorry about your husband."

Mr. Lavenger had told her to use the pretext of her husband's death along with government red tape to justify her trip out to San Francisco. *I'm sure he is under that understanding,* Emily gathered.

The roar of the DC-3 was rivaled by the hard pounding pulse in Emily's throat. "No turning back now." After the brief but effective revelation, Emily settled back into her seat and opened the briefcase, quickly grabbing the manila folder.

The military envelope was sealed with a button and tied with wax string. Looking over her shoulder, she began to unwind the string, counterclockwise, three times. Feeling the smooth, recognizable texture, she pulled the photo out first. Thick dark hair appeared over the fold. Rugged and handsome, he brought her back to Lavenger's office.

Lavenger kept it simple and precise with the paperwork. All times and schedules were predetermined and exact. Emily was to go to Hemming Military Hospital in San Francisco. She'd aid in drawing blood from the soldiers who fought in the jungles of the South Pacific theater.

There she would first meet Sergeant Francis Munro. The description was brief but informative. Emily browsed his profile. "Munro" was what his fellow soldiers and friends called him. "His presence can be felt in a room," it read. "A decorated soldier from his service in the Philippines-Midway Guam. He was experienced enough for leadership, but his stubbornness has cost him advancement. His was an enlistment instead of the draft."

The more Emily read, the more she thought of her Matt. *Valor*, *honor*, and ultimately, *sacrifice* were the words that specifically entered her mind. She allowed the sadness in, and from it came a certain calm.

Thirty-two years old this month. Considerably older than Matt, but similar. "He's stubborn, daring, and confident. He grew up south of Boston in a town near Plymouth, Massachusetts, called Kingston. He came from a family of cranberry growers on Cape Cod."

Instantly, Emily remembered Captain Bailey and the *Annabell Rose. How could that be? That's no coincidence,* Emily mused. Reading on, she began to plan out a conversation, in case her looks and perfume failed to allure. "Wounded in battle, Medal of Honor twice, three Purple Hearts…" *This is no ordinary guy.* Emily began to feel a sense of pride and put her notes away.

On the plane, while the twin propellers hummed, Emily found herself in and out of consciousness, trying to sleep throughout the remainder of the flight. Even the turbulence over the Rockies failed to keep her up for long.

The Blood Trail

So far, everything was on schedule and going according to the plan. Greet and inform the soldiers, collect blood, and look for Sergeant Munro. The line, although orderly, was winding out of the door. The First Marine Division was island-hopping across the Pacific, cleaning out hard-held Japanese positions. Stealing any and all their jubilant youth.

Nurses were drawing blood, and Emily checked each form for completion. She weighed every soldier, noticing the same pattern of weight loss. Malaria strains varied in the South Pacific, creating this opportunity for an encounter with the sergeant. Emily became more relaxed with the assembly-line-like fashion of the hospital routine, and in her preoccupation, she did not recognize the sergeant from his photo when he did appear.

"Here, ma'am," said Sergeant Munro, handing her the form. Emily's eyes scanned the name: "Francis S. Munro." Her hands were now visibly shaking as she tried to steady the scale.

"Ah, 185 pounds. Sound right?" she asked.

"Heavier than I look!" he said while smiling directly at her.

"Here long, soldier?"

"Few days...rest and relaxation is all."

"Going to the show tonight?" Emily asked.

"No," he replied. "Been with these guys every day for nine months. I need a break."

"Who's holding up the line?" was heard from out the door, along with a few sounds of "Shhh!" alongside moans, ending with a murmur of "Munro."

"Well, miss...," Munro began.

"Oh, my name is Emily."

"It was nice meeting you, Emily."

"You too, Sergeant. Maybe I will see you later, I'm going out with the nurses, to Harry's. Why don't you join us? You and a few of your men."

Munro paused. Emily was stunning, and their eyes locked, causing him to stutter. "Y-yes. How's eight?"

"We get off at seven," replied Emily.

"Perfect. See you there."

Emily was full of emotion—joy, excitement, and courage. *I can do this. I have to do this.*

Harry's House of Cards!

Strings of seashells and woven palms decorated Harry's, an ironic setting for the men who had just been fighting in a tropical hell. Harry's was a popular place, with lots of sailors and Marines as its regulars. Some were in the First, but not Munro's platoon.

If you didn't notice the stripes, you would have mistaken him for an officer—he earned and exuded that respect from others. Slightly graying, the thirty-two-year-old was fearless under fire, and his willingness to speak out made him the man among his men. The thirty-six-man platoon that spearheaded the raid on the village in Saipan was now only twenty-one.

Weeks before, Sergeant Munro and his platoon were chosen to lead a raid on a Japanese stronghold. Their orders were to destroy a radio installation and ammunitions depot, gather intelligence, and destroy the enemy. Simple as that.

Captain Weathers, their superior, had an intelligence report on a Japanese base camp, and along with the sergeant, they formulated a plan to destroy the emplacement with one platoon and a few frogmen.

Input from an E-class soldier, although an experienced one, wasn't protocol, but in this case, it was necessary. Several prior raids in similar circumstances produced devastating losses, and they needed a fresh outlook. On the destroyer *Cassin* days before landing, Munro convinced his superiors that a night mission, establishing dominating positions prior to dawn, was imperative.

Intel put the Japanese soldiers on the western beaches in a special celebration, autumnal equinox. Frogmen from the *Cassin* destroyer mined the beaches and bobbed in the breakers for hours, waiting for the festivities to begin. Attacking an angry enemy fixed on revenge required cover from the darkness rather than holding back until dawn. Munro's plan made perfect sense, and night preparations were underway.

Munro's platoon came ashore farther south and silently worked their way into position above and around the village. Music filled the damp sea air, and the half-moon cast a dim, eerie light on what seemed a vacant camp.

Like a shark sensing its soon-to-be kill, one of the frogmen, a Filipino named Lamassa, swam along the beach beneath the waves, cautiously making his way ashore. His detonator bag was hidden and poised for devastation. It was his call. When he decided to detonate, hell would follow.

Hundreds of Japanese were scattered on the makeshift dock and shoreline. Munro's men were now ready. Three 50-caliber rifles were positioned on surrounding slopes in the jungle and the road heading up from the targeted beach. Around the village itself, men dug in the soft island sand. All in all, there were two motor teams, five light machine guns, sixteen M1 Garands, four 30-caliber water-cooled machine guns, two bazookas, and three flamethrowers. The men were wired tight and ready.

Munro made the rounds, checking his men's positions and passing out last-minute encouragement. He scattered a few of his best men among the squads who were green, and checked his Thompson one more time. As his bolt closed, the first series of explosions ripped up the beaches. The second wave was on delays farther up the jungle paths.

Sirens sounded and men scrambled. It was near 2:00 a.m. when the Marines opened up. Confusion and sake were their allies, and they made the most of the acquaintance. The Third Platoon fought hard, but so did the Japanese, stubborn to their last breath. Marines of the First Division were using anything and everything to snuff them out.

Horrific screams of anger and despair echoed between rounds. Familiar names were being drowned out by Japanese war cries and exploding shells.

"Smallie! Smallie!" cried a Marine.

"Stay down, Dewy!" yelled Munro. "I'll get him."

Jim Smallie was torching a bunkhouse, his silhouetted weapon making him a priority target. Just as his tank was running out, a bullet from an Arisaka 99 knocked him over.

Dewy was trapped by rapid fire and screaming for his friend. He was held tight to the ground. Smallie lay still, more in shock than dying. Munro stripped off Smallie's thrower and rubbed his hands over his torso. "Wet, shit." Smallie was hit bad, and the sergeant's cries for a corpsman didn't produce.

Hearing his sergeant shouting for the corpsman was too much for Dewy, and he sprang from his hole. Lighting up the jungle with a full magazine, he charged for Munro. His last thought was to save his friend as a Japanese bullet tore through his head. Now half of his skull was leaking from his helmet. Dewy landed a few yards behind Munro with a thud. "Dew!" the sergeant shouted, but it was too late.

Smallie had taken one in the chest. Munro managed to get him to the beach, where he found Andy, the corpsman.

"Three dead and three wounded and more on their way, Sarge!" Andy shouted.

"Look, this guy was hit in his chest, take care of him." That was the last time Munro saw Jimmy Small alive. He bled out on the beach. Higgins boats raced in, and the remaining men loaded the dead and wounded. The M1s could still be heard popping rounds, but they were becoming more sporadic.

Dawn gave way to a grotesque scene. Body parts were strewn all over the beach, a repulsive effect of the land mines. More than half of the Japanese division was destroyed, and the white sand looked like it was painted pink and red.

Munro searched the huts for surviving Japanese, torching every one he exited. The last Jap bugle called out at 06:00 in a futile attempt. A handful of Japanese soldiers emerged from a well-hidden bunker, only to be cut down by an avenging 50-caliber.

The officers' quarters remained upright among all the burning buildings. Ghostly shadows danced behind the flames on the jungle leaves, some reaching up to fifty feet tall. Images of fire and screams of the dead echoed above the ascending ashes, the souls of the damned released.

Marines surrounded the grass and wooden structure. "Stand down, men!" shouted a lieutenant, but they openly fired anyway. Orders from the lieutenant fell on deaf ears as each man emptied his gun. Lieutenant Campbell was pissed but understood their anger.

"Marines, to the beaches!" yelled Sergeant Munro.

"I need two men to sweep for intel!" yelled Campbell.

"JJ!" Munro ordered.

"Here, Sergeant!"

"You and G go with Campbell! I'm going to see the dead."

In total, there were six wounded, and nine men had lost their lives, among them Captain Weathers. Weathers was someone who Frank Munro considered a best friend. They had actually grown up near each other and had chummed around together in their younger years. Close like brothers, they even went through basic together.

Those were always the best fighters. Two friends next to each other in battle was powerful. Sergeant Munro had witnessed and participated in great acts of courage in the last eight months, and having a close friend in the platoon had made it more meaningful.

The sharp horn from the band brought Munro back to Harry's.

"Hey, you okay, Sarge?" asked one of the men, a private named Foley.

"Yeah. Better now, Fole, thanks." His eyes now focused on Emily. The eyes, which could peer through an island jungle, now cut through the smoke-filled bar.

For the first time in nine months, the Third Platoon's feet was on American soil. The fighting Marines were now surrounded by a jungle of beautiful young nurses. The girls played along, happy to be out on the town with a bar full of soldiers.

Private First Class Lang, choking up, held his glass in the air, and in the midst of the crowded bar, he shouted, "Raise your glasses and lend an ear!" Slowly the crowd silenced. "My friends, raise 'em up high! For tonight was a gift, a gift from two fallen Marines. Smallie! Dewy! Thanks for sharing some of your heaven and not hogging all

the angels, because I'm surrounded by some tonight! Thanks, boys!"
They all held their glasses high in the air for the two fallen Marines,
James Smalley and Robert Drewhan. Then they bowed their heads
and drank to their sacrifice.

It didn't take long for Emily and Sergeant Munro to hit it off,
and they shared several stories, often shouting at each other to beat
the band. Some were funny family stories, some serious and personal.
Every story Munro told he would time so he could drink its final sip.
Breathing into it, he would place the glass quickly upside down on
the bar.

"Why do you do that? At the end of your stories, breathe in
your glass and turn it over?" Emily asked.

"To leave a little of the story, and maybe a little of me, right here
soaking in," Munro said as he confidently grinned.

Several stories and several drinks, along with some welcomed
contact, abolished both anxiety and time, and with it, all their
friends. Noticing the bar was near empty when they climbed out of
their booth, they laughed simultaneously.

Frank extended his arm to Emily, and she used it for balance,
causing the sergeant to temporarily lose his balance! As they walked
to the door. Emily placed Frank's arm around her shoulder. He
pressed her slender frame against him. Before he took another step,
Emily squeezed him tight.

"You're a real man, Mr. Munro. Some lucky gal you have back
at home," Emily teased, stuttering slightly.

Munro's head was spinning from the booze. "None like you."
He spoke honestly but laughed jokingly. "Emily, I thought about you
all day. I had forgotten about home, about women. I had my hands
full keeping these crazy kids alive, erasing the horror. Trying to hold
on to a nice thing, a pure thing, it's so hard, Emily…" His voice was
somber.

Leaning in to kiss her, he smoothly moved the hair covering her
neck with his nose. Slowly he drew in her scent, ever slightly touching the lobe of her ear. His next reaction startled even himself.

"I smell your perfume, and I'm gone! Off this rock! Woooo!"

"Okay, okay, you need to quiet down! Those MPs are beginning to notice you!" Emily jokingly whispered.

"Those guys wanna try and bust me to get me away from you! Boy, I'm better off not talking!" And with that, the sergeant kissed Emily long and hard, and then soft once more. He took her hand, and they made it outside Harry's without incident.

Emily was just a mess inside; part of her liked him, and part was feeling guilty and ashamed. But he was a good kisser, and before she knew it, she was under his arm again in the back of a cab.

Emily slid the condom off the sergeant and headed to the bathroom, her thermos of dry ice hidden behind the towels. Nervously she unscrewed the top and dropped it in. Instructions were to deliver it to the base mortuary, where it would be thoroughly frozen and shipped to the cryogenics lab in Los Angeles. It could be in the thermos for six hours and not a minute longer.

Emily paused before she moved toward the bed. Munro softly moaned in a yawn-type stretch. He slid over, tapping the bed. "Come on, darlin', I'm not gonna bite you now." With that, Emily was eagerly under his muscular arm. "Thank you, Emily..." were the last words she heard from him as her head hit his chest.

Munro woke to an empty room and an envelope. She had left a picture and an address along with a note: "To Frank Munro, a true savior." That was all.

Phase Two

"What do you mean *involved* with the funding?" Lavenger hollered into the phone, pounding his fist on his desk. "A senator! And he wants to discuss morality?" His face now flushed from his temper. "Look, you set up a meeting here, not some public place where he can filibuster me! Here! And soon we have problems of our own! I'll explain tomorrow when we meet. I'm driving down with Cole!" he said, hanging up the phone without any confirmation. "My team's data wasn't sufficient for the investors," Lavenger muttered. "He needs convincing! Some things must be both flesh and spirit, I presume! Being from Virginia!"

Lavenger closed the latch on his briefcase and leaned back in his chair, placing his feet on his desk and crossing them. He started tapping the switch of the desk lamp with the side of his foot, click off, click on, his method for calming himself. No particular tempo, just moments of darkness followed by light, in redundant discipline. His mind ripping over his strategy for phase two.

The drab olive Plymouth P11 had just pulled to the curb when Lavenger stepped past Charlie, the doorman.

"The early bird gets the worm," chuckled Charlie.

"Yes, and the wise owl is in bed before dawn!" was Lavenger's reply as he slid in the open suicide door.

"Morning, Joseph. I knew you would be early. Some things never change."

Joe was a lifelong friend of Lavenger's. Joseph Turner Cole, a military strategist and West Point graduate with political connections

32

in Boston, New York, the Vatican, and God knows where else. If Joe couldn't talk a man down, no one could.

"Joe, I will get you up to speed on the project. You may have a solution before we reach Underhill. Our research lab in Richmond is making headway, and we need additional funding for the bovine insemination. This location will be a front for these cattle, being close enough to Richmond in case any type of emergency may arise."

"A valuable consideration," added Joe.

"The pastures and security fencing will be explained plainly by the bovine observation," Lavenger continued. "Now, Joe, what have you heard of the war and our boys?"

Cole was pressed in the corner of the sedan, his hat barely showing his eyes. Looking out the window, he began, "Well, Mark, our advancement in Europe depends on the supply lines. I have suggested we employ a torpedo plane platform, like a mini carrier mixed with the escorts, overlapping and weaving routes. Also, we stagger shipments and diversify routes as well as deploy bombers out of Greenland. If we don't destroy that wolf pack, well, that war may go on forever!"

"Not without soldiers to fight, it won't."

"True enough, Mark. What about *our* boys?"

"Joe…"

"Unfortunately, Mark, there are many, but it has been a challenge to arrange these dates before one or several are killed."

"How many do we have so far?"

"Forty-four. Forty-four that I could set up out of one hundred and thirteen. I believe we have the diversity needed for the long-range plan. There are hundreds of recommendations coming in every day—pilots, sailors, and of course, Marines. I even had a pair of brothers come in. Their bravery reinforces our objective and may be something you can use on the senator," Joe replied to Lavenger.

"You know about that?"

Joe chuckled. "Yes, Mark. Would I be any use to you if I didn't? So how about you, Mark? How is it in your theater?"

"You know, Joe, you just need to get them back to San Francisco upright. Malaria-free and able to keep 'em sober enough to finish the job."

"Sounds simple enough."

And they both laughed.

The ride to Richmond was uneventful, other than the near miss of a rutting deer along the Delaware water gap. Cole's driver hadn't said a word for two hours, so when he spoke, both men turned an ear.

"There's a diner coming up. Place is pretty good. It's clean and busy. I recommend the hash."

"Thanks, Peter," Cole replied. "I think we we'll take you up on it."

The Underhill farm in Skinquarter was the perfect location for their growing experiment, well off the beaten path and naturally surrounded by the rolling hills. Three hundred acres of electric fencing and tall wire to keep the deer out. There were separate grazing fields of alfalfa, clove, and rye, two silos, and a livestock barn. It was just what Richmond wanted for the bovine, and just what CUF needed for their soldiers.

CUF stood for Courage Under Fire, a proper name for their project. Years of research in human culture and destroyed civilizations brought the three men to this farm that November day. Their plan was near completion.

The men stood silent looking at the farmhouse. Michael Robone, Mark Lavenger, and Joseph Cole, three men who concocted a revolutionary plan one night after dinner at Cole's house in Arlington, Massachusetts. They had concluded that the only reason civilizations fell, like the Jews in Israel, was that they had lost their courage to fight.

The initial conversation resulted in an argument that had taken three years to settle. It included every angle of what made a man courageous. Was it a gift like the Catholic Church and Christians believed? An invocation by a divine spirit, or the strengthening of one's own? Was courage more of an instinctive quality, something we were all born with, like a cornered rat or protective mother lioness, or was it like the champion horses' will, coming from a long line of genes, traits from parents and other ancestors?

The research was fun at the beginning, with frequent dinners and meetings over theories, but sobering when more evidence was being stacked on the gene pool. It was going to take more than historical corroboration to get funding for such a project.

Artificial insemination had only recently succeeded in New Haven. Doctors were trusting their hopes on stronger, healthier, and bigger cattle. It was Cole with his political ties who made this argument a resource of their idea.

The three men entered the Underhill farmhouse, furnished in traditional decor, with a formal living room. The men sat at a table, unloading their briefcases. Mark sat at the table's head. "First, let me get to the possible threat, *possible* because I don't know enough about this anthrax and tuberculosis that seems to be prevalent among the bovine specialists. I have been told that both of these doctors we have chosen contracted one or both of these diseases and they will be quarantined indefinitely, leaving our third choice, Dr. Havock, out of Cambridge. Cole, you have the file on him?"

"Right here, Mark."

"Okay, the nurses we chose are from the Midwest, both in pediatrics and general medicine. Both have military backgrounds. Michael, do you have their files from our investigator?

"Yes, Mark, right here," he said, handing it to Lavenger.

"Now, this house will be known from now on as Underhill. Simple enough, Joe? I have a team coming here this Friday to begin construction of the freezer and lab. I have the drawings and the layout, including the insemination room. The women can stay here for as long as necessary. We can leave the upstairs as it is and concentrate on this room and the lab. Funding will be under Richmond Bovine. Their workers and rustlers will be forbidden from the house. All involved will be screened beforehand, and a strict protocol of rules will apply." Lavenger, now smiling, continued on. "Michael, now, what can you tell me about this senator and how he found out about CUF?"

"Well, I wanted to tell you before we hung up yesterday, Mark, that he was involved in the Bovine funding. He's worried that if the news of government-engineered cattle in his district reaches the mainstream news, he's finished!"

"And he needs some financial reinforcement to persuade him otherwise?" Cole remarked.

"Of course," Mark added. "Talk about a hypocrite, thinking selected engineered cattle is immoral in this district! Has that idiot even been out in these hills? Mothers, sisters, cousins making up generations! Albinos running around like laboratory mice! Oops, sorry, Mike, your wife is from West Virginia, right? What is it they say about their women? If they ain't good enough for our family, they ain't good enough for yours?"

"Oh, I'll tell you what," Mike replied. "Next time you're at the house, you ask her." And some laughter followed.

Mark Lavenger started again. "Okay, gentlemen, let's agree, nothing specific over the phone. We meet here at Underhill one month from today with the doctor and nurses. Michael, continue compiling the lists of all the widows eligible for this project. Joe, we need a few of the women we used in stage one to convince and/or persuade the widows to partake. Do you have any in mind?"

"Yes, I do, several who proved valuable. What about you, Mark?" Joe Cole replied.

"Yes, one in particular. Can we agree on a number? Six?" Lavenger asked.

"Make it seven, Mark," Joe said.

"Have you come up with a price, Joe?"

"We can make it performance-based for our girls. Let's set a price for the mothers. Michael?" Joe asked.

"Based on the current cost of living, I will estimate it taking $8,500 on average to provide basic needs for a child for fifteen years."

"Wait, wait, you're not suggesting we give these women $8,500 and send them out the door pregnant, are you, Mike?" Lavenger asked.

Robone replied, "Well…on top of the $20,000 they received in death benefits, I think they may manage. What do you suggest, Joe.?"

"We don't just want to plant our country's future seeds and not water them, do we, gentlemen? Let's establish a fund and provide monthly support. That way, we know where these kids are and can more readily find out what we are paying for," Cole put forward.

"Okay, who's paying for this one, Joe?" Mark asked.

"Don't worry, guys like Senator Clemons grow on trees, and besides, this bovine process will net a nice, steady supply of cash. Meanwhile, I will get the government going on a widow's fund especially dedicated to children in or out of the womb."

"We will need more than just the thought of having their loved ones back in child form, Joe," Mike added. "We need to offer them something. I was thinking $5,000 up front."

"We have that kind of money, Joe?" Lavenger inquired.

"Mark, you worry too much about money. We have more than enough," Joe Cole assured. "Gentlemen, this is something we can someday feel proud of! We will never receive a medal, or fame, or honor, but this is our gift to America. We will soon find comfort in knowing that our sperm soldiers will never let our country be taken without a fight!"

"Amen," Mark stated. "Amen!"

News from Marietta

"What's that dog barking at, Max?" Martha Strong asked while tending to her husband. York was yelping outside.

"I don't know. I think I hear a car or something," her husband replied.

The dry leaves strewn across the gravel driveway made a crunching sound beneath the taxi's tires. The vehicle crested the road and slowed downhill toward the Strongs' home. Mrs. Strong watched from her bedroom window while tending to Mr. Strong.

"Who is it, dear?" Max asked.

"Oh, it's Emily, and she has Matty with her!" she said with excitement.

Martha hurried down the stairs.

The cabbie retrieved Emily's things from his trunk and remarked, "Hey, I remember this place. You're one of the riverboat people! Yeah, I took that boat up to Cincinnati to visit my folks. I remember that dog! He was always jumping off the dock, retrieving sticks."

"Yup. That's my dog, York!" Max Jr. replied, coming out of the house.

"Nice place you have here, ma'am."

"Thank you," said Emily, handing him his fare, plus a hardy tip.

"Thank you, ma'am, thank you. Nice to meet you."

"Nice to meet you also."

Emily watched the taxi drive off with York chasing behind. Drawing her breath as if for the first time, she bent down and hugged her little brother, squeezing him tight. "I missed you, Max, I missed you."

York returned and introduced himself to Emily's little Matty, who was desperately trying not to fall from the exuberant greeting. "Easy, boy," Max said, calming his dog.

Emily's eyes started slowly toward the house, climbing each step in her mind. Martha was standing on the porch, crying, when their eyes finally met. "Emily," she said, her voice starting to crack. Emily ran up the stairs.

"I'm so sorry, Em, I should have told you sooner. I'm so sorry."

"Shhh…Mom," she replied. "It's okay."

Pulling away, she called for her Matty. "Come see your nanny, Matty. Mom, I want to see Dad. Is he…?"

"He's fine, Em, go on. He's in our room."

Emily ran up the stairs, heading for her father.

Bittersweet was the news of Emily's return. The conditions were dour, but knowing his daughter was home strengthened Max Strong. His stroke left him blind in one eye and with weakness in his shoulder and arm.

Returning home to help with family business was what Emily and Matty needed. She did not return home empty-handed. Besides her son, Matthew, she brought determination and hope back to the Strong household. The five thousand dollars in cash wasn't necessary, but welcomed relief.

The *Annabell Rose* was dry-docked after Max's stroke. Business stopped completely with the boys off at war, and the family's savings was dwindling. Not wanting to add to her daughter's burden, Mrs. Strong tried keeping the news from Emily, hoping Max would recover quickly.

Emily had stayed in Derby, working in one of the factories, being a good wife and mom. Things were hard after Emily married Fitzy and left for New Haven. Brandon was killed while on deck duty on the USS *Hornet* some eighteen months ago. Driscol was part of an amphibious force in the European theater. They had not heard from him in six months. Max Jr., well, he would run the boat if his parents had let him, but nine-year-old river captains were in short demand. Having Emily back was just what Martha needed, and little Matty was the best gift of all.

"Dad, let me help. You can do this, I promise. Look, we can make those upgrades with the money I saved, have her repainted. Max and I will help you. I wrote out some advertisements I want you to read. One eye and all, Dad, you have to read these. I know this seems sudden, but you need to get back on your feet, Dad," Emily compassionately said.

Max Strong lay speechless, having already swallowed his pride months ago after the realization that the *Annabell* would be out of commission hit him harder than his stroke.

"First it was you, Em, then Brandon, then the *Annabell*...all gone. I was hoping to see one of you one way or the other—"

"Stop it, Dad! I'm here, and I promise everything will be fine. There are so many soldiers returning home and visiting family. We can get the route back, you will see," she said.

Max pushed himself up with his right arm. "Em, where is that little Matty? I want to see my grandson."

Emily helped her father get back on his feet, running advertisements in the Cincinnati and Pittsburg newspapers: "Relax and enjoy the view while traveling in comfort and style! All aboard the *Annabell Rose*, the riverboat queen, departing Pittsburg 10:00 a.m., arriving in Cincinnati! Monday, Wednesday, and Friday!"

Request for Service

Emily's enthusiasm returned with the lists of new projects readying the *Annabell* for Spring. Max Sr.'s desire to work returned also, even if his affliction staggered the pace. Keeping their minds off their problems, the two of them managed to draw up some plans that included heating a tent covering to get an early application of paint on the vessel. The interior of the boat and its engines were cleaned and prepped. All toll, Emily estimated the work at $4,300. A risk she felt was worth the reward.

"You remind me of me, Em," Max Strong stated proudly one day as he panned over the numbers. "And we're going to need to charge more."

"It will be worth it, Dad," Emily replied, smiling.

"Christmas is right around the corner. Let's see if we can get a better deal from some of the fellas at Jessy's boatyard. I'll have your mother take me down there tomorrow."

"Thanks, Dad. You up for it?"

"Yes. I'll wear that eye patch your mother made me. Matty will get a kick out of it!"

Emily and her father had never felt closer, and each day that passed brought more and more reasons to smile.

York was becoming Matty's best source of entertainment. Anything he threw into the snow, York would plow around nonstop until he found it. Sticks, rocks, toys, anything.

It was just before Christmas 1943 when another taxi appeared on the Strongs' drive, stopping up front, blowing the horn. "Telegram for Mrs. Emily Fitzgerald!" the driver hollered, stepping out of his vehicle.

Martha collected the telegram, clutching her chest.

"Sorry, ma'am, for startling you. I don't think it's bad news. Looks official, though."

"Thank you," Martha said. She looked at the letter. It was from Richmond, Department of Agriculture. From a Mark Lavenger. *What on earth is that girl up to?* she thought to herself.

Emily returned home from the boatyard with her dad. Sitting on the table was the telegram, but she hardly noticed. "You have a telegram, Em, from the Department of Agriculture."

Emily lifted the letter, her eyes immediately focusing on the name Lavenger on the envelope.

"What is it, Em?"

Emily's heart sank. "Nothing. Nothing, really. I applied for work everywhere before heading back."

"Well, open it, Em," her mother coerced.

Emily nervously opened and read the contents:

Dear Mrs. Fitzgerald,

I hope this letter finds you in good spirits. I am writing you in order to thank you for what you have done and respect your decision to dismiss further offers. I do, however, have another matter that I believe is more suitable for you, and it would help our cause tremendously. Please accept my offer to meet Thursday in Richmond. I have arranged the fares. In part, we are searching for a woman to provide comfort to fellow widows, like yourself. The work requires travel compensation, and other incentives also await. Please consider meeting with me, Mrs. Fitzgerald. I hope to see you Thursday.

Mark Lavenger

"Well, what did it say, Em?"

"Oh, I volunteered at a veterans hospital in West Haven a few days a week. Now they want me to take my act on the road. I guess only to the wives of fallen soldiers."

"What do you mean, Em? How does that make sense? The Department of Agriculture...?"

"I'm not sure about the department, Mom. You know the government. I do recognize the name Lavenger. Dad and I are ahead of schedule. I think I may go. It's only a half day."

"Okay, Emily, I'm sure you could use the money, seeing you spent all yours on that boat!" Martha said.

Her dad remarked, "I'll give you a ride to the station. What time does that letter say?"

Richmond

The train settled in a squeal just as passengers began moving about. Emily reached for her suitcase, noticing for the first time the teeth marks on the belt strap, no doubt a souvenir of Max's dog, York. More confident than she had felt at her last arrangement, Emily stepped onto the platform, shoulders squared. Curious and confident.

A man in a trench coat held up two signs, one read "Fitzgerald" and the other "McAdams." Emily began walking toward him when she was bumped into a slender woman with a suitcase in each hand.

"Excuse me," she said, stepping in front of Emily. "I'm Mrs. McAdams."

Oh, perfect, Emily thought as she introduced herself, reaching out her hand. "Hi, Emily Fitzgerald."

Lisa McAdams dropped her luggage and shook with both hands.

"Nice to meet you, Emily. Was it a long trip for you?"

"No, not so far. Pittsburg, actually. And you?"

"Okay, ladies, you two can get acquainted on the way," said the driver, snatching up their luggage.

The ride to Underhill was anything but quiet, with Lisa chatting up a storm. She relayed her adventures in Italy and England, where she met several of the hero soldiers, whispering in Emily's ear as to the number she had accumulated.

"Oh my god!" Emily said.

Lisa paused, then asked, "How about you?"

"One! One!"

"Well, I hope he was a good one!" Lisa said, and they both laughed. "Did you sleep with him?"

"Shhh...keep your voice down! Yes," Emily whispered.

"Oh, that's why—"

"What do you mean?" Emily asked, cutting her off.

"I don't know. You're not from my neck of the woods, I know, but I would really have to like a guy before I slept with him," said Lisa, now confusing Emily.

"So how did you...? Well, how could you have sixteen men and, well, you know."

Lisa smiled. "Honey, I would get them so worked up before I got them alone all I had to do was slip the condom. Then all they could do was make excuses and promises, saying they'd make it up to me in the morning. When morning came around, my sudden headache would incapacitate me, and I'd then send them on their way. I felt bad, but nothing like I would have if I slept with them."

"I hadn't thought of doing anything like that. I saw Frank, and he was so damn handsome, and I lost my husband..." Emily stopped.

"Oh, Emily, I'm sorry to hear that. I never married myself, but I'm sorry for your loss."

"Thanks, Lisa. Let's talk about something else. What about Lavenger? What do you think of him?"

"Who, Mark Lavenger? Oh, Mark, well, at first I thought he was kind of creepy...I wasn't sure. But after, when I was in Europe, he always sent me letters telling me how proud he was I volunteered. He even sent me flowers on my birthday!"

Barnyard Preparations

"Underhill is just ahead, ladies," announced the driver, making eye contact with them in the rearview mirror. Lisa reached into her purse and pulled out her favorite shade of red lipstick.

"So you must have liked those flowers," Emily remarked to Lisa.

"Yes, yes. And he's no boy either."

Lavenger was on the porch when Lisa and Emily arrived. "Welcome, ladies! There are refreshments inside. Come in out of the cold."

Moments later, another vehicle arrived. "There will be six of you here today," Mark commented. "The lavatory is at the top of the stairs, and your place at the table has already been determined."

Two women came in, Christine and Jennifer, greeting Mark with a smile. "You two can entertain yourselves. I have to make a call."

Lavenger had to prepare himself. He went into the other room and stood over a table, gripping the corners. He repeated to himself, "Steady, you fool." In front of senators and businessmen, he was a tiger; however, his demeanor changed in Lisa's presence, and he found himself in unfamiliar territory. Sure, he had had relationships, but mostly for convenience. Something about that woman drove him wild.

His thoughts were interrupted by the sounds of the third vehicle. *Thank God! Joe's here.*

As he looked out the window, his relief was reinforced when he saw Cole extending his hand toward the rear door of the sedan.

Which one is it, Jackie or Arlene? He saw black nylon and a shiny black shoe, then long black hair. *Arlene, definitely.*

Slowly standing from the ride, Arlene looked up at the farmhouse, the brisk winter air causing her eyes to flutter. "Go on in, Arlene," Joe suggested, holding out his hand one more time.

Jackie, still in the back of the car, looked up at the driver. The vinyl seat rubbing her bottom as she slid across made an unflattering sound, causing both to smile. "Don't blush on my account, ma'am. I know it's the seat."

Jackie just smiled and grabbed Joe's awaiting hand.

"Come on, Jackie, let's get this party started."

The farmhouse at Underhill had a far more relaxing atmosphere than their previous encounters' locations. The dining room table, where holiday meals were celebrated, still had napkin holders and a centerpiece, a small Dutch farmhouse with a windmill attached and salt and pepper shakers on either side.

The girls introduced themselves to one another as Mark checked the folders laid out around the table, making sure Lisa's was next to him.

Joe was pouring drinks and handing them out like a professional bartender. Slow and steady. It was hard to rattle Joe, unless his wife walked in.

Jackie had, by far, the biggest personality, with a contagious laugh and a big, beautiful smile. Her past was a tangled story of horror and uncertainty, but she hid it well behind her smile.

Christine and Jennifer had met in Europe and had worked together before. Christine lived in California, and they planned on staying the night, not wanting to sleep on the train. Jennifer was from Missouri, and she had grown up on a tobacco farm. Neither had met Mark or Joe, and they were recruited by Mike Robone, or Michael, as they called him.

Christine was a bright woman whose father was a drunk and whose mother had been overwhelmed in misery. She was surprisingly confident, however, her perfect posture almost more alluring than her pretty face. She was both stylish and outgoing.

Then there was Jennifer, who would be more relaxed on a horse in a lightning storm than in the Underhill dining room, never considering herself to be that attractive, which was an attractive quality in itself. She fidgeted with her hair and tugged at the hem of her dress while conversing, quick-witted and from a long line of Confederate patriots.

Jackie and Arlene had already met at the station. The two were opposite bookends with nothing in common except their work with CUF.

Arlene was quiet and very sexy, with jet-black hair. Her accent was slightly European, and her eyes dark, like her hair. Her family, sensing trouble when Hitler became chancellor of Germany, vacated and headed for America. Just twenty-three years old, she was educated and reserved.

"Ladies, can I have your attention, please?" Mark announced, standing at the far end of the table. "It looks like I'm casting a Hollywood movie here instead of trying to save our country, but amuse me if you will and take your seats at our table!"

The women looked over their places, their names on each folder. Joe walked behind Mark and pulled down a map of the United States, different sections outlined in six distinct colors.

"You may have noticed the color tabs on these folders are the same as on the map behind me, but before we begin, I want to thank you all for accepting this offer. For your loyalty, and most of all, for your continued secrecy in this plan I am about to expose.

"Thirty-eight years ago, this nation was involved in a war that destroyed almost two million American men. Moreover, most of these men were fathers who left tens of millions of children behind to be raised by their mothers. So some of you are thinking, 'No big deal,' right?" Mark received a few nods. "Well, we at CUF believe it was a big deal. Boys raised without men are more likely to take on the personalities of their mothers. Fine if their mothers were Joan of Ark, but the reality is that men who are sensitive make lousy soldiers.

"Joe, Mike, and I have spent years searching for that common thread that undermined the greatest nations in history. We, together with hundreds of years of war records, agree that most nations ultimately were eliminated or overthrown because they simply ran out of men who were willing to sacrifice their lives for those of their countrymen. Yes, there are examples of tactics and acts of God that could sway this argument, but the unnerving truth is that in war, there must be warriors.

"These men you have all met are such warriors. Looking into their lives as best as we could, we find no common denominator as to heritage or geographical location, race or religious belief. All we see that makes these men different from most is courage. Some say courage is a gift, true. God can turn water to wine, yet some of these men practiced no known religion. What makes these men different may be in their genes, the same as a champion stallion or prize bull. Here at the Underhill farm, our government is investing millions in a project to inseminate cattle from champion livestock to raise a herd of likewise heifers.

"Every minute of every day, we are at war. Women like you are losing their men. They are dying in defense of freedom and democracy on shitty little islands in the South Pacific and broad-ranging war fronts in Europe. Some here have felt that loss in their own lives. Emily Strong lost her husband while training natives in the Philippines. Arlene, I see you lost a brother. We all love this country, and that's why we're here, and if successful, this will be our greatest hour. Unfortunately, no one other than ourselves will know the method of this plan.

"Why you are here is far more important than what you are here for! All of you will be paid handsomely, if you will take this to your grave. CUF is not known by our government. This is a private undertaking with government backing. Some of you may be thinking this isn't possible. I say to you this: Booze was illegal for twenty-nine years, and there were still drunks on the street. Our government is busy looking left while we are walking right. This house, soon to be a facility for insemination, will be the first of its kind. If we can find others who will also agree with this ideology, then we will open more, but for now, it is just us. We are the fathers and mothers of our Sperm Soldiers.

"Earlier I mentioned the widows who are receiving letters, hundreds each and every day, containing the somber news that their husbands will no longer be in their lives. Some are alone, and some with children.

"The soldiers you have engaged with were selected not only by their heroism but also by what we consider to be a wide range of genealogy. Some were Greek, some Italian, Irish, Scottish, blue-eyed, brown-eyed, red-haired, etc. We feel we have an adequate supply to begin phase two. Now it is up to you women to help us achieve this goal.

"Each territory behind me will be handled by one of you. Lisa, you have orange, the northeast, from New England out to the Great Lakes. Jennifer, you have the southeast. Christina, California, New Mexico, Arizona, and so on.

"Now, here is the difficult part. It'll require you ladies to be both clever and prudent. Instead of sending letters through Western Union or it being delivered by cabs and clergy, you six women will present these personally to the grieving women and will need to become comfortable bestowing both sorrow and joy."

Jackie hadn't been the only one fidgeting. Mark took a long sip of water.

"This, I realize, will be difficult, but then again, you are offering them something more than a shoulder to cry on. Open your folders and look at the money we are offering to them, and then turn to page 2. A list of the benefits they will receive with the aid of CUF.

"Every one of you has a gift. You are all confident and, I believe, persuasive. If you can convince these women that their husbands were involved in a secret operation vital to this country yet so dangerous they were required to have their sperm frozen before partaking, to preserve their family, well, that is the game."

"Mark," Joe interrupted. "Mark doesn't mean *game* as in any way to make light of this endeavor. We are offering them something our government refuses to, a secure income to raise and care for a child. We here know they will believe that they are raising the son or daughter of their late husband. This, on the surface, may seem like quite a lie, but we have all gone down that road, and it took us here, to the Underhill farm. The questions you must ask yourselves are not simple by any stretch. I would like you to read the following pages set before you."

Joe Cole continued, now holding the floor. "In our research, we discovered what the aftermath of war did to destroy families here in America. We found thousands of letters in the presidential archives, some dated back to 1871. I confiscated the ones I considered prudent and copied some down. The theme that stood out the most to me was the despair and fear of poverty that these woman felt. Wives and mothers alike. If anything we do here can prevent the distress of how these families suffer, then, regardless of our lies, we will be providing for the patriotic American children of families who, on their own, would otherwise live in squalor. Eliminating any scene of duty or dignity after such a sacrifice placed on the altar of freedom."

Mark took over once more. "There are contracts for you all on the final page. Joe and I are going out for a smoke. Please feel free to discuss this among yourselves. I hope you all understand the clandestine nature of this endeavor."

Mark reached back to close the door, stealing one last glimpse of Lisa.

The room was still for a second, then Jackie blurted out, "Shit, I thought they were going to ask me to fuck the president or something!"

Laughter filled the room, which was a welcome change. Jackie lit a cigarette.

"Jackie, can I?" Jennifer asked.

"Sure."

The women all read, some at different speeds. Christine skipped to the last page.

"I'm signing on. Hey, where I live, women are paid next to nothing to slave on a factory floor, and for what? To screw the boss for a ten-cent raise! That is a crime, not this."

Emily read the letters, moved by the courage it took to write with such honor. "So you girls don't want to vote or anything?" she said.

"Vote?" remarked Arlene. "We all are here for one thing, so let's not get too wrapped up in the dogma of it all."

"What?" Jennifer asked.

"Okay, girls." Arlene stood up. "I come from a country, Armenia. The women there are treated like dogs, and without a man, worse than dogs." Her accent now sounded more pronounced. "Here in America, we are free, and I see big things in the possibility to earn this kind of money without any man. I believe in the cause, or at least I believe they do, and that's good enough for me. We are going to earn our money, trust me. We are going to look into the eyes of these grieving widows and cry with them."

Her voice crackled, but she continued.

"I decided before I took the train. I'm no whore, and I'm no maid. Women I work with give blow job to husbands for diamond earrings. To me, that's a whore. Taking sperm from a man who may die tomorrow, you all already decided to...you know what that meant. Now I decide to give life to someone who will cherish it. Where is the wrong?" And with that, Arlene signed and stuck the pen in the Dutch house windmill.

Emily signed without a word.

Jackie took another drag of her cigarette and concluded, "Hell, why not?"

One by one the pens ended up with Arlene's.

"Let's have a drink!" Jackie announced.

"Yes, let's!" said Emily.

And altogether they raised their glasses.

Battle Plan in the Pacific

Onboard the USS *Hornet*, Nimitz and the fleet commanders met with their Marine counterparts. The battle in the Solomon Islands was costly, but victorious. The United States was able to stop the spread of the Japanese Empire by exploiting its fringes, eliminating its supply line, and destroying more planes and ships than the Japanese could replace.

Working their way into the perimeter, commanders agreed to bypass Japanese strongholds and began an island-hopping campaign, establishing bases for the advancement on Japan. The Aleutian Islands and Rabaul were necessary stepping stones on their way to Tokyo. Every commander knew, once they hit Japanese soil, things could get worse.

General McGarther's army was preparing for a return Philippines campaign, which hopefully would stretch the Japanese thin along an already-vast war front. The next islands on the list were Tarawa and Makin in the Gilbert Island chain. The intel provided was laid out, and the battle plan broken down. Lessons had been learned, and tactics and coordination refined to what seemed a sound, doable plan. Somewhere along the line, there was a mix-up in the recording of the water depth off Tarawa, and the Marine amphibious forces paid for their error.

Marine Colonel Thomas Sutton called for a meeting of every sergeant, E6 to E9, aboard the transport ship *Guthery*. Three hundred Marines and their deliverers awaited the awful hour. Sutton wanted to ready them for the Tarawa campaign.

Frank Munro earned another lower stripe, bringing his title to sergeant major. The deck was filled with rough-and-tough leathernecks, most wearing their khakis, but all wearing their pride.

Colonel Sutton addressed the men with a direct and disciplined tone familiar to many. Among the men were some who had yet to be tested and some that were just worn-out. One way or another, they earned their stripes, and the colonel knew these men were the head of the spear. To achieve total victory, these brave men had to plunge that spear into the very heart of the Japanese.

"Gentlemen, the island of Tarawa is Japanese soil! They aren't just going to give it over to us—we have to take it! And when we take it, we take more than just a piece of dirt, we take what they swore to protect! We take a piece of their emperor's soul! Ready your men for battle and pass out the Lucky Strikes! We will overwhelm the enemy with a coordinated strike while our Navy provides close air support, and our big guns will soften up the beaches! God bless all of you who wear this uniform, and God damn those who don't! Marines, it is an honor for me to speak to you today. Let's not make this our last engagement! Dismissed!"

The ship was abuzz, most everyone wondering where they were going to get the Luckys for their men. Munro left the deck, heading to the lieutenant's quarters. He always checked who was driving his platoon ashore. On the wall, port side, was a list: "First Marines, Third Platoon, Boat 23, Lieutenant Jon McConell."

"McConell!" Munro shouted. "Lieutenant McConell!"

"Who wants to know?" remarked one of the sailors, his face buried in a novel.

"I do, fucknut!" Munro commanded.

Looking over his book, the young sailor replied, softening his tone, "He's below, going over his Higgins with his gunner. Some shit we're in, hey, Sergeant?"

But he didn't receive a reply. Munro headed to the bay in the ship's stern. The *Guthery* was a modern freighter converted to a transport, and her cargo bay was perfect for stacking the wooden Higgins.

"You McConell?" Munro asked the most experienced-looking man he found below.

"Yes, that's me," Lieutenant McConell said as he stuck out his hand. "Jon, call me Jon."

"Okay, Jon, I'm your first delivery tomorrow. Can you tell me anything about this shoreline that the big dogs aren't?"

"Well, they briefed us this morning, but something don't seem right. Looks like that reef is uneven on Red 2 and 3, and there is a distance of six hundred to seven hundred yards of shoals past that. It don't look deep enough, but intel says it's six to eight feet! Now this ain't my first go-round, Sergeant. Looking at the color of the water from the latest pictures, well, if that's eight feet of water, I'm twelve feet tall!"

Jon continued, "Colors' way off to be eight feet, and the way the waves were breaking on the reef looked funny to me. Look, the beach faces Makin. No way it can get pounded like that on the west side. That bright-colored coral will rip these boats open. I'll get us over that coral, but those shoals, fuck! Why do you think I'm down here? I'm loading three times the 50-cal under the turret, figuring on slugging it out in the shallows."

"Well, I appreciate the input, Jon. How's your gunner?" Frank asked.

"That's him over there, scared shit and green as hell!" Jon joked.

"That doesn't make me feel any better," added Munro.

"Me either. Hey, I'm finished here for the moment. Want some coffee?"

"Always." Munro smiled.

Like they had known each other their entire lives, the two began sharing stories. Jon was from a small town near Jupiter, Florida, Munro from a cranberry town in Massachusetts. Neither had ever heard of the other before today, what with the rotation of ships and the hundreds of landing crafts, but both had shared stories of the same islands: Guadalcanal, the Solomons, New Guinea, and the Papuan Peninsula.

"Damn, Jon, can't believe we haven't met. Big ocean, man," the lieutenant concluded.

"Yes, too big. Hell, I grew up in an icy fishbowl in the northeast called Cape Cod Bay. Ball-shrinking water with ten-foot tides. Here the water is piss-warm and can't rise or fall more than two feet. Why there's so much coral, I imagine. So your gunner?" Munro asked again.

"New."

"Yeah, my last guy got tore up by a Zeek spraying and praying while I was heading back for another platoon. Fuckin' mess, freaked out the boys climbing in," Munro said, shaking his head.

"How many you lose, Frank?"

"Twenty-three, same number as your boat! Some I knew, good friends, others I already forgot."

"Well, let's hope tomorrow the number stays where it's at now," McConell said solemnly.

"I got to check on my men. Nice meeting you, Jon."

"You too, Frank."

The whistle sounded and orders came down. Those in their bunks hit the deck and gathered their gear. November 21, 1943, was a bright, beautiful morning. What awaited the Marines on Red Beach was anything but typical.

An organized panic was what three hundred Marines looked like while readying for battle. Some talked in nervous fashion, some acted tough, while some said nothing at all. Every one of them scared, but like a fighter entering the ring, when the bell rang you reacted and you came out fighting! One thing the Marines in the First Division knew was how to fight.

"Second Platoon, ready! Over the side! Third Platoon, ready!" barked Munro. "Over the side!"

Munro went over first. Looking down, he saw his new friend Jon at the wheel. "Nice day for a boat ride, Jon!" he shouted, making short time of his descent. "Let's go, Merlino! Don't look down, boy! You can only go as far as the deck! Turner, Rasmo, help that fucknut find the horizontal!" One row after the other, they descended, four abreast.

"Let's go, men! You're holding up the puppies on board!" Munro barked again.

"I heard that!" Sergeant Kowalker piped in.

"Hey, you're no puppy, Kow, but half your platoon looks like they were just paper-trained!"

"After we take this beach, I'll put a crew together and we'll see who's got the puppies!" Kowalker joked.

"You hear this guy, Vince? We beat him, what, seven out of seven? Hey, Kow, Bernie up there?" Munro asked.

"Yeah!"

"Ask him who has the Luckys."

"I got you covered, Sergeant!" Jon shouted out now. "Clear the lines!"

Jon took the Higgins out to the staging area and started to circle. "We got twenty minutes before we break formation here!"

Jon threw a carton of Lucky Strikes to Sergeant Munro.

"Pass these out, guys! Thanks, Jon."

Lieutenant McConell found his bearing. Red Beach was six miles from the staging area. At 25 knots, he could make it there in fifteen minutes after they broke formation.

The mood on his Higgins was high as long as he turned away from Tarawa. Keeping in the same formation, eight boats per circle, four circles, and the decks of the *Guthery* were clear. Jon had to navigate through the fleet to reinforce the first wave, as long as his Higgins stayed afloat.

The big guns opened up on the tiny island, the roar of the Higgins drowning out the formation of P40s overhead. The flag was raised. Jon Broke formation, and the mood suddenly changed.

"Six miles out!" Jon shouted, and he hit the throttle.

The sea was calm, and the Higgins rock-steady. Jon checked his gunner. Randy Coin was holding tight to his .50. "Randy, lock it in! Three miles!" Jon checked his bearing. Red Beach was on his horizon. Black smoke from the shelling drifted left to right, and the formation of P40s began to strike.

"Five minutes!" Jon's heart began to pound. "Zeeks, nine o'clock!" he shouted. Coin dropped and turned. "Wait! They're too far out!" Jon shouted again. Coin watched while the zero lit up a P40.

"Three minutes! Three minutes! Randy, open up!" the lieutenant screamed. Randy pulled the trigger on his Browning .50-cal. *Thump-thump-thump.* Mortar shells began to explode.

"Reef coming up!" Jon said, reading the water. The boat to his right was hung up. "Randy, watch that crossfire! Focus on the beach! Focus on the beach!" Randy tried to steady the .50. The fire was coming from both sides.

"Eight feet, my ass!" Jon yelled as he powered his Higgins over the reef. "Fucking sandbar. Hold on!"

Running parallel to Red Beach was dangerous, but necessary. "Deeper water ahead!" Jon powered up his Higgins. "One minute!" he shouted, just as a mortar round exploded ten feet off his port. "Coin!" Coin was down.

Next, Frank chimed in, "Sully!"

"I'm on it!" Sully replied, taking Coin's place. Fran Sullivan was Munro's right-hand man. He should have been a sergeant but turned down the commission to stay in the platoon.

Fran put the hammer down straight into the beach. Tracers were pouring in from all sides. Jon powered down and shouted, "Clear the ramp!" *Thump-thump-thump.* The .50-cal rang out once again. "Light 'em up, Sully! Go, go, go!"

The shells from the destroyers left craters in the beach all the way from the water's edge to the jungle. Third Platoon hit the beach, and at this point, nothing no longer went unnoticed.

"Find some cover and put some shit on that bunker!" Munro was screaming orders. "Sully, let's go!" Looking back, he saw Jon power off, four tons lighter, in a rooster tail of foam and sand.

From five hundred yards out, Marines were jumping into the water, their boats floundering on the shoals.

"Walsh Reed! Get that .50 up and put some shit on that emplacement!" Munro continued. They were deep enough in to miss the heavy crossfire, but the jungle was full of Japanese. Pointing to a bunker that was pouring out lead, he screeched, "Marines, out in the shoals! Fucking crossfire! Where is the goddamn air support? Radio! Where's the lieutenant?"

"Dead, Sergeant," the radioman replied, visibly shaken, covered with his lieutenant's blood and bone. Munro pulled the private away until he could see the bunker. Every inch of Tarawa was sliced into grids.

"That bunker's on G67, a red one! G67, red one!" Munro called in strike after strike, setting up bombing runs for the Hellcats and 40s. With each explosion he prayed and cheered as the bombs ignited, redundant and futile, each one missing.

A voice over the radio spoke. "They've got a wall on both sides, sir, to protect from frags on a direct, and an opening at their ten and two!"

Munro spoke firmly into the mic. "I understand, sir. We're running out of mortars." Focusing on his men again, he added, "Swifty! You and Terra work your way up past that opening! You gotta try to put it in that bunker! Sully! Sully, where's Danny? Get me some C4 and a charge now!"

Danny Nolen wired a charge. "All of it, Danny!"

"Twenty pounds, Sarge? You sure?" he said, adding the other block.

"Danny, shorten the fuse! Shorten it! I want fifteen seconds. Do it!"

Sully looked at the fuse. "Sarge, wait!"

"Fuck this, Sully!" was all Frank said. "Walsh! Put some fire on that bunker, and watch my back now!"

Terra and Swifty made it to the bunker, forty yards ahead. The Japanese were now concentrating on the Marines out in the open, slugging through three feet of water two hundred to four hundred yards out.

"Marines, cover fire!" Munro yelled, and twenty-two guns pumped lead everywhere a Japanese tracer appeared. He then sprang up with twenty pounds of explosives and an unlit second fuse.

"Terra!" Munro followed behind Swifty and Terra. "Fuck, that's, what, eighty yards?"

"Looks like it, Sarge," Terra answered. "See that crater fifty yards out? I make it there and I'll kill those fuckers! Swifty, light me up!" With that, Swifty flipped his Zippo. Seconds later, there was an explosion behind the bunker. It, along with at least eight Japanese, was engulfed.

Red Beach was far from clear, but Munro's platoon fought their way to cover. Sully moved the men off the beach to the blown-out tree line, fortifying their position. Planes roared overhead, but they weren't all American.

Suddenly, the sound of a cloaked-out fighter filled the sky. Everyone looked skyward as a P40 with the nose on fire was heading up their six. "Second Platoon, watch your 6!" Sully shouted as the P40 hit the surf two hundred yards offshore. It smashed to the ground just thirty yards in front of Sully's forward position."

The Japanese were now shooting at the downed plane, and the cockpit was full of smoke. The roof had separated in the crash, and the pilot, a man they recognized as Pat, was visible, but motionless. "We gotta get that kid out of there!" Munro yelled. "Get some fire on those fuckers!"

Munro ran toward the plane, while Terra and Swifty laid down cover. Like a cat, he jumped on the wing and into the cockpit. He pulled the shoulder harness to his waist and grabbed Pat under his arms. Simultaneously, the sergeant was jacked with adrenaline and being burned by smoldering cloth and steel. Munro pulled up with tremendous force. A wet, hollow tear shot up his arms and through his soul.

The pilot was completely burnt from the chest down, yet his lungs were still attached to his waist and were left standing upright, gray and smoldering. Falling back, Munro realized he had just pulled a man apart. The smell of seared flesh and those smoking gray lungs caused the sergeant to vomit wildly. Sully and another man sprinted up next to the ruined plane and dragged their puking leader behind some downed palms.

"Sully, did you see that?"

"Fuck yeah, I did! Poor bastard! How's the sarge?" Fran shouted.

"Not good. He won't stop throwing up."

The medic made his way to Munro. The sergeant was bent over on his knees, with his helmet in the sand. His arms and hands badly burned. He grounded his head forward in a loud groan. "Get Sully," was all he said.

Sully came down next to his friend. Munro's mind and stomach were inside out. He couldn't get away from that smell. "Sully, you're up, pal...I'm blown out. Gotta take some morphine and get patched up. Sully, my fuckin' guts, man..." And with that they moved Munro to where the other wounded were resting.

The water behind the Marines was a deep shade of blue. The waves were dotted with pink, and so was the entire shore. Bodies floated motionless until the wake of a Higgins caused them to move. Second Platoon reached their objective, and Sully radioed out.

"Where's Munro?" the familiar voice asked over the radio.

"Laid out under some palm trees. He's fucked up!"

"Munro's hit?"

"No, just fucked up! We gotta get those bunkers on your left! Where's the lieutenant?" he asked.

"Dead! Yours?"

"Dead! Soon as these planes clear, we gotta call it in. I'm digging in!" Sully shouted.

"Gotcha!"

Sergeant Kowalker maneuvered his men, pinpointed the bunkers, and the naval team did the rest. Round after round exploded fifty to sixty yards from their position. Sully looked back at the second wave while McConell wove his way back through the shoals and lowered his ramp.

More Marines hit Red Beach, and the Navy walked the rounds farther in. Jon signaled the corpsman to load the wounded, Sergeant Munro one of them. Sully took a quick count. Thirty-six men hit Red Beach an hour ago; his count was now at twenty-three, seven wounded, six dead.

"You crazy bastard, what the fuck were you thinking?" Sully shouted.

"Sorry, Sully. We got those fuckers." And he almost smiled but was overtaken by his pain.

Jon looked down at his new friend, burnt and loaded with morphine. Men waiting with rope-tied litters hauled the wounded, while medics and Navy men helped transport them. Jon then received orders on where to pick up his next load.

The Marines fought for three days to take Tarawa and lost a total of three thousand men. A thousand a day, plus double that in wounded, those that had been wounded during the fight.

Munro's flagship joined a fleet heading back to Pearl Harbor. Among the wounded were six yellow prisoners, a rare find and an unwelcomed cargo, especially for the wounded soldiers. Bad news traveled fast, and soon every soldier who could heard new Japs were on board and prompted the wounded to yell their disgust to any upright sailor in earshot of their bunk.

"Tell those yellow bastards my platoon is gonna eat their comrades' livers!" one Marine yelled, provoking others all around. One angry Marine proclaimed his platoon was going to take the black rubbers the Japanese government gave out and would fill them with the gold teeth they took out of dead Japs. "Rattling them at you while we fight! Show 'em my black sack of teeth, Sailor! Ask where they want me to send them to back home!"

The Marines of the First received orders to return home, giving Munro time to convalesce at Pearl Harbor. The hospitals were busy, with nurses treating various wounds, but mostly overrun with disease. Malaria took more Marines down than bullets and bombs. Hospitals and stations across the two islands treated the soldiers and readied them once more for action.

Back home in Marietta, Emily Fitzgerald packed her suitcase for an emergency trip. Christine in California had over fifty prime candidates in her region and needed help. Emily agreed, of course.

Her son was safe with her parents, along with her government position, Widows of the Fallen.

Emily left three or four days a week, traveling to various towns all over the Midwest. Not telling her parents she was flying to California was not an issue now that her job was so secretive. Extending it one or more days, with little notice.

Emily's plane landed at Treasure Island, where the Pan American Clipper was waiting, tied to the pontoon docks. The Navy seized the little island two years prior, installing giant searchlights, equivalent to almost one and a half billion candlepower. When turned on, these lights could be seen up to a hundred miles away.

Christine was waiting for Emily when she departed the plane. Weeks ago, they were at Underhill, now on some island in San Francisco Bay. Rain was falling lightly. Christine stood beneath the entrance light under an oversize black umbrella.

"Emily!" Christine called out. Emily smiled as she ran under her purse, heading for her blond friend. "Emily, your plane leaves in half an hour!"

"What plane? I just got here."

"We have to talk. Mark sent me this," Christine replied, holding out a familiar-looking envelope.

Inside, the two sat down at the refreshment counter. "Coffee?" the barista offered.

"Yes, please," Emily replied.

"None for me, thanks," said Christine. "Emily, it's about Frank, Frank Munro, you know…"

Emily started to blush and pushed away from the bar. "You know about that? I didn't think what I did was public information."

"No, no, it's not like that. Mark told me because he didn't know how to tell you or ask you. Oh, Emily, Frank was wounded. He's lying in a hospital bed in Honolulu, and Mr. Lavenger—I mean Mark— wanted you to see him. Emily, he's not wounded physically…well, not really. Here, here, it's all in here. Mark sent it to me." She handed the envelope to Emily. "He needs some help! I don't know, just read it. Tell me you'll at least read it."

"Of course I will, Christine. I just…well, I just haven't heard his name since, and his letter, I didn't return his letter. I was ashamed and…you know."

"Oh, Emily, we all know! But he is alive, and Mark thinks you can help."

Emily took a quick sip of her coffee and opened the letter:

CUF Chairman Mark Lavenger

Dear Emily,

If you're reading this, then you have been told Frank Munro was wounded in action and is hospitalized in Honolulu. Frank sustained second- and third-degree burns on his hands and arms while trying to save a downed pilot. His act of selflessness and courage, which caused his external injuries, also set off a reaction to his body internally, causing him to vomit profusely, which led to dehydration. Although there are staff present who have spoken with him— and they believe he is of sound spirits—they can't explain his description of a "fleshy smell" he claims is burnt in his nose and brain. In other words, he is constantly smelling the burning flesh of the pilot he tried to save.

Please, Emily, he is a necessary asset for the military and, of course, a friend to you. Your travel and time will be compensated. There will be a uniform waiting in Honolulu with your name on it.

Sincerely,
Mark Lavenger

Emily put down the letter and continued to sip her coffee. "I have fifteen minutes, Christine. You know I'm more than a little nervous."

"About Frank?" she asked.

"No," Emily replied. "About that giant boat with wings that's going to fly me to Hawaii!"

"No better way to travel over water, Emily. I take them up the coast whenever I can. Trust me, they're great. Honest!" Christine leaned over and took Emily's hand. "Good luck, Emily. I have to go. Hope to see you soon, okay?"

"Sure. We will meet for coffee," Emily said, and they smiled.

Emily was impressed by the M-130 Clipper. Sitting in her seat, she was just above the waterline. When the powerful twin engines turned into the wind and throttled up, in moments, the aircraft was airborne, climbing into the rainy black night. The Martin M-130 cruised at 150 miles per hour. Its boatlike body was wide and more comfortable than any other plane of its time. Though it was luxurious to those with the means to fly in one, the cost of a round-trip ticket from San Francisco to Honolulu was $1,500 in 1936.

Emily had no trouble falling asleep in the oversize plush chairs. The eight-man crew was composed of veterans, and long hours of flight were mere routine. Filled mostly with medical supplies and nurses, the M-130 roared along, a lifeline to and from the States.

Emily woke to bright blue sky and miles of empty ocean below. "Breakfast is served 08:00, ma'am," the steward said. "Feel free to stretch your legs." She stood for the first time in half a day, heading for the lavatory. Friendly, tired faces broke into smiles as she passed.

Emily obviously hadn't been planning on this encounter; she had only brought clothes and toiletries for her business with CUF. Looking through her purse for lipstick, she opened her perfume, placing it down on the counter. Taking off the kerchief that was tied around her neck, Emily did her best to freshen up.

The flight was set to arrive at noon. At some point, Emily spilled some perfume on her kerchief, filling the lavatory with its fragrance. Emily stuffed it back into her purse, trying to keep its odor contained, and went back to her seat.

Breakfast was being served and included fresh fruit and eggs. Emily was taking it all in, trying to morph the successful amenities these aircraft had into the quaint *Annabell Rose*. She used her time thinking of patterns, colors, menus, even alcoholic beverages she could incorporate into her family's riverboat.

The captain interrupted Emily's daydreams. "We're approaching Pearl Harbor. On the port side you'll see what remains of the *Arizona*." A few of the woman rose to look over. Most had actually already seen Pearl at eye level.

Two women climbed into the empty row in front of Emily. "Oh, gosh!" they murmured when they saw the broken fleet. Emily was drawn to the activity below. The amount of ships, ships that were becoming larger by the second. The Clipper throttled down, then slightly up, the hull skimming the surface, gliding softly, sinking into the harbor, its water still stained from its destruction.

"Welcome to Pearl Harbor! Thanks for joining us, and have a safe trip!" Emily watched the others gather their things. She followed those whom she assumed knew their way to the hospital.

Cabs and buses were shuttling people all around Emily. She followed the other nurses from her flight to a bus stop. Moments later, a bus marked HOSPITAL arrived.

Emily readied her mind. She had to tell Frank she had moved and didn't receive his letter. Hopefully, he wouldn't mention it.

Emily introduced herself to the receptionist when she arrived. The woman pointed her to the assembly room, which was now a makeshift supply room.

The atmosphere was busy, and the staff moved purposefully. The one woman in the supply room was the only exception. "What?" she said, reluctantly looking up from her magazine.

"I'm Emily, Emily Fitzgerald."

"Take a seat." Ruth Chobit finished what she was reading and then proceeded flipping through the ledger. Without saying a word, Ruth walked over to the shelves on her right and slid both her hands under a neatly folded uniform. Walking back, Ruth stopped at her desk. Her manikin-like pose caused Emily to hold her gaze a second or two too long. "I haven't got all day, miss," Ruth said.

Emily grabbed the pen tied to the ledger with a string. She almost pulled it off the desk, its string being shortened over time. She signed her name and took the clothes from Ruth's outstretched arms. "Thank you," Emily said, smiling when she walked out of the room.

Kill 'em with kindness, she thought, something she remembered her father always telling her. *I'll ask someone else where to change.* And she was directed to a locker facility by a kinder staff member. "Could you also find out for me, while I change, where I can find a patient? Frank Munro. No-*e* Munro."

"Okay, Ms. Fitzgerald. Have that for you when you return."

Emily's uniform was plain, and she felt like it was anything but flattering. She took her kerchief and rolled it under her hair, tying a simple square not in the front.

"Ah, 237, Ms. Fitzgerald," the woman said, pointing to a staircase down that hall.

Emily found herself walking slowly up the stairs, being passed by a rush of nurses. "Burn Ward," a sign at the top read, with an arrow pointed toward metal double doors.

Emily walked the hall, focusing on the room numbers, not the bandaged soldiers who lay motionless like cryptic mummies. She read the room numbers in her mind, *233...235...237.* Emily paused before entering Frank's room. There was a pail next to his bed and intravenous lines in both of his arms.

Emily quietly approached as the dark, sleeping man lay still. His deeply tanned skin emphasized by the white decor. Emily noticed a tear streak from the corner of his eye, revealing his sorrow. Slowly she leaned forward to kiss his forehead. As she did not want to wake him, her lips barely met his skin. She didn't intend for the end of her scented kerchief to tickle Frank's nose, and he awoke suddenly, startled.

The familiar smell of Emily from their first and only night together filled a nose that had previously only smelled death. Emily was pulling away when Frank grabbed her arms. "Emily, Emily, it's...I can't believe it!"

Just then, Sully and a few of his men entered the room. They had been up prior but thought their sergeant would be shipped back home. They recognized Emily from Harry's. All tipped their heads, showing respect.

"Frank," Sully said, pointing to his new stripe. "E-7! And I get to stay with the Third! We'll talk later! We're going to hang out in the cafeteria." And just like that, the two were alone.

"Wow, they are either awful hungry or awful nice," Emily said.

"Both, I would say," Frank said with a smile. He was smiling for the first time in weeks, and he felt his face crack. He began asking Emily frantic question.

"Frank, I'm not here long, only two days, okay? My things were sent to the hotel near the airport. Frank, I heard you were injured. I'm so sorry, Frank, so sorry!"

"Why are you sorry, Emily? I knew what I was in for."

"No, sorry I didn't return your letter," Emily solemnly replied.

A moment of silence was only interrupted by an intercom announcement.

"Emily...I was gone out there, gone. I lost every bit of care and just became a machine. That pilot brought me back. Helpless, screaming, and burning. All that relentless shooting at him after he crashed got me to feel human again. In a split second, I had thought, What if that were me? And I just ran up to help him."

Frank looked weak, far from the vibrant man she first met, but still handsome. Even in his condition, she found herself more attracted to him than ever before.

"I have to tell you, Emily, I was thrilled we met, but," Frank said, grunting as he tried to reposition his weight, "I'll admit, I was sad when I awoke alone."

"I wish I could tell you my reasons, Frank. Someday I will, but for now, I just came here to see you."

Frank didn't stop to question his feelings. She had just pulled him straight out of hell, and she would never understand how much he had lost on that battlefield. The rush of fresh emotions energized Frank. Sitting up in bed and carrying on with his beautiful guest was more than uplifting.

"Emily, could you do me a favor?" he said, suddenly serious.

"I'll try, Frank."

"Can you go to the cafeteria and pick me up some sort of sandwich?"

Emily smiled wide. "Here, Frank," she said, then untying the kerchief, she laid it on his pillow and kissed his lips. "Don't go anywhere, Sergeant."

First Sign of Life

By June of 1944, the Underhill farm was approaching two dozen CUF babies. The women, all in their first trimester.

Progress in the Pacific as a result of the island-hopping strategy brought America closer to Japan. American industry churned out war machines, shipping them to every corner of the globe. Newsreels were on our soldiers' sides and played to the charitable nature of a free-living citizen. "Buy War Bonds." Their advertisements and slogans dominated the backdrop of city life, and pictures and newspaper headings reinforced unity.

Together, with one great cause, America fought back the spread of tyranny and oppression, winning battles in the Far East and vast West Pacific. All at home joined in the fight; neither age nor sex mattered. Jobs were plentiful for anyone wishing to work, and in an era where if you didn't work, you didn't eat, jobs went fast!

Can drives popped up across the fruited plains. "Knife for Life" slogans were a hit in California. All types of scrap metal were being salvaged to quench the appetite of an American war machine. Businesses and markets that participated left baskets at their doors for donations. The factories and workers were working around the clock, with commerce, opportunity, and pride in mind. They were all part of something, something that couldn't be defeated.

Life on the river for the one-eyed captain was also humming right along. The repairs and upgrades on the *Annabell Rose* were completed, and contracts signed. Having to shuttle freight was easier than transporting people, and the pay was better. Emily's dreams of turning her father's riverboat into a small luxury liner faded with time. Little Max became quite a mate, and of course, his dog had to come along too.

Emily was home as much as she was away, and her little Matty was growing like a weed. Martha had another boy in her life, bringing joy back to her family, keeping in her heart the memories of Brandon, her eldest. Her middle son, Driscol, was wounded slightly during the Battle of the Bulge and was sent to an army hospital in France. Seemed he was "porcupined," as they called it.

Tree fragments hit with ordnance blew splinter-like fragments into the targets. The tree that hit Driscol was at his 6, and he literally had an ass full of splinters. "I guess he got pretty intimate with those nurses, having his rump poked at every day for three months," Frank said when he heard the news Driscol married after his recovery. He stayed in France after his papers came through, and he had married his chosen nurse one month later in March.

The sergeant stayed in touch, and so did Emily. They wrote often, and Frank was able to visit in the fall after his burns were completely healed. Frank was given several more decorations for valor, but his mind was not on a different kind of trophy.

During his visit, he had tried taking Emily and Matty up to see his parents, but timing and weather would not allow. Frank's platoon, along with a few others, was taken off the line for a special training operation somewhere in New Guinea. He joined them eight days later.

His mission was top secret, which meant no one on the base had answers, only speculations, based on the practical nature of the training. Wherever they were going, it was steep. Every other man carried a fifty-foot rope equipped with a foldable grappling hook.

Once there, the Marines trained relentlessly, climbing and throwing grenades, both phosphorus and the pineapple. Night after night they broke down the doors of the wooden structures, yelled "Marines!" and carried one-hundred-pound bags of sand, sometimes while they descended the ropes. The training, although tiring, was a welcomed break from the jungle and being on the front line.

The men who stayed on from the original First in 1942 rose in rank and honor. They were now seasoned veterans—Munro now a captain, Sully a lieutenant, and Campbell and Swifty E-6 sergeants. Altogether, there were 106 Marines. Sergeant Kowalker, now also a lieutenant, was instrumental in taking Tarawa, knocking out two pillboxes with the remainder of his platoon. It had been three days of horrific battle, wiping out most of the entire division of Marines, three thousand wounded on Tarawa alone.

Now they were back training at a hidden base in New Guinea. Cloistered in the jungle compound, the Marines lived in pine barracks equipped with a genuine mess hall. The entire base was no larger than a hundred-acre farm. Set in a thick, damp forest surrounded by hills.

There were five buildings where the Marines practiced what was known as guerilla warfare. Stalin's Red Army would say about guerilla warfare, "First the grenade opens the door, followed by the machine guns." Good, sound tactics if you were indiscriminately killing everything in the room.

The Marines were learning to react to rescue situations. Although they were kept in the dark about the majority of the details, the men knew one thing for certain: they were going back to the Pacific.

The Marines were not the only ones dabbling in special operations. The Navy, too, introduced advanced frogman training and commissioned new, more modern ships. Their latest, a fast battleship named the *Missouri*. The fourth Iowa-class battleship. They improved the landing crafts and tripled the number of LVTs, or Alligators, as they were so fondly known. Everything the Navy did was in preparation for a massive amphibious invasion.

With the expansion of the US fleet came recommendations and commissions. For his bravery, knowledge of the waters, and sheer survival skills, Jon McConell's abilities as a Higgins navigator were noticed and rewarded, landing him a commission on the *Missouri*. He was now involved in the strategic planning and execution of amphibious landings.

Jon took several LVTs for torturous runs, testing their seaward capabilities. The fact that they rolled over the reefs with exceptional ease made them the most dangerous weapons in the naval arsenal, in his opinion, and he made good use of their power.

Firstborn

Lisa McAdams stood nervously alone, waiting for the delivery room door to open. *I hope it's a boy,* she thought. "Where's that Mark?" she said aloud, looking at her watch.

The delivery room in Boston General Hospital was moderately busy, with three little newborns squirming in their cocoon cotton blankets. Marie Stephens, the first woman to in vitro a child, was due August 8. On the day of the sixteenth, after one too many false labors, the luster of the project had been dulled for the men of CUF.

"It's better if we're all not there!" Joe remarked harshly on the phone. "The last thing we need is to be seen with these babies. Think of the implications, Michael! You want to be in pictures too? Okay, I'll call you when I hear from Mark. Yes, he's going back up. Lisa's been there for days. Yes, well, he's pretending it's his wife, okay, so it works for him."

"Joe, I guess Mark didn't tell you…," Michael began on the other end of the phone. But he didn't have to say any more. Joe knew instantly, but he didn't comment. His intuition had been right. Mark and Lisa were officially shacking up.

Can't say I blame him, I guess, Joe thought to himself. He smiled and lit his pipe, settling into his burgundy armchair. Joe also knew Mark would bring it up to him in an awkward fashion, during a crisis, to limit any sort of response. *I think I'll give him a pass. That Lisa would have been my choice too.*

A few hours later, as Joe Cole sat behind his desk, his gaze fixed and frozen to the phone, it was now his turn to dial Michael. Mike Robone was out playing with his daughters. He had bought them each bow-and-arrow sets, and they were target-shooting in the backyard. He was pulling arrows from the large canvas-covered target when he heard the phone ring.

"Mike, it's for you." Rachel Robone stood at the door with a peculiar look on her face. "Here, Secret Agent Man, it's Joe."

Mike smiled, taking the phone from his curious wife. "Joe! Tell me, old buddy!"

"Yes, Michael, it's a boy. Nine pounds, three ounces."

"Nice!" Mike said, feeling the relief. "When we celebrating? Private, of course!"

"Look, that was only the first. We have births scheduled almost every other week for the next four months!" Cole reminded him.

"Look, Joe, about what I said about Lavenger..."

"Forgotten, Mike. I'll make arrangements for everyone, and you make sure you bring your wife. She and Sandy can scrutinize Lisa together. It will be more fun for them."

"You're a rotten bastard, Joe!" Mike answered.

"Yeah, I'm not worried about Lisa. She is very self-assured, and there's just no substitute for youth. We will speak soon," Joe Cole concluded.

"One more thing, Joe. The boys are investing a lot of money with these guys out in Utah. Something big is brewing!" Michael said.

"I'm on it!" was all he said before hanging up.

Cole worked in and outside the government. Contracts, overseeing military investments, and assuring top standards all across the board. These were just a few of several areas of expertise Joe immersed himself in. Finances were his specialty. Where Michael investigated leads and companies for both CUF and the military, Joe took that knowledge to the market, creating a sustainable fortune for children and families of CUF.

Back in the delivery room, Lisa introduced Mark to Marie Stephens. "Congratulations, Ms. Stephens! He's beautiful!"

"Can you see him out there, Lisa? Can you see my baby? I want the nurse," Marie said.

A nurse, Evelyn Singer, had worked the birth ward for six years. She overheard and understood Marie's desire to see her child, and hearing her converse with that sharp-dressed couple, she made herself attentive. "I'll get your son, Marie."

"Have you thought of a name?" Lisa whispered to a tired Marie.

"No. Well, yes, but I'm not sure. His father always wanted a son named John. John Stephens."

"Sounds like a good lawyer's name," Lisa said, taking Marie's hand and smiling.

"Here he is, Ms. Stephens." Evelyn entered the recovery room with the little soldier in her arms.

Mark stared intently. He was one of the few who knew the real father, at least the pictures and history of him. The real question banging around his mind was how well his wife, Lisa, knew him. He decided he didn't want to know.

Joe had sent him the pictures and information of the hero soldier the night before. Ironically enough, his name was John, John Gabriel. Killed in action while on a raid in Rumal.

John Gabriel was a flyer with seventeen confirmed kills under his belt. Far from the Navy's top ace, he had still been a selfless flyer of a Grumman Hellcat. He flew some of the toughest missions in the theater. Thick flack and experienced Jap pilots early in the campaign had downed him twice, and he had come back stronger every time. He was also the first fighter to touch down on Guadalcanal.

"John's a great name, Marie," Lavenger told the new mother.

"Take him, Mark, hold him. Go ahead," she offered.

Mark fumbled for a second, then held up the infant John like a trophy, bringing him in gently and pressing his own chin on John's head. "Your dad would be proud, little man, very proud."

He handed the baby to Lisa, who had pulled a chair closer to the bed. "Lisa, I'm going to grab a coffee. Can I bring you anything, ladies?"

"No, thank you, Mark," Marie replied.

Lisa just shook her head and went back to snuggling Johnny.

Back to the Pacific

Training was over, and the now elite force of the Marines' First Infantry was about to deploy to Japanese soil. They were secluded from other soldiers and purposely kept in the dark about the ongoing campaign. Transferring to Pearl Harbor, they were assigned to the *Missouri*.

The new ship was the fastest in the fleet, turning 35 knots. Now officially dubbed the Sea Dogs, the Marines from the First traded their blue and red patches for ones with a growling face of a cartoon dog.

The battle-tested and well-rested Marines boarded the ship enthusiastically. Looking over the rail and overlooking the gangplank were officers involved in the planning and overseeing of the Chichijima invasion.

Munro was the first up the ramp, saluting sharply. "Permission to come aboard, sir!"

Captain Callaghan saluted sharply back. "Permission granted, Captain."

Munro stood a pace behind the captain, who saluted every man. Eighty-six of the hundred and six Marines who began their training five months ago in New Guinea walked proudly up the gangplank, each one saluting orderly. All wore their khakis with caps to match. Jon noticed Munro and smiled, elbowing the ensign next to him. "I know that guy. Some others too. I took them to Tarawa."

Iwo Jima was a six-week campaign. The Americans fought, won, and planted a flag on Japanese soil. One hundred forty miles south was a Japanese base called Chichijima, or Father Island. This island was the largest in its chain and was supplying the soldiers on Iwo during the nearly seven-week battle. There was something about this particular island the Navy waited to tell, something that would turn soldiers to savages, rumor had it.

For months now, reports from different Japanese listening posts were revealing war crimes taking place on the Father Island. Indigenes who were captured on an earlier raid told stories of a certain Japanese officer who was cutting out the livers of his prisoners and sharing his cannibal cuisine with other Japanese.

One step closer to Japan, taking Chichijima was the next logical step. This volcanic rock, with steep hills and reinforced antiaircraft emplacements, made for a difficult and complex invasion. The Japs on this island had prepared for the customary invasion style of American Marines, meaning it was well equipped with long- and short-range mortars and, of course, the ship-sinking eight-inch guns, all of which were dug in, covered with concrete, and camouflaged. Only after their phosphorus tracers streamed out could their exact location be pinpointed. Veteran gunners hunkered down in these emplacements. It required a strikingly precise invasion, one with a fair amount of deception.

Many of the Marine officers wanted to carpet-bomb the island, which would have been an effective but highly lethal method. Doing so would've undoubtedly killed their own pilots. Killing downed American pilots was not going to sell war bonds, but rescuing them would.

The radio towers on Chichi were not new to the Americans. Several sorties were flown, probing their defenses. There were two practical and obvious areas you could invade. They were mined heavily, and obstacles for prohibiting amphibious crafts were strategically placed, intended to stall any landing force, while the long mortars and guns were enabled for slaughter. A number of pilots died for the information leading up to June of 1945. An additional twenty-two pilots were known to have been taken alive, the reports consistently told.

The fortunate flyers landed far enough from the island where an American submarine lurking below rescued them. Watching the air battle over the island from the forward periscope, commanders searched the sky for smoking planes and parachutes.

The sailors of the deep saved whom they could before the eight-inch guns were turned on them. Picking them up fast enough to keep the eight-inch Jap guns from zeroing their positions, Gato-class submarines patrolled the waters off Chichijima, sinking Japanese supply ships and, on occasion, rescuing downed pilots.

Munro left the briefing room with a knotted stomach. Reaching down into his pocket, he pulled out that kerchief Emily left at his side all that time ago in the hospital. Her scent was faint, but Frank still buried his nose in it, pretending to wipe it when the brass walked past. Finding out about the alleged cannibalism on Chichijima brought Frank back to the overpowering smell of burning flesh that had once invaded his nostrils.

He had barely kept himself from vomiting, his reaction not at all unique. Several of the Navy officers in the briefing room were visibly sickened. Frank began focusing harder on the landing site and specialized craft. He was surprised when he realized he had failed to notice Jon McConell. They acknowledged each other with a nod before Jon began disclosing their soon-to-be-executed plan.

"New tactics are being applied, along with some exceptional old ones. The LVT-3s we are using have long-distance radios, 20-mill cannons, and single .50-cal camouflage netting to help hide the Gators' low silhouette, plus we have every twenty-five square yards of ocean charted out to four miles. If an enemy patrol boat happens along, our guns will knock it out without issue."

Everything was laid out and described in detail. The procedure had been designed to mislead the Japanese into thinking they were watching out for a large invading force. During what they called the rescue stage, the *Missouri* would shell the north face of Hill 407 while steaming directly for it, creating the final diversion.

The brass cleared the room. Frank took a long, slow breath and eased down his shoulders. He saluted Jon as he exited, his hat under his arm Jon reached out to shake. "Last I saw you, you weren't looking so good," Jon said.

Frank was putting the kerchief back in his pocket when Jon noticed the sleight of hand.

"What's that, Frank?"

"Oh, a little something…it's nothing, really. I'll tell you later."

"We have an hour before the briefing of your men. Let's get a coffee," Jon declared.

"Sounds good," Frank replied, and he followed Jon through the ship to its galley.

Once there, Jon sat at the end of the tabletop, while Frank poured his coffee. He got right to the point. "What happened out there, Frank?"

"It was weird, hard to explain. You know when you're in it, I mean, bullets whizzing past and just hell all around?"

"Yeah, seen it," Jon mused out loud.

Frank continued, "You know when there is a moment where everything kind of just slows down enough to make some sense?"

"Yeah."

"Well, you saw that plane go down right over our position, right?"

"Yeah. That was a hard one to miss," Jon said, chuckling slightly.

"I know, but what no one saw were the Japs beating feet through the jungle, trying to get that pilot. I was hit with a surge of energy— maybe it was just competitiveness, I don't know. I know I wanted to get there before they did, and I ran over everything, jumped on that bird, and lit those Japs up! A second later, I was lying on the ground with half a flyboy on me, still smoking!"

"Fuck! Frank, that is sure something you'll have to tell your grandkids!"

They both began to laugh, despite the dark nature of the story.

"Yeah, well, hearing about those bastards cooking our boys…" Frank lowered his voice. "I felt a little fucked up." He then pulled out Emily's kerchief and showed it to Jon.

"Now the story behind that must have a much better ending, hey, Frank?" Jon said.

"I'll tell you when it's over," Frank said, laughing as he smiled.

Munro addressed his Sea Dogs, now assembled on the rear deck of the *Missouri*. *Sea Dogs* was a name derived from the term *Devil Dogs*, which Japanese soldiers called the Marines at Guadalcanal.

"From the beginning of our training at Wet Hill until now, there hasn't been any information describing this mission. Absolutely nothing has been revealed to any man standing before me. Moments ago, I was told why exactly such secrecy was imperative." Munro paused, taking a moment to look over at the row of officers in front of him.

"We have two very important objectives." All their attention was on the captain as he glanced into the eyes of his friends and soldiers. "Men, there is an island called Chichijima, translating to Father Island. Our first objective is to scale the steep volcanic rock walls protecting the radio station compound on this island and elim-inate it, along with all its Japanese soldiers. The station is presently heavily defended. It is also being used as a prison for downed Navy flyers.

"Our second objective, gentlemen, should be evident. It is imperative that we locate and rescue all the American Navy pilots held captive by these assholes!" Munro paused while the men grew restless. "No use sugarcoating it, guys. Our Navy airmen are being tortured, killed, and if reports have it right, eaten on that island."

Munro went on, pointing toward the bow of the *Missouri*. "The Navy doesn't want to blast her guns, and the Air Force doesn't want to carpet-bomb the hills, because of fear of retaliatory fire."

Moving to the map he had hung on a portable board, Munro pointed out the radio tower and transmitting station. "We will scale these barriers of coral, rock, and jungle here! Using the cover of night, we'll set our explosives around the transmitters and position ourselves for a coordinated attack, coming from the air and sea. Be ready to strike an hour before dawn, 0500 hours tomorrow. When we attack the village, we kill every Jap in and around these five struc-tures. Look familiar, everyone?"

"Yes, sir," answered the Marines.

"Inside one of these buildings our flyers are being held captive. Let's keep that in mind. Watch your backdrop and search before you destroy. Our preparation for this mission was tough, but our duty can only be described as honorable. Gentlemen, I will turn the invasion details over to the commander."

Jon stepped forward, squaring his shoulders. Sully and Campbell recognized Jon from Tarawa and knew he was the real deal.

"Our photographs of Chichijima reveal a weakness in its gun placement. This weakness will be exploited by the location of our invasion and from the cover of night. A steep west bank overhanging the beach is without any known emplacement because of its poor trajectory. We will deceive the enemy with a mock raid on the southwest portion of the beach. Frogmen will deliver explosive devices, removing LVT obstacles, and preparing the bluff. Their guns will be trained on approaching attack boats and cruisers drawing fire for the demolition teams, here and here!" Jon said, pointing to specific locations.

Turning from the map, Jon then looked at each and every man in the room. "Fighter bombers and Corsairs will keep the guns busy, and once the demolition teams are extracted, the fleet will move out, giving the Japs the appearance of a morning invasion.

"The last run from the air will be from a strike force in Ramul. The Corsairs will buzz the airfield, keeping their pilots out of the sky, and diverting their attention to the southwest. We will already be eight miles from shore, waiting for dusk, before we close in.

"The explosives are set for 0600 hours. At that precise time, we will drive the LVTs under the overhand, keeping us hidden from their guns. Once we're under that overhanging cliff, you'll deploy, and our LVTs will stage there." The men were silent. Jon continued, the intensity of his voice increasing. "At dawn, we're going to shell the beach along with the southwest face of that rock. Make sure you're not still on it. The buildings and emplacements are labeled, and copies of this map are available. Questions?"

"Commander?"

"Yes, Lieutenant?"

"The Japanese still patrol the waters, correct?"

"Yes, Lieutenant."

"Are there any plans involving patrols?"

"Yes," Commander McConell replied earnestly. "I believe our LVTs will be camouflaged and tucked in along the rocks. We're hoping that will be enough, but we have several options, Lieutenant. Let's hope we don't need to exercise them!" And with that, Jon reached up to pat one of the massive sixteen-inch guns. The men laughed; it was a welcomed relief.

Jon continued, "While the Gators are hidden beneath the ridge, the guns from our ship, the *Missouri*, will be trained on our position. Any ship approaching will be shelled while our lieutenants in the LVTs call in ordnance. Men, Admiral Halsey himself will be in on this fight! He extends his blessings and welcomes you back to the Pacific!"

Evening fell on the men now dubbed the Sea Dogs. They checked and rechecked their gear continuously. Nets were slung from the side of the *Missouri*, and the troops descended to the Higgins boats, then transporting the men over to a merchant ship where their camouflaged LVTs awaited. The sea was calm, but that was the only relaxing element. Munro and his men were still buzzing over the cannibalism speculation, and their hatred for the Japanese on Chichijima grew potent.

Jon took the ride to the transport ship along with his lieutenants. There were no Lucky Strikes passed out on this ride. The Marines understood they were partaking in a stealth mission, with no room for the softening of their defenses. Concealment was key for a successful mission.

Entering the bow of the transport, Jon went over the weapons on the four LVTs. Each had a standard .50-cal machine gun on the starboard side and a twenty-millimeter cannon on the port. All were equipped with special underwater exhaust, allowing for maximum quietness, and Jon assured the men that they had been tested and were ready.

"Men, all eyes are on this mission," Jon said as the chatter turned to silence. "As we departed the *Missouri*, Admiral Halsey was on his way to take over as captain of our ship. Our ship, I believe, is the pride of the fleet! You all saw the guns, but what you didn't see was the armament of seventeen-inch Navy steel! Gentlemen, make no mistake, this is not the Coral Sea or Guadalcanal. We will not leave you for a moment. The *Missouri* can withstand anything the enemy will throw at us, and we will not hesitate to charge Chichi with guns blaring! But remember, keep off the southwest face! Marines, enter your LVT, and good luck!" Jon saluted the men, who were left feeling inspired and confident in their unfolding destinies.

The bow opened up to a dark sea as the Gators fired their engines, the roar of the motors echoing off the walls in the holding bay. Down the steep ramp into the sea, one by one, instantly the roar turned to a hum as the four Gators took to the sea, circled single file, and headed for the isle. The Sea Dogs were on their way to a mission so unbelievably gruesome their silence spoke volume. "Six miles out," the lieutenant said, holding his fist closed then sticking up one finger. "Still not a word."

The Gators were four abreast, and at two miles out, they slowed to 4 knots. "Two miles out." As the motors slowed, the heart rates rose. "Stay cool, boys," Munro stated, "stay cool," feeling the tension in his boat. "One, one." He held up one finger, the outline of the cliffs now blocking out the starlit sky.

The LVTs eased into position under the shoreline cliff, undetected. "Reed, Walsh, Murph, throw the hook," Munro whispered. The men threw, one by one. Reed's hook didn't grab and fell in the water with a splash.

"Shit!"

"Easy, Reed," Munro replied. "Reload and fire. Let's get this."

The two LVTs hooked six knotted ropes on the jungle vines covering the volcanic rocks. The small swells and light breakers did not inhibit the Sea Dogs' ascent as the two gunners abandoned their posts to hold the ropes once the last man left the deck. Silently, and without incident, the men climbed the ropes and dispersed into the steep jungle, just like they had trained for over the last four months. The lieutenants pulled the camouflage hanging on the inside of their crafts and deployed them with their light sea anchors.

Munro, Kowalker, Lang, and Feroli organized their men and moved as quiet as they could toward the village, just two hundred yards up the dense slope. Lights from the buildings began to flicker through the jungle's twisted ridgeline. The Sea Dogs spread themselves along a line just inside the shadows, utilizing the broad leaves and jagged stumps. Their enemy was completely unaware. Music was playing in one building, and movement in and out of what was known to be the transmitting station could be seen.

It was now 4:00 a.m. Kowalker and his men were to circle west, and Lang and his men south, both setting up their .30-cals in a crossfire on the compound. Rain began to fall from the heavens, and it was a godsend. The rustling dried jungle debris now muffled by the Pacific pour.

At 04:00, they began moving like snakes through the twisted vines. Munro watched fiercely through the curtain of rain, checking his watch every quarter turn. Sully moved down the line, checking his men.

"I hope she fires in this rain," Mugsy said after Sully patted his shoulder with assurance.

"Fear not, son. We're going to fuck these Japs up at dawn," Sully said without emotion, then moved on.

When he reached Lang, he made a deliberate effort to check the position of the .30-cal. "You don't want to swing too far left, Sergeant." Sully cut a thick piece of bamboo and stuck it in the muddy ground. "Nothing past here, you read me, Sergeant?"

Lang didn't respond right away, and Sully grabbed his earlobe, damn near pulling it off along with his hat. Lang came out of his trance. "Sully, one of my guys from back home could be in there or could be eaten already." His voice darkened.

"Focus on the mission. When the beach erupts, kill every fucker you see run from those buildings. Munro will get your bud."

Sergeant Lang had planned on being a flyboy like many who entered the armed forces. He joined up with his lifelong bud, Steven Flamos, in 1942, but hadn't made the cut to become a Marine pilot—something about his bearings being inverted. Flamos, on the other hand, was as comfortable inside out as he was right side up. Both had grown up in Brockton, Massachusetts, a city just south of Boston.

Flamos was shot down over Chichijima a few months ago, and when Lang heard they were going, his mind went dark and blank. All he could think about was that the Japs were eating American flyers on the island.

Munro checked his watch: five forty-five. As fast as it had come, the rain was gone, leaving a wet sheen on every leaf. Trickling sounds, along with a trio of insects, filled the air. Their melody was soothing, keeping their hearts still. Munro scanned left and right, checking his men. "Any minute now," he whispered to Murphy. "Pass it down the line and get Feroli over here."

The rose-colored sky revealed wire along the windows of the building set back farthest, Munro noticed. "That looks like some sort of mesh on those windows, and there's wire, you see it?"

Feroli squinted. "Yeah, definitely wire."

"That's where they are. Pass it along quickly. Keep the fire off that building," Munro instructed. He grabbed Walsh, who had his BAR trained on the staircase of what looked like a bunkhouse.

"Quick!" he said, grabbing a handful of shirt. "Tell Kow not to fire on building three, hurry!" Munro rubbed his thumb across his muddy watch: 06:03. "Damn it!"

The sound of a low-growling gear and high motor revs grew louder—an enemy 10×10 plowed up the muddy trail from the direction of the airfield. The barracks began to stir, and the first Japanese soldier stepped out of the radio building with a cigarette in his mouth and a lighter in his hand. He turned toward the truck, not knowing there were fifty guns trained on him, and flipped open his lighter.

The first explosion erupted underwater, followed by another, and another, each growing louder as they approached the shore. Horns and sirens sounded, and men scrambled out of their bunks, shouting. The Marines waited until the compound began to fill, their fingers deep in their triggers.

Sully's team was to take out the leaders. As soon as he saw the Japanese captain draw his sword, he parted his head like a canoe. Instantaneously, the three .30-cals opened fire and began cutting the Japanese down. Riflemen poured out the fire and sniped at every falling Jap.

"The Jap truck! Take out that truck!" Munro screamed over the volley of fire. Two separate hits from the bazooka teams blew it in half.

Planes buzzed overhead and began diving on the airfield half a mile away, keeping the Jap flyers in their holes. Munro signaled cease-fire, and he and two dozen men charged the buildings. As their feet hit the mud and gravel yard, the first shell from the *Missouri* struck the southwest face of Chichijima, sending a shockwave through the hollow rock.

The island shaking like the world coming off its axis, the Marines staggered as they charged the buildings, some stopping to confirm the downed were dead, with a bayonet stab in the chest. Feroli reached the door first but was blown off his feet by an after-shock. The Japanese were heading off the southwest ridge, away from the shelling, toward the camp. Although the enemy men had been stunned at the volume of fire, it was nothing compared to their surprise at the Marines running through their buildings.

Kowalker's men engaged the Jap soldiers and directed the fire, slowing their pace. Feroli was on his back, watching the sky as a Corsair tipped its wings and dropped a two-hundred-pound bomb on the road leading to the airport. "Munro!" he yelled. "We got trouble coming up the road!"

Munro signaled Lang to flack right and ran toward the bunk-house door, slamming his right shoulder into it, handle-side. He didn't feel the electric jolt over the instant pain of his now-shattered collarbone. Feroli grabbed the latch and was once more on his ass. "Fuck this!" Munro yelled, pulling out his .45, blowing chunks off the door.

"Marines! Marines! Anyone in here?" Two more Dogs reached the building and readied their weapons. "Go! Go!" Kicking doors in, they broke right and left. Behind them, hell was loose, and gunfire was ripping up the structures.

Munro entered the metal building, his eyes locking with a young flyer chained to the floor. In a second that seemed to last fifteen more, he turned to see three other flyers, all in chains. "Is this it, is this all of you?" he questioned, kneeling down to look at the stunned airmen.

"Yes," one replied.

"Look, Lieutenant!" Private Murphy shouted. "There are at least four empty chains!"

"Where are the others?" Munro asked again.

"He took them, he took Stevie!" one of the airmen said, bowing his head.

"Murph, get the cutters now!" Munro yelled. "We're going to get you off this rock, boys!"

Outside, war was raging on. Lang moved his men to cover the road leading to the airfield. The Corsair pilot tried to stop the fleeting convoy heading up the mud trail, but his two-hundred-pounder missed, leaving only some jungle debris in its wake.

Munro yelled for Sully, "Sully, get the mortars on that trail! Lang is in trouble. Have Walsh and the extractors get these guys down the cliff! Fuck, where is all that fire coming from?"

Munro scanned the battlefield. Bodies and blood covered the ground. "Demo! Demo! Blow that fucking place!" he cried, barking out orders while pointing to the radio building. Taking charge, Munro had his men wire the radio tower and the buildings. "They want these bunks. They can have them! Feroli, where's Feroli?"

"Dead, sir."

"Gather the men, move them to the ridge. Tell Kow to radio the *Missouri*! Tell them we have four, and keep on pounding that hill!"

"Yes, sir! What about Lang, sir?"

"I'll get Lang. You get your ass over to Kow!"

Munro grabbed Murph and Foley and headed for Lang's position. He could hear the .30-cal and the men screaming racial slurs at the Japanese.

"Reed! Reed! Where's Lang?" Munro asked.

"Sergeant!" Reed pointed to the road.

"What the fuck! Lang, get your ass up here!" Munro yelled. Sergeant Lang emerged from the opposite bank covered in blood. "Are you hit, Lang? Are you hit?"

Lang looked Munro square in the eyes. All he could say was, "Where's Stevie? Did you get Stevie?"

Munro shook his head no. Whistles were blowing from the north. "Lang, they're coming, we've got to go! We got four, we got four!"

Lang looked over at Reed, who was opening another case of .30-cal ammo. "Did they eat Stevie?" he asked.

"I don't know. What the fuck, Lang! We don't know where they took him, but he's gone, Lang, he's gone! Come on, let's go!"

Lang began to groan and growl. He looked back at the span of jungle he had emerged from, blood still wet on his face. "Reed, leave the .30!" he yelled, then sprinted toward its position.

"Marines, we're leaving!" Reed ordered. He and his men ran across the open road and compound, heading for the cliff.

"Lang! Lang!"

Sergeant Lang did not respond with words; instead, he lifted the .30-cal, threw a belt of ammo over his shoulder, and ran with the gun, tripod and all. His screams could be heard along with the firing of the gun long after he ran out of sight.

Below the ridge, the boats were filling up. They lowered down the wounded and dropped their dead into the water with respectful haste. Munro, Foley, Kow, and Murph held up on the ridge, the last rounds of Lang's .30 now silenced.

"That's one angry Marine," Kow said before he twisted the detonator. Fire exploded and sheet metal blew hundreds of feet into the air.

"Radio! Radio!" Munro yelled down the bluff. "Call it in on this position and let's get the hell out of here!"

Before the four Marines could grab the ropes, a shell from a Jap Cruiser exploded to Murph's right, blowing him clear off the bluff and sending rocks tumbling down on the LVTs below. The Gator gunners were busy pulling the deceased Marines out of the water and didn't notice the Cruiser. Looking out to the east, Munro saw the *Missouri* bearing down on Chichijima three or four miles out. Four massive shells exploded around the Cruiser as they turned to run.

Frank was about to lose his line of sight with the *Missouri* when, suddenly, as if someone had picked the enemy vessel up and broke it on their knee, the Japanese Cruiser lurched forward, buckled, and broke in half. Six hundred yards off the coast, the USS *Finback* slammed two torpedoes into the starboard side of the Cruiser, ending her for good.

Munro and Kowalker were the last on the ridge. "Kow, I can't climb down. I busted my shoulder. I'm jumping! Make sure you pull me out, you bastard!" said Munro.

"Fuck it, I'm jumping too!"

Both Marines headed over the cliff, still holding their Thompsons. Walsh thought they were Japs and swung his M1, ready to shoot.

"Hold your fire!" Sully yelled. "Those are ours! Two crazy fuckers!"

"Sully, pull my ass up. My shoulder's busted!" Munro said, sounding exhausted.

Seconds later, the three Gators cleared the rocks and were in open water. "Move! Move!" Kow yelled as the shells started hitting the bluff.

Looking out from the *Missouri*, Admiral Halsey charged in with his forward guns blasting, then turned twenty degrees port and let loose with his guns again. He then abruptly turned forty degrees, starboard, and their volley followed.

The guns from Chichijima concentrated on the rushing battleship, which shrugged off every round. Turning again port side, she displayed her might as the sixteen-inch guns pounded the hillside, creating a beautiful distraction for the LVTs.

Once the crew was aboard the *Missouri*, Munro, Kowalker, and McConell went over the mission.

"How many did you lose, Frank?" Jon asked.

"Six dead, thirteen wounded, one MIA."

"None of us would be here if you didn't sink that destroyer," Kow added.

"True, but that wasn't our kill. Admiral Halsey had that submarine stationed offshore. We lost a lot of flyers trying to take out that transmitter, Frank. The old man wants all you guys to stay on board a while. He told me there is something big brewing. How's your shoulder?" Jon asked, changing the subject.

Munro had his right arm in a sling. "Should be fine in a few weeks," he replied.

"We'll arrange a burial at sea for your men at 1800 hours, and we'll include the missing Marine." Jon took out a notepad and looked over at the men, obviously still distraught.

"Lang. Sergeant Robert Lang," Kow said.

Munro just shook his head and rubbed the back of his neck with his good hand. "He lost it, I guess. Either that or he had some vengeance for his bud, a flyboy named Stevie Flamos."

"The four you brought back are mighty grateful," Jon added, trying to lift their spirits. "They are being questioned, and I'll have a full report for you by tomorrow. Frank, you and your boys did exceptional today. Help yourselves to the coffee. I have to report to the bridge." Jon saluted the Marines and headed out.

Kow and Munro sat quietly. "You want to do something for me, Kow?" Munro asked.

"Ahh...I would say anything, but I'm afraid it could be too crazy," Kow replied, and they both chuckled.

"I want to write a letter, but I can't move my goddamn right hand."

Without hesitation, Kow took out a pencil.

"Dear Emily," Munro began.

A Growing Concern

"Emily," Martha called. Emily was still in a deep sleep. "She's hardly home at all lately, and when she is, she sleeps most of the day!"

"Calm down, dear, it's seven fifteen. You know she got in late."

"How would you know?" Martha snipped at her husband.

"I heard York barking on the porch, must have been 2:00 a.m."

"Two fifteen, if it makes any difference to you," Martha countered.

"Someone got up on the wrong side of the bed this morning. Morning, Matty."

Little Matty Fitzgerald stood in the doorway, rubbing his eyes. "Morning, Papa," he said with a slight yawn.

"What about me?" Martha added.

"Morning, Nanny!" Matty walked over and hugged her waist. "Where's Max, Nanny?" he asked.

"Oh, I imagine he's on the dock with that dog of his. You sit up with Papa and I'll make you pancakes."

Matty quickly climbed the large maple chair near his papa and started kicking his legs with excitement.

"You have ants in your pants, boy?" Papa said, laughing.

Matty laughed with him and said, "No, Papa. You're silly! Once, I had some worms in my pockets, when I was fishing with Max."

"You be careful on that dock, Matty. Don't go out there alone, now," Papa said, grabbing ahold of his hand. Pulling the child close to his good eye, Papa said, deepening his voice, "I'm watching you, boy!"

"Stop it, Max. You're scaring him!" Martha quipped.

"It's for his own good, dear," Max replied.

"Listen to your papa, Matty." She handed him a glass of milk. "The pancakes will be ready shortly."

"Morning, Mom."

"Emily." Martha paused, somewhat awkwardly. "I didn't hear you come down."

"Any pancakes for me?"

"Sit here, Mommy!" Matty said, full of excitement. "I'm going fishing with Max today!" Matty said, his little legs kicking up a storm.

"Is Papa going too?" Emily asked in a soft voice.

"Papa, are you coming fishing with me and Max?"

Just then, Max stepped into the kitchen, slightly out of breath. "Dad." He paused. "I was listening to the radio on the boat. They said the war is over! It's over! The Japanese surrendered!"

Martha quickly switched the radio on, and everyone stared at the yellow glow above the dial. "An unconditional surrender was signed aboard the USS *Missouri*..."

"Frank's on that ship!" Emily said, beaming.

"Oh, Emily, it's finally over!" Martha said as she delivered a plate of hot pancakes to her grandson. "Sit down, Max. We will celebrate over breakfast."

"Cook up the bacon, Martha," Max Sr. said, "and we will listen to all the details. What does this mean for you, Emily?"

"I'm not sure. Just as soon as I know..."

Ring-ring, ring-ring. The phone on the wall sounded.

"I'll get it!" said Emily. "Hello? Yes, I just heard! What does that mean for CUF, Mark?"

Lavenger paused on the other end. "Well, I'm sure we will be busy for the next six months. There are still a few hundred thousand boys scattered all over creation. Cole mentioned a recovery plan for the dead. Don't worry, Emily, Cole and I are meeting this afternoon. I will be in touch. Keep your appointments. There are several more on the way."

"Okay, Mr. Lavenger."

"Hey, did you know your boy was on the *Missouri*?"

"Yes, I did. How exciting! I can't wait to hear the details."

"Okay, I'll be in touch."

"Your boss?" her father inquired.

"Yes. He was excited, as you can imagine," Emily responded.

"What will this mean for our cargo shipments, Max?" Martha asked.

"I have several contracts that are not military related, but we can always haul people again," Max Strong said with a smile, sipping his coffee.

"Yes!" Max Jr. exclaimed, a tight fist raised in the air. "Mom, I'm taking Matty fishing."

"I'm going too," Papa said, pushing himself away from the table. "Martha, plan on catfish for dinner. Come on, boys, we have dinner to catch." The three of them hurried out the door.

Emily sat quietly, uncomfortably trying to think of something to say to her mother. "Mom..." She paused. "I know I have been away working, and you have been such a help with Matty. This job I have won't be needing me for too much longer, maybe six months or so. Mr. Lavenger will tell me when I am no longer needed. I have more cases coming, and I have a surprise for you and Dad."

"Oh?" Martha said with her back to Emily.

"I was going to wait until next week, but since the boys are off fishing, I was wondering if you and I could go into town. There is something I have to pick up."

"Sure, Emily. Let me clean up."

"No, I'll clean the kitchen. You go get ready."

Martha smiled at Emily. It felt like it was for the first time all week. "I'll be right down."

Emily pulled the Plymouth around to the front of the Strongs' home and waited for her mother. The news of the war's end was non-stop, and the cheers of celebration could be heard over several radio stations. Martha got in with her hat in her hand, and Emily shifted the car into gear.

"Dad told me you have been driving."

"Well, with his blind eye, I just can't trust him on these narrow roads. The river is one thing, but he makes me nervous."

"He made me nervous when he had both eyes, Mom, especially when he would speed over the town's river bridge and the boards would lift up as we raced over them!"

The women laughed and enjoyed each other's company on the winding country road into Marietta.

"What is it we are getting, Emily?"

"You will see. I want to surprise you," Emily said as she geared down to turn onto Main Street.

"Wow, look at all the people!" Chairs and tables were being set outside businesses, confetti and banners were scattered, and newspaper boxes were empty. "I know your father would like a paper, Emily. Let's hope they will have some to deliver."

Everyone in town had a wide smile and a spring in their step. "Good news travels fast, now, doesn't it, Emily?" Martha was feeling the excitement.

Emily turned the corner onto Center Street and pulled into the Ford dealership.

"Is there something wrong with the car, Emily?"

"No, Mother, not unless you hate the color of that coup over there," she said, pointing to a deep-blue '44 Ford.

"Oh, Emily!"

"Yup, I bought you and Dad a car!"

"Us? Emily, how could you afford…oh, Emily, it's beautiful! Your father is going to flip!"

"I wanted to thank you for everything you have done. I know I have been, well, you know…I had to show you my appreciation."

Martha leaned over and hugged her daughter. "Emily," she said, "let's get a closer look at that car."

"You go ahead. I have to check on the paperwork and see the salesman about a spare key. Oh, and, Mom, after, could you go to the post office and see if I have anything? Box 23, okay?"

Martha looked the car over, the shine from the wheels to the window trim momentarily dazzling her. Her joy was only interrupted by a mail truck that pulled up. Martha walked into the Marietta post office across the street.

The clerk did not recognize her but knew of Emily.

"Emily Fitzgerald, number 23," Martha said as she approached the counter.

"One moment, ma'am. Great news today, hey, Mrs. Fitzgerald?"

"It's Strong, and yes, excellent news."

"Oh, the riverboat Strongs?" Martha nodded and smiled. "Here you go." She handed her three large manila envelopes and one small worn letter addressed from Frank.

"Thank you," Martha said and headed across the street. Emily was standing beside the coup. Martha could see the salesman cornering her with a devilish smile. Martha watched Emily turn him toward the rear fender, taking the key from his hand and causing him to stumble back, hitting his knee on the bumper.

"Careful, son," Martha said. His face flushed from embarrassment. "Emily, you have a letter from Frank," Martha emphasized loudly, sending the salesman away sheepishly.

"Enjoy the car," the salesman said before he ducked back inside.

Emily thanked her mother. "You certainly didn't look as though you needed my help, Emily. I just thought it would be fun to poke at that man."

"Here, Mom, you drive the coup. I'll take Dad's car."

"Absolutely not! I'm not driving that car without your father in it. You enjoy the car, Emily," Martha said with a smile, mocking the salesman. "I will meet you at home."

Emily took the envelopes and placed them on the passenger seat. On top was a handwritten, weathered-looking letter. She took it and placed it on her lap, started the Ford, and headed down onto Main Street, past the barber shop, causing quite a stir.

The sexy blue coup exaggerated her beauty, and with joy in the air, smiles everywhere seemed directed at her. Emily couldn't help thinking of Matt, her Fitzy, how this war both hurt and helped their family.

She clutched the letter as she drove the winding roads back home. *I wonder what he's up to now*, Emily thought, her mind now focused on Frank. She hit the accelerator and sped home.

Martha pulled the old Plymouth down the gravel drive toward the barn. Emily was right behind her.

"Should we hide it in the barn?" Martha asked.

"No! I will park it right up front. They won't know whose it is."

"Did you have chance to open Frank's letter, Em?" Martha asked as she walked around the car.

"No, Mother."

"Okay, Emily, you know we never talked about it." She paused. "But we understand. Matty is going to need a father, and well, Frank seems like a nice man. We just want you to know—"

"We," Emily interrupted.

"Your father and I want you to know that it's okay. We don't want you to be a martyr, Emily, and so many boys, and men, were lost. You deserve a second chance is all."

Emily approached her mother. Tears had begun to form in her eyes, and she reached out and pulled her mother close. "Thanks, Mom." And they embraced each other lovingly.

"Come now. We better get a few scallions for that catfish tonight," Martha said, holding her daughter's shoulders. "You're a fine woman, Emily. I saw the way you handled that man at the car dealership today. You...you learned a lot growing up on the rivers. You know I used to regret that, but I saw today it was no mistake." Martha took her daughter's hand and led her around to the spice garden. "You go read that letter, Em. I'll get to dinner."

Emily still had tears in her eyes as she walked toward the *Annabell Rose*. She climbed on board, hopped up in the helmsman seat, and reached forward for her dad's pocketknife. After opening the blade and examining the letter's various stains, she slipped the blade in and cut it open.

Dear Emily,

If you think my penmanship has drastically improved, well, don't get your hopes up. My arm is in a sling. It's Kow—he's the one writing you for me, my Emily.

My papers came in and I decided not to re-enlist. I was hoping when I am back in the States,

I could take you on a road trip to meet my parents. I don't know when, of course, but it will be before Thanksgiving. Tell your parents I give them my regards, and all the boys here say hello, especially Sully. They say I'm lucky, being alive still, and to have you. I don't believe in luck. I do, however, believe in you.

Say hello to Max and Matty for me. Tell Max there is a dog on board. He is a Jack Russell terrier, but we affectionately call him a jerk russell! He bites at the back of our heels when we pass by. Still nice to have a dog on board. We will talk soon.

Love,
Frank

Meeting of the Minds

Cole opened his door. "Come in, come in, ladies. Make yourselves at home. Sandra is in the kitchen. Go right in." Joe Cole turned his attention back to his CUF colleagues. "Well, boys, we did the best we could with the time we had to work. There has been no reluctance for the most part from the widows, and seven out of ten of the babies born are male."

"Let's celebrate!" Mike said, heading for the library.

"Hold on, Mike. I was thinking out on the balcony. It's a beautiful August night," Joe persuaded, opening his jacket and exposing a pocket of cigars.

"So how's married life, Mark?" Joe asked, putting his hand on Mark's shoulder, guiding him out to the balcony.

"Excellent! Seriously, it is great," Mark replied, causing a sarcastic laugh from Michael.

"Give it time," Mike said, and the three lit their cigars.

"As long as we're together and don't get in lost in wanting our egos stoked, I think we can continue for another six to eight months, plus nine, of course," Mark Lavenger joked. They laughed.

"How are our girls doing, Joe?" Mike asked.

"Excellent, Mike. Like I said, there are no problems currently, and as long as CUF is making money, well, we can be assured no one will stray."

"Yeah, all bets are off if your investments come crashing down, Joe," Mark replied.

"Well, boys, we invest in gold, and everything I can do to convert our assets to gold, I do," Cole stated.

"What about the living fathers, Joe?" Mark added. "Any count?"

"Currently, there are still seven alive."

"Is that a problem?" Mark questioned.

"I can't see that it would be. The chances of them having sex with some girl born with their genes are seriously remote. Look at the age difference!" At that moment, both Mike and Joe looked at Mark. "Well, ha, funny, you jealous bastards," Mark said. "I'm fifteen years older than Lisa, big deal," he finished smugly.

"Let's make sure we are prepared for everything. We will keep track of them through their military records, VA appointments, and issued checks. It's the soldiers themselves I'm worried about. Some of those little girls could meet our boys. I began a location chart, and I will add the heroes. I'll go, what, two generations deep?"

"Yeah, if you live that long," Mike added, poking at Mark. "I will keep you up to speed regarding our soldiers. Just remember why we began this project. Gentlemen, Russia is already acting up, spreading communism all across Europe. We should make it a point to get together twice a year."

Mark remarked, "Great idea. Let's have the girls choose where, and we'll choose when."

"Nice, Lavenger. I like that," Joe said. "Gives Sandy the impression she is steering the ship! Come on, let's go rescue Lisa from those two women in there."

"What's that supposed to mean?" Mark asked with a naive tone.

"Never mind. True what they say, love is blind!"

Treaty Signed

Frank and his Sea Dogs were now part of Hallsey's Big Mo. "Having those Marines on board means something," he would say when he saw them on deck.

Frank had time for convalescence, and he and his men took part in the Battle of Okinawa. Steaming south in early August, Hallsey took his flagship in range of Japan and released his sixteen-inch guns on her. It was August 9 when he called all hands on deck.

Facing all he could south, the men of the *Missouri* stood and witnessed the destruction of Nagasaki Island. A bright light and a circular rippled shock wave lit up one corner of the sky, followed by a building mushroom-shaped cloud. Moments later, Japan surrendered.

The ship was abuzz with energy. Jon McConnell met Frank in the galley and shook his hand. "It's over, Frank. We lived to tell about it."

"Planning on writing this down, Jon?" Frank replied.

"Hope to someday. I plan on fishing mostly." They poured a cup of coffee and stared into each of their cups.

Absentmindedly Frank reiterated, "Yes, fishing. That reminds me, I got to get a letter off."

One week later, Jon, Frank, and the rest of the crew of the *Missouri* stood at attention and welcomed the Allied British commanders. August 29, the Big Mo steamed into Tokyo Bay.

September 2, they were back on deck and witnessed General MacArthur signing the unconditional surrender of the nation of Japan. Jon couldn't help but smile as he stared down the proud

Japanese, and Frank found his fists were clenched during most of the ceremony. He felt that the admiral wanted his Sea Dogs on deck for the fear factor, and he instructed his men to stare down every Jap that dared eye contact. The ceremony lasted twenty-three minutes; the Japanese commanders each had taken their place at the table and signed.

It was September 25 when the *Missouri* at last sailed into Pearl Harbor. The Sea Dogs then boarded a plane and headed for the mainland, leaving Frank no time to phone Emily. He hoped his last letter would reach her before he called. His anticipation caused his back to sweat.

Frank squirmed in his seat. "What's wrong, Munro?" Sully asked.

"Nothing, Sully. Just anxious."

"About what, Frank? Hey, we're above ground. We made it! That's all that matters!"

"You're right, Sully, you're right. I'll settle down when we land."

"You'll settle down now!" And Sully pulled a flask from his sock.

"Nice, Sully. Thanks." Frank tipped his head back and poured the bourbon slowly down his throat.

The transport arrived without incident, and the men of the First and Third said their farewells.

"Sully, Campbell, Terra, it's been quite an experience. Let's not be strangers," Frank began.

Campbell spoke up. "Okay, listen up, you guys keep in touch! We are gonna meet in two years' time up in Boston. I will be up and running with my fishing boat, the *Labrador*. We will talk shit and catch fish!"

"Sounds like a plan, Campbell," said Frank.

Frank did the math in his head. "Ah, 5:00 p.m....that's 8:00 p.m. there or 7:00 p.m. I'm calling."

"I have to make a call, boys. Something I have been wanting to say." Munro turned to his friends. "More times than I can count we kept one another alive while hundreds of Marines died all around us. Not knowing why we are here now, I can only say thanks to you and

God Almighty. I am going to make the most of it starting tonight! I hope you all do the same!"

"Amen," Campbell said, and they shook hands. Frank Munro walked slowly away.

The phone rang three times before the operator answered. "Marietta operator!"

"Maxwell Strong, please, 626," Frank said in a determined tone.

"Just one moment."

Frank was more nervous now than ever as he listened for the receiver to pick up.

"Hello?" The woman's voice sounded a bit muffled.

"Hello," he said. "It's Frank Munro, calling for Emily. Is this Mrs. Strong?"

"Frank! Frank, it's Martha. So nice to hear your voice. Congratulations! Frank, we all saw you in the paper on the deck of that ship. It was very exciting! Where are you?"

The knot in Frank's stomach began to ease. "I'm in San Francisco, Mrs. Strong. I just arrived. I am taking a train east, and it leaves in twenty minutes. I wanted to say hi to Emily, if I could."

"Oh, Frank, Emily isn't here. She is working…oh, I think somewhere in the Cleveland area, but she will be here tomorrow around noon. How are you, Frank? Emily told me you were injured."

"It's fine, Mrs. Strong. Really, I am fine, happy to be heading back home. Could you tell Emily I called?"

"Of course, Frank. Do you plan on stopping by, Frank? I know Emily and the boys would like to see you."

Frank was speechless, his heart in his throat. "I would like that," he said. "I think my train will be there sometime Tuesday. I will call when we stop tomorrow to make sure it's okay."

"Sure it's okay, Frank!" Martha said. "Emily has looked forward to seeing you. Just make plans to come here first, unless there is something keeping you."

"No, no, Mrs. Strong. Thank you. I will make sure to come."

"Okay, then, Frank, make sure you are on the train to Parkersburg. It's the closest stop. We will see you on Tuesday."

Martha hung up the phone. Frank had the receiver to his ear and his mouth still opened. *Well, that was easy,* he thought. *Now to figure out how to get to Parkersburg by Tuesday.*

Frank settled into his seat as the miles clacked away. Stations came and went, conductors called, whistles blew. There was plenty to see, too. Frank watched the people hop on and off, seemingly without a care. Some reminded him of men he knew, and some he didn't or could not forget. A menagerie of dead bodies appeared in his mind at times as passengers bunched up at a doorway.

At one stop, a young sailor boarded the train and took the seat just in front of Frank. His curly blond hair and fair complexion made him the spitting image of Sergeant Lang. Frank could just about feel the image of Lang standing on that jungle road dripping with blood. He reached into his pocket for Emily's now-torn kerchief, crumbled it, and brought it up to his nose. The scent was gone, but it helped him to think of her.

The images of the war flashing in his head were welcomely interrupted by kind voices of two female passengers speaking lovingly to each other. Seeing warm embraces, hardy handshakes, and big smiles were the best relief. Everyone looked so happy, and why not? No one was trying to kill anyone—no one at all. Frank took a deep breath. *One more day, one more day,* he mused, closing his eyes. *Chicago, I have to get to Chicago, and the mid-Ohio transit.*

Frank sat quietly in the diner car, carefully holding his coffee as the train rounded the hill and began to gain speed. "God, I'm anxious," he said out loud to himself. "I have to relax…relax, no way! I'm going to bust if I have another sip."

"How is everything, sir?" the waitress asked with a crock of coffee in her hand.

Frank covered his cup. "It's great, everything is great, miss! How long to Parkersburg?"

"I'll check for you, Captain," she said with a big smile, looking back twice as she walked away.

Frank looked sharp in his uniform, and the chest full of combat medals didn't hinder his appearance.

Moments later, she returned. "Just over two hours, Captain. Four more stops."

"Thank you, miss."

Frank extended his hand. Placing the pencil she was holding in her hair, she took Frank's hand. Looking him in the eye, she said, "No, Captain, thank you. We are all very proud of you Marines." She turned to walk back up the aisle, then stopped and looked at him once more. "Oh, the gentleman who was sitting over there." She pointed to a booth across the car. "He paid for your breakfast." She smiled and turned with her crock. "Coffee? Coffee, anyone?"

Frank was amazed by his reception from pure strangers, from the people who were back in the States, working in factories, mills, and keeping up with the war's demand. Seeing a uniform meant something. When the heroes returned home, they were a part of the greater good. They were victorious.

The rolling hills of Ohio were one of the most beautiful places on Earth. Late-morning mist hung in the cool saddles below the ridge. Fall colors of yellow, red, and orange painted the forest. A storm front approached from the southwest, pushing with it tropical air. Leaves began to blow and turned inside out as the sky darkened.

"Six minutes!" called the conductor. Frank tipped his head and grabbed for the helmet that wasn't there. His mind flashed to the first time he had met Jon McConnell. *Six minutes,* he thought, back in the present. *I have to freshen up, yes.* And he took out his kit from his duffel bag.

"Parkersburg Station!" roared the conductor. Frank stood before the train stopped, and when its brakes grabbed, the momentum carried him to the door. He looked back at the passengers and smiled. "Good luck," a few of them said, returning his smile.

Frank felt lighter than air as he stepped onto the platform. Rain began to fall like an open faucet. The station itself wasn't very busy, and a quick scan didn't produce a familiar face.

Frank slung his duffel over his shoulder and headed to the station front. Not with unsure strides, but walking cautiously. When he opened the glass doors in Parkersburg, he couldn't help notice a dark, sleek Ford coup parked out front. What he missed was the slender figure hidden behind an oversize umbrella.

"You like my car, Frank?" Emily asked, tipping the umbrella, showing her beautiful face. Frank stood motionless, his heart pounding at the sound of her voice. Frank was within arm's reach, and they both took a step toward the other.

Dropping his duffel bag, he embraced her. Emily swung her arms around Frank's neck and kissed him firmly, clutching him tight. "If you knew how good this feels, Emily...," Frank whispered, not easing a muscle. Emily kissed him once more. "Come on, Frank, let's get out of the rain."

Emily was more at ease than Frank had ever seen her before. She talked and laughed as she drove back to Marietta. Emily had already made up her mind about Frank out in Hawaii, although Frank never knew. He was used to being in charge of things, including his feelings. That was about to change.

"Emily," Frank said, "before we get to your parents', I want to know if you've given any thought to visiting mine."

Emily answered immediately. "Yes, Frank! Silly, of course. I already mentioned it to Max. You know he will want to take his dog. At least he's always clean."

"Max?" Frank asked.

"No, his dog," she replied.

Frank laughed. "Well, York is part of your family, isn't he?"

Emily said jokingly, "Yeah, so's my mom. You want her to come too?"

"Oh, I don't know, maybe. I think your mom likes me," Frank said.

Emily stared at him with an unkind face and her brow up. "You're not safe yet, mister," she said, breaking her stare with a smile. Both of them laughing, it was the best Frank had felt in years, and the ride didn't seem long enough. Frank recognized the hills near her home and the smell of the river.

"Okay, Frank, we're here," Emily said. "Prepare yourself." Emily rolled the Ford slowly down the gravel drive. York had heard her slow down and ran up the grassy hill, keeping pace with the car.

Out on the front porch, the Strong family sat with little Matty.

"Awful nice of your folks to be waiting, Emily." Frank felt his throat tighten.

"You know, Frank, they're just good folk," she said, looking over and grinning.

Matty ran over and hugged his mom. Young Max walked over and shook Frank's hand firmly. "Good to see ya again, Mr. Munro," he said, throwing up his best salute.

"Frank, just call me Frank."

"Okay, yes, sir!" Max said, reaching down to pat his dog. York sat wagging his tail, waiting for approval.

"My duffel bag is in the back, Max. Think you can bring it in?"

"Sure!"

"Mr. and Mrs. Strong," Frank said with authority, "good to see you again."

Martha and Max sat patiently as Frank approached their home. Martha got up and walked down the stairs, admiring his uniform and all the medals pinned to his chest. She hugged Frank firmly and patted his back, then pulled away. Brushing the medals on his chest, she said, "Frank, we're so proud, so glad you could come!"

"Hey," Max Sr. said from his chair, "that one's taken, Frank, but the lady behind you is available." And he broke out in laughter.

"Oh, Max," Martha quipped. "Always the comedian."

"Well, get up here so I can take a good look at ya," Max said. "So you were on the *Missouri* when the Japs signed. That's some story, Frank. You'll have to tell us all about it after dinner."

"Yes, sir," Frank replied.

"Now let's eat. I'm starving! Been smelling Martha's roast for hours," Max Strong said, getting up from the porch swing. "Frank, I set some clothes aside if you wanted to change, but don't feel you have to. Just wanted you comfortable."

"I don't know how it's possible, Mr. Strong, but I feel more comfortable here and now than I can ever remember."

"Oh, Emily, we have another charmer," Martha said, grabbing Max's arm and leading him in.

Emily still had Matty wrapped around her leg. "Okay, boys, let's see who can run to the kitchen first. Ready…go!"

"Hey!" Max yelled. "Not fair! This bag weighs a ton!"

Matty used all fours to climb the porch and reached the door first, Max not two steps behind.

"Just leave it there," Frank said. "I'll get it."

A ruckus and tumble was heard after Max ran into the house, followed by Martha yelling, "No running in the house!"

Emily paused at the stairs and looked up at Frank. "Sure you're ready for this, soldier?"

Frank walked down the stairs and took Emily's hand. "Been ready my whole life, Em."

And they kissed long and slow.

Emily and Frank visited friends and family around Marietta. Emily drove Frank into town to meet the locals, keeping him in uniform and causing quite a stir. Everyone liked Frank; his bright smile and resolve was a welcome sight. Shopkeepers and clerks came out of their businesses to shake his hand. The pharmacist even bribed him with a chocolate malt, saying, "It's on the house, Captain." Frank was overwhelmed by the love and admiration. Emily let him soak it in, always following just behind.

Matty took to him immediately, and York, Max's ever-faithful dog, was always bringing him a stick to throw.

Trip Back East

Martha packed up food and handed it to Emily, kissed her, and wished the couple a safe trip. "Now you better get out of here before Matty wakes. I'll tell him you're working. He'll understand. Your father's taking him fishing."

"Fishing!" Max Jr. said, climbing into the back of the Ford. "Aww..."

"Max, we're going to do a little fishing ourselves, I promise," Frank said, settling him down.

"Have a safe trip. Are you sure you want to take that dog?"

"Ma!" Max Jr. yelled.

"Okay, okay. Bye, Emily. Bye, Frank." Martha waved, looking him square in the eye.

"Thanks again, Mrs. Strong. I'll take good care of them." Frank shifted the Ford into gear, grinding the mechanics slightly, causing Emily's face to scrunch with the noise. "Oops, I'm a little rusty," he said, easing out the clutch.

Emily waved bye once more, and they headed down the driveway.

The sun had not yet risen above the hills as they drove out of Marietta, and the cool fall air was a little more refreshing than Emily liked, but she didn't complain. York's head was hanging out of the rear passenger window, and as long as they left him like that, he never whined.

Max had hundreds of questions, mostly about the war, but Frank always managed to steer away from any detail of battle. Mostly he told of his friends and talked of his time on the ships, which made Emily very pleased. She had heard of the horrors of war from the dozens of women from CUF and didn't want to know how many men Frank saw dead or killed himself. His uniform decorations were of a combat veteran and enough conviction for her.

Miles rolled by, and the seven-hundred-mile journey passed quicker than they all could have imagined. A sign for Newburg appeared ahead, and Frank got Max's attention. "There's a pretty big river coming up," Frank said.

"Yeah, I know," Max said. "It's the Hudson. My dad told me all about it, how it started up in Lake Champlain and ran right through New York City. It's not as long as the Ohio."

"Oh," Frank remarked. "I forgot we had ensign in our presence."

"What's that? Like a captain?" Max asked.

"No, but not far from it." Frank looked over at Emily and smiled. "There are some rivers where we're going, Max, all near the ocean, and the fishing this time of year will be spectacular." Then Frank said under his breath, "I hope."

"Really? But we didn't bring any gear."

"Not to worry, Max. I have all the gear we'll need."

It was about three when they crossed the Hudson. No one made a sound, just stared at the beautiful cable bridge and rough, muddy water.

"Wow," Max said after they crossed. "I didn't think it was going to be that big."

Emily motioned to Frank that a pit stop was necessary, and Frank pulled off near Danbury, Connecticut. "I will fill the car, Em. Max, here." He handed him a dollar bill. "See if you can rustle us up a few cold Cokes."

Emily let the dog out of the back seat, and he ran toward the wooded lot behind the service station. "Looks like I'm not the only one," Emily said, smiling as she walked away.

"I'll see if we can get him some clean water, Emily," Frank said.

The serviceman walked out under the sign "Balchune's Auto Service." Frank greeted him and shook his hand.

"Welcome back, Marine. Walter, Walter Balchune. Check under the hood?"

"Yes, sir, please," Frank replied, admiring the man's grip.

"Nice car you have here."

"Thanks, but it's not mine."

"A loaner?"

"No, it's Emily's. I mean the girl you saw who walked past you."

"That was no girl, son," the man said firmly. "That's a woman!"

Frank smiled and nodded. They chatted as the man cranked the fuel into the ten-gallon gas tank.

"Where you heading?" he asked.

"Back east, to my folks' house near Plymouth, Massachusetts."

"Well," Walter said, "they are doing a lot of work on Route 84, before you get to Hartford. If you don't mind me telling you, take Route 34. It's about ten miles ahead. It connects to Interstate 95. Might be quicker. Takes you through New Haven."

"I may just do that. I'm familiar with 95. Thanks, sir."

"Hey, don't mention it. Nice family you have, Captain, and that's one strong-looking dog."

"Yes, he's quite an animal. The boy has him trained well."

"Okay, seventeen gallons. Pay the woman inside. She's my wife!" he said proudly.

"Will do. Thanks again," Frank replied graciously. Walter headed back into the bay, where he began wrestling with an exhaust system. *Solid grip on that old man,* he thought. *That muffler doesn't stand a chance.*

Frank mentioned the detour through the valley toward New Haven, repeating what Walter told him.

"Okay, Frank, I know that area well. I lived there when Matthew was stationed in New Haven, and worked there for years."

"Emily worked at a torpedo factory," Max piped up.

"Oh, nice," Frank said. "You never told me about that, Em."

"Yeah, Emily, tell us how you made those torpedoes that sank all those Jap destroyers and U-boats," her little brother beckoned.

Emily turned to the window, her eyes filling up.

"Maybe you can just point to it if we pass by, Em," Frank said.

"No, no, it's okay, I will, but can we make a stop at a bakery? I want to visit a friend and pick up something for your parents."

The sleek Ford drove into a hairpin turn at the Steven's Dam, and Max was amazed at the nearly two-hundred-foot drop and white water flowing from the turbines that powered the factories downriver. The glacier that once carved out the pass left deposits of granite and shale, and the narrow road finally flattened out when they reached Derby. It was four fifteen, and most of the factories were still in first-shift mode, with moderate foot traffic.

"Okay, over here on the left, this narrow brick building. Here's where we assembled the torpedoes. The components come from the surrounding factories."

Frank and Max were baffled at how small a place it was.

"Straight ahead is Saint Michael's, just past it. There. Tyberski Bakery, park out front. I will only be a moment. They make the best sourdough bread around." Emily was visibly nervous as she stepped out of the car. "Be right back," she said and hurried into the small bakery.

The bell above the door rang a familiar chime, and Mrs. Tyberski looked up from behind the counter. The woman looked as if she was staring at a ghost, initially. She blinked her eyes and smiled. "Emily, Emily, my Emily!" she cried, coming around the glass case along the rack of assorted bread.

Emily held out her arms, and they hugged each other. "Oh, Emily, it is so good to see you! Where's little Matty? Tell me, is everything all right?"

Emily was choked with emotion. "Yes, everything is fine." And she hugged her once more. "I am with my little brother, Max. He's out front with a man I met, a serviceman."

"Oh, have them come in!"

"Well, maybe Frank, Mrs. Tyberski, but my brother brought his dog and it won't let him out of its sight."

"Oh, Emily, I'm so happy you found someone."

"Really? I was afraid you wouldn't approve, and I was worried what people would think."

"Shhh...now, you listen to me, Emily, life is for the living. We all know how you loved your Matthew, but he's been gone a long time. The world has enough martyrs, Emily. We don't need any more."

Emily finally allowed herself to smile as tears were falling down her cheeks.

"Here"—she took a piece of fresh baker's cloth—"take this and go out back and freshen up. I'm going out to see your family."

Mrs. Tyberski pushed open the door and walked over to the Ford. York's head was out the window, and he began to whine and wag his tail. She petted his head and opened the passenger door.

"Emily is freshening up. Step out of the car and let me take a look at you," she said to the handsome Marine.

Frank gladly complied and walked around the rear of the car.

"Well, now, you're a fine-looking man. Strong, too. You're going to make a fine husband." Frank didn't know what to say. "Come on in. Let's get you some fresh bread before the factory unloads and I can't talk."

Frank entered the tiny bakery as Emily stepped out of the back. The smell of fresh bread filled his nostrils, and he let out an "Ahhh." Mrs. Tyberski smiled. "Where are you heading, Emily?"

"We're going to Massachusetts to visit Frank's family. We left Marietta around five this morning and have a few more hours to go."

"You're not leaving empty-handed, I hope."

"No, ma'am," Frank said, his eyes dashing from loaf to loaf.

"Good-looking and polite—better hold on to this one, Emily!" The couple smiled sheepishly at each other. "Here, Emily, here are two loaves of fresh sourdough bread, your favorite." Emily watched her bag the bread like she had a thousand times before.

"Now hold on, you two. I have something else for that boy and his dog." Mrs. Tyberski maneuvered around the bread racks and disappeared. Returning, she said, "I have some heels for that dog, and look at these." She held out a white box filled with cream pies. "These are something the girls and I whipped up! We call them victory helmets."

Emily and Frank peered into the box at six chocolate cupcakes with the tops cut and filled with whipped cream. "These won't make it to your folks' house," she said and laughed aloud.

"Now, you two run along, but I want to see you back here on the way home, Emily, promise?"

"Yes, yes, Mrs. Tyberski, thank you. Thank you so much," she said while reaching into her purse.

"No, Emily, these are on me. You take care of your man and stop back, you hear?" Emily kissed her and thanked her once more. "Frank, it was nice meeting you."

"Very nice meeting you also, Mrs. Tyberski."

"Have fun, you two. I have to get ready for the rush." Just then, cars began to pull up, and Emily and Frank excused themselves as they left the narrow entrance.

Emily was smiling from ear to ear when she opened the door. "No, York, not for you."

Max wanted to know what was in the box, and they all grabbed a helmet and bit into it. Like the hum of a quartet, they all said "Yum" with a mouthful and drove off.

After finishing their first one, Emily wanted Frank to tell them what his home was like and who would be there waiting for them. "I don't really know if anyone will be waiting on the porch, but I'm sure my parents have something planned for later. My mother has eight sisters, and all claim to be direct descendants of the original *Mayflower* Pilgrims."

"Really? How interesting," Emily said sarcastically, joking with him.

"Yes, it's true. But my father's side is a bit of a mystery. I believe they came through Nova Scotia, dropped the *E* from Munro, and settled here. I never knew my grandfather, and my dad never mentioned him. Most of my aunts married well, and at least two of them are in the cranberry business. The have houses all over Cape Cod and along Kingston Bay. You will see tomorrow. It will be dark when we arrive, but you'll see."

"And your home?" Emily questioned.

"Well, it's hard to explain. It's different from a country home. It was built in the 1700s and overlooks the bay. There's a widow's walk."

"What's that?" Max asked.

"It's a place on the roof with a railing around it. Wives of sea captains would go up there, awaiting the return of their husbands from sea." Frank reached over and patted Emily's leg.

"Some became widows, I guess," Max said.

"Yes, some I'm sure did. Well, anyways, there are several rooms. My little brother should be there, John. Berry season should be over, and he won't be a stone's throw from my dad, the cranberry man."

"Sounds nice," Emily said.

"Real nice," Max added.

"Max, you're how old now? Ten?"

"Yes. I'll be eleven in January."

"Hey, that's when John was born, January 23."

"I'm January 11. How old is he?"

"I think he's either eleven or twelve, I can't remember, but I remember the day he was born. My dad made sure the driveway was clear of snow for two weeks before he was born so we would be sure to get out."

"Was there a lot of snow?" Emily asked.

"Yes," Frank said with exasperation. "That year it snowed almost every day, and I missed a lot of school keeping that driveway clean! I didn't mind. School wasn't a big priority to me."

"Well, that explains your letters," Emily said, laughing out loud.

Frank blushed. "Well, I had other things on my mind, I guess."

"Like what, Frank?" Max asked.

"Like hunting brant and sea duck."

"What's a *brant?*" Max asked.

"It's like a Canada goose, but a bit smaller."

"Oh, those taste good," Max said.

"Exactly," Frank added. "Most of my family liked to fish, but I was the only one who took to hunting. If I had a dog like yours, I would never have graduated."

Max smiled and petted his dog.

Max dozed off somewhere around Providence, and Emily slid over, resting her head on Frank's shoulder. "It's been a great drive, Frank, really great."

Frank squeezed her with his right arm. "Close your eyes, Em. We'll be there soon."

Frank eased on the brakes as he pulled into the driveway off Route 3A. The winding road never woke either of them. The lights were on outside, and the white pillars cast a shadow where Frank parked. "Okay, we're here."

Emily rubbed her eyes, reached back, and shook her little brother. "Wake up, Max."

"I'm up, I'm up." York began licking Max's face. "Aww, stop, York!" he yelled, then patted his head. "Stop, okay, boy?"

Frank opened the trunk just as the front door of his parents' home opened. Frank's mother, Ann, ran down the steps and hugged her son. "Francis, oh, Francis!" She let go as fast as she grabbed him. "You must be Emily! Ann Munro!" she said with a warm smile that could be seen through the dark. "John," Ann called, "John, it's your brother and guests. Come out here and help!"

A wiry young boy skipped down the stairs as Frank was coming around the Ford. "Wow, nice car! Is it yours, Frank?"

"No, it's Emily's," he said. "Get over here, you little monkey!" Frank grabbed his brother and nearly threw him up onto the roof.

"Now, Francis, don't you two start. Emily, forgive his manners. He hasn't seen Francis in almost four years," Ann said.

"You don't have to explain," she said as she pulled her own brother around the door and smiled.

"Who do we have here?" Ann asked.

"Max, ma'am, Max Strong." His accent emphasized his name. York was running all over the front yard.

"And whose handsome dog?"

"Mine, ma'am," Max said proudly.

John came running over to see him. "Mom," John said, "this is the kind of dog I was telling you about! Awww, they are the best!" York let John pat him vigorously.

"Well, he's welcome in too," Ann said. "Come on, let's get out of the night air."

"Mom, can Max and I stay out in the yard for a while?"

"It's okay with me," Emily stated.

"If Emily says okay, but not too late. And stay away from the water for tonight."

"Okay, Mom," John replied.

"I swear, Emily, that boy of mine, he could get wet in the desert!"

"Where's Dad?" Frank asked as he entered the hall.

"Well, we weren't sure what day you would be here, and your uncles were having trouble with their flatbed. They had a full load and nearly lost it on the way to market. He went off this morning with all the rope we own!" Ann answered. "I can't imagine him being any longer. I thought it was him who pulled up."

"Where did it happen?" Frank asked.

"You know your uncle James. He had some idea he could get more berries on that old truck. Then something happened. He didn't say."

"I thought you would be done with the harvest by now, Mom."

"Me too, but they decided to wet-pick the Carver bog even after your father told them they're almost twice as heavy that way. James never listens," Ann said. "Emily, why don't you come in the kitchen and sit down?"

"Mrs. Munro,"

"Call me Ann, please."

"Ann, I have been sitting all day. I would love it if you would show me your home. It's beautiful."

Ann took Emily's hand and walked off into the house. "Francis, bring those suitcases up to your room and check on those two boys. You had her long enough."

Ann and Emily were like old friends. Emily had noticed Frank's Boston accent when they first met, but years away from home had dulled it. Ann, however, had lived in Massachusetts her whole life, and Emily had to listen carefully when she was speaking, not wanting to mistake words unintentionally.

"I hope you like a good par'ty, Emily," Ann said. "My sisters have been waiting a long time for Francis to meet a nice woman. Oh, and come home safe too! We have a party planned for tomorrow afternoon, that is, if I can find my husband by then!" Both of the women laughed.

Ann showed off pictures of Frank in his youth. "I never saw Frank without his uniform on, Ann."

"Funny, I could never get him to dress up, not even for church. Now look at him, all neat and trim."

It was obvious Ann was proud of her Francis, but she was even more humbled by his service. Ann began to cry. "Emily, I heard so many things about that rotten war! Promise me he won't ever go again, promise me!"

Emily took Ann's hand. "Didn't he tell you?"

Ann stopped and listened.

"Frank didn't re-enlist! He told me he served his time and it's over!"

Ann hugged Emily. "Oh, thank God, thank God! He wouldn't have done that for me, Emily. He must love you dearly."

"No, Ann. I would like to believe that, and you're very kind to say it, but I think Frank had had enough. Enough sorrow and killing. He's a Marine, and the Marines are sent to the most horrible places on earth."

"I hope you're right, Emily. So many boys my son knew never came home, so many they never found."

"Well, he's here now, Ann. I don't want him to see us crying," Emily said as both of them wiped their tears.

It was after midnight when John Sr. finally pulled into his driveway. He noticed the Ford immediately and walked around the car, admiring it immensely before heading in. Max, York, and John Jr. were sleeping in John's room, and Frank, Emily, and Ann were still up in the kitchen, talking.

"Son," John said, standing in the threshold. Three heads turned simultaneously.

Frank got up as if a general had entered the room. Ann just said, "John, where on earth have you been?" He never heard a word; he just stared at Frank.

"You know, Frank, since you've been gone, there are a lot more ducks around." And he smiled and hugged his son. John was a tall and lean man, and his hands were as strong as iron.

"Emily, this is my father."

"She knows who I am! Emily, Frank told us all about you, but he never mentioned you were this beautiful!"

"Oh, I see where Frank gets his charm," Emily said, extending her hand.

"Charm! Frank, well, that's a first!" And John laughed. "I guess you went to charm school?"

"Come on, Dad," Frank said.

"Now, John, leave him be," Ann stated.

"No, he's right, Mom. I charmed my way through the Pacific and made those Jap generals surrender with my charm alone."

"More like that killer eye of yours, son. Emily, did he tell you about the time he shot two brant from the widow's walk?" John Munro asked her.

"No," Emily replied.

"Remember, Anna? It was about 7:00 a.m. one Sunday. Anna likes to go to the seven fifteen Mass. We were out front when we heard a gunshot. I looked up and one brant was falling like a pinwheel and the other landed on the hood of the car! Remember, Anna, he was, what, about twelve years old? Yeah, I knew those Japs were in for it!" And John laughed, taking a seat at the table.

"Okay, Dad, no more stories about me for now, okay? Tell me what happened with Uncle Jimmy."

"Oh, that fool was smoking a cigar, driving the berries out, when the head of the cigar fell on his lap, burning his crotch. Then he drove the truck with his burning crotch into the bog! Took us all day to unload those berries and load them back after we pulled him out!" Everyone laughed.

"You got to know my uncle, always with a cigar hanging out his mouth," Frank told Emily.

"Yeah, this time he got lucky. Wait till Eleanore sees his burnt pants!"

"Okay, John," Ann said, "these two had a long day."

"Hey, whose car? Yours, Emily?"

"Yes. Do you like it?" Emily said, already knowing his answer.

"A little fancy for me, but yes, it's very sha'rp."

"Well, why don't you and Ann take it to church tomorrow? Here are the keys," Emily offered.

John paused and looked at Ann. "What do you say, Anna? Let's give them something else to talk about tomorrow."

With that, they all got up and retired for the night.

The Family Cookout

Emily looked out the window of the bedroom at all the commotion unfolding outside. Frank, his father, and the boys were rolling barrels out of the barn and pairing them with planks of wood for makeshift tables. Ann was wiping down some chairs.

Emily looked at the clock. It was 9:00 a.m. Noticing the curtain move, Frank looked up and smiled. He was wearing blue jeans and a plaid shirt. The sun was hidden behind the clouds, and Emily followed the sloping backyard with her eyes down to a marsh, then a bay, then to a long strip of beach. Behind it was the ocean.

"God, it's beautiful!" she said aloud. "Just beautiful."

Getting dressed quickly, Emily walked out into the cool morning air.

"Good morning, Emily. Sleep well?' Ann said, noticing her first.

"Yes, Ann, very well, thank you. I can't believe it's after nine."

"I changed my mind about your car, Emily. It fits me just fine," John said, earning him a funny look from his wife.

"Oh, that's all he needs!" Ann replied. "Come on, everyone, inside for breakfast. The party doesn't start for four more hours. We have plenty of time."

"Maybe for you, Anna. I told the boys we would check the traps I baited Friday," said her husband.

"Can I, Emily?" Max asked.

"Sure, but have something to eat first."

"All of you, let's go!" Ann said with authority. "Don't mind us, Emily. We get up early."

"I don't," said Emily. "You remind me of my parents."

"I made blueberry muffins, and there is coffee on the stove. Help yourself. I'm going down to the cellar to get some linen."

The boys sat at the kitchen table, passing around the tray of muffins.

"Emily, Frank tells me you ran a riverboat back in Ohio," John Sr. inquired.

"Well, my dad had a stroke, and I took over it until he recovered."

"Great! Then, you're coming with us! I need someone dependable to steer while I hook up the pots," John decided.

Frank just shook his head. "I'll see you in a couple of hours, Em. I promised Mom I would help her set up the yard."

"Okay, boys, grab a muffin and let's hit the road. Emily, we will take my truck and the boys and that dog can ride in the back. Okay, boys?"

"Yes, sir," they both said, running out the door.

John liked to tease, but when it came to the boating, he was all business. Emily knew more than he expected, and so did Max. "I'll take the bowline. Emily, you get the stern," John commanded.

"Come on, York!" Max called. York was busy sniffing the smells left over on the dock. However, as soon as John fired up the engine, York jumped right into the boat.

The thirty-four-foot down east lobster boat was painted a dark green with a white pilothouse, and it cut through the water like a knife. Frank mentioned that his father had a boat, but never told Emily its name was *Anna. How ironic,* Emily thought. *What are the chances?*

"Emily, when we round this beach, it may get a bit choppy. Always is when the tide comes in," John warned.

"What's that?" Max asked, pointing to a round steel house.

"That's Bug Light," Little John said. "It's there so we don't hit the rocks."

"Yes," John Sr. said. "We don't want to hit the rocks now, do we?"

York had his head out over the side of the vessel, getting as much air and waves as he could, but still kept his balance. The two boys were making a game of walking back and forth with the surging tide.

"How much tide do you have here, John?" Emily asked.

"Well, it's near a full moon, so just over twelve feet, I imagine. See that bay to our left?" he asked, pointing to Kingston Bay. "She just about empties out on dead low. You'll see later on. Okay, Emily, we have the first trap coming up. It's the green-and-white one over there. Here, take the wheel!"

Emily stepped behind the wheel, looking out at the sea. "Starboard side, John, coming up!"

John had a long gaff ready. "Okay, Max, I'll get the first one, you the next. Then you, son, okay? Just watch me."

Emily eased back the throttle as she steered to the buoy.

"Okay, Emily, got it. Neutral!" John took the buoy and pulled it in, then hooked the rope around a pulley on the gin pole and hauled the trap up. The two boys and York watched as the trap came up out of the green-blue water. "Oh, yes, looking good," John said as he swung the trap up.

Max was amazed at the size of the lobsters in the trap. "Wow, how many are there?"

"Well, let's see," John said. "Junior, get the burlap bags out."

Opening up the trap door, he grabbed the first one behind the head. "Here's a keeper!" As he held it up, its multicolored claws opened, ready for battle. "Watch it now, kids. These babies bite!"

"Wow, we have crayfish back home, but nothing like this!" Max said.

"Same family, I'm sure, Max," John said. "Okay, see this one? It's full of eggs, so we let it go." John held the lobster up to York, and he sniffed it. "Watch it, boy. This thing won't let go." John threw the lobster over the side, and before Max could say no, York jumped in after it, disappearing under the surf. The dog popped up a few seconds later with the lobster in his mouth.

"What the hell!" John said. "Don't let it bite him!"

"Too late!" said Max. York shook his head several times in a frenzy, sending the lobster flying out into the water yet again. "York!" Max yelled. "No!"

York swam around, looking for what had just bitten him, sticking his head underwater. "Sorry, sir," Max said, embarrassed. "York, come." Max went to the stern and held out his hand. York swam over and pushed against it, climbing back into the boat. Both Johns stood with their mouths open.

"That was amazing! Where...how...how did you teach him that?" Little John asked Max.

"Well, my dad taught me how to help him into the boat, but he learned to dive by himself."

"See, Dad? I told you I want a dog like York, a Labrador retriever!"

"Wait till I tell Anna this one!" John Sr. said, laughing and shaking his head.

"Max, tell him to shake! Watch this, Mr. Munro," Emily said, setting the stage for her brother.

Max took York to the stern and backed away. "Okay, boy, shake! Shake!" York understood the command and shook off the cool sea water.

"Max, that's some dog, some dog indeed," John said, still awed by the performance.

Max was three miles high and couldn't hide his pride in his dog.

"Okay, we have five keepers here," John Munro said, holding up a big four- or five-pounder and a few small ones.

"Those are like crayfish," Max said.

"Yes, and if you boys are planning on fishing later, we'll keep them for bait." John pointed to the next trap and sent the first one back. "We have six more in this line from here to the tip of the Gurnit," he said, pointing to the lighthouse on the cliff. "Okay, Emily, let's get another."

Emily was at home on the water and drove the *Anna* like her Ford. John and the boys hauled in the six remaining traps and filled two burlap bags full of big, healthy lobsters. York stayed in the boat, occasionally whining when they threw one over. Emily turned and headed back to the Bug Light.

"What is the name of that beach, Mr. Munro?" she asked.

"Plymouth. Plymouth Beach. And that rough patch to your left is Brown's Bank. Over to the right there is the Plymouth Rock, where the Pilgrims landed. They're building some sort of wall around it 'cause some fools were chipping it with hammers, trying to sell it! Have either of you ever had lobster?" John asked Emily and Max.

"No, but we grew up on crayfish and catfish," Emily replied.

"You are in for a real treat, then. I told Anna to have her sister bring sweet corn, and we will have a real old-fashioned boil. I dug a bushel of clams Friday. It's going to be a great party, yes, sir!" John Sr. said enthusiastically.

When they reached the dock, John pulled a burlap bag out of the water. "I let the clams filter out here so we're not eating dirt later on tonight," he said, smiling at his ingenuity.

"I'll pull the truck down," Emily said as she headed up the wharf.

"Some sister you have there, Max," John Sr. said while he watched her walk away.

"Yeah, she's okay for a girl." This caused both the boys to laugh.

John drove his truck around to the barn and grabbed two bags of lobsters. "You go ahead in, Emily. We will take care of these."

Emily looked at the yard and was impressed with the makeshift tables and chairs, enough for over forty people. The sea breeze fluttered the tablecloths held down by arrays of pumpkins and gourds. It was picturesque.

Frank was out fulfilling a list his mother had given him, and Ann was busy in the kitchen. The first car rolled in at 11:45 a.m., followed by one or two every few minutes. It was a Yankee reunion for sure, and each car and truck had at least one child. Frank had started a fire before he left, with what looked like a witch's kettle on a tripod. A charcoal pit smoldered, and there was a thirty-gallon barrel of root beer at the head of the table, with dozens of large mugs.

Emily wanted to help in the kitchen, but Ann wouldn't have it. "You're our guest, but if you must, could you keep an eye on my husband? He'll get to talking, and I don't want those lobsters overcooked."

Emily introduced herself several times before Frank returned. He was once again out of uniform, and initially Emily hardly recognized him. He walked up the lawn carrying a bushel of apples and a brown bag of what looked like explosives. "How was Captain John, Em?" Frank said sarcastically.

Emily smiled and took the bag from the top of the bushel. "Frank, be nice. Your dad is funny. We had a great time. What is in here?"

"I picked up a few fireworks, sparklers, and some ladyfingers, for the kids, Em. Did you catch a lot of lobsters?"

"I would say so. We have at least three dozen. I lost count after the fifth pot," she replied.

Frank put the apples down and took Emily's hand. "There are a few people I want you to meet, but first, I want to show you something." Frank led Emily into the house, up to the second floor. Opening the attic door, he coaxed her up.

"Frank, what are you up to?"

"You'll see. Trust me." Frank took Emily up to the widow's walk, where he had stored a metal bucket with two bottles of beer in it on ice. Emily was too taken by the view and didn't see the pail until she heard Frank open a bottle on the rail.

"Here, Emily." Opening one for himself, he raised the bottle toward her, and they clanked the necks together. Frank stared at Emily before speaking. "Em, I hope you know...know that I owe you my life."

"Frank," she said, trying to interrupt him.

"Shhh, let me finish. Before we met, I had forgotten about home, about life. I only thought of the mission, my men, and well, killing." Frank lowered his head. "Since that night I met you, all I wanted to think about was you, and staying alive meant something. So I just wanted to say thank you, Emily. Thanks for taking a chance on a roughneck like me."

Emily lunged forward and kissed Frank. "Now you shush!" she said. "Frank, about that night. I...I..." Emily's mind was spinning. She wanted to tell him the truth about why she was there that night, but why? What good would it do? Pausing gave her a chance to formulate her thoughts. "Frank, when I lost Matt, I felt my life was over. I had a son and there were so many women who had more to give than me. If anyone here is a savior, it's you, Frank, it's you," she said instead, her eyes welling with tears.

Frank clicked his bottle on hers once more. "To us."

Taking a sip, Emily said, "Yes, to all of us," looking at the family gathering below. "I thought you took me up here to shoot a goose!" she said, erasing the levity.

"See, I knew hanging out with my dad was a bad idea," Frank joked. Both of them laughed and enjoyed their drinks. "I'm not in any rush to go down there, Em. God, get ready for about five hundred questions! See that one there?" He pointed to his aunt Eleanor. "She's going to tell you I'm part Indian. That one there with the beehive, smoking? Her husband is a letch."

"Which one is he?"

"There, with that dapper hat and suspenders."

"Frank…," Emily said, cutting him off.

"Okay, I'm just warning you."

"Frank, I can handle myself around your family."

"I know, I know. It's not for you, it's so you understand when I turn him upside down. Then you won't get mad!"

"Frank!" Emily hit his arm. "You better not."

"Kidding, Em. Let's just watch. Oh, here comes Bernie. See? He's setting up the horseshoes. Oh, boy…"

"Frank, this place is just beautiful. Everything is," she commented. Pointing to a monument across the bay, she asked, "What's that?"

"What?"

"That statue on the hill."

Frank pretended not to see it, causing Emily to hold out her arm. Walking behind her, he pulled her into his body and whispered, "Oh, that's my hero, Captain Miles Standish."

"Which war was he in?" Emily asked.

"He was the captain who protected the Pilgrims from the Indians in the first years. He was of small stature, but he had big balls—lots of courage, sorry. He was a little redhead they called Captain Shrimp, but not to his face. The first year, the Pilgrims were starving, and the clams and quahogs on those flats out front here kept them alive.

"Well, there were a few Indians who were trading with the Dutch for years before and grew weary of white men. They suffered from European disease and were dying by the thousands. They hated the Dutch fishermen. When Indians began harassing the settlers and kept them from digging, Bradford, our first governor, set a meeting in the public house."

Emily just listened as Frank held her close.

"Miles Standish asked one Indian about the knife he wore around his neck. The cocky Indian said it was a trophy from a Dutch queen and that he had killed the man who owned it with a matching one from their own Indian king! Well, that Miles reached across the table, pulled the knife from his neck, stabbed him in the heart, stabbed the Indian next to him, and ran after the one watching at the door, killing him also," Frank retold the story, getting excited.

"That's your hero?"

"Yes, underrated and outnumbered, he did what was necessary, odds against him."

Emily looked at Frank contently. "Men" was all she had to say, grinning and shaking her head.

The party was in full swing, and John Sr. was telling everyone about how Emily drove his Anna while he pulled the pots, and about Max's dog, York. How he dived underwater, grabbing the lobster when it was sinking.

Every family has a blowhard in its ranks, and cousin Ned was theirs. Always the expert, Ned was trying to undercut Senior, talking about his Dalmatian. Max was running around with the kids but had overheard a few of his stories about this Dalmatian, but said nothing. John Sr. became animated, and the conversation got heated. "Your dog is a pain in the ass!" John said to Ned. He called over York and handed him a piece of lobster.

As they sat for their meal, Ann moved next to Emily, showing her how to crack the lobster and split the tail. Everything was great, and Ann's sisters brought a variety of home-baked pies: blueberry, pumpkin, apple, and one not so familiar, strawberry rhubarb.

Later, when the party broke up, Ned overheard Frank telling Max and John he would take them fishing later on when the moon was up. Ned, of course, invited himself.

All the family loved Emily and was so impressed by her little brother's manners. Ann was, of course, proud of Emily withstanding all the questions and unfamiliar faces. Frank was busy catching up with the men and spent most of the afternoon pitching shoes.

It was near nine at night when Frank called to the two boys, who were running around with sparklers. "If you two want to go fishing, you better get your gear!"

John Jr. told Max, "Come on, we have some poles in the barn."

Max didn't know what to expect but was surprised when his new friend came out with two poles, about nine feet tall, and shiny black reels. "Wow, what kind of reels are those?"

John read the side. "Says Penn Squidder, whatever that is. All I know is they work great."

Junior and Max loaded the poles in the back of the pickup. John Sr. yelled to Frank from the porch, "Where ya takin' 'em?"

"I figure Damon's Point, North River."

"Tide's right for sure. Better bring the bridge gaff. Been catching some big ones over there."

Frank thought he could sneak away without Ned seeing him, but he wasn't that lucky. York was already in the bed, and the two boys in the cab. "No room, Ned. Sorry," Frank said as nice as he could.

"I'll follow you!" Ned ran for his car.

John was excited to show Max this fishing spot and talked about the striped bass that went up the river at high tide.

"You did bring bait?" Frank asked.

"Of course," John said. "Dad gave me four short lobsters. They're in the back."

The ride to North River was about twenty minutes, and the two boys shared fishing stories, John with his bass and Max with his big catfish.

"What about you, Frank? What's the biggest fish you ever caught?" Max asked curiously.

"Hmmm…" Frank took his time to build up the story. "I don't know how many pounds it was, but one year, before you were born, Little John, Dad had a rowboat and rowed us out to the Bug Light. There were fish breaking all over, and we threw out a hook with two big sea worms on it."

"What's a *sea worm*?" Max asked.

John answered instantly, "They're nasty with big black pinchers. They bite you! Don't they, Frank?"

Frank laughed. "Yes, but they don't hurt."

"Yes, right," John said sarcastically.

Frank continued, "Well, the worms hit the water, and Dad handed me the pole. I wasn't much older than you two, and a huge bass grabbed the worms and took off. I held on for dear life. It was so big I couldn't reel it in and it was pulling us all over. Dad was laughing and yelling 'Don't let go! That's a new pole!' Well, it finally tired and almost towed us around Clark's Island in the process before I could get it next to the boat. Dad grabbed it by the gills and pulled it in, almost tipping us over!"

Max and John hung at every word.

"I guess it was a little over four feet long, and fat! Like a pig!"

"As fat as Aunt Bunny?" John asked jokingly. Max spit—he laughed so hard, having seen John's aunt at the party earlier.

"Yeah, that's not very nice," Frank said, laughing himself.

The harvest moon cast an orangey glow over the North River. Frank told the boys where to cast out their bait. "The tide's almost slack, so give it some line," Frank told them.

Ned was pacing on the dock, which hung over the tidal river, while York sat patiently, looking out where the lines were going in. "My Dalmatian knows when I take him fishing. He barks when I have a bite." Frank just squinted his eyes every time he spoke.

"Hey, where's the fish?" Ned barely got the word *fish* out when John's line went tight.

"Got one!" John yelled, rearing back and setting the hook, his big pole now bending like a question mark.

"Max, get your line in. I'll get the gaff! Ned, make sure he doesn't get pulled in!" Frank said as he ran back to the truck, just twenty yards away, and grabbed the bridge gaff. He paused when he saw it coiled in the pickup bed. Six months ago, he was throwing a hook like that onto the cliffs of Chichijima.

John was a good angler and fought the fish like a pro. Ned was barking orders, but John kept the pressure on, grunting as he reeled. The fish splashed when it surfaced, and John gave it another hard pull. Frank threw the bridge gaff over John's line and pulled it snug, planting it in the struggling bass's side.

Hauling it up, Max was astounded. When the fish hit the dock, they all celebrated, and York gave it a quick bite, circling around.

"Okay, Max, get your bait out. They're in," Frank told him. Max thumbed the Squidder and cast the lobster into the channel, flipped the drag, and held tight. It couldn't have been more than two or three seconds when Max yelled "I got one! I got one!"

Reeling down, he set the hook and began the fight of his life. Ned tried stepping in, but Frank kept him back. "Let him do it, Ned. This kid can fish!" All of them watched as Max battled the monster bass. York was still circling the fish flopping on the dock, pawing it as if he could hold it still.

More line was being taken out than Max was reeling in, but the long pole was too much for it. "Keep the pressure on, Max! I think it's getting tired," Frank said with encouragement. Max finally gained his line and cranked down, pulling on the rod. The bass finally surfaced and rolled, and Frank threw the gaff once more. He hauled up the big bass; it finally reached the dock.

"Wow, that's a monster!" John yelled. Both basses were over forty inches and fat from a season of feeding.

While the boys admired their catch, York began whining, looking out at the water. "What's wrong, boy?" Max asked, trying to see what York was looking at. One hundred yards out, York spotted a buoy coming in with the tide, cut off most likely by an unaware boater. York paced and whined, and Frank noticed the dark spot bobbing out in the moonlight. So did Max.

The dock at Damon's Point was at least ten feet above the water. Max gave the command. "Get it, York!" And York never hesitated. He leaped off the dock and swam headstrong to the buoy. You could see the V wake coming off his back in the moonlit water. He grabbed the buoy and headed for shore. Hitting the beach, buoy in his mouth, he made his way up to the lot and ran down the dock, dropping the buoy at Max's feet.

"Your Dalmatian do that?" John said to Ned with a smile. Seeing that Ned was angry, Max gave the shake command. York shook, spraying water all over Ned. He cursed as he headed for his car, and the three on the dock broke out in laughter, petting York and celebrating their catch.

Emily waited on the back porch with Ann and John for the fishermen's return, sharing stories and enjoying the beautiful fall night. Peepers were singing their last songs of the year, and an occasional bat flew by the moon.

"I hate those bats," Ann said aloud. "I remember one night, when Francis was about fifteen, John was out on the bogs when Frank noticed on the wall in the den a bat clinging just above my chair. Just as I looked, it began to fly around the room!"

"Oh, how awful, Ann!" Emily said.

"Well, I covered my head with an afghan and was screaming. Frank grabbed a broom and swung the stick end up just one time! One time, Emily, he sent that bat into the wall, knocking it unconscious!"

"Frank has the eye!" John Sr. commented.

The squeak of the brakes and headlamps announced their arrival. The boys ran to the porch, telling their fish story and wanting everyone to come see. York strutted around with his trophy buoy, wagging his tail.

"Looks like you had quite a night," John said.

Emily admired the catch and thanked Frank with a kiss.

"I'll get the fillet knives," John Sr. said, dropping the truck's tailgate to use as a table. Frank washed off the reels and put them away.

"I'll get a lantern, Francis," Ann said.

Emily learned more about her man that evening on the porch than on her long drive to his home. How his parents counted on him as a young man with their family business, and how his friends admired his courage.

Frank filleted the bass while his dad held up the light. "I have some nice bait for my traps," John said, holding up the first rack. "Tomorrow, Frank, I want you to look at the flue in the holding pond on Number One. I can't get it to stop leaking."

"Okay, Dad," Frank said.

John placed his hand on his son's shoulder. "When you get a chance."

Frank just smiled and kept cutting up the catch.

"Baked bass tomorrow, Anna?" John inquired with a loving tone. "What a day!" he said, putting the last rack into the burlap. "What a day."

Munro Bog

Emily was up before the boys, but not before Ann. They grinned at each other as Emily poured herself a cup of coffee.

"What are you making?" Emily asked.

"Just a cranberry nut bread, John's favorite," she replied, looking over as she mixed away. "I hear you're going to visit the bogs today."

"Yes," Emily answered. "I'm excited to see how your business works."

Ann looked humbly at Emily and smiled. "Frank was a big help around here. We fall behind with a lot of things. John isn't as young as he used to be, but don't tell him that. He started lobstering three years ago and, like with everything else, became very good at it."

"I saw firsthand with the lobsters," Emily said with excitement.

"Tell me about your business, Emily," said Ann.

Emily froze, thinking Frank's mother wanted to know about her CUF employment. "Oh, I just try and help widowers fill out the paperwork, direct them to the many different funds the government has to offer."

"Oh, I didn't know that," Ann said, filling the two bread dishes with her mix. "Frank told me you were in shipping?"

"Oh, I am. Well, my family is. I help my dad with his boat, and my mother does the bookkeeping."

"Let's talk about that. It sounds much more…well, pleasant," Ann suggested.

The two women chatted while they sat drinking their coffee, and listened as the men stirred above. John and Frank came down at the same time, and York followed close behind.

"I gotta get me one of these Labrador retrievers, Emily," John said as he entered the kitchen.

"Labrador," Frank said out loud. "You know what? Someone I served with has these dogs, or he did."

"What? Who?" John said with a demanding tone.

"Calm down, John, let Frank tell you," Ann said, calming him instantly.

"Yes, I remember. Don, Don Campbell. We served right to the end. He has a boat over in Scituate he calls the *Labrador*, a fishing boat he was fixing up."

John grabbed the phone and started grilling the operator.

"Look at him, Emily, like a spoiled child!" Frank mused out loud.

"I heard that!" he said with a grin, returning to his conversation with the phone operator. "Okay, got it, thanks!"

"Dad, I was on the train from San Francisco with Soup—I mean Campbell."

"Soup? Who wants soup for breakfast?" Young John said goofily, walking into the kitchen with Max.

"No one. Now shush," John Sr. said. "Go on, Frank."

"I was saying that he might not be home yet. He has a girlfriend in Western Massachusetts somewhere, Linda. I don't remember if he was staying there."

"Doesn't matter," John Sr. said. "We're going over after we find what's going on with that flue."

Ann and Emily took care of the boys and got them ready for their next adventure. It was a cold morning, and John was fussing over the bog not being flooded. "I'll take the boys in my truck. You and Emily follow behind." John was focused on his berry plants but knew it was too cold for them to ride in the back.

The Munros owned three bogs, all in the area of Kingston and Carver. The Number One, as John called it, was in Kingston, and it was set back. Emily was happy to have Frank all to herself, and she began poking him playfully as he drove her car.

"Oh, don't get me going, Em. We're almost there."

Emily laughed. "Frank, I miss you," she said, grabbing at his thigh.

"Okay, okay, we're here."

Turning onto the dirt road, Emily didn't know what to expect. Ahead of John's truck and through the dust he was kicking up was a large opening. John turned into it, and Frank followed.

"This is our Number One," Frank said proudly.

Emily stared at the thirty acres of maroon fields with high grass banks, surrounded by bright-red and orange maples. "Frank, it's…it's beautiful!" Her eyes were wider than he had ever seen them.

The Number One bog produced more berries per acre than most bogs in the area, mostly because it was full of healthy young vines. John worked very hard making sure it was flooded before the first frost and made sure the plants had enough sand on them, spreading it all over the ice evenly when the bog froze over.

"Over here, you two!" John yelled.

York jumped out of the bed and began sniffing the ground. Frank walked with Emily over to the high bank, where John and the boys parked their truck. Emily could see mist rising above the old Ford pickup, and behind the bank, a still four-acre pond with the reflections of fall mixed into the misty surface. She knew she definitely saw a piece of heaven there that morning.

"Frank, look at this." John pointed to the flue they had installed six years prior. "I took out three boards, and nothing!"

Frank walked the bank and knelt down to look into the pipe. York followed and was sniffing all over.

"What do you think, Frank? What the hell plugged that pipe so far up?"

York wanted to get into the pipe, but it was too tight. He began to whine and stick his head in.

"Dad," Frank said, shaking his head, "I had a feeling when you told me, it's those damn muskrats! Too late to trap them, and we will risk blowing the flue if we try to use an explosive. Hey, what about old Stanley?" Frank looked up at his father. "You know, the old trapper who lives next to the hardware store?"

"What about him?"

"Does he still have those little dogs, you know, those terriers?"

"Yes, great idea, Frank."

"You go see if he'll come down here with his dogs. They will fit in this pipe for sure. I'll put the boards back in the slots and wait here. Take the boys with you, Dad, but leave York, okay? You don't want to start a commotion over there," Frank said.

"Come on, boys!" John was gone in a hurry.

Emily and Frank watched the truck as it turned into the wooded dirt path leading back to the road. Grabbing a handful of Emily's bottom, Frank said, "You want to tease me now, Em?" in a frisky way.

"Yes!" she said as she started running to her car.

Frank and Emily made love in the Ford for the first time in almost a year. Emily was concerned about the time, but Frank reassured her they had over an hour at least. Frank didn't last ten minutes and needed a break to recover.

"Just stay as you are," he said, putting on his pants. "I forgot to put the boards in the flue."

Frank secured the boards and washed his hands in the pond. York watched his every move. Looking back at the coup, he saw Emily rolling down the window and waving something out of it. Frank wasted no time finding out what it was, and they were soon locked in lover's grip. This time, he had more control.

York began to bark just as the two lovers exited their car. John had persuaded Stanley to come right away. All Stanley wanted was the muskrats and permission to trap on John's bogs.

York was circling Stanley's pickup as soon as he pulled in, whining. Stan opened his door, calling to John. "Good-looking dog, John," he said, walking to the back of his truck.

"Thanks," Max said, smiling.

Stanley, John, and Frank met at the back of Stan's truck. Max quieted his lab, and the obedient dog listened and sat on the grass bank anxiously.

"What's the plan, fellas?" Stan asked.

Frank spoke up. "What can those dogs do, Stan?"

Stan rubbed at his bearded chin before he answered. "I got three Jack Russell terriers in those boxes. One is quite a digger, and two are nasty little bitches! They will kill anything in there, I'm sure of it!"

"You have a harness, Stan?" Frank asked the trapper.

"Yeah."

"Okay, if we lower one dog down the flew end and send another up the pipe, we'll at least have 'em pinned down," Frank concluded.

Stan opened the box in his truck bed, and three small white, brown, and black muscular dogs jumped out, running all over the grass bank, sniffing and relieving themselves. York sat and whined as Max told him, "No, stay."

Stan put a harness on the one he called Shiner, a male with a black patch of hair over his right eye. Frank walked the harnessed dog up the bank and lowered him down the flue. Barking and whining all the way down, instantly he began digging and pulling at branches with his teeth.

Next, Stan picked up one he called Jin and put her in the twelve-inch cement pipe protruding from the grass embankment. The other skinny Jack barked and jumped up to the opening. Stan said, "Easy, Becky," and held out his arms. Becky jumped in his arms, and Stan let her go in the pipe.

Hollow barking and god-awful noises were coming from the pipe. John, Emily, and the boys stood with York on the bank. Stan stood at the end of the pipe with a burlap bag. Jin dragged a muskrat to the end of the pipe and dropped it right into Stan's bag. Shiner was still digging like mad and ripping the nest apart. Jin went back in with his sister, Becky, and both were biting and being bit by the cornered rats.

Suddenly, a muskrat got by Jin and headed for the opening. Stan tried catching it, but it shot under his bag and ran to the flooded trench surrounding the bog. "Get it!" Max said, and York leaped down the bank.

The muskrat made the water and was swimming away when York dived in, grabbing it by the head. Turning in the trench and swimming back with his trophy, York climbed out where Stanley was, looked up at his master, and bit down hard. You could hear the crunch over the echoed battle.

Emily turned away and could not watch. The boys couldn't see enough. Dropping the now-dead rat at Stanley's feet, York stood ready for more. Jin came back with another dead one, and the barking slowed down. Shiner was still at it on his end, and Becky dragged out a big muskrat while Jin was mauling another.

Stan opened his bag and Becky jumped out of the pipe. Blood was trickling out near her mouth. Jin dragged the last rat out and jumped down, getting a drink from the flooded trench.

"Okay, Frank, pull up my Shiner," Stan said, with John relaying his message.

Emily wasn't too upset and began petting Shiner to calm him down, leading him to the edge of the pond to get a drink.

"How many did you get?" Frank asked.

"The Jacks got three, York got one," John Sr. said proudly.

Stan took his trophies back to his truck and called his little dogs. One by one they jumped in his arms and he put them back in the box, rewarding them with a hard scratch on the back and neck.

"That was incredible," John said.

Stan took off Shiner's harness and placed it in the cab. "Okay, my job is done now."

Frank walked to the bog end of the pipe and looked in. He could see light from the pond end, but he could see that the pipe was still jammed. "Dad, do you have that bridge gaff in the bed?"

"Let's see." Frank and John walked to the old Ford. In the bed was the gaff and the buoy York had recovered.

Looking at the two boys, Frank said, "Okay, I have an idea, but I'm going to need one of you to help. Dad, give me your jackknife."

John handed Frank his knife, and he cut off a six-inch piece of the buoy and tied the gaff rope to it.

"Okay, the flue opening is too narrow for me to get down, but if I lower one of you boys down with this gaff and you feed this piece of buoy into the hole Shiner made in that nest, I think the water will carry it out so we can pull that nest free," Frank instructed.

John Jr. looked at Max. "I'll do it," Max said confidently.

"Now, Max," John Sr. said, "you don't have to prove—"

Cutting him off, Max said, "Any of you ever try noodling?"

"Oh!" Emily said out loud, shaking her head.

"What's that?" asked Senior.

"Back home in the Hire River, we dive into a sunken car and try to get big catfish to swallow our fist, and then we pull them out."

"Come on!" John Jr. said in disbelief.

"No, it's true," Emily said. "My older brothers and their friends would do it, and the water was nothing but mud, but you never did, Max."

"Not that you ever knew about," he said with a smile.

"Only if you want to," Frank said, and the others all agreed.

Frank took Max's hand and lowered him down the nearly seven-foot hole. Max pushed the float through the hole with a stick and fed through the line.

"Now, take the gaff hook and wedge it in near the bottom," said Frank.

Max understood what he needed to do. "Okay, all set," he said, his young voice echoing in the hole. "Pull me up!"

Frank reached down and pulled him out of the hole. Emily put her arm around her dirty brother.

"Now, let's see if this works." Frank began lifting the boards from the flue, and the hole began to fill. Water began running out the end into the flooded trench.

"Hey!" Stan yelled. "I see it!" He pointed to the end of the pipe.

John Sr. looked over the berm to see the piece of buoy dangling down with water falling off it. "Son of a gun, it worked!" he said.

"Not yet, Dad." Frank leaped down the bank and tightened the line. Looking up at Emily, he pulled the line around him and tightened it, smiled, and pulled with all his might. They all saw the veins in Frank's neck bulge, and suddenly he fell back into the trench, followed by bushels of twigs, sticks, and leaves.

"Oh, Frank!" Emily began to laugh, as did John and the boys.

Frank got out from under the rushing water, using it now to rinse off. "It wasn't pretty, but effective."

Emily went to her car to grab a blanket, while Frank climbed the bank.

"That was some show, son," John said.

"I see why you are where you are, John," Stan said, extending his hand. "You make quite a team."

Frank took off his wet shirt and began wringing it out.

"Wow," Little John said, looking in awe at the scars on his brother's back. "How did you get those?"

Max and Frank's father looked at them too. "Son, I had no idea," John Sr. said with concern.

"What ya think they were doing over there, John?" Stan said, and he shook Frank's hand.

Emily returned with the blanket and put it on her man.

"Don't worry about it, Dad. You either, boys. I made it out all right."

"Out of what, Frank?" Emily said, puzzled.

"The war, hun. They saw my scars."

"Don't let your mother see them, Frank. She…well, just don't," John Munro said solemnly.

Frank looked at his father, and for the first time in his life, he saw his eyes welling up. "Dad, I'm okay, really."

Junior was firing off questions when Emily interrupted. "I want to get Frank dried off and you, Max, cleaned up."

"We will see you back at the house," John said, composing himself.

Walking away, Frank asked Emily, "Do I look that bad?"

"No, not at all, Frank." And she squeezed his shoulder.

"Dad!" Frank yelled before his father got into the truck. "After dinner, I'll drive over to Campbell's with you!"

John waved, and they headed home. Frank described the operation of floating berries, how they loosened them from their vine and used booms made from boards, corralled them, and scooped them into barrels.

Emily had a great time and let Frank know it. "I'm not just talking about the dog show, Frank," she said, nudging him in the ribs. Frank's smile was as wide as ever, and he didn't need to reply.

Anna had a big dinner ready, and after the men were clean, they enjoyed a quiet meal. John and Frank had business over in Scituate and left shortly after. John drove his pickup, and Frank eased into the seat.

"Dad, a lot happens over there. Yeah, I have a few burns, and I was shot a few times, but I'm one of the lucky ones, trust me."

John stared straight ahead, not wanting to show emotion. "You never wrote us about those things," John said, "about being shot, those bastards!" He raised his voice and gripped the wheel.

"Dad, I'm okay. Hey, as long as Emily doesn't mind, what do I care?" he said, chuckling. "I'm going to marry her, Dad."

John looked over at him. "You better, son. I guess that's God's way of rewarding you, so you better!"

John pulled up to the firehouse on Route 3A. There were two men sitting in chairs out front. "Either of you know where 77 Driftwood is?"

One of them got up and walked over to their truck. "Sure. Who you lookin' for?"

"Campbell," Frank said as he leaned forward, looking in the man's eyes.

"Campbell, Campbell...hey, Joe!" he yelled back to the second man in the chair. "Campbell, he's the one with the dogs, right?"

Joe shrugged his shoulders.

"No matter, Driftwood..."

John drove out of the station with a renewed smile. "I hope your friend is home, Frank."

"Yeah, me, too," his son said.

John pulled down Driftwood Road and pulled into number 77, noticing the porch light was on. "Looks promising, Frank."

Frank stepped out, and they both walked up to the door. The barking dogs caused the inside of the house to stir, and before they knocked, a middle-aged woman came to the door. She looked at Frank, and then at John. "Can I help you, gentlemen?"

Frank spoke. "Mrs. Campbell, Mrs. Campbell, I'm a friend of Donald's, from the Marines."

"Who's there, Ma?" a familiar voice shouted.

"Soup, get out here!" Frank said with a smile.

Mrs. Campbell stepped aside, hearing her son behind her.

"Munro," Don said. "What, you miss me already?" He extended his hand to John. "Don Campbell."

John shook it firmly. "John Munro, Frank's dad."

"Ma, invite 'em in, come on!"

Mrs. Campbell wasn't expecting guests, and it was after 7:00 p.m. "Don, why don't you men sit out here and I will put on some coffee?

John spoke. "Out here is fine, Mrs. Campbell. We don't want to impose."

"Oh, you're not imposing. I haven't finished my dishes and—"

"Ma, it's okay, Ma. We're fine, trust me," Soup reassured.

Mrs. Campbell disappeared behind the door.

"Sorry to call so late, ma'am," John said.

"Sit down, Frank, Mr. Munro, sit. She is fine. She hasn't had any men in the house besides me since my dad died, that's all." Turning to Frank, he said, "So what happened with Emily?"

"You know Emily?" John asked.

"Yes, we met in Hawaii. Sweet, isn't she?" Soup said, smiling.

"She's at my dad's now," Frank said proudly.

"Your dad's...you always were a hard charger, Frank." And Don laughed.

"Soup," Frank said, stopping his laughter. "Emily brought her little brother and his dog."

"Dog, yes," John said. "A black Labrador retriever."

"What's he look like? Is he a stud?"

"He's great, Soup, just great. I told my dad you might know where he can get one. He's crazy about this dog."

"Hold on a second." Soup got up from the porch and walked down his front steps, disappearing into the darkness.

A slight rattle sounded, and they heard a dog running around the corner. Up the stairs came a handsome yellow bitch wagging her tail. She jumped up on John. "Get down, Dufas!" Soup said firmly, the Lab excited to be free from her chain. "This is Daisy, one of my females."

"One, how many do you have?" John asked, still patting her square head.

"Two now. My oldest died when I was away. Daisy was just a pup when I shipped out, so I haven't had chance to work with her."

Daisy was a tall yellow Lab, friendly and lovable.

"I didn't know they came in two colors," Frank said.

"They don't—they come in three! Black, brown, and yellow. I have a brown one, but she is knocked up. My sister met a guy who knew a guy and he had a good dog. Anyway, May, my brown, is a good bitch, smart. I used to take her out on the water before, well, you know."

John and Don Campbell hit it off right away, talking about their boats and the Massachusetts Bay fishing grounds. Mrs. Campbell brought out a beautiful tray of coffee along with neatly sliced pound cake. They all thanked her, and Frank asked her to join them. She kindly declined but extended an open invitation to Frank and his father.

"How long are you going to keep Emily up here, Frank? I want to get a look at that dog. Dufas here is coming into heat."

"We are here until Friday. Em has to get back."

"Bring your dog by, Don. My Anna would love to meet another one of Frank's friends." John was enjoying himself between the two Marines, sipping coffee. He listened to Soup talk up what a hero Frank was and learned more about the war that night than he had from four years of reading the newspapers.

"What about Linda, Soup?" Frank tried asking anything just to change the subject.

"I stopped at her folk's house and took her out. They had me stay in the barn out back!" They all laughed. "I guess they didn't trust me, and they were right!" he said, laughing even more.

"Their barn? Well, you were right at home, then," Frank said, trying to keep it rolling.

"Yeah, yeah, I couldn't take it. They were on me worse than the Japs! So I told Linda I would get her up here. She's coming this week."

"Perfect! Bring her by, and invite your mom too," John said.

The men talked and laughed until midnight. John made sure they had each other's numbers before the porch light went out.

"That's some character, Frank."

"You're right, Dad. He's also a damn good Marine."

Meeting of the Minds

Mark Lavenger poured a cup of coffee and brought it out to the porch. Leaning over, he teased his wife with the cup. "Tax," he said, looking for a kiss.

Lisa wrapped her arms around his neck and gave him a sexy, long kiss. "You're a tax collector now?" she questioned, smiling as she took the cup.

"I was just reading about General Patton. You know, his cousin was the most decorated Marine in current history. Looks like it runs in the family," Mark said matter-of-factly. "We are invited over the Coles' tonight, darling, I hope you don't mind."

"Not at all. I like Sandy and what's her name?" Lisa said, being playfully rude.

Mark laughed. "The Robones can't make it, so it's just us four."

Mark loaded his briefcase as Lisa packed their clothing for their weekend trip to the Coles'. Keeping track of the newborns at Underhill was becoming easier for the men with the help of Lisa. They made a good team and a fine, handsome couple, even though he was fifteen years older.

Lisa liked the "splash of gray," as she called it, and his rugged look. Mark liked everything about his young bride, especially the feistiness she brought into their bedroom. It kept a spring in his step and a smile on his face.

After the Underhill farm was in full operation, Mark built a more-than-modest home overlooking the Huntsville Reservoir in Black Mountain, Pennsylvania. It wasn't what Lisa would have chosen, being from South Boston, but Mark picked the location more for logistics. It was 365 miles from Skinquarter, Virginia, and 320 miles from Boston. There were several means of transportation and the privacy they might need in case things imploded.

They both enjoyed the train and having a comfortable sleeper car, but it did take considerably longer than driving. Mark didn't mind the nearly ten-hour drive, and he and Lisa had a few favorite stops along the way.

As one drove Route 2, a road that wound through the Berkshire Mountains, there was a restaurant that sat high up overlooking North Adams, Massachusetts. The Eagle's Nest was a hotel and restaurant that was one of their special places. Dubbed the Mohawk Trail, Massachusetts had some of the nation's oldest heritage, and whenever they entered the town of Concord, Mark would always say, "Here's where it all began, Lisa."

The Coles had expected the Lavengers before eight, having cooked a turkey for dinner. Mark and Lisa didn't make any unnecessary stops, but they did have a small incident outside Greenfield.

Having stopped at the Eagle's Nest for a late lunch, the two snuggled in the front of their Dodge while the cab heated. The mid-November sky was gray and lifeless and emphasized the cold. Lisa never minded warming her man and was always playful in his arms.

Leaving the Nest, they noticed several cars and trucks parked along the road, in areas where there were no houses. "Must be hunting season," Mark said aloud. A number of young men who returned from war, some never firing their weapons, were still in killing mode, and the local white-tailed deer were on the move. Coupled with the oncoming rut, it made for a perfect opportunity to bag a big buck.

Back on the road, Lisa was chatting with Mark, saying something about visiting Gloucester, when, without warning, three does being chased by a rutting buck jumped in front of their car. Not slowing or covering his brake, Mark didn't realize the buck was following, and he hit it flush, broadside, sending it flying in the air. Its forward momentum carried it over the shoulder, sending the animal tumbling into the field.

Slamming the brakes hard enough to squeal his tires, Mark skidded the big sedan onto the shoulder and stopped, sliding into a hayfield. Lisa pulled her white knuckles from the dashboard.

"Are you all right?" Mark asked with heavy concern.

"I think so. Oh, look at that poor deer!"

"I plan on it," Mark said, getting out. He walked to the front of the Dodge and inspected the damage. One headlight was broken, and the chrome rim holding it dangled. The heavy bumper was dented, and his grill pushed in, slightly touching the radiator.

Mark looked over his left shoulder at the buck lying lifeless in the field. "Come on out, Lisa," he said. Both were slightly shaking as Lisa took Mark's hand, and they walked over to the beast. Staring at its magnificent rack, Mark bent down and grabbed the buck's antlers, lifting its head. Its tongue hung limply from its mouth, causing Lisa to turn for a second.

The sound of impact and the squeal of the tires echoed throughout the valley. Several hunters came from their stands to check out the source, and in minutes there were a half dozen walking toward them, all carrying rifles. Mark didn't move from the beast, and neither did his wife.

"Gonna keep it?" the first hunter to arrive asked, smiling at Lisa.

"No!" she said sharply.

Mark stepped toward the men, who were now circling the kill.

"Yup, that's him, all right!" one man said, looking at his friends for approval. "Been huntin' him for three years now. Guess I should have used my car instead of this old rifle," he joked, holding out his old Springfield. "You two all right?" he said in a much more serious tone.

"Lucky he didn't go through your windshield," another man said.

"Yup, that's what happened last week. Almost killed a man on this same road," another commented.

Mark squeezed Lisa's hand. "Guess we were lucky," he said to the group of hunters.

"Better check your Dodge for damage," the first gentleman said.

"I looked briefly. I don't think it's too bad," Mark said. "Come on, let's have a look."

Mark, Lisa, and the man with the Springfield walked back toward the Dodge. The sun was setting, and the temperature was dropped noticeably.

"Better sit in the car, Lisa." Mark opened the door.

"Let's have a look!" The man rested his gun on the fender and popped the hood. "Yep, see here? Pushed your radiator back into the fan. Didn't break nothing else."

The five men were still looking over the deer, pulling on its antlers and admiring his size.

"I live on that farm just yonder. Got some tools. Fix you right up."

Mark was happy to know he was more friendly than he looked. "Your Springfield, were you in the war?"

"Yep. Brought it back with me from Austria. You two wait here, I'll get my tools."

Mark stopped him. "Wait, sir, I didn't get your name."

"Bill, Bill Dobbins. Those two in the green plaid jackets are my boys. The other two, never saw 'em before. Here." Bill handed Mark his Springfield. "You keep an eye on her while I'm gone." Smiling, he added, "Careful, she's loaded!"

Mark looked the gun over. It was a 1917 306 Springfield standard issue. Lisa stared out the windshield at her husband, gun in his hand. It was the first time she saw him with a gun, and she liked the way he looked.

Mark held it up, sighting it away from the men up toward the shy, shouldering it and bringing it down. Walking over to the passenger side of the car, he smiled at Lisa, who was trying to look concerned but instead broke out in laughter as soon as he opened the door.

"What?" he asked her sheepishly.

"Nothing! I didn't say anything." And she laughed even more.

The two young men walked over and introduced themselves. "Hi, I'm Paul, and this is Tommy." They both looked at the gun in Mark's hand. "My dad's gun," Paul said.

"He has another one with a scope on it," Tommy said, sounding as if it weren't anything special. "You two from around here?"

Turning to the two men in the field, Paul yelled, "Hey, they're keeping it! You two better move on now. We're gonna dress it for them!"

Mark could talk to anyone about anything at any time, and soon the four of them were chatting about everything from the Nest to one of Mark's favorite subjects, the battle of Lexington and Concord.

The two young men were fresh home from the war; neither of them had the chance to fight. They were drafted in '44 and were now just eighteen and almost twenty.

"My dad was in World War I. Doesn't talk about it much," Paul said.

"Not many men do, son," Mark said.

"What about you?" Tommy asked Mark.

"Well, I'm what you call a tweener, too young for World War I and too old for II."

Just then, they heard a tractor heading up the road.

"You don't want that deer, do ya?" Tommy asked.

"No. You can have it," said Mark.

Tommy pulled out his pocketknife, thanking Mark while he walked away.

"All this land yours?" Mark asked Paul.

"Yep, from the Deerfield River, two miles down, to the base of those hills off yonder."

"It's beautiful," Lisa said, bringing a smile to Paul's face.

Bill pulled up on a big yellow-and-white Massey Ferguson Tractor towing a hay wagon. Paul walked to the wagon and placed his rifle gently in the bed. "Get the chain there, Paul."

Bill climbed down and secured the chain to the grill. "Paul, I brought some blocks. Put 'em under the rear tires." Paul didn't question his father; he just did what he was told.

"Now I'm gonna try and pull that grill out. I want you to get in and stand on those brakes," Bill said to Mark. Mark got behind the wheel and pressed down hard. Bill gently tightened the slack and revved up his tractor. The Dodge began shaking as it was being pulled, but the blocks dug enough to pull the steel frame.

"Okay," Paul said, "don't turn her over just yet. Let's check that fan."

Bill moved the fan with the belt still attached, his hands like iron. Mark watched as he checked the distance between each blade, bending the ones he knew were out of line. "Okay, start her up and we will check for leaks," Bill said.

Mark started the Dodge, and the three of them watched for leaks. "Fan's a little off, but I think it will get you to where you want. Just don't push it. Can't do much for that light." Mark was very thankful and reached for his wallet. "No, you don't." Bill waved his hands. "But if you want to leave that deer…," he said, as if the couple was thinking of keeping it.

"No," Mark said, handing him two twenty-dollar bills. "And you're also keeping the deer. I insist!"

Bill looked at the money, and then over at his boy, who was busy cleaning the deer. "Tell you what? You keep that rifle and we'll call it even." Mark didn't know what to say. "Better unload her before you drive off. Don't want to get caught with a loaded, having a busted headlamp and all."

Mark shook Bill's hand. "Bill, thank you. Those are two fine young men you have, sir. I won't forget this."

"Can't imagine you would," the hunter said cheerfully. "You two take care now."

Bill and Paul walked over to Tommy, who was wiping his hands in the grass. Lisa watched as Mark unloaded the Springfield and placed it in the back seat. "You are unbelievable," she said, shaking her head. "What are you going to do with that?"

"Teach you to shoot, Lisa," he said, shifting into gear. The Dobbins waved as they drove off. "Wait till Cole hears about this one," Mark said, his smile as wide as the crescent moon.

By the time they reached the Coles', it was near 9:00 p.m. Mark wasted no time telling Joe what had happened, while Lisa and Sandy left the two alone and opened a bottle of wine.

Lisa kept her place in the Back Bay and turned down Sandy's offer to stay. Lisa still had several cases pending and planned on staying in town for a few weeks. Mark and Joe had serious business to discuss regarding their future.

"Senators?" Mark questioned, his voice sharp with a tone of surprise.

Joe Cole explained, "Mark, listen, I gave this a lot of thought. We need to persuade Congress to invest in the future of this country. Mike is out west, looking into a new project regarding jet engines, and Kelly Johnson's team is looking to build a plant to accommodate his goals. As senators, we can direct more funds toward his projects and take a little for ours."

Mark looked a bit pissed. "Senators, Joe! You know I hate those bastards! I feel as though I would be the biggest hypocrite in the world—that is, if I got in."

Without knowing it, Mark was living in a district of Pennsylvania ripe for the picking. It was Joe being in Boston with the blue bloods that would prove difficult.

"How are you going to crack a race up here, Joe?"

"I'm not. I looked over the best location for a victory, and it's Florida, Mark."

"Have you discussed this with your wife?"

"I told her we were going to buy a vacation home and get out of the cold. She was thrilled. If the vacation home turns into something, well, a bit more luxurious, I don't see that as a bad thing," Cole mused loudly.

"And the Senate race, did you discuss that?" Mark asked.

"Sandra is a team player, Mark. She has been with me through every endeavor. This will be good for the both of us."

"I love the optimism, Joe. I just hope you know what you're doing."

"*We* know, Mark. You're going to win in Pennsylvania, and I am going to take Florida by surprise, and together, we are going to do what we do best."

"Keep chopping wood, I know." Mark was pacing at this point, trying to digest the whole political entrée. "How many are we up to now, Joe?" He changed the subject.

"The girls have done well, especially that one you have! Last I counted, we have eighty-nine slotted and seventy-seven inseminated since June. Things are going well, Mark, and as long as we keep up with the payments, I see no reason to follow the plan. I'm aiming for three hundred and fifty with the widows," Joe determined.

"I hope that is enough. I just wish we started earlier."

"Not even close, Mark. We have to get the hospitals involved, educate the public of the possibilities. I believe we will have hundreds of hospitals by the end of the decade performing insemination, and if we can recruit the right nurses, we should ensure the sovereignty of America in the years ahead."

Wedding Bells

The summer of 1946 was a time of great expectations. The war's end created new beginnings for millions of hardworking Americans. Factories transformed from making weapons to producing innovative products like appliances, luxury automobiles, and household gadgets. Americans were getting married, building houses, and it seemed like the sky was the limit.

It was also going well for Emily and Frank, whose wedding invitation landed on the desk of the new senatorial candidate, Mark Lavenger. Emily kept in touch with Lisa, Christine, and Jackie, who were now involved in recruiting the nurses necessary for the hero expansion. The best part of the new plan was that CUF didn't have to pay for them. As long as the hero supply was properly cared for, each hero had the potential to produce a thousand soldiers apiece.

The wedding was set for August 22 in Marietta. Frank sent for his wartime friend Jon McConnell to do the honors, and several of his Marine buddies were there.

Max Strong had converted most of the *Annabell Rose* back to its original purpose, and several of the guests had unique accommodations on board. Max also had several tents on his property and crafted makeshift bunks in his barn. The town of Marietta welcomed the remainder of the guests in their hotels along the river.

Soup and his girl, Linda, were married shortly after she arrived in Scituate, and Sully and Kow were a few towns apart. Kow had a bought a big Dodge sedan, and all four drove down together.

The Munros came by rail and auto, bringing with them twenty-eight and one yellow Lab named Sally. Max Strong and John Munro took no time getting acquainted, and John was impressed with the *Annabell Rose*. The two juniors took up where they left off, but this time with two dogs.

Guests who were planning on staying arrived early, and Emily and Frank were busy entertaining. Mark and Lisa were invited on board and found their stateroom to be both comfortable and elegant. Martha and Anna had spoken several times over the last year, and they made everything look easy.

When Kow arrived with Sully and the Campbells, Frank didn't hesitate to show them their rooms on board. Jackie and Christine arrived together by cab, taking the train from California. Both of them were anxious to see Emily, and the three of them disappeared, but not before the two bachelors filled their eyes.

"Who're the skirts?" Sully said, looking at Frank.

"Friends of Emily's. They worked together for some time during the war."

"Linda, why don't you go in the house and find out which one of those women will be with which one of us during the ceremony? So Sully can relax!" Kow suggested. Sully just smiled.

"Are you sure it's Sully who wants to know?" Linda said, elbowing Soup in a playful way.

"She busted you looking!" Kow said, rubbing it in.

The four men stood on the deck of the *Annabell Rose*, looking out over the muddy current. Frank was leaning on the rail between them. "I haven't had a chance to thank you guys for coming down," he said humbly, his head bent down. "I have something for each of you, something I think you will enjoy."

"You got that blonde for Sully?" Kow said, erasing Frank's seriousness.

"I'll let her decide that, okay? Listen, you remember the last raid we were on?" Frank turned serious again.

"How could we forget that, Munro?" Kow said, his voice now somber.

"Well, you remember Jon, Commander McConnell?"

"Yeah, sure," they all said.

"Well, seems that we did something, something the brass recognized as above and beyond. Jon is bringing them here tomorrow. I just want you guys to know how much I appreciated you having my back is all, and when I told Jon that we would be here, he told me about...well, you'll see." Frank stopped.

Just then, Lisa and Mark walked out on the deck. Frank knew Mark was Emily's boss, though they had never met formally, and his wife was one of her friends. He introduced himself and his fellow Marines.

"I'm going in to see the girls," Lisa said, kissing Mark on the cheek. All eyes were on her as she walked away, including Mark's.

"She's one beautiful woman," Soup said.

"Yes, I'm a lucky man," Mark replied, holding out a handful of cigars. "I don't want to intrude but thought you men would like to have an evening smoke."

They all took a cigar from Mark, Sully biting off the butt and spitting the end over the side before Mark could take out his pocketknife.

"What is it you do?" Kow asked.

"I work with the government providing funds for widows," Lavenger said.

"A G-man!" Sully commented, taking the lighter from Frank.

"Who wants a drink? I brought some bourbon," Mark said, trying to lighten the mood.

"Bourbon! We're in whiskey country, man! Fuckin' bourbon." Sully sounded genuinely upset.

"Okay, take it easy, Sully," Frank said. "I got you boys covered. Mr. Strong has a cousin who brought his own, some smooth shine as he calls it. Be right back."

"You know, providing funds for widows isn't my only job." Mark was trying to find an avenue in.

"What else, Mark?" Kow said, pulling on his cigar and blowing it toward him.

"You boys are familiar with the Gators, LVTs, the Browning BAR, and bazooka?"

"Yeah. What do you know about them?" Sully said with little expectation of an answer.

"I got the funding for all three of those," Mark bragged.

"How's that?" Soup asked.

"Okay, well, everything you men used during the war has to be approved by Congress. During the hearings, men like me represent the manufacturer and push for funding. I have to convince senators to appropriate money for equipment. Those LVTs were a hard sell. Took three months and a lot of persuading to get that vote."

"What kind of persuading?" Kow asked.

"Across from the Arlington Cemetery, separated by the Potomac River, is Marine Avenue, near the National Mall and a waterfront restaurant these Senators like to have lunch in. I arranged for a little demonstration, an unauthorized demonstration. I directed three LVTs to cross the Potomac, over Ohio Drive, through the Tidal Basin, and right up onto the parking lot of their favorite watering hole!" Mark continued.

"Nice," Soup said.

"Hey, those LVTs saved our asses," Kow said.

Frank returned with a glass milk bottle of whiskey and five thick glasses. He noticed his friends were all getting along better than when he had left. Frank placed the glasses on the rail of the deck facing the river and poured each three quarters full. "Take one," he said, and Frank raised his glass. "For the ones we miss and those we don't."

"To Lang," Kow added. "To Lang."

The Marines toasted. Mark drank down the whiskey; it was smooth, but it was strong, and he felt all the way to his stomach.

"That's good shit," Sully said, coughing a little.

"Thanks for the drink, Frank," Mark said, putting his glass down, standing up.

"Hey, where you going?' Sully said. "We just started! Hey, Munro, this guy saved all our asses!"

"Yeah, how so?"

"Those Gators, man, he got us those Gators."

Mark once again found himself among friends, and the men joked and sipped the shine on the deck of the *Annabell Rose*. They told him stories of one another's heroism and how they witnessed the Jap surrender on the *Missouri*. Mark was impressed and humbled by every account, how they joked with one another but with the utmost respect.

Inside the house, Emily was showing off her gown and pointing out the window to her girlfriends who were single. They all knew Mark from Skinquarter, and Linda, although a stranger, felt she had known them her whole life. That was the magic of the moment; it was surreal, and they all enjoyed one another's company.

"I'm going out there and having a drink," Jackie said. That was all the invitation anyone of them needed, and they marched out of the house and headed toward the men laughing and joking on the boat.

Sully saw them coming. "Oh, shit," he said in a joking manner. They all stopped and watched Emily lead them up the ramp, through the cockpit, and up on the dock.

Mark stepped up. "Gentlemen." He paused until they were all present. "Let me introduce you to my friends."

Sully and Kow were impressed, and Soup was, too, but didn't show it in front of Linda, in case he was on thin ice from earlier.

"Jackie Russo, Christine Mederos, Lisa Lavenger, I want you to meet America's finest Marines, First Lieutenant Don Cambell, Second Lieutenant Chuck Kowalker, First Lieutenant Fran Sullivan, and Captain Frank Munro." The men and women all exchanged greetings.

Kow walked over to Mark. "You know all about us."

Sully just said, "I like this guy!" and handed Jackie his glass.

"Careful, Jackie," Kow said, but she smiled and took a bigger sip than she should have, causing her to cough. "She's perfect for you, Sully!" And all the men laughed.

"I miss something?" Emily asked.

Frank responded, "Never mind. Kow was trying to forget the fact that Mark Lavenger knew everyone's name and rank."

The ten of them talked, laughed, and told stories.

Kow took Mark aside and asked, "What else do you know about us?"

"I have special clearance, and when Emily invited us here, I wanted to know who Frank considered his close friends. You men are heroes in the eyes of a lot of military, especially the Navy, for what you did on Chichijima."

Kow began to relax once again. "Kow," Soup said, "tell us the story of you and that Filipino girl when her old man followed you down to the beach and hid in the reeds."

"Yes, Kow, let's hear it," Frank said, all of them feeling the glow from the moonshine.

Kow was an animated storyteller and knew how to work his audience. All eyes were on him as he began. "It was while we were on leave around '44. These guys here and a few others took a boat over to Maui. Soup wanted to find a local who could take us out fishing. We all needed a break, and Honolulu was wall-to-wall GIs. We were on this ferry when Soup spotted this huge patch of saw grass seaweed about a mile from the landing. We weren't on the dock five minutes when he came back with this Filipino guy whom he was trying to talk to but couldn't understand one thing he was saying. Remember that little bastard?"

They were all laughing as Kow told how he wanted them to wait while he got his daughter, who understood English. "He kept saying 'No English,' and he had his finger up, so we walked over to this pub just off the dock and this little dude came in with this beautiful Filipino girl, right?" Kow looked for approval.

"Yeah, yeah, come on," Soup said.

"Soup here got the girl to ask her dad about taking us all out fishing, and he was jabbering away, slapping his hand into his palm. She turned to Soup and said, 'Twenty dollar, only take four.' Okay, so Soup, Sully, Frank, and this guy Lang ponied up five each. I figured I would stay and hang out with May. Remember, you fools were saying 'Mayday, mayday, Kow's going down!' She wasn't too thrilled, but we hit it off when you guys left. She took me swimming in some little cove down the road from her house and then invited me for dinner. It was an awesome day for me. These guys were trying to get the old man to troll around this weed patch, but he wouldn't."

Soup jumped in. "The little bastard was trolling with two cane poles on each side of his boat and had the line wrapped around his toes. He knew the dorado were near the grass, and they were running big. He didn't want his toes torn off. I was yelling at him to get closer, and we caught a few blackfin tuna before we got there. The old man was turning off, waving his hands, whenever I tried to get him closer."

Kow began again. "So while these guys were coming in, the old man cruised by the beachfront, saw me out in the water kissing his daughter, and disappeared around these rocks. It was about eight, and the sun was just going down, right? I was on the beach when I heard this noise, like a dog growling, and the reads were parting. May grabbed her top, got up, and ran off. When I turned to see why she was running, her father hit me with this cane pole and started screaming all types of Filipino, swinging wildly! I was getting welts all over me, and I was trying to pick up my clothes. I was butt-naked!"

They all started laughing.

"Yeah, you can't fight when you're naked! I was trying to cover up, and this little dude was swinging! All I heard was 'Whoosh' and a smacking sound. I finally grabbed the stick, and he was kicking sand and trying to get it out of my hands. So while I was grabbing my clothes, I was pulling this little Filipino around the beach. He wouldn't let go of the stick, and he was yelling 'GI bastard, GI bastard.' After I got a handful of clothes, I let go, and he chased me up this trail, but I outran him."

Frank was laughing the loudest and told everyone what Kow's back looked like when he caught up with them later. "He had welts that overlapped and were in five different directions!"

They all enjoyed reliving that moment. Sully just shook his head. "Tick tack Kow," he said, still shaking his head, bringing them all back to laughter.

They were all enjoying the story when two more guests arrived.

"Oh, boy, this will be interesting," Lisa said with a cynical smile.

"You don't know the half of it, Lisa," Mark said, checking his watch.

Arlene and Jennifer exited the cab, and Jennifer leaned into the passenger window to pay their fare, but the cabbie had already walked to the trunk. Handing Arlene her suitcase, he was reaching for Jennifer's when York ran up behind him, startling him, and he bumped his head.

Jennifer began petting the friendly dog and handed the man his fare. All eyes were on the two women as they began to walk down the grass slope, suitcases in hand. Sully looked over at Kow and nodded.

"Arlene!" Mark yelled, waving his hand. Jennifer pointed at him, and the two ladies walked briskly toward the dock. Up on deck, Mark looked once more at his watch. Lisa began to head down when Frank mentioned to the men to help with their luggage. Sully didn't hesitate and joined Lisa. Christine and Jackie smiled and waved at the girls, prompting Kow to ask Mark how he knew all these dolls. Emily had Frank show them their room on board.

The Strongs and the guests were curious as to who the new arrivals were. The deck of the *Annabell Rose* looked as though it was cut from a magazine. Mark introduced his last two women proudly, and they all exchanged hellos.

"Frank," Mark asked, "is there a plank of some sort on board?"

"Planning on jumping, Mark?" he asked.

"We're going to need something to welcome the next guests" was all Lavenger said.

Looking downriver, Mark began to smile. A hollow drone was echoing off the hills overlooking the river, and Frank, Sully, Campbell, and Kow all turned to see. The girls were chatting when the noise grew too loud to ignore.

Jon McConnell was arriving on a PT boat from Washington, DC. The battle-ready vessel, with its three diesel engines, was turning 36 knots, and the wake was bank to bank. Everyone on board, and everyone at the Strongs', stared at the gunship as it roared past and turned sharply around to settle port side. Jon McConnell and three officers were on the bridge, now putting their caps back on while the gunboat eased alongside.

Frank looked at Mark and smiled.

"Permission to come aboard?" Jon shouted.

"Sully," Frank said, "I need a hand." Frank knew the *Annabell*, and Sully followed him to the main deck to swing out a plank they used to load horses. Frank saluted the men on board as they threw both he and Sully their lines.

The *Annabell* was still rocking from their combat entrance, and the slap of the waves along the shore could still be heard after they shut the engines down. The two enlisted men stayed on board while the officers boarded the *Rose*.

Everyone in the house, as well as in the yard, was either on the dock or climbing on board, wanting a closer look at these new guests. Mark looked over at Emily and Frank's parents and signaled them to the upper deck. Max Sr. took his wife's hand and walked in through the helm and out on the deck. John and Anna followed. Max and John Jr. had already raced to the bridge with their dogs at their heels. Jon McConnell was carrying two bags, one an official-looking leather satchel.

The three officers stood shoulder to shoulder in their khakis, with gold piping on the shoulders. Mark spoke up. "Everyone, please, can I have your attention?" His voice was loud and confident. "The war department, along with the United States Navy and Marines, are here to present your men, Captain Frank Munro, First Lieutenant Francis Sullivan, Second Lieutenant Donald Campbell, and First Lieutenant Charles Kowalker with some very special awards."

Frank looked at Mark, and then at Jon. Sully, Kow, and Soup were as stunned as the rest of the crowd. Jon opened the leather satchel and pulled from it four black-and-white ribbons and four blue ribbons, and from them a Silver Star. As the bag was placed down, it made a funny sound and seemed full of something. He smiled as he looked at the men.

Jon spoke. "The officer who is presenting these awards today has never met these Marines in person. He did, however, watch them perform their heroism on the cliffs of Chichijima from his Gato submarine. When I told Admiral Halsey the Sea Dogs were gathering for a wedding, he presented me with these awards and told me Commander Whitten, the Gato commander that helped in the rescue, would do the honors."

One by one they stepped forward to receive their honors, each time drawing a great applause. Frank was the last to bow his head and accept his awards, bringing a tear to his mother's eye. The men stood shoulder to shoulder and saluted the commanders and then shook their hands.

They began to mingle with the guests when Jon stood up and announced he had something else to say. "Ladies and gentlemen, please, I have something special here in this bag, something for your Marines." Jon was holding the bag up. "There are hundreds, maybe thousands, of things that happen during war that go unrecognized. When these men rescued the flyers from Chichijima, the world didn't know what had taken place. Commander Whitten watched while these Marines, the Sea Dogs, as they were called, carried our wounded soldiers and the rescued airmen by roping them down steep volcanic cliffs, all while under fire from a Japanese destroyer.

"Commander Whitten sunk that destroyer, allowing these men to return to the *Missouri*. After they loaded the landing craft on board, I inspected the LVTs for damage and found these." Holding up a piece of volcanic rock, McConnell continued, "These rocks had fallen into the rescue boats when shells from the Jap destroyer tried blasting Frank and his men off the cliff."

Everyone stared up at Jon; there was no sound but his own voice.

"Looking at these rocks, I had an idea that I presented to Admiral Halsey. Each of you men here are leaders, men who saved our Navy flyers from certain death, and the US Navy Department wanted you to know they are grateful. These stones were cut, and on each one the name and rank of every Marine in each squad was engraved along with a special bronze unit citation."

Jon turned the porous stone to show the crowd. Placing it back in the bag, he lifted it up high and said, "To the Sea Dogs! The first and finest amphibious assault team in Marine history."

Everyone applauded and shook the hands of the men on board. Jon climbed down and handed the custom awards to his friends. Frank stared at the names on his stone, as did his friends. Holding back his tears, he thanked Jon and showed it to Emily, who had never been so proud.

"Let's get this party started!" Jackie yelled in her sexy Southern tone, causing the crowd to cheer.

Little John and Max were impressed by the young warriors and, along with Soup, asked to go on board the PT boat, of course wanting to check out the engines. The two juniors ran around to the bow to examine the .50s and marvel over the torpedo tubes.

As if Emily needed another reason to be proud of her man, after Jon's speech, she was beaming with joy, as was Linda, who never knew anything of Soup's heroism.

The wedding went off with military precision, and the two newlyweds were enjoying their moment. Frank and Emily had made history in more ways than one.

Washington Senator Cole

Mark left his home in Pennsylvania in a rush. He did not like the tone of Joe's voice when he asked Mark to "get his ass down here!"

Things were winding down after the war, and the fifties had just begun. The April weather had brought more rain to the region, and Mark's drive to DC took longer than he had planned.

When he arrived in Washington, he headed straight for Cole's office. After removing his dripping trench coat, Mark proceeded down the hall to see his good friend Joe.

"I don't give a shit about your intelligence report! I know those yellow bastards are pushing their luck. Russia is testing our resolve and pushing China into a fight! Oh, fuck Congress!" Joe was screaming into the phone.

Mark stood speechless at the threshold.

"I know we're not ready for war, but damn it, man, we're not going to sit by while the PVA force their commie ways on South Korea." Joe paused and pointed to the coat rack, seeing Mark's dripping coat. "There are ways around sending troops without congressional approval. You make sure you find out what Russia is sending those yellow bastards!" Joe hung up the phone and ran his hand through his hair, exhaling a huge breath.

"Trouble, Joe?" Mark said somberly.

"Mark, there is trouble brewing in Korea, and I don't think we're going to avoid it." Joe sat behind his desk and pointed to the leather chair in front of him. "Sit down, Mark. Take a load off."

"What's this about?" Mark asked before he had settled into the chair.

"Mark..." Joe paused. "Seems we're going to be expanding our program. Hey, close that door, will you?"

Joe looked tired. Mark could see it in his face. He must have been on the phone with senators and aides all day. Mark settled back into the chair and said, "Joe, I came as soon as I could. Now, what exactly are you talking about?"

Joe didn't hesitate; he had stacks of folders and reams of papers on his desk, and holding up a folder marked "Confidential," he said, "Mark, we hit the thousandth mark last week! The end-of-the-war push and the CUF initiative have these mothers and families 100 percent on board and with zero suspicion. Honestly, Mark, that idea of yours to send for these women and tell them in person instead of waiting for a response letter has made the difference. Because of us, our soldiers and mothers are being cared for and our program and its funds are secure. There is one little problem on the horizon, however."

Mark scrunched forward in his chair. "What might that be, Joe?"

Joe sat back in a more relaxed position, seeing the tension growing on his friend's face. "We're going to need to diversify, Mark, diversify."

Mark looked puzzled. Joe had just told him the funding was secure. "Joe, what are you talking about?"

"The soldiers, Mark, the soldiers! Look, we have a great start here, but they are all Anglos."

"Yes, we discussed this at the beginning, but there weren't many nonwhites in combat roles at that time," Mark replied.

"Not many, true, but I was researching the Tuskegee airmen, and they had some outstanding flyers over in Europe. Their record of bravery, above and beyond, is outstanding!"

"A little late for that, don't you think, Joe?" Mark said sarcastically.

"No, no, I'm not looking back here, Mark. I'm looking forward!" Joe paused.

"Korea?" Mark said.

"Yes, Korea." Joe handed Mark a folder. "I want you to take a look at that, Mark, and hey, that's FYI, okay? In it you will find the history of the Buffalo Soldier, dating back to its conception in 1861. The Army with its wisdom put a division together in '46, and they have been stationed in Japan under the Twenty-Fifth. They will make up the Twenty-Fourth infantry division. It's all in there."

"Am I to start recruiting black women, Joe?" Mark asked seriously.

"No, not at all, Mark. Remember Arlene, one of our ladies?"

"Hard to forget her, Joe," Mark said, smiling.

"When she was in Europe, she hired prostitutes to do her dirty work. I figure we can use the local talent there to make sure the job gets done. I will send someone we can trust to steer the boys in the right direction."

"Not a bad idea, Joe. I honestly thought we were pushing our luck with the girls, anyway."

Joe's phone began to ring. "Mark…" Before Joe could say anything, Mark got up with his file and walked toward the coat rack. Grabbing his hat, he thought twice before placing it back on his head. The rain had soaked through, and the lining showed it. Mark had even more on his mind, and he simply put the wet hat on. Pulling it down, he threw Joe a half-ass salute and headed out the door.

Joe was already deep into his conversation by the time Mark opened the door. Joe looked back and nodded as his eyes met Mark's. *Buffalo Soldiers, what next?* Mark mused to himself as he walked down the brightly lit hall.

The statehouse was bustling, and there was a nervous energy all around. Mark noticed the military sedan pull up as he exited the building. *General MacArthur. Oh, this can't be good,* Mark thought. The general quickly exited the car and walked briskly up the steps, pants pulled up halfway to his chest, stopping for no one.

Trouble on the Peninsula

Lisa Lavenger stood quietly, looking out her large picture window. The morning papers' headlines filled her head with regrets from the past: UNITED STATES MARINES STORM THE BEACHES AT INCHON HARBOR, KOREA.

Mark was back east, shoring up the contracts with Arthur Young at the Westland Aircraft Company in Buffalo, New York. A Bell 47 helicopter had been purchased by the Navy and the US Army and was transformed into the H13 Sioux. Mark had worked on that project with Mike Robone since 1947, but Mike had to forgo his responsibilities due to illness. That left Mark taking care of the military contracts that also funneled money to CUF.

Mark was proud of his work there. Lisa had joined him on some of these trips to Buffalo, and with a little convincing from her husband, she took several rides and fell in love with the dynamics of helicopter flight. "It's like the world moves and I'm standing still," she said, describing her flights, especially the ones over Niagara Falls. She only flew in the civilian version of the Bell 47; the military Sioux were being tested in secret. Mark was to arrive sometime that afternoon, unaware his wife was on the porch swing, holding the newspaper, watching the road below. The plush green Pennsylvania valley spread vastly over the lower horizon. With its shades of green and wisps of white mist, Lisa's view was a peaceful place on earth.

Seven thousand miles away, however, Squeaky and One-Time paused to look at the beautiful rolling green valley below them. There, heavy mist rose and drifted over the Nakdong River through the thick, plush underbrush. They set up on the infamous line known as the Pusan Perimeter. For the 12,368 soldiers that made up the Twenty-Fourth Infantry, this perimeter would define the Duce Four's fighting ability and readiness. These two men could not have foreseen the tragedies that lay ahead, nor could they have discerned the uncertainty of their commanding officers. They were good soldiers; they followed the orders they were given, or not given.

Preparedness and readiness was the initial problem in the onset of the Korean conflict. Clerks, cooks, anyone and everyone was thrown together to stop the immediate flow of communists into South Korea and, ultimately, Seoul.

The American military, now with the coalition of the United Nations, would have to assemble an invading offensive force to repel the communists, but before a major landing force was to assemble, the UN needed time.

Scattered in the South Pacific were four infantry divisions stationed in and around Japan. Their proximity and the timeline fit, but their leadership and equipment were both mismatched and outdated.

Before the hasty deployment was ordered, the men of the Duce Four had things pretty good. The US military had as many opportunities as men have desires, and finding something challenging was no desperate search. Men of the Duce Four participated in artillery challenges, not just with accuracy, but with speed.

The few commanders who recognized that they had less equipment but more athletic soldiers used this combination in drills. To make it more competitive, awards were given in the form of passes and furloughs. Major Blane would even sign off on a few extra day passes if a squad performed above and beyond. Competition among the ranks proved healthy. Although the Duce was short seven hundred or so combat infantry, their resolve appeared solid before they deployed, and it would be tested in days to come.

The South Korean Army that had been overrun by the North Korean People's Army, and the Twenty-Fourth Infantry, was sent out to protect the northern end of the line, thirty-four miles, referred to as the Pusan Perimeter, located in the peninsula of Pusan, Korea.

After the invasion of the North Korean People's Army swept into South Korea, they occupied Hill 409, the highest hill in the region. On the way to that hill were a series of smaller hills: Hills 102, 109, 117, 143, 147, and 153. These made up the knobs and valleys along their line. The enemy was stretched out over this line also and was constantly probing for weaknesses. Rivers, streams, hollows, and holes all presented their own deadly challenges.

The rolling hills of South Korea were a stark contrast to Lisa Lavenger's view from her rural home. Somewhere in the South Korean peninsula, a black soldier called Spade would witness and record the battle as it unfolded.

Men from the Duce Four had already received severe resistance; both enemy rifle and mortar fire caused five hundred casualties times five wounded before reaching their objective. The enemy had proved resilient in the face of fire. The Twenty-Fourth was now occupying three knobs overlooking several potential crossings with roaming expeditionary forces between machine gun and mortar positions.

Sitting in their freshly dug fox, checking their weapons, were Squeaky and One-Time. They positioned their .50-cal on a suspected river crossing and laid out their ammo boxes. One-Time, Sergeant William Cobb, and his feeder, Squeaky, joined the Twenty-Fourth at the tail end of WWII, both aged eighteen.

Because they were black, it was easy for them to stay together throughout basic training, and subsequently, they ended up in the same platoon. Squeaky, Kevin Johnson, was a quiet kid from the rural south. His best school friend was William, Billy Cobb.

William was called by several names, but slow or lazy was not one of them. William lived on his bike, and he had delivered papers on back roads to tar paper shacks. In the afternoons, he would ride to the store and do errands for his neighbors.

Billy Cobb's bike was his horse, and he cleaned and oiled it every chance he had. Billy was what Squeaky called him. One-Time was what everyone else in the Duce used. Billy, a funny and graphic teller of tales, always began his story with "One time," so it stuck.

Squeaky was "as quiet as a mouse," and he eventually became squeaky. It was a process; most guys in the Duce Four went for the names their friends chose. Corporal Lawrence J. Jones, or Spade, as he was affectionately called, had another alias: Too Dark. Too for the Duce Four, or "two stripes," and Dark because he was blacker than the ace of spades.

C Company moved into position on the east side of the Naktong River early morning on August 6, 1950. A hundred and four men set up in various positions. Major Blane was a prick about digging in, and as soon as their positions were established, they started digging.

Things were different for L and K Companies. Their lieutenants had the men take up defensive positions, digging in, but their captains felt there was no need because they, on the other hand, anticipated a short stay. This was the beginning of the nonmaneuvers taken before the North Koreans overran them, an albatross placed on the neck of the once-mighty Duce Four. The US Army's heavy gun batteries, necessary to defend the perimeter, were not defended properly, leaving them exposed to the waves of enemy troops.

Across the Naktong River were some two thousand light infantry troops from the Fourth NKPA. They were armed with rifles and light machine guns and moved quickly across the river into the American-held positions. When the fighting started, there were several areas where the NKPA crossed and focused on the American big guns. They massed attacks with pinpoint accuracy. They men of the Duce Four fought bravely but were overrun, giving up four Howitzers.

The United States had severely depleted its military after World War II. Along with the decommissioning of hundreds of ships and a half-million soldiers went a number of military leaders. Each branch suffered, and career veterans were in short supply. To complicate things, the military desegregated the Army in 1948, and the Twenty-Fourth lost leaders to other branches that were looking for officers. Understaffed and underequipped, the Twenty-Fourth Infantry Division was unable to make do.

It had been originally commissioned to be equipped with 142 tanks but, in reality, had only a dozen M24 light tanks and a handful of Shermans when they entered Korea, no match for the Korean/ Soviet T-34, a winner in battle all over Western Europe. The Duce Four was not the only division that suffered losses in men and equipment; the Marine Air Force had relied on the Corsair to provide air support against an enemy equipped with Polish-built Russian MiGs. It had been the equivalent to taking stick to a gunfight.

Worse over, the Twenty-Fourth and her sister divisions also lacked one-third of their authorized infantry and artillery commands and two-thirds of their antiaircraft complement.

Instead of their authorized strength of 18,804 officers and men, the divisions in Japan were made up of only 12,500.

As the closest division to Korea, the Twenty-Fourth was the first deployed. It was brought up from a strength of 12,197 men to 15,965 just before departing. The Twenty-Fourth, stationed in Japan, were closest to Korea when the North overran the 38th parallel and the "police action" started. American involvement was about to escalate with an invasion force landing in Inchon, but before any landing force could be orchestrated, a parameter of defense had to be established.

Naktong Valley: The Bowling Alley

Twelve thousand soldiers of the Duce Four poised, overlooking the Naktong Valley. Russia had had a more global view, looking at the once-superior military of the Americans, and needed an opponent to test their latest weapons.

When General MacArthur wanted to use nukes on Korea, he was relieved of his command. This meant conventional war and Russia was as good as anyone at supplying the weapons necessary. Not to mention the propaganda and desire to drag out a war and help boost their economy.

Too Dark was making his rounds when the first Russian MiG passed over. Distant rifle rounds echoed across the valley as the roar of a small plane astonished the Duce Four below. It was out about one-thousand-plus yards when Spade rolled over the sandbags protecting One-Time's .50.

"Squeek! Let's lay down some hurt! Now!" Spade yelled. One-Time was already locked and cocked. The MiG broke hard left and began to climb. One-Time was trying to get in front of it, but the tracers faded past the tail, as did the MiG. At that moment, it opened up.

The ninety-millimeter shells exploded all over the Twenty-Fourth's position. Blane was constantly moving up and down his line to keep in contact with his guns. Spade was about to jump when they heard bugles coming from below. Things slowed down as One-Time began exploding his targets. His short, controlled bursts were popping NKPA like grapes.

L and K Companies were overrun almost immediately, causing C Company's flanks to be compromised. Blane immediately moved a few men from each squad to prevent a pincer move. Doing every-thing he could, Blane helped carry ammo to the gunners while he encouraged his men. Dozens of Corsairs were engaging with MiGs overhead, mortar fire ripped up and down the line, and Blane saw every position to both flanks in full retreat.

Realizing his men were about to be surrounded, Blane and Spade battled to the far left position and began pulling back of the knob in a semicircle. One-Time's gun was smoking. Lieutenant Blane charged toward One-Time and Squeaky, green tracer rounds streaking over his head and rocks and dirt in his wake.

Squeaky heard him yelling, "Retreat!" just before a mortar blew him out of his boots. Spade stood wide-eyed. His CO was gone, the line was broken, and over sixty men of his company were either pinned down or blazing hell from their holes. The others dead or MIA.

Spade gathered up a squad and worked his way off the knob, pulling back while covering each position. "Billy, let's go, man!" Squeaky yelled over a burst.

"You go, I'll cover your asses," One-Time said.

Squeaky wanted to stay with One-Time, but Billy wouldn't have it. "Billy, come on!" Squeaky dived over the brim. The whistles and bugles seemed closer. "Grenade!" yelled Squeaky.

The first grenade landed in One-Time's position. Spade was twenty feet away and was blown back. Squeaky pulled back the bolt on his M14 and jumped back over the brim, Spade screaming "Retreat!"

Pop pop pop! Squeaky looked over at his lifelong friend. One-Time took the blast, and it opened up his right side to the bone.

"I'm done, Squeak, done! Go, man, go! Tell my mom I love her!"

Squeaky sprang to his feet and cleared the action. He peered over the lip and saw hundreds of enemy troops moving toward his position.

Spade reached over the brim and grabbed Squeaky. "Move your asses!" Spade saw the hole in One-Time, his intestines sticking out. "One-Time! Hold 'em off!" Spade and Squeaky slipped down the ridge to the creek bed and could hear Billy Cobb's .50-cal over the small-arms fire.

For the next ten minutes, Private William Cobb rained down hate on the enemy. Spade said it was a miracle Billy didn't die from the first grenade attack. Three times the enemy tried blowing One-Time out of his hole, and each time he took the hit. With his .50 spent, One-Time grabbed his carbine, knelt down to shoulder it, and bled out in a fighting position.

For two weeks the battle to secure the Pusan Peninsula raged on. Moments of bravery and heroism were being overshadowed by desertion. If the fear of dying by gunfire was not enough, dehydration was killing the troops. The drinking water from the rice paddies, the only available supply, was polluted with human waste.

More troops were landing while South Korea fled toward Seoul, beneath the 38th parallel. Leaders were born on the battlefield, though, and both Spade and Squeaky were promoted to staff sergeants.

Dark Mark

Lavenger's phone was ringing off the hook. Lisa was out shopping, while Mark had been pondering over the intel on the Bell. "Hello?"

Senator Cole was on the other end. "Mark, we have to get a girl to Seoul! We need to get some boys off the line and down to Seoul!"

"About that. Lisa is out. I'm not going to ask her, okay?"

"No problem, Mark. I already arranged everything, did it over the phone. Madam YumYum has plenty of Yankee princesses for our heroes. I already set up the delivery-and-courier system. All we need is someone to instruct. I had a call from Arlene. Seems she is more patriotic than I thought! She was more than happy to go coach up the girls." Cole chuckled.

"Joe, what's going on with the Saber? We need airpower, Joe!"

"Yeah, those dumb bastards cut out the defense budget, caught us with our pants down for sure. We will have ninety-seven on the line in three weeks. In the meantime, I will keep pushing to arm your whirl bird, and maybe we can put an end to this thing sooner rather than later."

"I hope so, Joe. America has no heart for this one. Public opinion is teetering," Mark said hurriedly.

"Mark, why don't you and Lisa drive down and meet me in Tampa? I have a few things I would like to go over with you two. Let's try for the weekend," Cole said.

"I will check with…," Lavenger began, before Cole cut him off.

"Mark, I have ensured CUF will survive. Any and all connections to you and Robone have been removed. No worries, my friend. See you this weekend."

Lavenger hung the phone up slowly and lowered his head on the receiver. A load of relief passed over him, and his mind was beginning to wonder.

Lisa was coming up the drive, and Mark headed out to help her. Anxious to see his wife, he moved with purpose toward the sound of her car. Mark couldn't hide it—he was easy to read. Probably why Joe trusted him so much.

Skipping two steps and smoothly opening her door, he made her smile. "Hi, Lise!"

"My, aren't you cheery," she said sweetly.

"Anxious to tell you the news, Lise! We're taking a road trip to Joe's this weekend. Congress is out of session. Joe and I can work a little from there, you and Sandra can relax by the pool. We'll take the boat out at night, and we can stay as long as you like!"

There was no response from Lisa, and Mark COULDN'T read her.

Turning around, Lisa held her arms out wide, as if trying to embrace the beautiful view. "I like it here," she said softly.

"No flights, okay?" Mark quibbled. "Just you and me in our car, nothing to do with CUF. You can pick any bed-and-breakfast along the way. Nothing but fun in the sun, promise?"

Lisa knew they were going to Tampa, although she was not as enthusiastic as Mark. She strutted up the porch stairs with two bags of groceries. Mark followed, breathing in her perfume with his eyes half-closed. It was the spring on the screen door that slowed them down.

Juggling groceries one minute and, in the next, suddenly, each other. Mark caught the edge of the door with his face, cutting his brow and creasing his cheek. He was still sitting there, laughing, when the blood began to trickle down.

"Oh, shit." Lisa saw the blood and startled her man. "You may need a stitch!" Reaching into her purse, she pulled out her makeup mirror.

Mark looked unsteady, trying to find his face in the small mirror. He finally focused and pulled open his wound. "No, Lise, we can just put some tape on it, okay?"

Cut or no cut, Lisa wasn't giving in that easily. She taped up Mark's face and sauntered around with a cold Schlitz. They were still crazy in love with each other. Lisa held out and teased her man relentlessly, but somewhere after 11:00 p.m., she gave in and the two took each other to bed.

The Drive to Cole's

Mark wound out second gear in the Dodge, rounding an inside uphill turn somewhere in Georgia. It was their twelfth hour on the road. When they hit the crest of Route 319, a sign read, "Welcome to Fitzgerald." Mark's mind raced back to his first CUF operative, thinking of Emily Fitzgerald, then to Lisa.

An uncomfortable moment was spared when Lisa saw a place up ahead. "Pull over there, handsome," she said as she rubbed her bare foot along Mark's thigh. "I'm feeling like I want to lie down a bit. How about you?" she said as seductive as she could. Lisa was very good at steering Mark's mind and was, in all seriousness, what was responsible for the success of the CUF experiment early on.

Mark pulled down the long narrow driveway toward the old plantation bed-and-breakfast. The hedgerow was overgrown and the rail fence missing some boards, but all in all, the property stood the test of time, surviving the Civil War, multiple hurricanes, and of course, the Depression.

Mark grabbed the hand brake and began to pull. The dust-filled drums squealed to a complete stop, turning the heads of the four croquet players. Their stare of disapproval prompted Mark to hit the horn when one stiff was about to strike the pole. Lisa chuckled, knowing her man was back to normal.

"Lisa, you want to give them something to talk about?" Mark whispered in his wife's ear. Mark looked like he had just stepped out of the ring with his eye taped up and red crease on his cheek. No wonder the players immediately looked down on the couple, speechless.

Lisa liked the intimidation and grabbed her man, kissing him firmly on the lips. The two lovers were later responsible for the destruction of the headboard, a fan, and a light fixture. The two road warriors had disappeared into their room and were not heard from till the crack of dawn, or crack of ceiling plaster, whatever woke the landlord first.

Morning gave way to a beautiful horizon. Thick smokelike fog hung in the lowland, and pockets of mist rose and dissipated over the rise. Mark stood in the window, looking out over the lush green rolling fields. He had already packed his things and was trying to snap his suitcase when he said, "Hey, Lise, we should hit the road. We have a six-hour drive."

Lisa was in the small bathroom, brushing her teeth. "What did you say about sex?" she said with a mouthful of toothpaste.

"Six, baby, six! Six-hour drive!"

"Oh, I thought you said you wanted sex before we drive." She giggled.

Mark turned and smiled.

"Well, do ya?" Lisa asked.

Mark was still weak in the knees. "They already cooked our breakfast, darlin'." Mark leaned in for a toothpaste kiss.

"You better find a good place to pull over before we get to Joe's, baby," Lisa said playfully. "Come on, Mr. Lavenger, we'll eat and run!"

Run they did through the rolling hills of Southern Georgia. The trip would have been an eighteen-hour drive straight through, but Lisa and Mark knew how to plan a road trip. They got the biggest chunk of the leg finished on the first day and had a short, relaxing drive on the second.

Cole's House

Joe pulled the door of his study closed and locked it. "Don't worry about the girls. Told them it was military business. You wanted to keep Lisa out, I get it, trust me. Look, Mark, let's have no delusions about this program. One day it may explode in our face."

Mark had his head slightly cocked to the left and bit down on his lip. Mustering a grin, he began to speak. "Mmm, about that..." Mark began to move around Joe's desk. "I have spent more time— more time than you know, Joe—with the reality and seriousness of what we did and are doing. We're playing God, and that in itself will be judged, my friend, so anything else, it's chicken shit."

"Exactly, Mark, exactly," Joe interrupted.

Mark held his hand half in and half out. He wasn't finished. "You have to be all the way in or all the way out. I'm standing in your study, Joe. I get it. I made my peace with God about it a long time ago. In my own way of believing, I am true to my faith, and why I agreed to carry on with CUF is this..."

Mark opened his palm and rhythmically beat it to "all," *smack*, "those," *smack*, "young," *smack*, "men," *smack*. "All those young boys who were killed before they ever got a chance to fight. In an instant, thousands of our boys were terminated. Blown to God knows where, never to fight, love, enjoy their beautiful country! No chance to ever return home to prosper. Tens of thousands who never raised their gun in anger, just wiped out—bombs, ships, aircraft. The means are endless. We focus on those who survived, those who are above-and-beyond brave. My reasoning is simple, Joe. I am offering a replacement vessel." Mark paused and bowed his head. "I am offering my God a vessel for a soul who was taken before his time."

Joe stood there looking as if he was about to laugh but refrained. He walked around to his cigar chest, took out two Cubans, and fumbled for his lighter. "Mark, I wish it were that simple for me."

"Look, Joe," Mark interrupted. "Get past how we got here, okay? If we were doing something so horrific, we would have been found out. There are blessings in this, Joe. We never forced anyone to bear a child. Those women who volunteered and those women who were out playing God, shopping for their perfect baby at the sperm bank…" He wrung his hands and paused in animated fashion. "Well…" He paused briefly again. "My motivation was, is, and will remain for the security of the country. Theirs, I'm not so sure."

"Harsh, Mark." Joe passed him a cigar and commented, "Passionate speech, my friend. Sure you won't consider running in South Florida?" Joe smiled sarcastically. The two of them fiddled with the ends of the Cubans until they were just right.

"Mark, in all seriousness, I know our intentions remain good. I just hope our secret stays with us. CUF is funding soldiers' families. We started the ball rolling, and it took on a whole new identity. Mark, don't you worry." Joe moistened his cigar, rolling it in his fingertips, then pointed it at his friend. "Having all the best swords in the world means nothing without the soldiers to wheel them."

With that, Joe flipped his Zippo and leaned forward to light up Mark's cigar.

Mark eased back in the leather chair and drew hard on the Cuban. "Damn, Joe, smoother than Asian ass." He laughed as he slowly exhaled. And so did Joe.

"Just not as cheap," Joe said, coughing and lighting his cigar. "Mark, just not as cheap."

Mark, Lisa, and the Coles enjoyed ten days in South Florida, boating, fishing, and enjoying the Deep South from the deck of Joe's thirty-two-foot Chris-Craft named *Clarabell*, his childhood goose. The boat had been built wide in the middle and narrow in the stern. It had two six-cylinder Perkins motors that, when at headway speed, completely drowned out the water breaking past the bow.

Back on the Road

Mark and Lisa left early the following day. Their intercoastal adventure had come to an end. They were anxious to get home, and they had a two-day drive ahead of them.

Mark was pushing too heavy on the gas pedal when he rounded a corner, and failed to see a young man on a bicycle.

"Ohh! Look out!" Lisa yelled.

Mark tried to tighten the turn, indicated by the squeal of the Plymouth's tires. Mark missed the boy, partly because he was able to reclaim his side of the road, partly because the young boy drove his bike off the road at the last second.

Mark slowed to a stop after looking in his rearview mirror. Up out of the grass on the side of the road popped Willie Jr., as he was called, after his uncle William Cobb.

Lisa opened her door before Mark could stop the car. "You all right, son?" she wailed.

"Yeah, I think so," Willie said. He stood his bike up and began to walk it out of the grass when it stopped suddenly. "Oh, my bike!" Willie skidded his bike up to an old fence post, studying the freshly bent rim.

Mark was out of the car and saw the distressed look on the boy's face.

"My uncle's gonna kill me! He's gonna kill me! He told me to take care of his bike, guard it with my life! I'm a dead man, ohh—"

"Calm down, son. What's your uncle's name?" Mark asked.

"William, William Cobb, sir. They call me Willie Jr."

Mark never made the connection. He hadn't taken a look at the names of the newest batch of CUF donors and hadn't noticed that a William Cobb was one of them.

The news that William was killed in action had failed to reach his family. He was on a list of prospective soldiers destined for Madam YumYum and a weekend in Seoul.

Mark popped the trunk and wheeled the bike over, holding the rear off the ground. "You said it is your uncle's bike?"

"Yes. Before he went off to Korea, he was delivering papers and groceries. That's my job now. *Was* my job. Oh, man, my uncle's gonna kill me!"

"Son, let's get you to town and get this bike fixed. Where is the nearest big town?" Mark said. Lisa already had the road map out, and the three set out to fix Willie's bike.

The boy had been on his way to pick up his papers. His route was twenty-three miles through the rolling hills, and the boy was solid grizzle from riding it every day.

"Willie," Lisa asked, "you said your uncle's in Korea?"

Mark looked down at his briefcase. "Do you know where?"

"Yeah, the Duce Four, Twenty-Fourth regiment," the paperboy said proudly.

"You know, Willie," Mark said, "your uncle should be proud that you're taking over for him. You could be fishing in the creek or chasing girls."

"Hey!" Lisa poked Mark's shoulder. "Don't tease the boy! What my husband meant is that he is impressed with your work ethic."

Willie Jr. just looked out the window. "Oh, there's my stop." Mark hit the brakes. "My papers." Mark stopped and picked up the delivery bag hanging under a makeshift roof. The bag weighed over fifty pounds, and the wiry Willie Jr. would deliver all eighty-seven of them by bike.

Mark rolled into McGurk's tire and service station outside Montgomery, Alabama. Mark asked about the bike tire and where he could get it fixed as he filled up his Plymouth. Willie was nervous, wondering how he would deliver the papers, fix the bike, and what to tell his parents about the white folk who had caused the mess.

At Wevill's Bike Shop, Willie Jr.'s fear diminished, and like a child, he stood in wonder. On the floor was a model JC Higgins bike with two huge saddlebags, two mini red taillights, and a SALE sign on it. Mark saw Junior immediately grab for it.

"Easy, son," a voice came from the rear. Mark looked over. "What can I help you fellas with?" Mark rolled in the banged-up bike. Mr. Wevill and Mark had a brief discussion, and Mr. Wevill approached Willie. "See anything you like, sonny?" Wevill asked.

Without letting go of the bike's handlebars, or even taking a look around at the others on the floor, the boy stated, "This one, sir."

"Well, let me tell you about this bike. A fella near your age came down here wanting this bike. He paid me half before I ordered it, and I haven't seen him since. That was one year ago, so I'm selling her."

"Sir," Junior said softly to Mark, "what's gonna happen to my uncle's bike?"

Mr. Wevill said, "Well, I might have a rim out back for that model, but it's not going to be fixed right away. It seems the links are bent, and I'm fresh out of that size chain."

Willie Jr. felt defeated once again; however, the feeling was short-lived. Mark had already secured the deal on the new bike, and after learning the boy was a deliveryman, Mr. Wevill told Mark he would fix up the old bike free of charge.

"Come on, Junior." Mark watched as Willie Jr. was just blown away with the whole experience. He didn't even feel the skinned knee and ankle that were both pink and weeping blood.

"Tell you what, Junior? Let Mr. Wevill get that new bike oiled up for you, and Lisa and I will take you to lunch. You and her can draw out your delivery route, and before I bring you and that new bike home, we will help you deliver the papers. No worries, my friend." And Mark smiled.

Junior was speechless. He had never been treated so fairly by strangers and was amazed by the generosity. The Lavengers were equally amazed by Willie's attitude and demeanor. After their lunch and after retrieving the bike, the three of them headed off into the country, delivering papers and telling stories.

Home at Last

Mark sat at his desk with a hot cup of coffee steaming in front of him. He opened his briefcase and fished out a list of soldiers, their matrix, and began his work ranking and determining their accessibility for extraction. It took him three times through before he reread the name and it dawned on him, Sergeant William "Billy" Cobb. *Junior!* he thought to himself. "Lisa!"

Lisa ran into the room, sensing something serious. She looked at Mark now standing with a folder in his hands, gripping it like it was alive.

"God, Lise, it's Junior's uncle!"

William Cobb was officially listed as MIA, but the report should have read KIA.

"It was there the whole time, Lise, right there at our feet. Junior's uncle, damn those fuckin' Koreans!" And with that, Mark turned away. He didn't want his wife to see his tears. He was shaken. "Lise, we will stop and see Willie Jr. when we pass through Alabama, promise."

Lisa didn't say anything, but later on, she silently cried while she prepared dinner. Things were quiet for the next few nights at the Lavengers'.

Spade Gets a Pass

Corporal Lawrence was now Lieutenant Lawrence Jones, a.k.a. Spade, a.k.a. Too Dark, and he was on a three-day leave to Seoul.

Too Dark sat quietly on the 10 as it roared down the runway. He knew enough to look at the crew to see if they were alarmed. They weren't. The flight was short and uneventful, and soon he was on his way to downtown Seoul.

Mark had no problem securing drivers and rooms for his soldiers, but Too Dark, however, was a little harder to corral than others.

"Stop here!" Too Dark said with authority. The brakes squealed as the driver stopped short. The smell of marijuana permeated the air of the car. "Hey, I smell something."

"You can get plenty of that where you're going, pal" was all he heard from the man driving.

"Yeah, where's that?" Too Dark said with attitude.

"A place called Madam YumYum's."

"Yeah, well, I'm not hungry," the soldier replied, stepping out of the car.

Mark's driver had orders, but he had no way of physically getting Too Dark back in his jeep. "Hey, tell you what, Lieutenant? I don't want to scrape you up off the floor of some opium den naked and afraid in two days, so if you want to find something to smoke, I'll go with you," he suggested, thinking quickly.

"What's your name?" Too Dark asked.

"Mike Riley."

"Yeah? Well, you don't look Irish."

"Well, my mother's Italian."

Too Dark walked back toward Mike in the driver's seat.

"Look, Too Dark, here's the thing. I served, did my time, they offered me this gig. Pick you guys up, drop you off, don't let you get fucked up by the one million gooks around here trying to rob you blind! So who cares if my name is Stinky Finger Steve? You and I are hanging out because I need the job, capisce?" Mike said with his fingers pinched within his thumb.

Too Dark smiled. He wanted to see if Mike was down. "Hey, I smelled hash or some rope passing through that intersection."

"I know a place. It's a few blocks over, and I will show you a few bars where you can walk to from your hotel," Mike suggested.

"Cool" was all Too Dark would give him.

Mike drove the military jeep down a small alley behind Tetra Noodles. Every window shade and blind was cracked open five stories high. All eyes were on the Yankees.

"Take a good look now, Too Dark. See all these eyes? Well, when you're all fucked up, you can't just blaze up anywhere. You gotta be safe, okay?"

"Cool. Yeah, man, I get it."

Mike now had his attention. Once they were in the alley, there was no beep necessary; the sound of the jeep alone sent out a runner. Mike signaled 1 and 4 and handed the boy five dollars. He returned with a glass pipe and four grams of finger hash.

"You're staying over there," Mike said, pointing at Mrs. YumYum's. "This place is as far as you should wander alone, okay?"

"Cool, cool, I got it. They let you blaze up in there?"

"Yes, and there are two bars nearby, but watch out for the opium," Mike told Too Dark.

"Yeah, I'm good with that, Mike. Thanks."

Mike pinched off a piece of hash and stuffed it in the pipe. "Hey, give me your lighter." Mike took a long pull as Too Dark watched the gray smoke pass through the tube. Holding the hit in, he handed the pipe to Too Dark. Pausing, Lieutenant Lawrence Jones took the pipe from his new white friend and they smoked up right there in the alley.

"So why did you leave the service?" Too Dark asked Mike.

"Well, I didn't really leave. They wouldn't let me fly Corsairs anymore, so I...well, yeah, I quit. Well, they asked me to leave because I was flying high in a different way, seriously." They both began hysterically laughing. "Yes, sir, that was a few years ago, in some mosquito-nest shithole in the South Pacific. Damn, they grew some great reefer out there, though."

"You flew high, man?" Too Dark said, still laughing.

"Man, I was rolling one with my knees and looked over my shoulder when some nip kid tried to blaze me up. I rolled reefer everywhere and lit his ass up. Tried opening the hatch before I landed, caught the landing gear." Mike took another hit and, while he was still holding his breath, started again. "They got me for damaging government property, blah, blah, blah. Truth is, I could see the sand flies better than anyone in my squadron. They all knew it, just couldn't handle the smoke. Not their poison."

Too Dark bumped Mike's fist. "Mike, man, you can come bang with us, but you're too white." And they both burst out laughing again.

"Thanks. Hey, you keep it in front of you out there, Too Dark."

"Shit, what's in front of me soon is going to be some smooth and sweet." Too Dark smiled, and it lit up the night.

"I will see you in a few days. Madam YumYum knows how to get in touch with me." Mike rolled Too Dark up to the lobby. "Hey, these girls are hot. No need to wander, man. Trust me there." And they bumped fists again.

Too Dark skipped the first step and settled into a smooth strut as he pushed through the lobby doors. Mike drove away smiling, high as a rat in a transport.

Cold as Hell

The onset of war proved to be the most predictive for the boys of CUF. The war looked like it was about to end when the Chinese decided to throw two hundred thousand of General Song Shi-Lun soldiers against twenty thousand soldiers of the Fifth and Seventh Marines and US Army, commanded by Oliver Smith and Major Almond.

In a historic battle of defensive retreat, the US military withdrew from the Chosin Reservoir, beginning November 26, 1950, until they joined their counterparts on a retreat across the peninsula on December 11, 1950.

With temperatures reaching twenty below zero, Nick Savignano trudged alone, following the man far in front of him. The staff sergeant was in his third straight day of constant battle and was beyond numb when the sniper round whizzed by, hitting the transport in front of him. He barely cared.

Nick was a handsome Italian American, strong and confident, from a city in the northeast, Brockton, Massachusetts. The northeast was a heavy recruiting area because of the similar climate. Nick was drafted and joined the 101 Airborne Division, rapidly moving up to staff sergeant.

Six days of keeping his men alive while still assaulting the enemy and killing them twenty to one had taken its toll. The action would burn out the best of them. Nick, or Sav, as they called him, took care not to keep all their guns slung around their shoulders. He also kept two Springfields in the cab of each of the transports for the squad sharpshooters.

Keeping a gun semiwarm helped keep it true. The extreme cold could warp the wood and shrink the barrels, causing all types of inaccuracies. Two of his best shots were Private Freddie Massa from Ansonia, Connecticut, and Corporal Edmond Sheppard from Pelham, New Hampshire. Both in their own minds were the best shots in the squad; it was not a bad problem to have. Keeping them alive and ready to fight…well, that was a different story.

Staff Sergeant Sav raised his hand three seconds after the bullet hit. Pointing at the passenger's rearview mirror, he removed his hand from his heavy mitten and made the gun signal. Out of the cab came the two rifles wrapped in a blanket. Sav moved his squad around the transport and grabbed his field glasses. His bloodshot eyes and drooping lid froze when it hit the metal rim. Holding his breath, trying not to fog the glasses, he scanned the rigid valley.

Two more bullets came in; one hit the transport, and the other a soldier's frozen foot. The foot didn't bleed for two days until he was in a mash tent. Sav caught a flash and saw three PVA soldiers decide to take potshots, while the mortar team was trying to set up in a frozen ground.

Freddie was scanning when his counterpart, Sheppard, said, "Got 'em, two o'clock, 500 to 550 foot elevation!"

The transport driver shut his truck off and gave Edmond his perch. "On you, Freddie. I'm taking the far left and working my way in."

Freddie squeezed the 150-grain Springfield, followed by Edmond. One fired while the other reloaded. Nick Sav's head was buzzing. The bolt-action Springfields sounded like music. When Freddie dropped the first Chinese soldier, Edmond gut-shot the mortar team target. He let him crawl off while he killed three more, then finished him off.

They loaded the guns back in the cab along with Staff Sergeant Savignano. Two of his men crowded in with him on either side, Jimmy Grasso and Paul Destefeno.

"Sarge, you need to catch a few Zs," Destefeno added. "We got your back, Sarge!"

Nick was pinned between two of his men in the warm cab. His frozen hands, legs, and feet were all pins and needles.

On November 30, the 101st Airborne was being overrun on the eastern bank of the Chosin River. Baker Company had begun the day with 156 men.

Baker's Company staff sergeant got the word that the Chinese had poured almost a quarter million troops on the United Nations force surrounding the Chosin. The US Military's Seventh and Fifth Marines and 101st Airborne made up the bulk of the twenty-thousand-man force. Alfa, Baker, Cobra, Delta, Easy, Fox, and George Company surrounded the ground around the Chosin. When the fighting began, and the whistles and trumpets blew, the boys of Dog Company would all have either killed or were killed in face-to-face combat.

Nick took his squad across a small ravine to an ambush point they knew was being used for a pincer move. The squad had four .30-caliber light machine guns, twelve M14s, two M2s, eleven M1 Garands, and six 9-millimeter light machine guns. His sixteen-man squad moved quickly into position and dug into the frozen bank. After probing the front defense of Able and Fox Company, Dog Company got hit front on, whistles blew, and motors rained in.

Sav calmed his men. He looked at the ones he could see and said, "Don't you stop firing until every Charlie is dead!" Sav could see the heads bobbing up and down, passing through the rocks and snow, now heading to their position. "Hold your fire, boys. I want the first burst by the .30s."

Just then, a division of PVA came into view. They were grouped tight and moved like a purple caterpillar through the pass. Nick smacked the helmet of Destefeno on the closest .30, and he began to let it rip. Three more Brownings joined in, and the rest opened up with their Springfields.

At first, the PVA ran back without firing but immediately regrouped and charged Sav's position. He was on the radio, calling in the 105s, when the first wave came in.

Freddie Massa was out of his hole, grabbing up all the .30-round boxes he could carry when the first 105 hit 1,500 feet away. The blast wobbled him. "Adjust 500, 223!" he called. *Boom!* Another round hit.

Sav walked the big guns in and called, "Check your fire!" To the sergeant of the 105, he screamed over the radio, "That was Danger Zero! I have a battalion of PVA, three hundred or more, trying to make their way around hill 87."

"Copy, Danger Zero."

"Grid 223, 4 and 6."

"Copy, Dog Company."

Sav put the radio down and yelled to his men, "We only have one another now, and Gordy with his 105s! None of you pricks better owe that limey bastard any money!"

Sergio yelled out, "Nothing to worry about, Sarge! Me and Duffy are into him for 500, so if we get killed, he don't get paid."

Laughter broke out, some of it sounding nervous.

"Here they come!" Caravetsa yelled.

When the bugle blower puckered up, Freddie dropped him at 220 yards. The first wave of 150 PVAs came pouring up the pass, stopping and firing wildly. Destefeno and Muller, on top of two of the Brownings, were locked in on gaps that would clog with troops once they tried to navigate the jagged slope. The passes were literally shut down with bodies.

Mortars rained in, and Sav's men were in deep. The first wave was stalled by bodies, and when the next wave came, Sav called the 105s, and the second wave turned the pass pink and black.

After four days of defending their positions, outnumbered ten to one, the US troops fought hard with frostbitten fingers. Death came to those who surrendered, to the enemy or to the cold. Those who fought lived, and surviving your first human wave of wild-eyed Chinese PVA would empower any young man, frozen or thawed.

Dog Company was on their third assault of the day when Sav ordered his men to pull back. He commanded them to dig in farther up the pass, while Muller and Destefeno stayed at the first Browning.

Stevo pulled the last few shovels of icy snow from under his MB jeep. The cold was brutal, and each time he made the snow beneath him crunch, a crisp, cold sound, it set his bones shaking. He could barely get his Zip to light after removing his hands from his frozen mittens. He pulled the 105 shell under the engine and began to roll an ear swab as steady as he could. He held it briefly on the dull orange Zippo flame and could hear his earwax sizzle as he struggled to move it toward the makeshift motor heater.

Stevo lay there warming his frozen hands as black smoke leaked up out of the hood. "Get ready to move, boys!" he screamed from under his jeep. "This smoke could bring a shell right down on us."

His crew was busy de-icing their Bofors Gun. Temperatures were dipping below zero, and he needed to light up the shells under both vehicles. Sergeant Stevo cut a few 105 shells about six inches from the rim. Filled with a mix of gas and diesel, he used the giant Sterno to warm his MB and Bofor carrier. "Don't worry about that sight, boys. They won't be overhead today. We gotta get hot."

Steve Costa led the Twenty-Fourth antiaircraft battery squad, Easy Company. His four-man squad consisted of a layer, trainer, adjuster, feeder, and radio. Sergeant Costa spotted rounds, identified enemy planes, and defended their position. He was easy to spot with his grease gun strapped to his back and heavy, thick beard. He was a joyful soul and actually had a lot of fun at war with his diverse group of friends and squad mates. Stevo was what most guys called him, but that was before Billy Dean.

Major Colonel William Dean was commander of the Thirty-Fourth before he was taken prisoner in the battle of Taejon. Stevo was a loader in 1950 when Dean's army was tasked to defend Taejon, a strategic city used for transpiration of food and weapons.

Dean's army was closest to Korea when the fighting broke out. His army, however, was overwhelmed, and panic struck throughout the lines as wave after wave of KPA poured over the men.

Stevo had been part of the five-man team whose job was to defend the CP against enemy aircraft. He learned quickly that with a few modifications to the Bofor gun, he could use it to take out almost anything.

Sav's Last Stand

Nick steadied his men after they rallied. "We've got to stay here, boys, till Destefeno—"

Sav was cut short by the squeal of a T38 track. "Move, move, Devely!"

Sav's men dived over the icy berm. Destefeno saw the T38 turret turn toward his buddies and opened up with his .50. Ripping rounds all over its face, he lucked out when a tracer made its way in and the tank paused. By the time Destefeno folded his bipod, an HE round blew a portion of the mound he was on clean out from under him. Falling and scrambling for his life, Destefeno made it to the basin with all his limbs until he was cut in two by the 38's machine gun.

Sav was calling on the radio, but there was no reply. The 105s had problems of their own.

Sav rolled through the dial to the motor pool. "Burski, Burski, you read me?"

Burski piped in, "Sav, that you?"

"Bursk, we're screwed, got a T38 heading up our pass. Destefeno's gone, man."

"Sav, all I got left is the Bofor."

"Tell that ginny bastard Stevo to move his ass!" was all Nick could say.

Sergeant Costa heard the T38s in the pass and knew they would end up taking out their rear. He had already cut the barrel transport mount, which lowered it another eighteen inches below level. Antiaircraft rounds were designed to explode on contact, by pressure and timing of the explosive, but with T38s, it was impossible to penetrate the armor with a forty-millimeter shell. Instead, Stevo used the maneuverability of his MB to help pull the Bofor around and above to a plateau with a window view of Sav's pass.

Sav was in trouble, for he knew behind the tank were hundreds of Chinese, and they only had the cover of a small icy berm. The T38's crew made a mistake firing three more rounds on to Destefeno's last position. Each round produced huge crowds of frozen rocks and snow, which Sav used wisely to move to a better defensive position.

Sav stayed in contact with Burski and relayed his new position. He could see the Bofor moving into position above and just behind him and knew it was too close to cover him. "Tell that greasy bastard I'm heading over to the outcropping on his 6, okay? On his 6! If I draw fire, he's got to open up, no matter!"

Sav knew he was going to be exposed briefly, but he had to move. His exhausted men, with the snot frozen in their noses and their blackened, sleep-deprived eyes, already looked dead. "Boys, we gotta move one more time. That tank will kill us all! Stevo's above us, and he's going to kill that fucker, you got me? Then we got to cover him while he gets off that ridge, roger?"

"Roger that, Sarge," the soldiers muttered through their icy breath.

"Okay, move!" Nick commanded.

They might have looked half-dead, but they still knew their jobs. Systematically they moved from knob to knob, just staying of of the 38's line of sight. Stevo's Bofor crew zeroed in on the pass below and had eight boxes of forty-millimeter laid out, sixty-four rounds and about thirty seconds of pure hell.

"Don't miss, Stevo" was the last thing Sergeant Costa heard before the 38 began ripping machine gun bursts in and around Sav's position. He held fire long enough for the Bofor crew to get it in the reflector sight. With the rear of the 38's engine compartment exposed from above and behind, a direct hit would surely cripple it if not completely destroy it. Stacking and storing extra rounds in the engine compartment was fatal.

Sav looked out at the 38 crawling up the pass, and he could see Costa's gun over to his right. Behind the 38, hundreds of Chinese regulars scurried among the rocks. "Two thousand meters and clos-ing," Sav radioed to Burski. "Tell Stevo, fire at will!"

Costa was over his perch and had a bird's-eye view of the valley. It was crawling with regulars. He snapped his head over to his crew and hesitated briefly to give the order to fire. He knew it could be his last. He held up his left hand and was trying to keep steady on the 38's rear when he lowered it once again. *Boom boom boom.* The boxer began raining HE shells that hit all over and behind the 38. The six-volt battery on the Bofor was frozen, and so was its sight.

Sav ran toward the trainer, who was now trying to hit a a tank, evading his fire. Sav jumped behind and started screaming adjust-ments just as two 40s hit a sweet spot and blew the rear of the tank completely off. Their deadly shooting drew the immediate attention of every gun in the pass, and lead, ice, and rock were lifting past their position.

Sav opened up from his outcropping and caused the Chinese to retreat for cover. Steve's crew raced to escape over the frozen hill, skidding and slipping until they were all back on the road below. Sav led his men over the cropping to the transports waiting on the road below.

"We're leaving this place!" Sav screamed with an exhausted breath. Hunched over, he had nothing left to say.

Stevo's jeep rumbled up, and he yelled, "Get in, Sarge!"

Sav pulled himself in to the MB and wrapped himself in a blan-ket. "You greasy bastard," he said with an immaculate smile. "You saved my ass!"

Costa and Savignano limped the MB through the ruts and holes left by the retreating Twenty-Fourth. They prevented the rear from being cut off and captured. Word spread rapidly up the convoy line. By the time it reached the front, the two held off three thousand and blew up three 38s. They were both now off to Seoul.

Stephen tightened his finger grip on his riser, pinning the arrow tight. November 21, 1963, was a few degrees below average in temperature, and the sky showed unstable weather clouds, which Stephen used to move with minimum silhouette. He learned from

Charlie T what he could get away with regarding movement in the forest. Low and slow, wait for a cloud and a rustle from the breeze, and slip in as quietly as you can. "Slow down, kid," he would repeat over and over when he first took Stephen out to scout deer. "Hunt your way to the stand."

Stephen remembered every word, but he still had to mindfully stop and concentrate. *Got to get to the stand...*

"No, slow down. No, stop, hold, say a prayer. Seven, step and stop," Charlie would tell him. "Don't sound like a predator."

Charlie Tartaglia was a second-generation Italian from back east. He served in the Navy on the USS *Lexington* and was credited with one zero and two torpedoes planed from his forty-millimeter Quad gun. Besides the numerous war stories Charlie would tell, his second love was bow-hunting white-tailed deer, and the stories proved full of advice.

Stephen was a better pupil of Charlie's school than the public one, and as his classmates spent the whole day talking about civil rights and going to the moon, Stephen was planning his approach.

Trying hard to fight the temptation to move quick to his stand, Stephen reigned himself in. He could see the twisted maple tree where he placed his crotch stand earlier that week. He had a few choices but decided on the maple because the afternoon sun split the two hilltops to the southwest, and the sun shone on the thick brush.

"Kid, you've got to find the thickest cover when the rut is on," Charlie T had once told him. Where the sun shines longer, the vegetation is thicker, and Stephen had chosen well. The sun shone in that particular bedding area until dark.

Sounds like we're still in rut, Stephen thought to himself. Ahead, he thought he heard a low grunt and some wet popping, but he dismissed it, thinking it was turkeys. Placing his turkey call in his mouth, he began to peck and pluck while scratching the ground with a stick.

Using his mock gobble, he moved around the thicket to his stand. The bedding area was a mess of saplings and briar that grew thick with the extended sun. After the loggers cleared the large hardwood, the canopy opened up, leaving new growth opportunity and access roads. Although steep and twisted, the old logging roads became game trails, and two skirted his stand.

Just as Stephen reached his maple, he saw a flash of white in the thicket, and suddenly he heard a low, deep grunt below. Through the whips he could make out a white square and black nose of a doe. She was frozen while the brush behind her was racking back and forth. *That doe might not be ready,* Stephen thought.

A doe would stay in the thicket, while the buck tried to penetrate her fortress, his wide tall rack tangled in the dense cover. Stephen knew he had no chance on the ground. His heart was pounding, he was late to begin with, but there was no way his mother was letting him skip school just to bow-hunt.

As he climbed into his stand, he could see the brush had stopped moving. Scanning frantically, he saw the buck coming to investigate. With his bow around his neck, he wasn't halfway up his tree when he saw bone. A huge white rack was moving through the saplings. Fortunately, it began blowing and moving a few leaf clusters above.

Stephen quickly climbed into his stand and slid the string of the bow past his face. *If he smells my tracks, he's gone,* he thought. Moving slow and careful, he knocked an arrow and pulled half-draw. He needed the buck to change direction. An animal that large didn't get that way from being stupid, and even with a warm doe around, they always put caution first. The monster buck froze fifteen yards out.

Stephen's stand was over a mile from his house, down a slow rolling hill with a south-facing slope behind it. Whenever his mother took him to the car dealership for service on her car, Stephen would sneak off to check out the forest behind. A trail leading up the ridge behind the dealership ended in a twisted maple grove. A hunter could get there in twenty minutes. The logging road down the road from Strong's Marine took three times that.

It was his third season hunting alone. Counting gun season, Stephen quickly had a dozen deer under his belt. He learned to plan his hunt after having been busted so often his first year. Earlier that week, he had his dad drive him behind the dealership, where he could stash his gear. He had everything in an old duffel bag, bow included.

Stephen's fingertips were purple from the string's tension, but he knew if he made any movement, his chance would be over. He had to hope for a good headwind and for the doe to get hungry enough to come out to feed.

The massive eight-point bobbed his head as Stephen looked for an angle, his senses on full alert. When the doe finally broke cover, it was ten minutes before dark. The buck turned and started to follow her; he had unfinished business. Twenty yards out, there was an opening. Stephen went to full draw and began internally begging for the buck to hit his opening. *Please, please turn. God, please.*

When the rack of the buck entered the window, Stephen launched his cedar spline. As he watched it turn and speed toward the target, he prepared for a solid lung shot. It hadn't been the best idea to shoot at a moving buck, but Stephen wasn't stopping the bruiser vocally, and he knew it.

His arrow penetrated just past the ribs, making a hollow *thump* sound on impact. Stephen instantly smelled bowels. *Shit, shit, oh, man, thank you, thank you, God!* He saw the buck move off with his tail down tight. "Oh, man, it's gonna be dark and I just gut stuck a monster buck!" he said out loud to himself. Heart pounding, shaking from adrenaline, he quickly slipped down his tree onto the dimly lit forest floor.

The temperature was dropping, and with night only moments away, Stephen had to decide. *Okay, get on his tracks and try and stick him again, or wait till tomorrow morning, skip school, leave him overnight to die, maybe coyotes will eat his guts...he'll be torn up.*

Stephen moved slowly to where he hit the buck. He found the cedar arrow lying on the wet, leafy ground. Examining it for blood, he didn't have to bring it too close to his nose before he detected bowel. He could see the large divots in the ground where the huge buck walked off.

Stephen stayed low in the brush but moved quick and quiet, stopping every six or seven steps, looking ahead for sign of his buck. He found some fur on a sapling and determined the wounded buck's direction. All the while he told himself not to push the buck; he was up against it, and he knew it.

Right as the almost-defeated hunter was about to turn and head back, he saw what looked like mist puffing up from ground. Stephen crept closer, using the trees to block his approach. The monster had settled behind a blowdown, and his heavy white breath was billowing up into the dim light of the forest.

Stephen changed directions and began moving above the bedded buck. Disoriented, it never noticed him. When his second arrow hit, it shattered as half of it slipped behind a shoulder through its ribs.

The buck exploded up out of its bed, tripping over the blowdown as it began its death run down the ridge. Stephen heard it pile up with a giant crash. An incomparable silence occurred after that moment, and time stood still. Every emotion erupted at once inside the hunter, and he didn't know whether to laugh or cry. He excitedly thought, *How am I going to get this beast out of the woods, and what's Charlie gonna say?*

Emily put the flour back in the pantry, looked over at the clock, and realized it was six thirty at night and she hadn't seen her teenager since she had left for school. "Elizabeth, can you go out and get your father?"

Frank was wrestling with a rudder cup and bearing when his daughter, whom he called his little angel, entered the barn.

"Daddy, Mommy wants you."

"What about you, darlin'? Don't you want me?" Frank said jokingly as he tried, one more time, to lift the rudder into position. "Lizzy, darlin', Daddy needs your help." Frank had inadvertently kicked the blocks he had ready, and they were just out of reach. "Lizzy…," Frank said, grunting.

Elizabeth Munro had just turned five and was as cute a little girl as one could imagine. She always wore some sort of hat, or scarf.

Tipping her head way back to see her father's face under her dad's old ball cap, Lizzy smiled. "Whatcha need, Daddy?"

Frank paused, admiring his little one, and smiled. "Bring me those blocks and those shingles, will you, darlin'?"

One by one Lizzy moved the wooden pieces and her father slid them under the rudder. Sitting with exhaustion on his rear, Frank pulled his little one tight.

"Couldn't have done it without you, Lizzy." And he squeezed and tickled her. "Now, let's go see what your mother wants."

Stephen wished he had some help and a flashlight. He was able to gut the big buck, and he had a piece of rope long enough to tie the front legs to its head, but this was a 250-pound mature male, and no thirteen-year-old kid was going to drag the beast up the ridge to the old logging road.

"Sorry, Emily, I had to finish that boat today. Lizzy came just in time."

"Well, if that son of yours were here instead of running around the woods like Davy Crockett, he could be helping you, and we could sit and eat like a normal family!" Emily continued. "You know, Frank, with all the wonderful things, amazing things, going on, you would think he might pay more attention."

Elizabeth spoke up. "What is *amazing*, Mom?"

Emily paused and changed her tone. "Well, Elizabeth, we are sending men into outer space, and one day they will land on the moon. Do you think that is exciting?"

"The moon!" The little girl giggled. "You're silly, Mommy." And Elizabeth ran off.

"Ever since we moved, Stephen has spent more time with Charlie T and in those woods than he has here!"

"Now, Em, you know we're all different. I don't expect him to be like me, and besides, Charlie is a gig man."

Emily turned away. She wasn't thinking about her son, rather the soldier she already knew he was. "Frank, I'm getting worried. He has been out there a long time. Can you…"

Frank pulled back on both lips and held his hand up, signaling he understood. He shook his head and headed for the door.

Coming down the driveway, walking like a rooster, was his boy Stephen, grinning from ear to ear. "You find a dollar on the way home?" Frank said sarcastically.

Stephen could hardly contain himself and erupted in a rant. "Dad, you wouldn't believe it! It is the biggest buck of my life! The biggest buck ever! I shot him twice! It…oh, Dad, it was so, so cool!"

Frank just let him run on and on. He knew he had to get it out.

"Dad, we got to get him! He's all cleaned out, promise! Oh, and I got to tell Charlie T!"

"Okay, calm down. Go tell your mother what happened." Stephen began to sprint away. "Hey, leave out the kill shot and guts, okay?"

"Yup!" Stephen cleared the first three steps and ran down the porch toward the front door, taking his bow off and quiver. Standing in front of the door and wiping his feet frantically, Stephen sounded more like their dog Molly than their son.

Emily came to the kitchen door. "Ma, Ma!" Emily stood in a classic pose, slowly crossing her arms. She watched her son wriggle off his hunting gear under the porch light. Stephen stood at attention before the door after he put his bow in the corner. Emily could see he was wide-eyed and eager to spill out his story.

"Ma, you aren't going to believe this buck! Oh, it is huge! I shot him twice, and Dad's got to go help me! Aww, it's huge! I can't budge it!" Stephen was trying to show his mother with his arms just how big the buck was.

"Stephen, you got him down? Is he dead or wounded?" she asked.

"Dead! Oh, yeah, Dad told me not to tell you about the shots, Ma, but aww, it was great! I hit him in the gut! I had only one little hole to shoot through."

"Okay, okay, you and Dad go get the tractor ready and I will make you both something for your trip."

Stephen was already running back outside before his mother finished, jumping all the porch steps. He hit the ground, fell forward, rolled, popped up, and kept running to the barn. Emily just shook her head. "That kid, honestly…"

Frank and his boy took their Ford and wooden trailer down the old coal road where it crossed the logging road. The going was slow, and the two were able to eat a sandwich each as they tried not to spill all their Cokes. Frank was fond of his bottle of Coke, as most soldiers were.

The moonless night gave way to laminated holes in its black curtain. "You comfortable?" Frank asked his son, balancing his rear on the fender.

"Yeah, and this beats walking," the boy replied.

A few low branches and thorn bushes had Stephen climbing from right to left on the tractor, aggravating his father. "Stephen, sit still!"

"Dad!" Stephen said as he grabbed the steering wheel and almost fell off the tractor again.

They reached a clearing just before the ridge, and Frank shut the Ford tractor down. As the last cylinder sputtered, there was nothing but dead silence. Sitting in the iron seat with a brilliant starlit sky before him, Frank was frozen in memory.

"Dad, Dad?" Stephen looked at his father's lifeless stare. "Dad..."

Over the last hour, Frank had several reasons to fall back to a where and when. He mostly avoided talking about the past, so much so that Stephen hardly asked him any questions about the war. The seat of that Ford was identical to the ones he had been accustomed to sitting in when he was stationed on the Hornet. He recalled sitting in the Bofor's seat, staring out at the night sky.

"Dad, Dad, come on!" Stephen was walking around the tractor with a lantern while Frank's brain switched from then and now. "Dad, you okay?"

Frank paused briefly. "Son, snuff that out."

"But he's right over there!"

"Shhhh, come up here," Frank said while tapping on the right metal fender.

Stephen obeyed and climbed up on the hood. The heat from the motor felt good, and he leaned forward, grabbed the wheel he was now straddling, and looked cautiously at his dad.

"Son." Frank took a sip of his Coke, lowering it as slowly as he swallowed, and he began again. "Son, as you know, I don't like talking about the war, what I did or whom I did it to."

"Correct," the boy said. Frank looked at his son, and Stephen nodded. "Okay."

"Oh, god." Frank took a deep breath and sighed. "Stevie..." Frank paused. "Killing for me was never fun. I envy your innocence and excitement about the hunting, and truly, I am proud of how you proved a kid from back east can hunt these bucks with the best of 'em." Frank was stalling; he couldn't begin to explain or even knew why he wanted to. Why should he tell his son about his experience with war? He just knew he had to, and sitting out there beneath the army of God's night sky, he began.

He started with the basics: training, shooting, weapons, ranks, and the ships he was on. He talked briefly about friends and how he met Emily. He held up his Coke bottle and told his son he teased his mother and told her they modeled the bottle after her. He shed a few tears about those who were lost and laughed about friends he had found.

Stephen didn't have to say a word or ask a thing; he was stunned and excited at the same time. Frank felt a bit lighter when he stopped, and he stood to stretch his legs. He spoke for about twenty minutes, making sure not to get too graphic, and tried not to paint any images of glory either.

Stephen's mind was stuck on a phrase his dad used moments earlier: "I was a king in a field of corpses."

Frank saw his boy staring blankly and had stopped talking. It was a lot to swallow for sure. "Okay, let's go get that buck!"

Stephen quickly snapped out of his trance and jumped off the tractor, swiping the lantern from the hood on the way off. "Follow me!"

Frank fired up the Ford and Stephen led his father toward the ridge. "Dad, leave her here. We are going to have to drag him up!"

Frank slid sideways down the ridge to the creek bed. Stephen had beat him to the bed, and Frank could see flashes of white bone.

His boy wrestled with the big male's antlers. "Wow, son, that is quite a trophy."

Stephen turned the animal and tried to show his dad the arrow's entry hole. "Come on, Dad, we have work to do!"

Frank grabbed one of the antlers and paused, looking at his hand under the swaying lantern light. "Damn, boy, this may be bigger than that buck Charlie got last year."

Frank began dragging the buck, while his son picked up the other side, and together, they made it about forty-five yards before taking a quick break. Breathing heavily, Frank told Stephen to climb up ahead of him. "I'm going to flip him and use his antlers to dig in on that steep part." Frank, manhandling the buck, began bringing it up and while sticking its horns into the steep bank. "Put your foot against that tree, Stevie, and pull with all your might!" Frank let his boy pull the beast over the rim, pushing the meaty rear quarters to help it up. Both of them strained, and Frank was breathing even heavier. He felt as if he was back in basic training.

They sat up and began to drag the deer toward the trailer. Frank needed his boy to help pull the buck up again on the high trailer. "Let me get a rope on him, and we can pull his head on first." They maneuvered him into position, and Frank flipped the body. The deed done, he held his chest, out of breath again. "Stevie, your mother's going to kill us."

Stephen didn't know what to think. His kill was in the wooden trailer, his dad just filled his head with things he had previously only wondered, and they had an hour or so to get back. His dad didn't say much of anything the entire drive home.

"Dad…"

"Yes," Frank replied.

"So can I ask you about that stuff once in a while?"

Frank smiled at his boy. "Sure, son." And he rubbed the wool cap on his boy's head. "Once in a while."

"Can we hang this in the barn tonight, Dad?"

"Yeah, but I'm not skinning it tonight, okay?"

"I know, I know, I will do it tomorrow," Stephen said.

Friday, November 22, was a day like most others. Emily had to return to Marietta to help her mom. Matt was off at college, and she attributed his good grades to sending him east. She loved her time in Massachusetts and her in-laws. She was there with them when President Kennedy won the election and felt like she was a part of something special.

Emily tried to keep current with domestic and global news. Silently she followed the escalation of the Vietnam War and the rise of communism in Southeast Asia.

Frank was struggling with his own thoughts. He left the family cranberry-growing business in an attempt to build a mariner on the Strongs' property. They used the *Annabell Rose* for weddings and occasional river concerts, but the clientele were cheap. Boat storage and repair were bringing in some money, but the fuel dock was the marina's greatest asset.

Emily had saved a considerable amount of money, and her investment in the old ferryboat paid off in dividends. Her parents had left her the seventy-six-acre riverfront property and the *Annabell Rose*, along with fifty-four thousand dollars in cash, which Emily spread out for her and her husband's venture. The best investment they had made was toward the material used to build the rails and cradle, important for hauling boats out of the river.

Frank and Emily lived between two large ports, and with all the tugboat traffic on the river, they knew their property could serve as a good alternative for emergency fuel and repair. They based their rack design on the hull blueprint of the common forty-two-foot tug. The rails were bought from a scrap yard, and they weren't good enough for the modern trains, but worked fine for their application.

Frank used the PTO on the 8N to turn the reduction winch. He had old phone poles signed on both sides of the rails, with old ark lights painted red and green. He extended out into the Muskingum River. Between working on boats and ferrying his clientele, Frank worked hard at building slips. He estimated the best size was for boats up to fifty feet.

The Strongs' marina was easy to spot with the *Annabell Rose* parked sharply out front. The fuel dock was run by Emily, and she had an electric bell wired from there to the house. Fuel customers would have to wait a few minutes for her arrival at times, but they never seemed to mind. They would admire the property and the old riverboat and, of course, Emily herself.

Emily returned from her errands with little Lizzy. Pulling into the driveway, they saw Frank backing around the tractor toward the winch. "Looks like your father is finished with that boat," Emily said to her daughter. Looking into the barn, she saw the huge buck hanging from a rafter. "Elizabeth, stay here where it's warm. I want to get a picture of the deer for your brother."

Emily helped Lizzy from the car and waved at her husband, holding up one finger. The two hurried up the stairs, braving the wind and cold. "Lizzy, want to get my camera? It's below the radio in the drawer," Emily told Elizabeth, always keeping her camera ready. With the new business and construction, she had detailed photos.

Turning on the television, Emily called for her daughter. "Lizzy, why don't you watch the president while I run out and take a picture for Stevie?" John F. Kennedy's limo had just turned into a crowded street, and Emily stopped and stared.

"Here, Mommy." Lizzy handed her mother the camera and sat in front of the TV.

As the camera focused in on Jackie, Emily spoke. "Lizzy, see how pretty the first lady is?"

Suddenly the president's head snapped forward and then back. Emily saw him grab his throat through a mist of blood, and Jackie was crawling on the trunk of the motorcade, trying to retrieve a piece of her husband's skull.

"Oh, god, they're killing him!" Emily shouted. Falling to her knees, she struggled for a breath.

"Mommy, what's wrong?" Lizzy said frantically.

"They are killing him!" Emily wiped tears between her gasps.

Chaos broke out on TV as Emily's eyes began to pour water. "Go! Get your father, Elizabeth!" she said sorrowfully.

Lizzy didn't know what to do. She had never seen her mother cry and felt horrible. The little girl didn't know what she had just witnessed, but she knew it was bad.

Weeping on her knees, Emily pleaded with her daughter, "Go get your father!"

Elizabeth ran out of the house crying. "Daddy, Daddy, come quick, they're killing him! Daddy, they're killing him!" Elizabeth was crying and running toward the barn.

Frank had just begun lowering a tug down the rails when he saw his little girl running toward him. He immediately shut off the Ford and came around the winch. Her fragile face was red and wet from crying. "Lizzy, what's wrong?"

"They're killing him, Daddy!" she said, still weeping.

Frank held her still. "Killing who?" he asked firmly.

"Mommy," was all Lizzy could say, and Frank scooped her up and ran toward the house.

Emily had picked herself off the floor and stood watching everything unfold on the television. She didn't hear the door open, but when it shut, she jumped.

Frank rounded the corner with his daughter in his arms. "Em?"

Emily reached out and hugged her husband. "They just killed Kennedy," she whispered in his ear, squeezing him tighter. "Oh, Frank, what did they do that for?" Emily felt heartbroken.

Frank tightened up and growled under his breath. "Those fuckers!" he said out loud, holding his two girls tight.

Lisa was setting down a dish of quiche, admiring its beautiful texture. Mark was out back, stacking firewood, when he heard the phone. "I'm not here, babe!" he yelled. It had been two hours since Kennedy was shot, and neither Lisa nor Mark knew a thing.

"What, slow down, Joe," Lisa said. "Oh no! No! No!" Dropping the phone, she rushed to turn the television on. "Mark, Mark!" she yelled.

Mark dropped an armful of wood and ran toward the door. He knew it must be bad. "What's going on, Lise?" he said as he ran into the kitchen.

Lisa stood in the living room holding the phone. She turned toward her husband with a tear rolling down her cheek and handed him the phone before she plopped down in a chair in front of the television set.

"Hello?" Mark said, looking at his wife, the TV, and all the reporters. "Joe, what the hell just happened?" Joe briefed Mark as best as he could. Mark was stunned. "This is not good, Joe. We're killing our own now!"

Joe was silent on the other end for a moment. Finally, he spoke. "We don't know anything yet. We got the shooter, that's all I know."

"Okay, okay, just keep me in the loop." Mark hung up the phone and sat on the arm of Lisa's chair. Reaching for her hand, he pulled it up to his face, kissing it and pulling her closer.

"Oh, Mark, who would do such a thing?"

"I don't know, Lise, but we're gonna kill whoever it was, count on it!"

Both of them sat and watched as the quiche grew cold.

Unlucky You

Emily spoke firmly into the phone. She was trying to settle her eldest son, who was now married and living in New York. "Please, Matthew, your brother has his own mind to make up," was the only thing Stephen Munro heard.

Frank called out to Emily, who had the phone cord now stretched around the corner into the living room. "Em, come on, it's your deal."

Stephen sat with his arms crossed. "Ma, even if I don't get picked, I'm going! I'm going to be nineteen, and I already waited a year!" He tried yelling loud enough for his brother to hear.

"What's he, some hippie now, Dad?" Stephen asked.

"Hey, enough. It's too cold right now for the hippies," Frank said softly.

Emily pulled her chair in and reached for the deck. "Anything, Frank?"

Frank turned up the radio. "Not yet."

Emily began to deal out the cards. All she could think about was how many younger versions of her husband and son were already dead. "Frank, can you just tell him, you know, just how horrible it is?" Emily looked at her husband with tired eyes. She had been carrying a lot of guilt, her cross to bear. She was never much of a churchgoer, but it did not stop her from employing God's name with earnest.

Washington correspondent Roger Mudd at the Selective Service headquarters broke into the broadcast. "Good evening. Tonight, for the first time in twenty-seven years, the United States has again started a draft lottery." Mudd rambled on about the history of the drafts and World War II.

The mood in the kitchen remained somber. For reasons unclear, Mudd explained that any numbers in the last third would most likely be drafted. There were 366 numbers, and the only one that mattered to Emily was number 330.

Her Elizabeth, now eleven, was quite sharp and calculating. "You don't have to be in combat to serve, you know," she said softly.

"Shhh, okay, here we go," Frank said.

The December 1, 1969, Vietnam War draft took 366 numbers, even on the twenty-ninth of February, and placed them in a box for males born from 1944 to 1950. An estimated 850,000 men would learn their fate as Colonel Mudd read out the numbers. In 1970, a year was added at the end of each following year, and the choice was now youngest to oldest. As the numbers were called out, parents and their children dealt with the immensity of the future in their own way.

As a family, the Munros sat at their kitchen table and played cards. Stephen left his cards on the table and watched his sister fiddle with the order of hers. "Two pairs, Lizzy?" he said sarcastically.

"Ah, 335" was called, and Stephen just sat with his arms crossed.

"Not even going to look?" Lizzy asked.

"Nope. Playing the hand dealt to me," her brother replied.

"And 330." Emily placed her cards on the table and stared at her son, while Frank silently watched her every move. Lizzy began to weep.

"I told you I was going, and now I have to," Stephen said unenthusiastically. "I'll consider the Navy, okay?"

Emily looked at him desperately.

"I will let you know." Stephen flipped over his cards. "Ha, ha, three Johnnys." And he smiled.

Frank burst out laughing as he folded his hands. "Okay, well, it's going to do no good worrying about it now. You won't be going anytime soon, so let's keep our heads up and—"

"And what?" Lizzy said. "Tell everyone my brother is going to Vietnam so they can call him a murderer?"

War protests were popular among the young teachers, and Elizabeth's would travel to Kent State to organize antiwar protests.

Stephen started, "Lizzy, you have to ask your teacher if she believes that all lives matter, not just ours. The North Vietcong murdered millions of peaceful people, Lizzy. They were only trying to practice their religion freely."

Emily looked a bit puzzled. She never thought Stephen cared about the reasons the US was at war; she just assumed he wanted to do as his father had done.

Spring on the river was a busy time, and now that they were short-handed, the Munros were facing a new era of boating.

Matthew Fitzgerald, now married, had become active in the war protests. He didn't call too often, so when the phone rang early Sunday morning, Emily was surprised to hear from her son. Matthew was back in Ohio and was interested in a visit, but the conversation soon turned into politics and the expansion of the Vietnam War.

President Nixon announced on April 30 that an escalation into Cambodia to end the war was a necessary military strategy. This sparked protests around college campuses nationwide.

Matthew wasn't a belligerent man, Frank and Emily having brought him up to see all sides of an issue. When Matt had decided on Hofstra University, his parents knew liberal ideas would be influential, but neither of them would have predicted his anti-American attitude.

Emily liked to blame his wife, Elisha, but deep down she knew her son resented the military that took his father twenty-four years earlier. "Matthew, please, your brother believes that all life matters, and you have to consider how communism and communists work! The same propaganda that is controlling them is controlling you."

"Ma, we're not robots and aren't going to follow our leaders to an early grave," Matt said.

"So you burn down the ROTC building, is that your peaceful solution?" Emily was heartbroken. Her son was angry, and the local newsfeed showed an expanding crowd protesting at Kent State. "Matthew, you and Elisha are taking this too far. You should respect the mayor and the governor's warning. They are talking about curfews and martial law."

The phone was silent, then Emily heard Elisha say, "Just hang up the phone, Matty," and he did.

Frank stood out on the rear deck, looking out at their marina. They had sold the *Annabell* to a museum in Michigan and invested their profit in floating docks and slips. He was rewinding the building process the property had endured.

Emily came out with a cup of coffee. "Thanks, Em," Frank said, leaning over the rail, staring out at the river. "I miss seeing her out there."

"Yes, sometimes I do too." Emily turned and asked Frank bluntly, "Frank, tell me about this brown-water navy?"

Mark Lavenger hung up the phone and started placing folders into his briefcase. "Can't believe those fools. What did they expect?" he said aloud. "They're calling it a massacre, four dead a massacre!" With the receiver under his chin, he was trying to call his secretary.

"Yes, Mr. L?" Lori said with her Southern drawl.

"Lori, I need you to call Delta as soon as possible. I'm on my to Fort Polk. Oh, and, Lori, call Lisa and tell her I will call her when I land."

"What number should I call?" his secretary asked.

"Our home," Mark said, angrier than he intended. Taking a breath and collecting himself, Mark continued, "Lori, my wife is away visiting her mother. She won't be home until three. If you could please call after three and tell her I will call her when I land." He paused. "Okay?"

Mark left for the airport in a rush. His office was tucked behind a marina on Merritt Island near Cape Canaveral. He had less than an hour to make his flight, and he wasn't shy when it came to hammering his '67 SS up Route 95 to Daytona.

Lisa convinced them to move after her mother had relocated closer to their friends the Coles. Mark always assumed some collusion, but he secretly didn't mind. He liked not carrying wood or shoveling snow.

The ninety-five-degree temperature outside, however, was working the big block 454. Mark had the AC blaring, and with his tack near 3,500 for the last ten miles, his motor went over 220 degrees. He had thirty-five minutes to make his flight. He powered the windows down and turned on the heater. He slowed to eighty and watched the temperature drop. Shutting the heat off, he kept it under ninety and left the windows down.

After he arrived, his mad dash through the airport helped him make the flight's last call. The fifty-five-year-old looked like a running back carrying his briefcase tight under his arm. His shirt was soaking wet by the time he entered the cabin and was shown his seat in first class.

Mark was a frequent flyer, and he got to know several pilots from the military and met several others along the way. "Hey, Mr. Lavenger," a copilot cheerfully said, remembering Mark. "Hey, I see you're a little, well, drenched," he said kindly. "I'll tell you what? We have a few extra Delta shirts, and I have a new pack of Ts."

Mark was embarrassed slightly, but also grateful. After catching his breath, he thanked Copilot Flynn. Mark stepped out of the lavatory looking sharp as he fiddled with his cuffs. He looked out through the open door to the coach and thought he recognized someone. Whenever it happened, he would wonder if it was one of the CUF kids who looked like their fathers.

"Excuse me, sir, we are getting ready for takeoff." Mark looked back as the stewardess closed the door. "Please," she said, pointing at his seat. The others in first class were now all looking.

"Anyone want a beer?" Mark said with a friendly tone.

"Sure, why not?" One, two, three of the passengers ordered their favorite. "Budweiser, please."

The flight to the Army field was a stopover from Dallas. Mark was one of a few who didn't board another flight; he had business on the base, and it would be a game changer.

It was during the midsixties when Mark had found a hull used for fast transport to and from the oil rigs popping up all over the gulf. The aluminum hull twin Detroit diesel boats had a 320-mile range at 25 knots, over a thousand miles at ten. Pushing 960 horsepower, these water taxis easily converted into troop transport, evacuation, patrol, and assault craft.

Mark struck gold with the hull design by Sewart Seacraft. The Navy bought the plans, and in forty days, they delivered the first four to the Mekong Delta. There were fifty upgrades and alterations from the original design, Mark's I, II, and III, each specializing it its own warcraft.

Mark had with him plans for the new LCM, or landing craft mechanized, for troop deployment in the Delta. With four thousand miles of river and the majority of the country population living on these rivers, the riverine forces of the Seventh Fleet were essential for the protection of the troops and goods being shipped to Saigon.

Mark had special clearance on the base and went immediately to a meeting room where a meeting was already underway. He liked the flexibility, pace, and diversity of his job. He forgot his promise to call his wife when he landed and was twenty minutes into the meeting when he realized it. Fortunately, they took a break and Mark found an office where he could talk.

Lisa's mother had been hospitalized with some form of phenomena, and she had initially been failing. Mark apologized immediately for his lack of concern and forgetfulness and was relieved when he heard she was on the mend. Lisa knew her husband and was sweet as ever.

"Lisa, I am literally in the meeting about the LCM, so I will call you when we're through. Love you."

"Love you too," she replied, and they hung up the phone.

Most everyone was talking about the National Guard shooting the students at Kent State. Mark knew they were distracted, but he knew he had to push for this transport vehicle.

Mark stood before the Navy Military Assistance and Advisory Group. After setting up his overhead slides, he cleared his throat. He needed to grab their attention, so he basically shouted, "If you want this war to end, gentlemen, then here is a means to that end!" Everyone stopped chattering and turned their attention to the new design.

"As you all are aware, the riverine warfare, or brown-water navy, has evolved from patrol and minesweeping to attack, search and rescue, and seal and troop deployment. This craft, gentlemen, holds three M60 tanks and 450 troops. Mechanically, it is the same as the Swift and PBR, so no retooling the motor pool. It simply delivers combat personnel faster, safer, and more efficiently than our counterparts."

Mark was flashing through the slides he had prepared. He knew the men in the room realized the swamp and jungle combination made large troop movement impossible, and the air cavalry could only provide light armament. He had detailed files on the specifications as he dispersed the designs to the panel. He continued clicking the projector.

"With the eleven-man crew and two-hundred-ton capability, these crafts, gentlemen, can get *our* boys on and off the battlefield." Mark did not need the hard sell; he knew the deal was dependent upon the availability, production, and costs. He had the numbers ready, and they were staggering.

One Small Step for Man

On July 20, 1969, millions of people found themselves glued to their TV sets as the Apollo 11 mission reached its climax. The hatch of the Lunar Module opened, and Neil Armstrong descended the stairs.

On blue Earth below, there was another small step for man. E3 Gunner Stephen Munro just hit the flotilla in the Mekong Delta. The smell of diesel reminded him of the base back at Mare Island. The docks were the same, but the water at Mare had been clean, and in Vietnam, it looked more like a river after a big rain in Ohio.

Just like Armstrong above, Stephen couldn't have been farther from home. River Float One was now his home, and his front yards and backyards were lined with Swifts and PBRs.

Swift Boat objectives in the Delta were used to eliminate North Vietnamese infiltration of both men and supplies by river and sea. They were a vital part of the supply line, but in addition, the Swift Boats delivered medicine and doctors to remote villages along the thousands of miles of moving mud.

In 1966 three separate task forces were formed. TF-115 was called Operation Market Time, TF-116 called Operation Game Warden, and TF-117 was called the Mobile Riverine Force. Operation Market Time was in charge of the coastal patrol, while Operation Game Warden took on the enemy on the backwaters of the Mekong. The Mobile Riverine Force was made up of Army and Navy forces.

Stephen stood at attention, awaiting his orders. His fellow enlisted men stood shoulder to shoulder in the moderately size office. He was hoping to be a part of the riverine force but was simply happy to be out "on the playing field."

Commander Nyhan paced before the five new faces, and his speech was brief. "Boys, you're now in the shit. Know how I know? Because I'm in it with you." He pounded his fist.

Commander Nyhan was a brute of a man, wide as he was tall. "I read your bios, and I'm impressed! Several of you volunteered to learn Vietnamese, and although that alone doesn't make you officer material, it's a start." Nyhan walked behind his desk and picked up his smoldering cigar, plopping back down in his chair. "Lieutenant Simmons here will call out your name and task force assignment."

Simmons began, "Listen up! When I call your name, grab your gear and head out to your assigned task force." The lieutenant stepped along the line, eyeballing the new meat. "Oliver, TF-116! Murray, TF-116! Ambrose, TF-115! Waski, TF-115! Lester, 116! Munro, TF-117!"

Munro clenched his fist and tightened his jaw.

"Something wrong, Munro?" Nyhan barked.

Munro turned to face his commander. "No, sir," he said sharply.

"Do you know what Mekong means, Munro?" he asked, suddenly softening his tone.

"Yes, sir, the Mother River, sir!"

"Mmm." Nyhan pushed himself up and walked around his desk. "Munro, let me show you around your new home."

Lieutenant Simmons didn't know what to think. He hadn't ever seen his commander behave like that to fresh soldiers.

All the enlisted personnel had been extensively cross-trained in every area of Swift Boat operation. During firefights, any man had the ability to take over for the injured.

Munro had three patches emblazoned on his uniform, but the one he wanted the most was the one his commander wore: Tonkin Gulf Yacht Club. It was a black-outlined junk with bright yellow and orange backing. "My family has a marina back home, sir. I think my dad would like your patch."

Nyhan smiled and led Munro along. "You're going to be part of an elite unit, Munro. Keep your nose clean and you will be running one of these soon." They had just walked past two PBRs, part of the Fifty-Fifth.

Nyhan stepped onto the Swift. "Commander on deck!" yelled the quartermaster. Ensign Malloy emerged from behind the deckhouse with a rag in his hand. He was helping Hurley with new injectors.

"How's that upgrade coming, Ensign?" Nyhan asked.

Ensign Malloy saluted his commander with a greasy palm. "Going well, sir. Ready for a test run at 06:00, sir."

"Very good, Ensign. Oh, this is your new gunner. I will leave you men to your business." Commander Nyhan waddled away with a blue smoke trail.

"Well, get the fuck on the boat, E3!" Malloy yelled.

"Yes, sir!" Stephen said.

"Stow your stuff port side bunk and start breaking down the forward .50. I'll introduce you to the crew at 05:00," Malloy commanded.

"Yes, sir," Stephen said again.

"Call me Skip, Gunner," Ensign Malloy said, his tone cooling.

"Yes, sir, Skip!"

At 05:00, the crew stood across the stern of the PCF, or Patrol Craft Fast, 112. Malloy addressed his men. "Okay, fellas, we're taking the big boss out for a run. Hurley got our two girls below ready for the prom."

The boys chuckled, and a few mashed fists with Hurley.

Malloy continued through the laughter. "If this goes well, boys, it means less bullshit and more bullets."

Munro looked around at his new crew.

"Okay, this is Munro. He's got the stern .50 and mortar," Malloy said, introducing Stephen.

Hurley turned to look back, but the other guys didn't bother. Munro was the fourth gunner they had had this year. Two had been killed in action, and two others severely wounded.

"Okay, shitsticks, get your stations in order! Munro, help Gerry with the lines!" Ensign Malloy barked.

Nyhan led his two advisers down the ramp and over to the PCF. It was 06:00 sharp.

"Ready when you are, sir," Malloy said. His commander looked at his guests and nodded.

Ensign Malloy throttled up the 112 and headed up the Song Hau Gain River. He put the PCF through a few routine maneuvers.

"When you pass those san pans, open her up!" Nyhan instructed, gripping the railing with one hand and holding his cap with the other. He smiled when the skip hit 31 knots.

Just as Malloy started to turn back, an MSB made contact and all hell broke lopse. The normal tactic was to speed away and gather two or three other Swifts before blazing up the shoreline, but they had civilians on board.

Munro had already loaded the mortar and had the lanyard in his hand. The MSB began taking direct hits from a recoilless rifle from the one-hundred-foot bank of its stern.

Commander Nyhan reached over Malloy to slow down the 112. "You got a fix on that shoreline, son?"

"Yes, sir!" Malloy said, adjusting his sights as the boat steadied. "Fire!" he yelled.

The first mortar hit past the hill, and the radioman of the MSB was now directing fire while Munro pounded the ridge. He stayed half-crouched and jumped the first few times the 81-millimeter fired. The first hit took out the electrical system and killed both engines. Small-arms fire poured down, and three of the crew were killed immediately.

Nyhan ordered his guests to remain below as they were going to move in to tow the mine sweep out until a tug could get to their location. "Malloy, you call up the wolves now, son!"

"I already did, sir. They said two miles!"

Nyhan was proud of his command and loved his H1UB gunships. The pilots had night vision, could and did fly in every weather condition, but most of all, he liked that they were all volunteers.

When Nyhan said he was in the shit, I guess he meant it, thought Munro.

The coordinating Sea Wolves swooped in. "Hey, you two are gonna want to see this!" Nyhan yelled down the stairwell. His two guests emerged in time to see a Huey unleash hell.

With a Minigun mounted on the rail, three floor-mounted M60 machine guns, fourteen rickets, and a .50-cal door gunner, these Hueys were the deadliest the Navy had.

"Who's flyin', Skip?" one of the men on board asked.

"Salt and Pepper!" Malloy stated.

"Yeah, baby!" the soldier cried, his fist pumping in the air.

The Huey opened up with rockets, followed by continuous bursts from the M60s and pilot-controlled Minigun. As they moved down the ridgeline, assessing their damage, one of the men, Jonesy, spotted TJ, one of the Wolves, who had his .50-cal already firing. In the Sea Wolf pack, any weapon you wanted to carry was permissible.

TJ wore a black Remington 1100 slung over his shoulder. After a few passes and in for the sweep, another Sea Wolf, Badger, walked the shoreline blowing smoke and debris. Then, three distinct blasts were heard as TJ pumped down three more rounds, considered to be his signature.

Salt and Pepper, a four-man effort, had the only two black gunners in the Navy, TJ Jones and Michael Poor. Neither one knew the other before they hit the flotilla. Poor was from the northeast, and Jones, Nevada. Navy crews were tight families, and the two had become fast friends.

The other half of Salt and Pepper, Lieutenant Jay Peters and First Lieutenant Paul Cardigan, were both twenty-five years old and experienced pilots. They had quite a reputation for heroics, but for also keeping their cool under fire. The combination rewarded them the best gigs.

Jonesy was on the radio with Badger as they sought out cover. Munro was still on the .50. As he pulled up to the minesweeper, the phosphorus smoke on the stern was a sight to behold, like a misty morning in the smoky mountains, only here it rained AK-47s.

Munro pressed his finger firmly against the break to keep from accidentally firing. It was a tense moment, but as the lines were secured and the MSB safely from shore, the crew and guests celebrated with cigars.

Look-Alike

The constant chirp, peep, squawk, and yawl of the millions of creatures in Vietnam had become white noise. Even the early-morning
minesweepers became just a buzz.

The 112 was on another delivery mission, this time to Tan
Chau. The three-day trip took them to the edge of Cambodia. Most
of the teams were not on board for the whole trip. They would get a
help lift or a pickup, drop-off close to a target. These boys were going
in secretly, and 112 was none the wiser.

Having a SEAL team on board the 112 had the crew boasting,
trying to impress their comrades. Munro was new to the game but
caught on quick. As he was cleaning the tube on the 81-millimeter,
he heard one of the SEALs call out, "Hey, Virgil!"

Munro heard a few chuckles and looked over at the members of
the team he could see. "Remind you of your old lady?" Munro said
as he gave the tube a hard plunge.

"Ohhh!" one SEAL sprang up. "We got us a wiseass here!"
Kevin Donovan was the youngest member of the team and had a big
chip on his shoulder.

The last thing Munro wanted to do was tangle with a fellow
crewmate, but he also wasn't willing to back down.

The deck of the 112 was wooden and roughly ten square feet.
Munro stepped forward as Donovan made his move. Stephen piv-
oted back around his gun and climbed onto his aggressor's back,
twisting his right shoulder. While struggling, the two fell onto the
deck, which aroused the rest of the crew.

Skip looked over his shoulder just as Munro slammed the larger
man onto the deck. Stunned by the hard contact, Donovan managed

to get the gunner on his back and was now twisting his left arm out of the socket.

"What the fuck?" Malloy yelled as the SEAL team closed in around the wrestlers.

"Stand down!" yelled the team leader. Keller Mac had been in charge of the team since 1967, and although he had no great love for Donovan, he knew he had to keep his team together as a pack so they responded as one.

Skip slowed the boat down to just a few knots and stood above the downed men. With his chest out, he started barking, reminding the men they were aboard *his* boat. The SEAL team stood and listened, all crossing their arms.

Donovan still had Stephen locked up when Skip tugged hard on his ear. "What, this not working?" he screamed sarcastically, stretching the lobe.

Resco, one of the observing SEALs, noticed Munro smile. "Something funny, Virgil?"

"Virgil?" Skip demanded. He turned and started laughing, which became contagious among the men.

They were all fans of *McHale's Navy* growing up, and Munro did resemble the gunner Virgil.

"Hey, Skip, who does he remind you of? Creepy, right?" Tommy McGraw said. The rest of the team agreed.

"Damn, I thought it was Danny when I first stepped on board," Resco said.

"Yeah, me too," another commented.

"You have any family in Michigan, Virgil?" McGraw asked.

Munro looked at each of them, still breathing heavily and full of adrenaline, and he couldn't even feel the SEALs holding him. "Nope. My family is from Ohio."

Donovan went to say something, but Resco shut him up. When they peeled him up off the deck, he had a darkening shiner above his left eye.

"If it was his right, you would be taking his place," Resco said as he dragged his teammate past Munro.

"Sorry, man," said McGraw, extending his hand to Munro. "Damn, if you don't look just like our Danny...man, it's freaky."

The three SEALs now stood around Munro. He was about to tighten his fists when McGraw asked, "Hey, is the captain cool?"

Puzzled Munro looked blankly at them. McGraw opened his field pouch and exposed his pipe.

"Oh, yeah. Yeah, I guess so. I mean, he can't smell it when we power up, but yeah. Some of the guys smoke," Munro replied, understanding.

Skip didn't mind when his sailors smoked weed or hash, but drew a hard line with artificials. "Seen a motherfucker claw his own eyeballs out when he dropped acid," he would tell everyone.

The SEALs were "all-natural, baby," as McGraw would tell it. "Look, Virge," he said, taking a long, slow pull from the pipe and exhaling in Munro's direction, "we go natural here, man, okay? We don't eat your food or smoke cigarettes, okay? We gotta smell no different than they do, roger?"

Munro listened to every word. They began describing the different sounds of the surrounding jungle, and he immediately thought of his friend Charlie T and how he had read that American Indians used sweat tents to eliminate the odors of a predator. "I do get what you're saying," he said. "I do a lot of bow-hunting back home, white-tail mostly."

That caught the attention of Keller Mac, who had just gotten through scolding Donovan. "So Virgil can fight *and* hunt."

The trip upriver was uneventful for the 112 after the fight. Stephen was learning all he could about the differences of the monkey calls to the green pigeon and parakeet.

"You've got to know the warning sounds, Virgil," Mac said. He had taken a liking to him right away, and with him as team leader, the others followed.

Donovan kept his distance as best as he could, and the crew, for the most part, enjoyed one another's company and the cooking.

225

"Hey, Resco, you better learn a thing or two from Willis over there. This is the best food we had on this boat in a year!" McGraw joked over their freshly caught fish dinner.

"If I had some fresh-black bass, well…" Willis was a modest chef. "When we pull in to Tan Chau this evening, have Munro—I mean Virgil—catch us up some."

"No shit," Resco said.

"Yeah, no shit. I swear the kid talks 'em on the line!" McGraw said, cleaning off his plate.

Munro had left for basic training with his two-piece rod and Garcia Mitchell spinning reel. Off hours on Merritt Island, he was fond of jigging for halibut and salmon. His pole and gear made it all the way to South Vietnam, and he was more than eager to show and share with his new friends some great mangrove carp and Punjabi fishing.

Like a private charter, he guided his captain to where a small stream flowed out into the Tan Chau, working his jig with the current so he only had to jig twice before he had a fish on. The men laughed and cheered as Munro shared rod and technique with the SEALs.

Heavy fighting broke out on the river before they reached the city, and Malloy informed the crew he was taking the Long Hoa. Everyone manned their stations.

"Anything you want us to do, Skip?" Keller Mac asked.

"Well, if you don't mind, I could use more eyes port and starboard. Gets pretty tight up in here." Malloy looked around at his crew. "We're going wide-open the next seven miles. You waste any sampan that gets near my bow."

Munro cocked his twin .50s and turned his turret ninety to ninety. Mac and Willis stood with Malloy.

"Tough kid you got there, Skip," Mac said while looking through his port window.

"Yeah, I guess I wouldn't have known. I mean, he is a damn good shot and has the balance of a cat, but shit! I thought your guy was gonna eat him up!" Malloy replied.

"Not the size of the dog in the fight, Skip!" Willis always kept it brief.

"Eyes on that sampan!" Skip was yelling over the screaming diesels.

"I think your wake's gonna drown him," Mac said jokingly.

"That fuckin' Zipperhead is up to no good!" Skip said as he powered by, flipping him off. "Today's your lucky day, fucker!" he said as his wake tossed the sampan over to the bank.

As soon as the wake broke the shoreline, AK-47s opened up from a fixed position. Munro saw the muzzle flash before the first round hit the stern. He turned and opened up on the sampan that was fumbling for a weapon.

When the first .50 let loose, two SEALs unshouldered their XM177 assault rifles, but by the time they were trained on the sampan, Munro had cut it in two, along with the NVC, who popped like a hot pumpkin. They both began returning fire, but at 30 knots, it wasn't a long firefight. Munro looked back at the helm and smiled, then turned back to the stern, training his .50 toward the port side shore.

"Like I said, Skip, tough kid," Keller Mac said as he smirked.

Skip entered the Mekong River at over 30 knots. He wasn't supposed to draw any unnecessary attention, and he immediately realized this as he saw a Navy LMC loaded with supplies navigating the current. He slowed to 12 knots and eased up her port side. They rolled along that way for another mile, making brief radio contact.

Although still in South Vietnam, they were riding up a bulge into the Cambodian border. Mac collected his team as the Swift turned her nose into the soft bank. "Skip, thanks for the ride!" The SEALs all jumped off and disappeared into the jungle.

"We will stage at FOB in Tan Chau," Skip told his crew. "Smoke 'em if you got 'em!"

One of the men still aboard, Monreal, took over the helm and swung the 112 with the current, slowly throttling up. The diesel smoke swung around the stern and lingered as they pulled away. The diesel smell triggered one of Munro's memories, and he solemnly thought, *I wonder what Dad's doing back home.*

Late-Summer Sadness

Frank turned the radio on as he pulled out of Ray's Service Station. "Proud Mary" was midway through as he began changing channels. His '63 Chevy pickup had a song of her own, and Frank would rather listen to her sing through the gears than some yahoo on the radio. His Lab, Molly, always joined Frank for a ride, and the two of them drove iconically through the rolling hills near home.

Frank turned the corner to see a fire truck and rescue truck leaving Charlie T's place and immediately pulled in. "Stay, Molly," he said firmly when he opened the door. Charlie always had two or three beagles running around, and he knew it would only lead to trouble letting a roamer like her out.

"What's going on?" Frank saw the coroner's car and expected the worst.

"Friend of yours?" asked a paramedic.

"Yes, mine and my son's. Is he…is he dead?"

"Yes, sir. Sorry to tell you. Must have passed away sometime yesterday, it appears. Died in his sleep with the TV on."

Frank stood bowing his head. "I've got to tell Stevie," he thought aloud.

"Excuse me, sir, but we have a few questions about his family or nearest relative," the coroner said, approaching Frank.

Frank was very cooperative, and together they were able to track down his sister in Providence, Rhode Island.

"What about the dogs?" Frank asked.

"Don't know, not my department," the coroner said.

"Well, help me load the dog box into my pickup and I will see to them, or is that not your department either?" Frank said sarcastically.

The coroner didn't say anything. He helped lift the dog box into Frank's pickup and drove away.

Can't imagine Charlie wanting that prick to be the last one to touch them, Frank thought. He collected the three beagles, then searched for their leads, bowls, and collars. They were all happy to see Frank loading their box, because they were accustomed to going to run rabbits after driving. The three began baying with excitement. Frank understood and played along. "Want to get the bunnies? The bunnies?" he asked as they bayed and wagged their tails, jumping into the box.

Frank wondered what Emily would think was worse, that old Charlie T died in his sleep or him bringing home his three dogs. Frank didn't have to wait long. Heading out of the house was his wife and daughter while he pulled the Chevy into the driveway. Frank's truck stopped with a squeak in front of the barn door. Lizzy ran over to see her dad and passed right by the box of dogs. Emily, however, walked over and noticed them immediately.

"Going hunting, Frank?" she inquired quite seriously.

Looking at Lizzy, he pulled her in for a hug and made a gesture that Charlie had died. His intelligent wife understood.

"Well, you know we have to tell Stevie," she said.

Frank held his little girl a bit longer. "Yep, as soon as Lizzy and I figure out where we can keep the three little pigs back there."

"Pigs, you bought pigs?" Lizzy climbed up into the truck. "Oh, Daddy, you're always teasing me! These are Charlie's dogs! That's Waggs, Biscuit, and Brandy." Lizzy never forgot a dog, any dog. She met these three over two years ago when Charlie dropped off Stevie after their rabbit hunt. She didn't seem to mind them hunting rabbits but scolded her dog, Molly, for always chasing them. "If we put the box in the goat pen, we could use that for them," Lizzy said, offering up her 4H project.

Frank and Emily knew she didn't care much for feeding livestock twice a day but knew it would teach her responsibility. "What about the goat we were going to get?" Emily asked.

"Rather take care of Charlie T's dogs," the little girl said. "Where did he go, on vacation?"

Frank looked at Emily before saying, "Lizzy, your brother's friend passed away, and there was no one to look after these dogs, so—"

"So we will," she said, finishing her father's sentence.

Emily stood with her arms crossed, warming herself.

"Girls, think you can help this used-up old man get this box off my truck?"

The three of them moved the dog box into the goat pen. "I'll get some more straw, Dad," Lizzy said as she ran off into the barn.

"Frank," Emily said sorrowfully, "that poor man died all alone."

Biscuit hopped out of the box after Molly ran off with Lizzy. She ran over to Emily and began circling around Emily's legs, wanting affection. Brandy and Waggs hid in the box. "It's okay, girl." Biscuit wept under Emily's hand. She was nervous and confused. There were no rabbits, no guns, and no Charlie T.

Frank, Emily, and Lizzy settled the dogs and headed down to their docks. Frank had cleared a half-acre behind the knob on the riverbank for parking, and it even had its own entrance off Route 60. He kept his customers as far from his house and barn as possible.

The Munros had been busy servicing their customers. Transient slips provided a new form of revenue as more and more pleasure craft appeared on the river, and Emily didn't have to convince Frank they needed to add a gas pump on the fuel dock.

Frank liked working on the river and particularly liked the challenges their marina presented. Anything having to do with growing the business, he was in love with.

Dinner was at six, and both Lizzy and Frank were hip to hip at the sink, washing up.

Emily couldn't wait to jab at her man. "Frank, who would you like me to use to install the new one-thousand-gallon tank?"

"What?" Frank sounded puzzled.

"Well, I can't expect you to do everything, darling. You informed me earlier you were...mmm...what did you call it?"

"All used up," Lizzy chimed in, wiping her hands and sliding in her spot at the table. "Like that rusty old tractor we drive by every day in Thompson's field, right, Daddy? When I asked you why they left the tractor out in the field all the time, you said it was all used up!"

Emily slid a dish in front of her husband. Placing her hands on his muscular shoulders, she lowered her head and, in a whisper, said, "I will let you know when you're all used up, my dear."

Frank eyeballed his wife as she walked away. Her apron strings were tied just above her bottom. "Looks good, Em," he said as he joined his daughter at the table.

"Lizzy, what are you planning on doing with those dogs?"

"What do you mean, Mom?"

"Well, they are hunting dogs. They need to exercise."

"Tell you what? You can take them out to Shad's farm this weekend," Frank said between bites. "I need to help Mr. Shad with the conveyor on his silo."

"Perfect," Emily said, and she joined them for dinner.

"Dinner's great, Mom," Lizzy said.

Emily managed to keep a diverse menu at home. In her years traveling for CUF, she enjoyed the regional cuisine. Frank always appreciated the effort, and a clean plate was his evidence.

Before they finished, the fuel dock bell rang. Frank got up immediately. "Don't eat all the dessert without me," he said to Lizzy, grabbing her side and tickling her.

Emily placed Frank's plate in the oven and left the door open. Looking out the pantry window, she paused to admire her man.

"Mom, what's for dessert?" Elizabeth asked.

"Oh, there are some cookies for you," she said loudly, "and pie for your father," under her breath.

The next morning brought more bad news with the *Marietta Times*. The paperboy was thrown from his dad's pickup while trying to avoid a collision with an Amish wagon, breaking his collarbone and fracturing three ribs. His father had to do both driving and delivering for him and wasn't too pleased.

He did enjoy his trip to the Strongs' marina, and of course, Emily. Jack Bailey drove the 56 home route in the rural area near town. Jack worked the third shift, so he picked up the papers and his boy and drove him for two hours while he jumped in and out of the truck bed like a springer spaniel. He would try to show off his skills coming down the Munros' driveway, pretending to surf the gravel, jumping. Friday morning, there was no young surfer.

"Hey, Jack, where's Jackie Jr.?" asked Frank as Jack Sr. handed him the paper.

"Aww, I launched him out the back when one of those pumpkin rollers was stopped on a curve. Should have knocked that buggy down the holla!"

"Jackie hurt bad?"

"Not too bad."

Just then, Lizzy ran up with her Molly and caused the hounds to start baying.

"Where's Jackie?"

"Hold on, Lizzy. Mr. Bailey was just telling me."

"Should have seen the little bastard—oops!" the man said, catching his language. "Aww, well, when I hit the brakes, I didn't realize Jackie was surfing again. He flew through the air like Superman, past my truck. He cleared the pavement and tumbled into a washout, broke his collarbone and three ribs."

"Ouch!" Frank said.

"I been telling him for years to hold on back there. I swear the kid thinks he in California."

"He's gonna be okay, right?" Elizabeth was a year younger than Jackie and liked watching him show off.

"See you got Charlie's dogs," Jack Bailey noticed.

"Yep. Lizzy is caring for them. We're going to run them today out at Shad's."

"Too bad about Charlie. Saw something in the paper about it. Looks like Monday. Gotta go!"

"Jack!" Frank yelled as he began driving out. "I can lend you my best worker for a few mornings if that will help."

Lizzy grabbed at her father's hand. "Really, Dad?"

Jack backed his C10 step-side up to the Munros'.

"As long as she rides up front with you," Frank said.

"Deal," Jack said eagerly, and they shook on it.

"You want to go now, Lizzy? I'm sure Mr. Bailey is about half-through, right, Jack?"

"Yep! Sure could use the help, and company."

"Can Molly come?" Lizzy asked.

"If she can ride in the back," Jack replied.

Frank led Molly around and opened the tailgate. Molly jumped in, wagging her tail. The loyal dog loved truck rides no matter where she sat.

"You can drop her at Shad's on your way home. I should be there by then," Frank said. He was proud of his little girl because she was so much like her mother, adventurous, tough, and kind.

Frank told Emily about Jackie Jr. and how Lizzy would be helping him out a few days a week.

"That was nice of you, Frank. Now you're not going to leave me here on this beautiful morning all alone, are you?" she said, using her seductive tone.

"Thank God I'm not all used up," Frank said as she led him back inside.

Emily walked to the fuel dock with her notepad in hand. The marina was quiet, but they had seven slips full and two transients for the month of August. The afternoon temperature was in the mid-nineties and humid. No one was out washing or waxing their boats, so Emily checked the tanks, calculated the gallons, and updated her books.

Sitting beneath an old sycamore, she began to write her son. She started with a few light stories, like young Jackie flying through the air, and about his friend Charlie. She promised she would attend his funeral in Stephen's honor.

Emily drafted the letter with precision and imagined how many mothers and fathers did the same, and wondered further just how many Franks and Stevies there were out there from her work with CUF. Emily didn't like contemplating that part of the program. She cut out the obituary for her son's friend, attached it with a paperclip, and sealed the letter.

The Panel

Senator Cole stood before the Congressional Arms Service with a stack of folders and an eight-millimeter projector under his arm. Most members of the service personally knew the senator, or at least knew of his reputation. The senator wasted no time.

"Before I begin, gentlemen, for the record"—he glanced at the stenographer—"to voice my negative approval about the venture our CIA will propose…" Cole looked the panel up and down before walking behind his film table. He wanted to take out any threat on his gunship proposal.

Opening a large manila envelope marked "Top Secret," Cole played up the theatrics. Pulling out one of the folders, he began to read, "If Operation Midnight Climax taught us anything at all, it was that LSD doesn't belong in bedroom, let alone on the battlefield!" Cole grabbed their attention as he spoke with disgust. "With all due respect to our CIA, I have to, as my duty, question what we call intelligence these days!" He knew they were gaining interest, or at least waiting for the punchline.

"Doping Johns and watching drug-induced sexual behavior is going to bring us what? Were these Johns really horny KGB agents?" The panel laughed a little, and Cole roostered up a bit. "What intelligence so vital to our country's security was revealed in those two-way mirrors?" His preparation and delivery were admirable, as he refrained from using too much of a sarcastic tone. "How much did we pay your agents to watch an LSD freak show while pounding down martinis? Wouldn't it been cheaper to interrogate the Beatles?"

A few more chuckles were heard from his audience. Cole feared nothing. He held up a folder marked "Operation Midnight Climax" and walked around his podium. "Here is what the CIA thinks we need in Vietnam!" He placed the folder before a familiar face, an army intelligence officer. Walking backward, he kept eye contact with what was now a captive room.

The two CIA officers who were up next looked tense. Their training didn't prepare them for this form of attack, and their squirming indicated their anxiety. Cole gave his opponents a quick look before he opened his movie case.

Cole knew these were low-level agents, and his net worth to America was greater than their perverted ideas. He felt no hypocrisy for creating his own form of supersoldier, and his conviction was now being supported by battlefield evidence. He was proud of his soldiers, and his assurance fueled his confidence.

Cole began loading the eight-millimeter reel. "What we need in Vietnam, gentlemen, is to stop the supply line coming in from Cambodia, not doping up our boys to create a whacked-out supersoldier!" As he threaded the reel, he continued, "No evidence exists that we will be more effective in combat stoned out on acid! We're not trying to reincarnate a band of berserkers or warrior-shamans, are we?"

Cole proceeded to introduce the Lockheed AC130 Spectra Gunship. "You want to change the game, gentlemen? Put a game changer on the field or, in this case, in the air." He paused, then asked, "Please dim the lights."

Cole spoke while the panel watched an outstanding display of versatility and power on the screen. "We now have the capability to deliver more firepower, and we no longer lack in defense, what with the new Pave Pronto modifications. The magnetic signals detect and destroy ingestion systems like those used on the Ho Chi Minh Trail." The upgrades sold themselves. "These planes will be around for a long time, gentlemen. The 130 platform is as diverse as your imagination." Cole, as usual, was loaded for bear. He had a folder full of recommendations from several branches and from test facilities.

The senator was masterful with his delivery; he highlighted problems, found solutions, and reinforced the practical application. Together with Lavenger, the two men were responsible for arming half of the Army and Navy alone. In addition to his gunship upgrades were upgrades for a small naval branch he helped push through. One in particular wound up reuniting friends and even changed one young man's life forever.

Dirty-Water Lockup

Malloy sent Monreal and Munro off the boat and into the marketplace.

"Skip got a taste for that gook food now?" Stephen Munro asked.

"Yeah, that and something else," Monreal replied.

"Yeah, I smell what you guys have been cookin'," Munro said as he ducked under and dodged the lot market awnings.

"Well, anytime you want to join us or..." Monreal stopped speaking, suddenly smelling what he was looking for. "Keeping your nose clean to Commander Nyhan means keeping the needle out of your veins," Monreal said as he began to laugh. "Hey, listen up, Virgil. Skip and the rest of the crew...none of them drink. We all like the Thai stick, and me personally, I like the finger hash, and I smell some over there."

The two were about to go into a shabby-looking building when they heard someone shout, "Hey bạn đang làm gì đốpassed!" Monreal turned to see a South Vietnamese lieutenant standing in the middle of the muddy road with his finger pointing at him. "Dang làm gì đó?" he barked, which translated to "What are you doing?" in English. Monreal and Munro looked over their shoulders at him. Neither bothered saluting; no one in the Ninth Army had ever saluted a soldier from the South Vietnamese Army.

The SVA lieutenant knew it was a hash house, and although it was not permitted, marijuana and hash were hard to regulate among the troops. Marijuana grew everywhere, and hash houses were common.

When Dave Monreal didn't answer the lieutenant, he became belligerent. As he walked aggressively toward Dave, he screamed in a high-pitched voice, "Tên của bạn là gì?" What's your name?

Monreal had had enough. He was a first-generation Filipino American, and everyone assumed he was SVA from a distance, but Dave was thick and muscular. "I'm not a South Vietnamese soldier, and I don't speak Vietnamese," he said angrily in the man's face. His brashness caught the attention of four other South Vietnamese Army soldiers and two of the crew of the PBR.

When the lieutenant pointed his finger hard into Monreal's chest, Dave twisted his wrist with his right hand, dropping him down while smashing his left elbow into his face. When his men jumped in, so did the brown-water boys.

One of the seamen from the PBR was a tall blond kid they called Pitta. Seaman Ken Pittman missed Ranger's school by two inches, and that was how he ended up a crew member. Quickly and forcefully, Pitta struck one of the SVAs with roundhouse kick to his neck, and the only thing that saved it from breaking was the enormous M14 slung around his shoulder. Stephen immediately swept the closest soldier to him, and both he and Pitta collided going for the third.

The petty officer of the PBR was a Midwesterner from Michigan, Captain Hines Myer. His crew called him Oscar. He yelled, "Hey, no! Stop! Pitta, I swear, you bastard." Pitta had the lieutenant in a choke hold facedown, and by the time they pulled him off, his face was green.

When the South Vietnamese Army's version of the Military Police pulled up, the battling men all stood up and stood together. "Okay, boys, let's not let this get out of hand," Munro said, "but if one of those guys hits any one of us with those clubs, all bets are off!"

Things were tense, and the Navy boys didn't want to end things quietly. After the rumble, Pitta saw a local boy he did business with named Van. "Hey, what's your boat number? That kid will help."

"Ah, 112," Monreal and Munro said in unison.

"Van, get to the 112 and tell them what happened, okay? Van! Go to the 112! Okay!? Hiểu, okay?"

Van waved and ran toward the river.

The MPs took the four SVA men and put them in a tent with two armed guards standing under the flap. The lieutenant whom Monreal choked wasn't able to speak, and that was a good thing.

Van made it to the dock and talked his way onto the 112. "Hey, you, Navy," he said in almost-perfect English. "Your men, MP locked them up, okay? Hiểu? SVA locked them up."

Malloy and another man on board, Gerry, grabbed a weapon each and headed to the post. Things instantly went from bad to worse when they were denied access to the base and to their men. When Malloy began shouting and demanding that his men be released, the camp commander, a one-star border defense general, came to the gate. He was not amused with the lack of respect and discipline.

"I see where your men learned respect," the general said angrily.

"Respect! How about protocol, General?" Malloy cried.

"Skip, be cool," Gerry said under his breath. He was thinking more about self-preservation and the fact that they were outnumbered.

"My CO will be on the wire, General. You'll want to think about changing your tone when you're speaking with him!" Skip grabbed Gerry and walked away, looking back several times, wanting to continue but restraining himself. "Smell that shit when we passed that gray-and-white building?"

"Yeah," Gerry replied.

"Take care of business, and I'll meet you at the boat. I need to call the commander." And Skip Malloy was off.

Nyhan was out testing upgrades on the PBR jet drive. He wouldn't be back for hours, and Lieutenant Gallagher was in charge. Malloy gave Gallagher what little information he had about his men and the pending assault charges.

When Malloy's radioman, Gerry, returned with the goods, the two shut the radio down and lit the pipe up.

"Skip, how long can they hold them?" Gerry asked.

"Fuck if I know! Commander will get the message. He'll get 'em out, trust me."

Malloy and Gerry spent the rest of the day bartering with the locals and cleaning their weapons. They had two or three days before they were needed for the extraction.

Commander Nyhan had been spending his time testing the new jet drive pumps. With him was Admiral Jon McConnell, Frank's old pal. The new pumps delivered more power to the jet drives of the PBRs, and with the hundreds of miles of rivers in Vietnam, some too shallow for the Swiftys, it was a vital upgrade for the SEAL teams.

When they were finished, Nyhan was impressed. The Mekong Delta was famous for its shifting shoals, and on their way back to the flotilla, an LCU was hung up, trying to head up a tributary.

"Take me over there," McConnell said, pointing to the LCU.

"These guys get hung up all the time on the sandbars. We'll get a tug over to him," Nyhan stated.

"No, no," McConnell said. "Get me that captain on the radio."

The radioman dialed in, and Jon introduced himself. The young captain sounded nervous.

"Son, listen, power up and slam on reverse!" Looking over at Nyhan, Jon held up his hand as if to say "Hold on." Jon continued, "Walk that rudder back and forth!"

The LCU began to free itself. "Nice job, Captain!" Jon turned to Nyhan. "Those aren't any different from the Higgins I ran in the Pacific. Let me show you how to get those LCUs over these shoals."

Jon positioned the now-free LCU outside the shoal. "Okay, Captain, listen up! I want you to power up and head straight for the shoal. When I tell you, you're going to kill the power and ride your wake right over, roger?"

"Roger," the young captain said. He powered up the LCU to 12 knots.

Jon was ready on the mic. The LCU was pushing tons of water with its flat bottom and front. "Kill, kill!" McDonnell shouted into the mic as soon as the LCU was thirty or forty yards out. By the time the throttle dropped, the bow was a few feet away. The whole craft was lifted and floated over from its own massive wake.

Jon turned to Nyhan. "That's exactly how we got our boats over miles of razor-sharp coral reefs." The admiral had earned distinction in how he read the water in WWII, and his climb up the military ladder was in part because of his particular skill.

"This is a cakewalk, Commander. Get your boys up to speed on that maneuver and you will save a lot of time and bullshit," Jon said.

Nyhan was impressed. "You want to stick around a little longer and coach 'em up?"

"Love to, but I have to get back to the Kitty Hawk at 09:00 tomorrow. Now, where's the kid I came to check on?" Jon inquired.

Jon McConnell and Frank Munro did not speak or see each other often, but that didn't mean they did not keep track of each other. Long before his son was deployed, Frank had talked to Jon at length about the war and necessary strategies to win it. It was Jon who ran the background on Charlie T and where and when he had served. He promised Frank he would check in on his son when he was deployed.

For Nyhan, the one he needed to tow the line was sitting in a South Vietnamese Army's Military Police tent on the Cambodian line. "We've got a Delta Hilton up in Four?" he asked his lieutenant. *Four* stood for the Mekong.

"Yes, sir, in Tan Chau," was his reply.

The YRBM, or Delta Hilton, was a floating helipad. Although susceptible to mines, they were moved and positioned along the Mekong River.

"Jon, I will get a bead on your boy, and I'll meet you in the mess hall on the barrack ship." Nyhan scrambled to his office and got on the horn. He finally got through to his counterpart at the FOB in Tan Chau. "So no one killed? Shot? Stabbed? They didn't have any dope on them, and they weren't drunk? Sounds pretty weak, striking an officer. You do know Monreal is a Filipino?"

"Let them cool down and I'll get 'em out tomorrow."

"No, that is a negative. Look, Admiral McConnell is here, and we're taking a Wolf up there in forty minutes. You've got twice that to get that kid back on his Swift, roger?" Nyhan demanded.

The radio was silent for a moment, and then, "Roger that, Commander, will do." It took a butt kiss or two from a military liaison officer called in, but they were almost back on board.

"We got a forty-five-minute ride up the Mekong to Tan Chau, Admiral, and I cannot guarantee your safety," Nyhan told him.

McConnell climbed into the Hilo and strapped in. Salt and Pepper made up the crew, and they took off showing Admiral McConnell the flotilla and base below.

"Last chance, Admiral," said Nyhan.

McConnell twirled his index limply. "Let's get up the Four!"

The Hilton at Tan Chau sounded more luxurious than it actually was. Most of the emphasis was placed on keeping it from being mined, and it had been discovered that the best way to do it was to have as many sampans full of families as possible keeping watch. The children of the surrounding fishing villages were willing to help, and they were all rewarded for it. When a Huey came in to land, however, the activity had a tendency to escalate.

The Huey powered down, and Nyhan and McConnell stepped out.

"Officer on deck!" Lieutenant Stevens yelled. Debris was still swirling across the deck, and some of it wrapped around the lieutenant's legs. Kicking it off while saluting, he led them off the pad. "Welcome to the Delta Hilton, Admiral!" Stevens said confidently.

"Where's the 112?" Nyhan asked.

"Sir, seems the SVA have a beef with one of your boys."

"Monreal?" Nyhan said, figuring he knew.

"Munro," Stevens corrected. "Seems a few of those gook soldiers have a hair across their asses 'cause he embarrassed them. I don't know. Munro didn't know what their beef was. He spoke to them in the little Vietnamese he knew and could only understand a few things they yelled back. Apparently, he took out their best guy in the may-lay, and now that guy wants a piece of him, bad."

McConnell knew something was wrong. "What's this all about?"

"Fine," Commander Nyhan said. "Let 'em have at it! Bare knuckles, right here, right now!" He was not going to be pushed around, especially not by an SVA officer.

When Monreal heard what was going to take place, he immediately volunteered, as did Pitta. "You boys watch our backs. We will let this play out!"

Ensign Malloy then stepped into the SVA tent with two MPs on each side of him.

"Hey, they got you too, Skip?" Munro said with a nervous smile.

"No. Shut up and listen." Malloy sat on the bunk across from Munro. "Virgil, if you want to get out of here, you've got to fight one of their guys."

Munro stood up immediately. "Let's go!"

"Wait a minute now!" Skip wanted to help prepare him.

Munro turned to his skipper. "I know who it is. He's been eyeballing me ever since I dropped him this morning."

"Okay, son," was all Skip said.

Admiral McConnell stood among the crew that blocked off the street in front of the South Vietnamese Army CP. There was an uproar of shouts and whistles.

Out of the gate came their young friend and warrior. "Take off your shirt, Virgil!" one of the men screamed wildly. Munro handed his shirt to Skip and turned toward the compound. He shook his body as if it were made of rubber. His hands and arms were waving like a monkey's, mocking the SVA. Munro could actually feel his crewmen chanting, "Virgil! Virgil!"

The admiral turned toward Michael Poor, one of the onlooking men, who was rooting Stephen on. "Is that Munro?" Jon asked.

"Yes, sir, they call him Virgil. Something to do with that TV show *McHale's Navy*," Poor answered.

Munro's heart was pounding as the SVA walked out their "champion," Private Ngai Do. The SVA soldiers were all clenching their fists and chanting "Do-do-do!" mocking the Americans.

"This could get ugly," McConnell said to Poor.

The two men began circling each other, and it seemed as if they would both strike at any moment.

The CO placed his soldier before Munro. Munro wasted no time and unleashed a left uppercut. A spit-tangled tooth spun momentarily in front of the stunned crowd. Munro followed the left with a straight right and mashed his opponent's face and nose. The first blow sounded like a hollow coconut dropping on the sand, the second one like it hit concrete.

Instantly the street filled, and Munro was swarmed with Do's comrades. The commander blew his whistle as Nyhan snatched up an SVA private and threw him into the road. Pitta pulled Virgil from the pile, and Monreal cleared out a path toward the road. TJ started pumping rounds in the air with his shotgun and froze most of the men. The SVA CO was now blowing a whistle frantically as he tried to collect his troops.

Nyhan had his .45 out and had it pointed at an SVA private who was still trying to instigate a brawl. "Let's go, boys," he called out as they backed down the road to the Tan Chau market.

Munro did not realize his father's friend was among them. He was right in the middle of the pack as they escorted him back to base, rooting and congratulating him, pushing his shoulder and rubbing his head. At five foot eight, 175 pounds, Munro was all gristle.

"Your first time, sir?" Poor asked the admiral, both still catching their breath.

"Son," McConnell said, laughing between breaths, "my first deployment was on the USS *Johnston* at the Leigh-hey Gulf. I was saluted by the fuckin' enemy. Look it up!" The admiral looked at the tag on Poor's shoulder. "Hey, you any relation to Salem Poor Gunner?"

"Yeah, what Poor black ain't? He had four wives!" And they both laughed.

McConnell walked the docks over to the 112. It had been quite a day for the boys, and they were planning on a little celebration.

"Heads up!" Gerry said, seeing the admiral approaching their stern.

"Permission to come aboard?" Jon asked.

"Permission granted," said Malloy while saluting.

On the deck were several weapons, including an AK-47. "Who belongs to that?" Jon asked.

When Stephen Munro heard what the admiral said, he recognized his voice. It was similar to what he had said when he asked about Stephen's dog during a visit in Massachusetts. Munro turned, saluted, and smiled. "Jon, I mean...Admiral McConnell!"

"Steve!" Jon said, and he stuck out his hand. "You put on quite a show. Didn't you know you're supposed to bow first before starting a fight?"

"Yeah, I knew, but if you're going to eyeball me all day like some badass, well, that's what you get!"

"I see your time in Brockton, Massachusetts, paid off." And they both laughed. "Here, Steve." John handed him an envelope. "This was all the information I could dig up on your friend Charlie. Sorry. Told your dad I would come check on you."

Munro looked puzzled.

"You didn't know?" Jon paused, then asked, "When was the last time you got mail?"

Jon didn't have long, but the two sat and talked briefly about the similarities of Mekong and the Muskingum back home.

"Steve, I'm gonna sugarcoat this to your old man. No need to worry the folks, right?" Jon placed his hand on his young friend. "I've got some great spots back home." Jon looked at him seriously. "And I want to take you and your dad, so keep your head down, Stevie. This place is unforgiving"

He had no sooner finished than Poor came down the dock. "Admiral McConnell, sir, we're ready, sir."

Stephen gave Poor the heads-up, and he shook the admiral's hand. "Tell my dad I'm safer here than I was working off the wheel of the *Annabell*. And thanks, Jon."

Jon turned to see the man he only remembered as a fourteen-year-old kid. "I'll tell him."

Munro took the envelope and headed for the 112. He was looking forward to telling his friend back home about his adventures. He knew of a Catholic parish, a Saint Mary's in Long Xuyen, and he planned on lighting a candle for Charlie T. Before he could hitch a ride south, he had work to do.

Nyhan met the admiral on the helo deck of the Hilton. They had to yell over the wash of the rotors.

"You know, that kid of yours would be perfect for the crew of one those new PBR SEAL boats," Nyhan said, talking about Munro.

"Yeah, I know, but I can't recommend him *and* tell his dad I'm looking out for him," Jon replied.

"Jon, when you are here in Vietnam, it don't matter where you are, you're in the shit." Nyhan paused and looked Jon in the eyes. "I learned a few things too." Nyhan shook his head and lowered it in sorrow. "Everyone is where they are supposed to be."

Jon looked at his new friend and took in his wisdom.

"Jon, one man gets blown to bits, and the man next to him is untouched. Everywhere I go, I feel it is where I belong, okay? I'm here. Virgil is up here, and not by chance! He is here for a reason, no?" Nyhan reassured.

The two climbed into the Huey and buckled up.

Jon had seen more death by explosion than most men had seen sunrises. He had survived the sinking of his destroyer, the USS *Johnston*, after it faced down Taffy 3, a four-battleship convoy.

His vessel had literally been blown out from under him immediately after torpedoing a battleship and sinking a number of destroyers and pilot ships. He could have limped back to the US fleet, but when the *Johnston* saw ships positioning for attack, he turned back toward the Japanese fleet. Jon clung for his life on pieces of floating debris. He watched as massive iron giants collided in battle.

He was adrift in his memory when the Sea Wolf left the Hilton. He snapped back to reality when TJ cracked off a few rounds.

"Pepper!" yelled the crew of the 112. "Light that bitch up, Hurley!" They all squeezed into the pilothouse. "Virgil!"

"I'm coming!" Munro squeezed through the door.

"Shut that door, Virgil," Skip said.

"Fishbowl!" Monreal said, laughing, and they began passing the pipe. "Virgil! Virgil!" Monreal said in a mock chant, pumping his fist while exhaling hash smoke.

The next morning, the crew wanted something fresh.

"Dave, you and Gerry head to the market." Before Skip finished speaking, he heard, "You don't learn too quick there, do ya?"

Pitta was in the turret of the PBR next to the 112. "If you want or need anything, sir, use Van or another local kid. Stay out of the market."

The skipper knew whose backyard he was in. "Okay, you're right, thanks. Can you call him over?"

Pittman called Dave over and pointed out a few of the sampans that sold the best food. "Van is a good kid, but don't give him too much or have him get too much at one time."

Seaman Ken Pittman was as new to his boat as Virgil was to the 112. He grew up in a DC suburb, played a little guitar, and impersonated a few late rock singers like Jagger, Ray Davies, and Fogerty, but his best was his mocking of Neil Diamond.

Like most new meat, he had replaced a crew member who had been either wounded or killed. His PBR mostly ran supplies and medicine to the Red Cross and various religious volunteers all over the Mekong River and Delta. They were a part of the Hearts and Minds campaign. They had been shot at just like anything else that moved in Vietnam. The seaman he replaced had taken an RPG blast off the rebar concrete gunnel. His torso had been severed into two, and he bled out in a minute and a half.

Word had come down that a two-man listening post was needed as soon as possible. Malloy had the Wolf delivering men to the Hilton. The 112 needed to travel eight miles north into Cambodia.

"Hey, Pitta, we could use another gunner on this run. You up for it?" Malloy asked.

Without saying a word, Ken dropped below, coming back up with his rain gear and M16.

Malloy was impressed. "I will square it with your CO. Virgil, show him where he can stash his gear."

The crew was on standby when they heard the Sea Wolf rumbling up the Mekong. It was basically a touch-and-go. Two Rangers hit the Hilton helo deck running. They saw the 112 from the air and hustled with their eighty-pound packs down the ramp toward the boat. The men were Corporal Rich Pasacarnis and Specialist Dave Fogg.

I wonder who they pissed off, Skip thought. These were not two grunts that pulled a suicide detail; they were Rangers going who knew where. Most two-man posts were a few yards outside the wire, and they were protected by a wall of claymores. Dropping two men off alone here was, well, suicide.

Placed out as advanced scouts, these two-man posts provided the best early warning system available. The men who pulled the duty often felt totally expendable. These two Rangers looked tip-top, however, and Malloy questioned his opinion.

Malloy and the crew took the Rangers up a tributary at Thong Lack over the Tan Choa into Cambodia. Pitta took the M60 alongside Dave, who was tucked in the nest on the .50s. Virgil at the aft .50 was the most exposed. His armor vest and ammo box were his only shield.

Gerry stood on the gunnel by the door, holding his M79 grenade launcher. He had his left leg up on the gunnel and his M79 pressed against his hip. He didn't want to look routine today, not where they were going.

The river was low, and as a result, fewer mine sweeps were possible. The enemy used every resource it could scrounge. Each log or piece of floating debris was a possible mine. That fact caught the crew's attention as a sampan with four fishermen on board pulled up a mine. Apparently, it was tangled in their net. When it exploded, every gun on the 112 swung toward the boat as Skip pinned the throttles forward, putting distance between them. He planned out on a sharp turn, right in line with a fixed-positioned M20, 75-millimeter recoilless rifle.

At one thousand feet per second, the twenty-pound shell penetrated the pilothouse, blowing out Skip's eardrums and stunning Hurley. Thankfully, it did not hit anything solid enough for detonation. As it passed through the pilothouse, it skipped off the river and onto the jungle slope before exploding.

Monreal opened up, concentrating his fire on the smoke left from the shot some three hundred yards upriver. As the 112 was closing the distance, a round flew below the nest, ripping through the aluminum and fiberglass shell. The pilothouse filled with smoke, and Hurley was struggling to get on his feet. He began coughing and calling, "Gerry, Gerry!"

When the round passed through, its percussion knocked Munro from behind his gun and into a catch net on the stern. Gerry, who had been standing in the door, was gone. Pitta and Dave were full-on engaging the enemy, and the two Rangers who were stowed below were pulling each other off the deck and out the door.

Munro sprang off the net and headed for the helm. He plowed into Hurley, who was trying to pick up his skipper.

"Virgil, shut her down!" Hurley pulled himself into the door, which was immersed in white smoke. Munro throttled down, and through his smoky starboard window he saw tracers coming from the bank. "Ranger! Get on the .50! Ranger! Get on the .50!" Munro needed to spin the 112 and maneuver it past their line of sight.

"Gerry! Where's Gerry?" Corporal Pasakarnis scrambled to the aft .50 with Fogg on his heel.

Fogg scanned the river and saw what looked like a seaman floating facedown. "There, there!"

Munro could barely see through the thick smoke. "Two o'clock, off your stern!"

Rich was now engaged with the enemy, who was raking the water all around Gerry. Pitta and Monreal were now engaged with the small-arms fire. Virgil slammed the port engine in reverse and the starboard forward, spinning the 112. He slammed the port engine forward and pinned both throttles. The jet drives tore through the murky brown water, causing what looked like a root beer float topped with diesel smoke.

Pasakarnis opened up on the .50 as Fogg scrambled for a boat hook. Putting the port side between his crewman and the hot bank was priority. Skip and Hurley were conscious, but clearly out of the fight. Pitta was hanging from his M60, trying to concentrate his fire on the bank.

Fogg jumped in the river, grabbing Gerry by his life jacket. He was faceup and alive. Fogg helped Monreal pull Gerry onto the deck and headed back to the nest. He never saw who was behind the helm or noticed Richie on the .50. He scaled the smoky pilothouse back to his nest. Gerry was groaning and spitting up water.

Munro had a choice, turn and fight or head for cover. He chose the latter.

Specialist Fogg was the best medic on the Swift that day. He rapidly examined the three men down and didn't feel an immediate medical evacuation was necessary. "They are stable!" Fogg yelled.

Munro had other concerns. "Monreal, you and Pitta look out for mines!" he yelled. Munro drove the 112 back around the curve and slowed to an idle. He looked over his crew, who were still on their feet, and through the smoke to those below. He tried to talk to his Skip, but Malloy's hearing was gone, along with Hurley and Pasakarnis.

Dave hopped through the door. "Skip! Aw, man, and Hurley! Neither one can hear a thing!" he said. "Both look dazed and are curled up, moaning."

Gerry was breathing heavily, and Fogg was taking off his life jacket and gear. "Lost my thumper," Fogg said as he stuck out his hand to his friend Dave.

Dave turned to Munro. "Nice driving, Virgil!" He took over as second-in-command, while Munro grabbed two tubs of .50s and headed to reload.

"Hey, man, I got this," Munro said to Ranger Rich.

Rich barely heard him over the ringing in his ears. "What?"

Munro saw him squinting, trying to hear. "Hey, man, sit down over there and get checked out, okay?" Munro led him over to an engine cover and sat him down.

"I'm okay," he said but realized his ears were ringing something awful.

Munro gave him the stay signal and went back to his gun. He looked over at the two up in the nest and asked Pitta if he needed another .30 cal.

Monreal was racing the Hilton forward and was informed he must proceed two miles up to drop a package. "Roger that, sir." Monreal informed the crew, "We've got a problem here."

Fogg stood up and walked toward Dave. "I've got to have someone with me that can hear, okay?"

Pitta looked at Munro, who was looking at Dave and Fogg. "I'll go," Pitta said.

"What?" Dave turned.

"Yeah, I'll go too," Munro said.

"Virgil, you're not going anywhere! Pitta, you know what this guy is asking?" Dave asked.

"No, but I missed my shot at the Rangers once," said Pitta, and he hopped down to the deck.

"Okay, okay, we gotta get you ready," Fogg said, then he filled the crew in on their opponent. They were going to spot for a squadron of B52s that were on call. He and Parsakarnis were stationed on the trail monitoring movement. They had to choose a safe position out of range. "Look, I got a SEAL team out there already. Now I'm short a skip and engineer."

"Yeah, but you can gain a good gunner," Munro stated.

Fogg was adamant. "Pittman, can you read a map?"

"Yeah, of course!" Ken was a seaman in Vietnam who could read any map.

"A map's not what you need to read if you want to make it, Pitta," Munro said.

Fogg looked at Munro. "And what needs to be read?"

"The signs! Knowing the different calls of the birds, the monkeys…," Stephen said.

"What do you know about that?" Fogg asked sternly. He didn't want to be arrogant, but he *was* a Ranger.

"Pitta, look, man, pay attention to the sounds, okay? I've got a few things for you." Munro went below and came up with his AK-47, assorted clips, rounds, his radio, and MREs. "Here, take what you need and take this," he handed him his AK.

Ken looked over the weapon. "I'll take my M16."

Fogg told him to take both.

"I will show you how to take it down. It's simple, only eight parts total." Ken watched as Virgil tore down the AK and put it back together in under a minute. "These fuckers are tumblers," he said, handing Ken his clips. "I wouldn't try to hit anything over three hundred yards, Pitta, and don't spray and pray. Keep it on semiauto."

Fogg helped Pitta get suited up, and he took what he could from Rich. Pitta had no idea what he was walking into. One of their extraction options was a jungle pluck in a basket of a Huskie, or getting snatched up by the low end of a balloon cord by the nose of a plane flying at over 150 miles per hour.

Dave had them check each other's gear and their radios. "I am not driving right back into that M20," he said.

"I can try and drop some hurt on 'em, Dave," Munro said, stroking the 81-millimeter tube.

"You got smoke, right?" Dave asked.

"Got a case of red phosphorous right here," Stephen said. Red phosphorus along with white phosphorus smoke were used for smoke screens, but firing from a 25-knot platform upped the ante.

"We got about four hundred yards before the next curve! We don't know what's behind it, but we gotta go!" Dave said. The crew looked at one another. "Munro is going to paint that jungle red, and we're going to boogie on by!"

"Roger that!" Munro said, and he began opening up his ammo case. He signaled to Rich to help feed him the rounds.

As a Ranger, Rich was trained in all weapons. "Just yell in my left ear!" he said, yelling himself.

Dave gave Munro the signal, and he and Rich began lighting up the jungle with red phosphorus. Munro gripped his lanyard and made his adjustment. Rich dropped in the RP rounds. Munro estimated, pulled the lanyard, and repeated. They got three rounds off before Dave hit the first turn.

Dave pointed the 112 at the far bank where the river broke right. He straightened her out and kept her as steady as he could, trusting in the mortar smoke. Munro's shells were exploding in, over, and along the river. A few hit the water and splashed, and a few hit beyond the bank and were inhaled by the jungle.

They had three good hits on the bank ahead, and the cooler current pulled them across the water. Pink and red smoke wisped by their faces as the Swift ran the gauntlet. When they hit the far corner, the jungle reappeared, more vivid than before.

Dave slowed to 20 knots and called for Rich to take the twin .50s.

Munro had to relay, screaming in his left ear, "At 20 knots, Dave calculated! Fifteen miles!"

Munro helped Fogg and Pittman off the bow and passed them their gear. Kenny handed Munro a letter he pulled from Richie's armored vest. "That's his," Pittman said, pointing the letter toward Rich. "My baby don't care."

What a strange thing to say, Munro thought.

Ken was nervous and grabbed the first lyric that made sense to him.

"I want my AK back, Kenny!" Munro said out loud as he watched him follow Fogg into the brush.

Back to the Hilton

The muddy eddies and current swirls could be seen down the port side of the 112. Munro was helping Gerry rewire relays and patch up a hole from an M20, and Dave was on his file, making his morning mark.

"How many feet you have to go, Dave?" Gerry called out with a screwdriver in his mouth.

"Six feet, three inches," he said, standing up with the triangle file in his hand.

Dave used his thumb's width to measure his inch, and since the rail on the gunnel was thirty feet, he figured an inch a day.

Gerry passed the time another way. He kept track of the number of "dust-off calls" he heard over the radio during the day. A "dust-off call" was a four-man medieval crew that flew unarmed to the battlefield to evac soldiers. Gerry ran out of carving space on his radio in three months' time. It looked like a Boy Scout camp outhouse seat after jackknife award weekend.

Virgil did some quick math. "You broke forty days, man," he said, helping Gerry.

Dave hopped off the bow and onto the deck with a soft thud and headed to the CP.

"You must have shit when that 20 knocked you into the river."

Gerry was quiet. He was a gearhead, mostly, but Hurley was a better mechanic. He had pictures of old hot rods and the latest Chevys tapped on the hull alongside his bunk. He had just received a 1969 pace car photo, which he kept in his vest pocket.

Whatever it is you need to reach for when you're living so close between life and death, pin it up in front of you! rang through Munro's mind. It had been advice his father, Frank Munro, gave him before he deployed. "Imagery, visual reinforcement, and visualization is a window back to the world you know. Your reason to continue on, a light at the end of their tunnel," Frank had told his boy.

For Munro, his world was a bit different, and so were the walls he chose to pin his dreams. He enjoyed the moment and all that it offered. Rarely thinking of home, he filled his mind, studying the people, their clothes, body movements, and how they worked, fished, and lived. He studied and patterned them like he did the white-tailed deer back home. There were moments and places on that Swift that actually brought him back to the mighty Muskegon. The wooden deck of the 112 as he scrubbed it and looking out the round windows of the pilothouse when he drove it.

"Heads up!" Dave said while he climbed on deck. "Skip's fucked! Blown eardrum and a jacked-up equilibrium. Hurley has some percussion head trauma, and that Ranger Richie, he was sent back to the Ninth."

Gerry and Munro stood in front of their new skipper. "So we getting a new skip, or are…?" Gerry began to ask.

"Not we," Dave said sharply, interrupting. "Yeah, I'm taking over the 112, but you two are getting reassigned."

"Where?" Gerry asked.

"Right here! You two are taking that PBR back upriver to extract those SEALs!"

Munro looked to where Dave had just pointed, at a thirty-foot gunboat tied up tight to the Hilton.

Dave continued, "Seems those two sticks we dropped off were calling in a huge hit, something called Midnight Thunder."

"What else?" Gerry asked, instinctively knowing there was more bad news.

"Virgil is going to be gunner's mate, so he gets a raise, and you"—Dave looked at his friend—"you, you're the radioman on that ass glass piece of shit! Fuck, I'm pissed. I liked you guys!" Dave was fuming. He didn't care about being captain; he would rather be alive with his crew for forty more days.

The Mission

The SEALs flowed through the forests and marshes of the Vietnamese jungle like so many of her tributaries. Donovan was the ripple on that water, and the team took notice. Their mission was to mine a bridge that was clogging the Ho Chi Minh Trail, providing a maximum enemy concentration and an enemy-rich target.

Midnight Thunder's work as spotters had been altered by an influx in enemy movement. The NVA were killing villagers by the hundreds. They left their burnt bodies lying like dead dogs. The first one of these villages appeared smoldering just below the team as they closed on their target. Scanning the village for the enemy, Mack held his men and swept through.

As the rest of his team carefully entered the Mong village, Donovan's eyes were fixed on the dead Mong. "What the fuck is that green shit coming out of their asses?" he said, nearly puking.

"That's the guacamole," Tommy said.

"Yeah, man, I remember the first time I saw that shit. It was coming out of the head of a Maine lobster." Barrows and Rico laughed.

"Stow it," Mack said, "just over a click, gentlemen."

The images were already burnt into Donovan's mind. He must have turned to look back a half-dozen times.

"Mouse, on point!" Mack wanted him to regain focus. "Look sharp, troop," he said as Donovan passed him.

The bridge at Phnom Penh was woven into the side of a step ridge, making it a perfect bottleneck, but also very hard to hit from the air. With the trail being used mainly during night patrols, the NVA bunkers were literally all around them. They had a narrow win-

dow to wire the bridge, detonate it, and escape the grid they occupied, and as soon as night fell, they went up the skirt of the bridge
and had their way with her.

The Crew

The Wolf touched down, much to the dismay of the EOD divers checking for mines.

Munro and Gerry were about to meet their crew at a briefing at 14:00.

Gerry and Virgil stood outside the CO's office, waiting for orders. Out of the door came a seaman and petty officer, followed by Lieutenant Gallagher. The two snapped up a salute for their lieutenant.

"At ease," Gallagher said.

"Hey, Rich, how's your ear?" Gerry asked the seaman. He didn't look at Gerry or return with an answer.

"Still blown out, I guess," Virgil said, laughing.

"What's funny, Munro?" asked Petty Officer Murphy.

"Ask Rich," he said, still smiling.

"Who's Rich?" Murphy asked.

Gerry and Munro looked at the seaman and then back at each other.

"Ranger Rich, the one who was half-deaf," the lieutenant said. "He went back to the Ninth, I was told."

"Yeah? Well, then, that's his twin brother," Gerry said. It was an awkward moment. Munro and Gerry seemed so sure.

"Maybe that Thai stick blurred your memory," their lieutenant suggested.

"No, sir," Gerry said as he sharpened his eye at the lieutenant.

"Okay, boys," Murph said, "I'm curious how this new and improved vessel is gonna handle. Heard we have some new fiberglass chimes on the bottom of her."

"Yes, and a few other upgrades," Gerry corroborated.

"Gerry, right?" Murph asked. "Get up-to-date on those new jet drives. Hey, Butler, fuel and dope! We are having a draw on what to name her after Butler gets out the fuel."

James Butler was from Buffalo, New York. Seaman first class and an above-average volunteer who showed exceptional courage while he was a gunner for the Ninth. He volunteered for the brown-water navy after surviving his second crash. A Swift Boat patrol rescued him near Bien Hoa. "I figure I can swim better than I can fly," was the answer he gave his CO when he asked for a transfer.

"Munro," Murph said.

"Virgil, sir. The guys call me Virgil."

"And they call me Fuel Truck, but not to my face. You guys will call me Murph."

"Roger that, Murph," Stephen replied.

"Go untie that STAB and bring it over to the 116," Murph commanded.

Virgil liked driving the STABs, or SEAL team strike assault boats. He and Monreal used to race around the float base in the middle of the night while wearing night vision goggles. "Just going on patrol, Skip!" Monreal would yell as they took off to smoke some hash with their shipmates.

Murph waited until he had the three on the deck of the 116. "Virgil, you're on the twin .50s. See how good your eyes are. Gerry, you're next to me, navigation radio. Engineer Butler, you're on that fancy M60 with the ceramic plates." Murph was as wide as he was tall, and the nickname Fuel Truck fit.

"Murph seems pretty cool," Gerry commented as he reached for his chart.

"Rule number one." Murph held up his finger like he was addressing a child. "Everyone drives the boat. Number two, everyone learns the armament. Three, the radio. Four…"

The boys were all cross-trained, and on the first test run, they all switched positions. Captain Murphy was impressed with the 116's performance and how his crew handled the helm. It was immediately clear to him that Virgil either had more experience than the others or he was just a natural. What he would soon find out was that it was both.

Extraction

Orders came in, and Murph informed his crew on where the three extraction points were located. He drew circles on Gerry's map. "Depending on the heat, we will try to get 'em out. Sea Wolf is on standby, told me nine miles."

At 03:00, they set out wearing night vision with a STAB in tow. As they sped up the canal and crossed the Mekong, the 116 passed the intersection at 28 knots; with the upgrades, their top speed was now 34 knots.

Mack had his SEALs ready to move. Baros and Reco were ready with the detonators. "The jug is full. I repeat, the jug is full!" When they clicked the detonators, it sounded as if Armageddon had begun.

"Big dance, big dance!" Mack hit the mic for the last time. "Let's move!"

At 03:00, the airfield at U-Tapao, Thailand, was stacked with an array of the Seventh Air Force's B-52s. Operation Midnight Thunder left the wet runway, fifty-seven minutes to target.

Mack's team needed to move, and the night provided them with the best opportunity to stay hidden. The team pushed for the closest extraction point and put some distance between Midnight Thunder and themselves.

"Midnight Thunder, Midnight Thunder, this is Ski Patrol," Mack called out over the radio.

"Go, Ski Patrol" was heard from the other end.

"Big dance, big dance." Dave began communicating and calling out grids.

Intel had the enemy moving heavy, and they were dead accurate on the trail. Pittman was on the starlight and was relaying to Fogg where he saw the heaviest concentration. They were two miles northwest of the bridge, with a long but broken view of the trail.

When the bridge blew, Dave and Mack called in "Big dance" once again. The VC were pinned in the valley, with their escape route cut off by a five-hundred-pound bomb.

When the first five-hundred-pounder hit, Pittman felt it in his chest. As they walked in closer, he felt they were going to crack the earth. Fogg was shaking, trying to read the grid and stay cool on the radio. More bombs hit, but they missed. After 250 five-hundred-pound bombs exploded in a three-mile valley, the kill zone moaned with pain, and once it was over, the shriek gave way to absolute silence.

Murphy slid the 116 into the the grass and killed the motors. It was 07:00, and the light rain deepened the plush green backdrop of the jungle.

Virgil watched as the trees slowly unwound around him. He saw a flock of beautiful green parrots move along the treetops, squawking. He cocked his .50, and Mack's team appeared on the bank.

"There they are," Murphy said, pointing ahead.

Virgil popped out from behind his .50s. "Murph, don't...don't start the motors."

"PBR, this is Big Dog. What's the problem?" Mack sounded anxious.

"Murph, along the far bank there is movement, under the canopy. Watch." Virgil pointed out the birds and how they were tracking what was under them.

Murph acted quickly. "Okay, listen up, we're going to cause a diversion across from that bank. Virgil, eyes on the bank. Big Dog, hold tight. Butler, get some smoke on that bank. Gerry, you hop in the STAB, and when we pull away, you sweep in for those boys."

"Roger that, Murph," Gerry replied.

"Butler, start cranking," Murphy commanded.

Butler placed a belt of WP rounds through the M18, the hand-cranked grenade launcher, and began peppering the bank. Murph hit the throttles, leaving Gerry in his grassy wake. Gerry fired up the

STAB and headed to the team. When the 116 hit midriver, the bank ahead exploded with SKS and AK fire.

Gerry swung the STAB into the undergrowth, and the team spread out in firing positions. Mack gave the go, and they plowed through the brush onto the river's edge. Virgil was hammering the bank as Murph danced the 116 across the channel.

"Butler, get on the .60!" Murph cried out, spinning the 116 around.

Virgil could see the STAB pushing water. Butler fired until he lost sight of the bank.

"Virgil, take the helm!" Murph said. He frantically wanted to help Gerry and check the 116 for damage.

"How is she, Murph?" Gerry asked as Virgil eased them alongside the STAB.

"Looked like you took a few rounds," Mack chimed in.

"Mack, you get to split your team. Too shallow for an eleven-man crew," Murph said.

"Got it! Tony, Mike, with me. Tim, Mouse, you two keep up," Mack decided. Then he asked, "Hey, Gerry, got anything to smoke?"

"Smoke 'em if you got 'em," Murph said, and he grabbed the chart from Gerry.

Gerry dropped below and came up with his pipe.

"What happened to the Swifty? Too shallow?" Mike asked.

Gerry filled them in as they passed the pipe, even managing to tell the boys about Virgil's fight with the SVA gook.

Butler and Virgil were still looking tense from the firefight. They were both white-knuckling the handgrips when Mack called. "Virgil, jump over and take a pull man."

Mack, Tony, and Mike were kneeling behind the helm, passing Gerry's pipe. "Virgil, why didn't you try BUDs?"

Virgil took a long pull, still feeling pretty tight as he kneeled down. Blowing out his hit, he asked seriously, "How many times have you fired your gun?"

"Well, it's not about that," Mack said.

"Ahhh, well, just a question."

"Three times in six months." Mack leaned back; he was high and very relaxed. "Three firefights is all."

"Well, that's why," Virgil said. "See, I love to hunt, bow-hunt, as you may not know, but here…" Virgil took a long pull. "Over here, Mack. I love to burn the powder."

Coughing out smoke, they all laughed.

"You're a killer, Virge," Tony said. "I'll get in the nest, okay?" he said, leaving Virgil with Mack and Mike.

Mike called Butler over, introducing himself and his leader, Mack.

"That's Ranger Rick," Virgil said, and he laughed.

Gerry heard what Virgil said and started laughing. "Ranger Rick! I'm calling you Ranger Rick, fuck it!"

Gerry was stoned and took the pipe. "Take a pull, Ranger Rick!" He said to Butler in a humorous tone.

Butler was easygoing but mean enough behind his .60.

"Hey, man," Virgil said to Butler. "Your twin was good on the gun too." And he passed him the pipe. "It's freaky, man. Are sure you don't have a cousin or brother in the Rangers?"

Boys to Men

Mark Lavenger liked his home in Florida and his job with the military. Lisa was busy with her mom, and instead of rushing for a routine dinner at home, Mark and Lisa took turns choosing restaurants. They talked about business and about their friends the Coles, but Lisa was really interested in the program. Tonight, her choice was the Blue Coral, an outdoor bar.

When she came back from the ladies' room, she snuggled up to her husband and began to pry.

"Lise, I would rather keep you from this." Mark was being kind. "Why go there?"

"Okay, can you at least tell me how many were in Vietnam?" she asked.

"Yeah, 1,322. So far, 442 were killed in action, 415 of them decorated, 653 wounded, and 277 frontline soldiers in various divisions and branches of our military!" Mark raised his wineglass with a touch of a salute.

"Mark, have you seen any of them? I mean recently, not when they were young?"

"Well, Joe keeps track and fills me in. I've got to tell you, Lise, these kids are above and beyond average. I mean Medal of Honor, heroic shit!" Lavenger told his wife.

"Well, I just wondered if some of them looked alike."

"Lise, there were hundreds of different CUF warriors. I imagine there may be a few who look alike."

"Mark." Lisa snuggled up to him tight. "You ever regret not having one of our own?"

"Yeah, Lise, I do, but the flag-covered coffins streaming home changed my mind," he replied. Mark knew his wife knew a little something about life. He had to wrestle a bit with his conscience over the years. At first, he thought he would adopt a Vietnamese child but switched immediately to a puppy. "A child would really change our life, Lise."

"Oh, you think so?" she responded sarcastically.

"Yes. Do you really think we could road-trip with a baby, help out your mom, go wherever, whenever?" Mark said seriously.

"Well, when you put it that way, yeah, I understand, of course. But you could do what you do, and I could be a mother for the first time."

"First time!" Mark laughed. "Oh, I can recall a few times."

Lisa dug her fingers into his ribs. "I'm your mother, all right," she said while tickling him.

"Well, Lise, there are a few thousand orphans in Southeast Asia that would just love you dearly."

Lisa pulled away and stared at her husband.

"Think about it, Lise," Mark said.

"I have," Lisa replied.

Cole waited patiently for word from his CUF contact at the Honey Hotel. Mark and Joe had ceased talking about their work and anything else related to CUF business over their home phones. They had been using the US mail to exchange information, or sometimes resorting to communicating through overseas contacts.

It was late in the day, and Joe Cole's office was quiet, quiet enough to hear his secretary's heels in the hallway as she returned from the mailroom. Cole was expecting the latest numbers on CUF heroes. Secretly, he kept track of the number of Valor, Cross, and Honor medals his boys accumulated.

Joe had been busy "milking heroes," using beautiful Thai women in three different Bangkok brothels, adding more ammo to their arsenal. His justification was that it was too bizarre of a concept for a country to ask a virgin kid to lay his life down before he ever lay next to a woman. Mark and Joe were both merit-based men, and they believed their boys earned it.

Murph called his men to the deck of the PBR. For the past couple of weeks, his crew had been speculating that Murph was actually part of some branch of the CIA. He had the ability to seemingly appear out of thin air. Each of them had a gut feeling he was not just regular Navy man.

"Listen up." Murph looked at his young crew. "Those two sticks you dropped, one got airlifted, and the other, last they saw him, he was firing off his AK and moving southeast."

Virgil knew, as did Gerry, that it was Pitta who was on the move.

Murph continued, "He made contact twice, so we need to go three clicks upriver and wait for further orders."

"What did the Wolf say, Murph?" Virgil wanted to know everything.

"Wolf said it appeared he was surrounded and they couldn't get close enough to him, what with all the fire they were taking. One of their H13s got shot up, killed the copilot."

"He's in the shit," Gerry said as he headed for his charts. "Virgil, you're driving. Butler on the .50s."

The 116 headed upriver. Four days ago, the men had been a bit more optimistic about seeing Pitta again.

"Tell me about your boy," Murph asked Virgil and Gerry, and they filled him in. The questions and answers helped Murph paint a picture.

"No way he will be near any town or village. He's at least six foot four," Virgil said.

"Yeah, I got that from his report," Murph said, "and I agree, he's too tall to be trying to fit in with coolie clothes." And the three of them laughed. Murph let Gerry and Virgil navigate, and he gave them opportunities to complete his thoughts and words. "Virgil, what would you do if you were in Pitta's shoes? You have to have been here about the same amount of time he has."

Virgil laid out a few scenarios, and some were quite clever.

I hope Pitta is as clever, Murph thought to himself. He knew what lay ahead.

Virgil hid the 116 in a tributary under dense cover. Gerry was scanning the channels. There were no dust-off calls in the Cambodian valley they occupied.

Pitta had one advantage over his shorter enemy. When he ran, it was easy for him to outpace them. Avoid and evade the enemy was his plan. After the blown extraction, Pitta was without map and M16. He had left them on Extraction Point 1. Before he could climb in the basket with Fogg, the LZ lit up with small-arms fire. He had thrown his pack and rifle in and was about to jump in himself when a tracer hit the cable just above his hand.

He had unslung the AK and returned fire, which was a fortunate move. The enemy thought it was friendly fire and hesitated. Now Ski Patrol was down one and he was on his own.

The air strike had split up the VC, at least those who survived it. They monitored the airwaves for dust-offs and extractions. Their main focus was on the area surrounding the freshly hit valley.

Pitta kept his contact brief and communicated on ridges where the enemy couldn't guess his next direction. When he called in over the radio that he wanted to hear some Creedence, he was hoping the enemy weren't fans as well.

There were only a couple of places Murph figured he could emerge on the river based on his location, and they were both a mile apart.

"We're going to ease up a half-click and drop you two off," said Murph.

"Who, sir?" Butler asked.

"You and Virgil, gear up. Butler, you're the RTO," he added.

Butler would be in charge of carrying flares, two smoke grenades, an areal ID panel, map, radio accessories bag, machete, and a flashlight. In addition to the ammo and C rations, the extra weight could add upward to ninety pounds. Luckily, Butler was strong both mentally and physically.

Murph handed Virgil a map of where they would be headed, and on it he had circled where he figured Pittman might come out.

"We can't hope for him to pop smoke and then wait to see if we can even get to him. There are VC patrols in the area, heads up out there. Butler, you are Badger 1 on channel 223. Check your radio. Virgil, if we get held up back here, you two will have to get close to the border."

Gerry and Murph eased up the river. "We're exposed for the next half mile, Gerry. What do you think?"

Gerry grabbed the rail and pulled himself into the nest. He simultaneously cocked his .50s and tightened the strap on his helmet. He twirled his right finger, and Murph hit the throttles.

The PBR lurched forward, catching the attention of Virgil and Butler, who were climbing the steep bank. The two clung to the vegetation as they watched the 116 sizzle out of sight. They were alone in Cambodia, and if they were captured here, no one would come for them.

Virgil was in charge and took point. He wanted to sit overlooking the game trail that led to the river, figuring Pitta would too. Not five minutes after they stepped off the 116, they heard gunfire coming from its intended direction.

Murph slowed the 116 a quarter of a mile from his extraction point. He was trolling slowly along the opposite bank when he made contact with the enemy. Gerry returned fire, but the 116 was getting ripped up from both sides of the bank. Their only choice was to try to draw the enemy fire upriver away from Virgil and Butler.

"Keep firing! Keep firing!" Murph was screaming while rounds bounced off the helm.

Gerry had been hit and was bleeding out. Murph needed cover and turned into an irrigation canal. He pulled Gerry in through the canopy and assessed his wounds, not noticing at first that he was bleeding from his head. He stuffed a bandage into Gerry's wound and propped him up. "You gotta hold on, Gerry."

Murph was in two feet of water when he spun the 116 around and blew back out into the river, the radio microphone in his hand. "Request dust-off!" was all Gerry heard before passing out from his wounds. Murph was out of options; he had to take the 116 back into the gunfire to save his crewman.

Butler and Virgil heard the twin .50s roaring and paused. "We gotta get into position and wait for word," Virgil said.

Butler settled in above his partner and monitored the radio. Virgil held his M203 across his lap. They were both breathing heavily from the climb when they again heard the motors of the 116.

"Badger 1! Badger 1!" Murph spoke to Butler over the radio. "Badger 1, over! Badger 1, gotta bring it on back! No time for guests! Badger 1, be two clicks below the red circle. I will be waiting." Murph moved quickly, leaving a brown wake that grew wider as he faded.

"We're on our own," Butler said. The two sat still, waiting for the jungle to settle down.

Butler was the son of a Korean War widow whose husband died in 1950. He was nineteen, an all-star at Bennett High School, and he had a job working with his stepfather in a metal fabrication shop. Butler and Virgil shared two things in common, their passion for fishing and football.

Butler was a CUF soldier. His biological father was killed in Italy in 1943. The man had earned his honors during the Avalanche Campaign when the Fifth had invaded Italy. His company had the pleasure of halting the German advance along the Sale River.

Polish immigrant Dominic Grabovski had shown courage when he single-handedly took out a Panzer tank with a fistful of phosphorus grenades. After killing the tank crew, he fought his way through the infantry. He received a congressional medal of honor and a visit from Arlene in Paris.

Virgil watched the trail and, in particular, a monkey who was moving along the canopy but not squawking. "We've got something here," he stated, and both men chambered a round.

Virgil held his hand in a fist, saying, "Hold your fire. If they ain't friendly, let 'em pass by." He chose a clear vantage point over-looking the valley below. "It's our boy. Check his 6."

Virgil dug out his binoculars and handed them to Butler. Pitta was moving fast. "He either heard the gunfire or he's being pushed," Virgil said softly. "Keep checking his 6." He watched Pittman move through the thick vegetation covering the game trail. At six foot four, he wasn't hard to spot.

"Looks good behind him, Virgil," Butler said as he started gathering his gear.

"Okay, I'll signal Pittman and you move up the ridge," Virgil said.

"Roger," Butler answered.

Virgil waited for Pitta to get close. "SEEEE SUUU!" he whistled commonly.

Pittman froze; he thought he was done for.

"Hey, give me back my AK!" Virgil called out.

Pittman felt relief rush over him. He looked thoroughly exhausted.

"Pitta, we've got to get over this ridge as soon as possible," said Virgil. "Glad you made it, man, seriously. The enemy is close."

They both helped each other up the wet jungle ridge to Butler, who was waiting with water and an open MRE. Pitta had a pounding headache. He was dehydrated, and because he had been on the move constantly, he could only manage to find a few pieces of fruit a day.

"That was the best shit, man. Thank you, Richie!"

"No, he's not Richie," Virgil corrected.

"Not this again," said Butler.

"Look, Butler, I told you, this Ranger could be your twin brother," Virgil replied.

Pitta looked confused. "Don't break my balls. I'm not in the mood, okay?" he said, squinting as if the light was cracking his brain open.

"Pitta, we will rest up here," Virgil said.

Suddenly, Virgil dropped on one knee and pointed his M203 over the ridge. "What the hell is this?"

Pitta was getting to his feet when a monkey ran into their camp and took some of his food. "Hey, Doe-Doe!" Pitta called the monkey. "I remembered what you told me about the game here, and two days ago, I made friends with this guy."

Virgil grabbed a piece of white bread and held it out. The monkey calmly came back and took it gently out of his hand. "This must be someone's pet."

"I thought the same thing." Pittman was opening up his second can of B-3 pork steak. "He isn't the least bit afraid, and he's sharp, man. Really!"

"What do you call him?" Virgil asked.

"Doe-Doe."

"Let's hope he is our good-luck charm," Butler said.

The two miles back to Vietnam would only take six minutes of travel in the PBR, but the river was hot. The three had food for a few days and waited until after dark before they decided to move off the ridge. They followed the river to a village they had passed along the Mekong.

Butler scanned the rice paddy fields with his Starfire. "Virgil," he said softly, "there is a huge buffalo out there where we gotta cross. What are we going to do with the monkey?"

Virgil had been carrying the monkey on his back. "If he can hang on to me when we cross that opening, he can have a free ride."

"Listen," Butler said, "if we get out there and that bull charges us, are you going to shoot it?"

Virgil looked at Pitta, who was looking at Butler. "Yeah, fuck it, I'll shoot it," Virgil said, and he chambered a round. "Follow Butler, Pitta. I'm right beside you."

The three men had a two-hundred-yard rice paddy to cross in front of them. The moonless night helped conceal their otherwise-obvious silhouettes, but the splashing could be heard from the hootch nearest them.

The buffalo was startled and began to holler, which helped mask their splashing. The bull ran from them, and Munro, finding it hilarious, broke out in laughter. It was contagious, and the three laughed until they were able to catch their breath, stopping just inside the tree line.

They had made it and were now that much closer to their extraction point. Word spread fast, and Nyhan ordered two PBR boats to head out toward his men.

When Butler radioed in that they had Ski Patrol, the base RTO pumped his fist. "Roger, proceed to Alpha 1!" He had to be brief. He followed protocol and assumed they were being tracked.

Doe-Doe followed the men. He climbed up and through the jungle trees, which seemed to settle the other animals. When Doe-Doe began to screech and chirp, Virgil held his men back. He could see the direction the monkey was looking. Virgil signaled for them to evade and cover as he moved around a rotted tree. He could hear a patrol heading their way.

Butler and Pittman tucked behind a blowdown and readied for the worst. No matter how loud the birds, bugs, and other animals were, one's heartbeat is all that can be heard when the enemy is near.

With Doe-Doe barking and jumping around, they found themselves distracted. They had to move quickly to their positions. Munro, Pittman, and Butler all said their prayers. They knew fire could rain down on them at any moment.

After a few minutes, mistakenly thinking the coast was clear, Butler called out for Virgil just as an NVA private stopped to move his bowels two hundred yards from where they were hiding. The private froze and Doe-Doe climbed above him, barking and chattering. He was almost on top of Virgil when he stopped. Virgil clenched his rifle; he could see the side of the soldier's face. Butler froze in his position and could see the NVA peering in his direction.

Munro sprang from his position and smacked the soldier in the neck with his rifle butt, stunning him and knocking him down. Butler and Pittman joined in, and the three of them bludgeoned the NVA to death.

"Okay, we're officially fucked when they come back for dung heap here," Virgil said, wide-eyed and breathing heavily. "We're less than a half mile to Alpha."

"First, we drag his ass to the river." Pittman grabbed the soldier's weapon, an SKS with a retracted bayonet. He gathered his ammo and grabbed his collar, pulling the dead man like a dog.

Butler joined him and they moved quickly to the bank. "No way!" Butler spotted a sampan tied to the bank, a green twisted dock alongside it.

"Which one of you guys is going to stand out there and row that fucker down the river?" Pittman wanted to know.

"Oh, man," Virgil moaned.

"What's up, Virgil?" Pittman asked.

"Okay, strip that VC and give me his clothes. You two guys are too tall and too light. If I can cover you guys in the fishing nets, I will row us out of here," Virgil advised.

They knew it was risky, but only had a small amount of options. Virgil put on the dead man's clothes, and they stuffed him under the roots protruding from the bank. They were able to load up their gear and position the nets.

"I want that monkey." Virgil was trying to get Doe-Doe into the boat. He had a C ration in his hand and lured him in. "Got him!" Virgil put Doe-Doe in the boat with a can of white bread and grabbed the two long oars. He had experience rowing plenty of boats back home, but never a sampan. Luckily, he knew how they worked and was able to swiftly push off the dock. He stood dead center behind the huge crossed oars and began to paddle out into the channel. The enemy would be seeking out army men, not a fisherman in coolie clothes.

Virgil ordered Butler to get on the horn, and with that, Badger 1 was home free. When two PBRs rounded a corner in tandem, Butler popped the smoke.

"Badger 1 is in the sampan! Badger 1, I repeat, Badger 1 is in the sampan!" The call came across the radio.

The smoke grenade started lighting the fishing nets on fire, and Butler almost flipped the boat over while trying to put them out. Doe-Doe was climbing all over Virgil, and he almost found himself in the river when Butler moved. Virgil was still trying to pry the monkey's hands off himself when the PBR skippers eased up on them.

"You guys want a lift, or are you going to row that piece of shit back to Saigon?"

Pray with Me

===================================

Virgil hitched a ride downriver on one of the PBRs to a small village called Long Xuyen. He wanted to find a church. He wasn't able to keep Doe-Doe, so he gave the monkey to a fishing family who traded with the 116. His one condition was, they had to keep him and not eat him.

Virgil was prepared for his journey, bringing with him a few barter items, some money, and a fearless attitude. Murph hooked him up with a Monitor who was already heading downstream.

The crew of the Monitor's tiger barge made it look like a frat house boat, with awnings and towels blowing in the wind. They were a fun bunch of guys who tossed the football and Frisbee whenever they felt like it.

Virgil settled in the armored taxi and shared a joint with a seaman. "This is a sweet gig you guys got here," he said.

"Yeah, it's better than Charlie's backyard," one of the men said.

"I thought the rivers were Charlie's backyard?" Virgil blew out a huge hit and began to cough, making his new friend laugh.

"You want to mow Charlie's lawn?" the seaman asked with an awful Chinese accent. He pointed to a flamethrower on board and laughed some more.

The floating tank armament made it nearly impossible to attack. Mines were its only real enemy, so the captain of the Monitor followed behind the minesweepers as they methodically trolled the waterways.

Virgil had a basic sense of where the church was but needed a little help navigating. Every time anyone mentioned Charlie, it struck a nerve. He had once only associated or considered the name in a positive light, but they murdered it in Vietnam.

Virgil filtered through the marketplace, asking a few vendors where the church was. "Nhà thờ công giáo?" he asked as best as he could, which translated to "Catholic church?" and he would then make the sign of the cross.

He took the route a woman pointed out. Her smile convinced him she was on the up and up, but when he came to a bamboo bridge hung across a nasty, muddy canal, he had his doubts.

The single-bamboo-log bridge arched like the rainbow. It had one handrail made of smaller bamboo tied with natural cordage. Virgil was about to attempt a crossing when two children climbed on from the opposite bank. He observed their technique and was amazed at how they hardly moved the structure, more so resembling half of a spiderweb than a bridge.

"Well, if I only weighed sixty-five pounds, I could do the same thing," he said to himself. He smiled at the children who walked the bridge like it was merely a log on the ground. What he did notice was that they had removed their sandals when they crossed, so he sat and took off his jungle boots.

"You going for swim?" Virgil heard a young woman's voice ask from behind him. Caught by surprise, he had his hands full of socks and shoes when from behind a village hootch stepped a dainty young woman as beautiful as a freshly picked Asian flower.

"Hi" was all he could muster. Virgil knew that he looked very out of place standing there flat-footed. "What time does the tide come in?" he asked, trying to make a joke, which was lost in translation when he tried to explain.

"What are you doing here?" she asked.

Virgil was nervous as she began walking softly toward him.

"The church. Nhà thờ công giáo. Saint Mary's," he said as best as he could remember.

She was close enough to touch, and Virgil stuck out his hand. She did not move but simply bowed her head. Virgil was embarrassed and bowed respectfully.

"I'm Virgil...well, I mean Stephen."

"You not know your name?" she asked.

"I'm Stephen. The guys call me Virgil."

"What guys?" She smiled, teasing him. "My name is Ha' Chu'."

"Gesundheit!" Virgil said, and he laughed to himself. "Ha' is your first name?" he asked sincerely.

"Yes, and you like the name Virgil?" Ha' inquired.

"At first no. My real name is Stephen Munro." He showed her his name tag.

"You pray, Munro?" she asked.

"Yes, I do, Ms. Chu'! Is the church over that bridge?" Stephen asked.

Ha' started taking off her sandals and replied, "Yes. You follow?"

Ha's beauty was breathtaking. Virgil had seen hundreds of Vietnamese girls with their families working in the markets, and he had seen the hookers who visited the flotilla, but not one could compare to Ha'. Virgil wasn't shy with the ladies and had managed to stay single after high school.

He watched as she delicately placed one foot in front of the other, holding the skinny bamboo railing with her left hand. Virgil waited for her to reach the far back, and then he proceeded to follow. Stephen had great balance, and his confidence showed in his speed.

Ha' watched him navigate the narrow bridge. He hardly looked down because he was preoccupied with staring at her. He noticed where the bamboo wasn't supported, and as if he were on a springboard, he launched himself onto the bank. She did not seem impressed, so Virgil sat on his pack and put on his shoes.

"Not far. You no need shoes," Ha' said as she began to walk ahead, looking back at Stephen. The church was just beyond a small grove and sandwiched between two cement buildings on a busy street.

"Did we really have to cross that bridge?" asked Stephen. In front of him was a bustling Vietnamese city.

"I wanted to see if you would follow me," Ha' told him.

"Where did you learn to speak such beautiful English?" Stephen was being generous.

"The missionaries." And she pointed at a small, quaint church.

Virgil crossed the asphalt road to Saint Mary's Church, still carrying his footwear. There was a basket for shoes and sandals beside the worn white door. Ha' placed her sandals inside, wiped her feet, and opened the door slowly. Virgil looked at the shoe basket and placed his boots in. He noticed the wear marks on the threshold and on the white door. *Good sign,* he thought.

Inside, the door light revealed turquoise adobe walls and a single cross above a bamboo and Thailand rosewood altar. Each station of the cross had been hand-carved, and their detail slowed Virgil to a crawl.

Ha' continued toward the altar and genuflected, blessed herself, and then disappeared into a dark room. Virgil couldn't hear her footsteps anymore—the whole church was silent. The smell of past burned incense clung to the wood and the walls.

Virgil walked slowly up the aisle. To the right of the altar were a dozen unlit candles and a statue of the Blessed Mother. The stained glass window above the cross provided little daylight, but what light it did provide was now directly on Virgil's face. A wave of peace fell over him as he looked softly at the cross. He used to look at his crucified Lord and say, "There is the bravest man I know," but at that moment, standing there in a mission church in South Vietnam, he thought of nothing.

He was calm, calmer in that moment than he had ever been in his life. He stood there for just a few seconds, but it could have been an hour. At the precise moment he began to think of his late friend Charlie T, the sun broke through the clouds. The colorful streams of red, orange, green, yellow, and blue beamed through the glass, engulfing the young soldier in what looked like the healing rays from God's immaculate heart.

Virgil felt the warmth of those tinted rays and closed his eyes tighter. A tear squeezed out, and as it ran down his face, his new friend Ha' walked in. Stephen was in a state of total adoration, absorbing God's rays. Frozen in the moment, she watched the tear roll off his jaw, collecting sunbeams on its way to the floor. Joyfully she thought to herself, *What devotion!*

Virgil exhaled a laborious breath and opened his eyes slowly. He looked at his new friend Ha' and then moved to the candles, knelt down, and dug out his Zippo. He lit a candle and placed it before the Blessed Mother, bowing his head and praying for his friend's soul.

Ha' waited quietly. She had seen several soldiers at Mass on Sundays, but never one here on a Thursday.

Virgil blessed himself again and stood up. He looked over at Ha' and smiled. She returned his with a shy smile of her own and said, "Would you like to meet the sisters?"

"I would, but can we go to lunch first?"

Ha' nodded and took Virgil's hand. They both squinted hard at the blazing sunlight when they opened the door into the courtyard.

"We eat here with the sisters, okay?" she said.

Virgil was smitten; he would have followed her into a mine-laced rice paddy.

Five sisters of Saint Mary's mission entered from a squeaky wooden door out onto the courtyard, all of them carrying plates of Vietnamese food. Virgil started squirming to get his pack off. He began removing every C ration from it as they approached. He had used his socks to cram cans of beef, pork, and white bread in what looked like giant sausage links.

Only one sister was an American, although they all spoke English. The Filipino nuns were hard to distinguish from the Vietnamese women. Virgil was severely outnumbered.

One of the nuns rang a bell, and several children from all ages and both genders ran out into the courtyard. The dining tables were wobbly and, like a lot of things around the mission, in need of repair. Virgil was introduced, and the children all seated in their respected places.

The Dominican Sisters of Peace Mission was a refuge for orphaned children. They fed, clothed, and educated them all. A safe shelter was provided until the women succeeded at finding the orphans adoptive families.

The children stared at Virgil but were very polite, saying hello as best as they could. Sister Eleanor led the prayer, and everyone bowed their heads. "May God continue to bless this mission with food, safety, and friends." She looked up at Virgil and smiled.

Somewhere in the middle of it all, a Filipino sister, Lailani, asked Virgil, "Are you the Virgil who beat up the bully Do?"

Virgil almost choked when he swallowed. Everyone at the table was looking at him, and suddenly it became church-quiet again. "Yes, that would be me," he said sheepishly, raising his hand half-heartedly.

Suddenly, two teenage girls ran over and hugged Virgil, thanking him. "Girls," Sister Eleanor said kindly, "let Mr. Virgil enjoy his lunch." It seemed Stephen's reputation preceded him and word spread fast among those who were terrorized by Do's crew.

Do and his SVA soldiers had taken the two girls' brother away to fight. To make matters worse, they had also lost both of their parents. Their mother had been overcome with disease and their father fell victim to a mine. Their brother had been their caretaker when Do's men came around.

The SVA men had tried to abuse the two girls when their brother, Chan, fought back. He was immediately seized and dragged away. Neither had heard from him since.

Private Do had had a ruthless reputation long before Virgil arrived in South Vietnam.

"He was an angry child and an even angrier young man," Sister Eleanor said.

"You did good by these children, Virgil," said Lailani.

Virgil did not speak; he poked at his plate of food and forced down a bite, although he was feeling slightly choked up. "Sister, I see your mission has seen a lot of action. If it is okay with you, I would like to return with some tools and fix a few things."

"That is very nice of you, Virgil," Eleanor replied.

"We have tools here!" Ha' said abruptly, then apologized for speaking out of turn.

"I have till 5:00 p.m., then I have to catch a ride upriver to Tan Chau," Virgil offered.

Stephen was more handy than his father had been at his age. The toolbox they handed him, however, looked like it came over on the *Mayflower*. He noticed a screwdriver and pulled it out. He looked around and spotted a shutter hanging crooked and loose. "I'll start over there, and when you clear the tables, I will fix them too."

Virgil loosened each screw and filled the worn-out holes with wood slivers he carved from a broken hammer handle. When he tightened the first screw, it squeezed loud and caused the children to make an "Ew" noise. Virgil tightened each screw, making each squeak more dramatic. Ha' laughed as she helped ready the tables for repair.

Virgil was a big hit at the mission. The boys wanted him to throw around a baseball with them, and one had an old leather mitt. Virgil did the best he could to put them in a throwing position, but it would take more than a few minutes' lesson. Virgil had worked up quite a sweat, and when he put away his tools, Ha' brought him a washbowl and towel.

Ha' did not live at the mission, but she had attended school there when she was young. Her parents were killed by the VC in 1963, and the sisters took care of her until they located an aunt living nearby. She helped out at the orphanage whenever she could. Her aunt was a dressmaker, which explained her beautiful dress.

"I would like to see you again, Ha'," Stephen said.

"I will walk back to boat with you?" she asked.

"Yes. First, I will say thank you to Sister Eleanor." Virgil said his thanks and goodbyes. He then asked the sister for a pencil and paper.

She handed it to him with a sense of strictness. She felt a little ashamed when Virgil walked over to the two teen girls to take down their brother's information.

"I'll do what I can, Sister, but I can't promise anything," Virgil said, holding up the piece of paper. He handed the pencil to one of the girls, who returned it to the sister.

Ha' walked to the front of the church, where they had left their shoes, but the basket was empty. "We gone long time, Virgil."

Stephen giggled.

"What funny?" Ha' asked.

"Oh, nothing." Stephen simply found his new friend to be adorable.

"Come, I will buy us both new sandals," she said.

On the way back to the river, Ha' led Stephen to the market, where they could buy sandals. He was trying to find a way to ease into a kiss while they were sliding on their new sandals.

Ha' wanted to, but not in such a public setting. She conveniently led him between two vendors and stopped and reached for his hand. It felt stronger and bigger than most men's.

Stephen's heart began to pound as he slid his hand between Ha's hair and her neck and pulled her in for a kiss. Before it was over, he already imagined another. He pulled away from her lips, staring in her dark eyes. "I want to see you again, Ha', but I don't know when." Stephen hugged her tight.

"I come to Tan Chau. See you there?" she asked him.

"I could be out on a mission or back in the delta, Ha'. I will be back in no more than ten days, I promise." Stephen didn't know what he was saying. He would say just about anything to her, and he tried desperately to hide it.

They stood there hugging and kissing until Stephen heard the mine sweep heading upriver. He knew his ride would be minutes behind.

"Virgil, please be safe," Ha' told him.

"No," he said quickly. "I will just be me. I don't know safe, okay?" He wasn't laughing. He hated pity or worry. "I don't want anyone to worry, okay, Ha'? Worry does not fix anything. If you have fear, say a prayer for me, okay, Ha'?"

She only understood that he asked her to pray for him, and that was what she planned to do. When they pulled apart, Ha' looked up at Stephen. "Please come soon, Virgil."

Stephen could think of nothing else on the way back to the flotilla in Tan Chau. When he hopped off the monitor onto the dock, he headed straight for the 116.

"She ain't here," a seaman First Class said, looking at the empty slip. Stephen didn't recognize the new meat and headed for the CO.

He stood outside O'Neil's office. The CO of the 116 Mobil Ravine Force was busy lecturing the new EOD Divers.

Commander Nyhan's MRF was now up in Tan Chau, and it was imperative they work round the clock. He was uptight for good reason—the area to defend had been tripled. The 116 had 187 men total, Nyhan's near 700.

O'Neil was on his third tour and on his way up. "Stephen Munro, don't bother coming in."

Stephen didn't know what to think. He had been standing in the green metal hallway for quite some time already.

O'Neil walked out of the office and put his cap on. "Follow me, Seaman. We're going to see the commander."

Now Stephen was worried. *Was Ha' Chu' a spy?* he thought to himself. *Be cool,* he reminded himself. He hadn't said or done anything, and he had always thought the commander liked him.

Stephen followed O'Neil up the ramp and into the stairwell leading to the bridge. Commander Nyhan had an office, but he liked to do his business on or near the bridge. Both men entered and saluted.

"O'Neil, you two come out here. I want to talk to you both," the commander said firmly. He grabbed a navy bag and walked out toward the gun battery.

O'Neil followed quickly, but Stephen took his time. It was his first time at the helm of a boat that size. He climbed out of the hatch and walked toward his officers. Mesmerized, Stephen had already forgotten all about the reason he could be there, and he quickly refocused when the two stood shoulder to shoulder, looking directly at him. He stopped and stood at ease with his hands behind him.

"First Class Petty Officer Munro, step forward," Commander Nyhan said sternly.

Boom boom! Stephen felt like his heart exploded.

O'Neil pinned the eagle and stripe insignia to Stephen's chest and handed him his patches.

"O'Neil, you have better things to do than stand around here," Nyhan said, understanding his situation.

"Make sure you pass the word to his crew," O'Neil stated to the commander.

Nyhan shook Stephen's hand and congratulated him. "Proud of you, son. You showed me something, and now I've got something to show you."

Nyhan took him over to the port railing overlooking his fleet. There were two new PBRs, equipped with attack armament, tethered to a Swift. "See those new PBRs? You're going to be the skipper of number 77 there out front."

Virgil stood wide-eyed, staring down at the attack boat.

The commander continued, "The two boats will work in tandem. We're meeting tomorrow at 09:00 to go over tactics and techniques. That should give you time to go over her."

"Yes, sir," Munro said respectfully.

"You have done well to earn this, son. Don't fuck it up!"

"Yes, sir—I mean, no, sir, I won't!" Stephen said. He was beyond excited.

"What do you think of the armament, Munro?" Nyhan said, lighting his cigar.

"I think I'm going to burn some powder, sir!"

Nyhan laughed a bit. "That's one reason we chose you. Now, drive her like you stole her, son!"

"Yes, sir, I will, sir. Thank you, sir!" Stephen saluted sharply and headed to his boat.

Lucky Mae

Stephen took off for the bunk ship. He spotted Monreal and told him the news.

"We're gonna have to celebrate!" Monreal said as he shook Stephen's hand.

"Yeah, but first I gotta check out that boat." Virgil looked around the bunk ship, wanting to collect two of his crewmates.

Gerry and Butler heard the news, and they congratulated him accordingly.

"Have you guys seen Pittman?" Stephen asked.

"Yeah, he was seeing a few guys about putting a band together for the party this weekend," Butler replied.

"Party?"

"Yeah, Nyhan is having some bash for the Seawolf, and Pitta wants to get in on it!" Mark Gerry was a good mate to have; he kept track of the crew and what was going on.

"Let's go check out our boat, boys," said Stephen.

The meeting at 09:00 preceded the meeting on the 77. Stephen began to go over the rules. "Rule number one, everyone drives the boat."

Munro was early and sat in the back; the other skippers were on deck, talking. The commanding officer began explaining the reasons the Navy was making changes to the drop-off and extraction locations of their SEAL teams.

After an ambush killed three SEALs during an extraction in My Tho, the Navy realized they needed more firepower, and two boats were always better than one. By developing a safe field of fire protecting the 6, through basic tactical arrangements, the two PBRs would work together by laying down cover fire from standing and moving positions. With the additional armament of a mounted M134 Minigun, the two PBRs were capable of duplicating cover fire from the Seawolfs, but from a horizontal position.

Training began immediately following the meeting, and Stephen's crew were put through the paces. They were shown how to engage in fire while maneuvering the PBR gunship through shallow waters and tight canals.

Their sister boat, the 113, was run by a Greek skipper named Flamos. His crew was made up of volunteers from several Swift Boats operating in the northern rivers and shoreline near the 38th parallel. They were familiar with the PBR's agility and speed but were not nearly as aggressive as the 77 while charging a bank or turning out of danger.

Stephen Munro was quick with his decisions and heavy on the trigger. He knew the boys of the 113 would try to outgun them as he stood at the helm of his ship with his binoculars. "Oh, shit! Mark, get on the radio! Tell 'em to hold their fire! Hold their fire!"

Pulling out his pistol, Stephen fired three shots in the air and was able to get their attention. He hit the throttles as Gerry reached them over the radio. "Tell them there is someone on the edge of the bank," he said to Gerry.

Stephen swung the 77 in close, confirming he was right. "Shit, it's a kid! Pitta, get that kid!"

Kenny had already leaped to the shore and was reaching for her when the wake rolled in.

"She alive?" Gerry asked.

Ken tried unrolling her from her fetal position. She was naked and cold, and God only knew how long she had been there.

"Check her for holes," Munro commanded. "Kenny, pass her up here! Gerry, get one of your shirts and a blanket! Pitta, oh, man, she lived through that barrage, man!"

All of the men were amazed.

"Take a look around the bank. Make sure we didn't waste anyone," Stephen continued. "Gerry, tell the 113 we have a little girl and we are looking for more indigenous persons." Stephen was trying to wrap the little girl in a blanket. "Mark, check those fucking maps and make sure we're firing where we are supposed to! This was supposed to be a restricted area!"

Pitta scanned the banks. "Gerry, tell the 113 we gotta get her to an aid station!"

Stephen had a shivering little girl in his arms and needed to get her warm. He asked her several times while drying her off, "Tên của bạn là gì?" or "What is your name?" Without receiving an answer, he pulled a dark-green T-shirt over her head. When the shirt cleared her ears, she loosened up enough to cling to him. "Hey, anyone have any chocolate I can give her?"

Stephen took the 77 to the closest aid station, just north of where they had been training. On the way, after a bar of chocolate, the girl said one word, "Mae," which Stephen assumed was her name.

A corpsman who had just come off duty was walking out of a tent with a red cross on it. "Wow! Hey, Sailor," he said to Stephen, who was heading past him. Grabbing him by the arm, the corpsman continued speaking. "You don't want to take her in there!" The man shook his head and mouthed *dead bodies*. An unsuccessful emergency surgery had just concluded in the tent.

"What do we have here?" The corpsman was trying to get a peek at the little girl who was tucked under Stephen's arm.

Stephen thanked him and explained how they came upon her.

"Bring her over here, Petty Officer," the corpsman said.

Munro followed the man into another tent. "She hasn't said much. Her name is Mae. She ate some chocolate, but it took her a while to stop shivering."

Just then, a call came in reporting more casualties.

"Look, I gotta scrub up," the man said.

"Hey, what about Mae?" Stephen asked.

"She looks okay and will most likely end up at an orphanage somewhere. Saint Mary's is about two miles upriver. She'll probably be placed there."

"Thanks, man. I'll take her there myself," Stephen said, and he headed back to the 77 with Mae still clinging to his side.

"Hey, Skip, is that your new Doe-Doe?" Pittman asked jokingly.

"No. Where we are going…well, you guys better behave, okay?" Stephen told Pitta.

Sister Eleanor

"Surrender your socks, boys, and stuff 'em with Cs! We're going on a little hike!" Stephen commanded.

Butler stayed at the 77, and the three walked through the Long Xuyen streets with Mae and links of tied socks holding their C rations. Stephen was certain he was being watched by every Vietnamese person because he was carrying one of their own. At one point, an old woman began shouting at the men while trying to take the child, but Stephen said firmly, "Saint Mary's! Sister Eleanor!" which seemed to settle her. They continued through the vendors.

"Wait here," Stephen said to his comrades, and he stepped into Ha's aunt's dress shop.

"GI, what you want? You want silk?" a woman asked from behind swaths of hanging material right after Stephen entered.

"Is Ha' here, ma'am?" he asked.

From behind a veil of silk peered a strong-looking middle-aged woman. "Oh, GI, you want something for girlfriend?" she said and smiled at little Mae.

"This is Mae. We found her," he told the woman.

"What you mean found her?" she asked.

"On patrol a few clicks—sorry, ma'am, a few miles downriver. I'm taking her to Sister Eleanor."

"Oh, sister take good care. Ha' there at orphanage, helping," the woman said, relaxing.

"Do you have something I can put on her besides this T-shirt?" Munro asked, pulling on the GI green dress.

Ha's aunt was a considerate woman, and she had seen her share of orphans. She gave what she could to help Saint Mary's. "I fix her up."

Mae surrendered into the woman's arms, reluctantly letting go of Stephen, and disappeared behind a curtain to change in the storeroom. Mae appeared moments later wearing a white-and-yellow dress.

"This was Ha's dress. Virgil, you be good to her," she said, looking straight into his eyes.

Stephen Munro now knew Ha' had told her aunt about him. "Yes, of course, ma'am. Thank you so much for helping Mae, ma'am." He held out his hand, and Mae tried climbing up his arm. "Come on, you." He scooped her up and headed to the street.

"Woo-hoo, look at you!" The boys were teasing Mae, trying to get her to smile.

"Just over the bridge up ahead, fellas," Stephen directed.

When the men arrived, Sister Eleanor was out in the courtyard with Ha' and some of the children.

"Virgil!" a few of the orphan boys yelled and ran over to see him. Ha' was standing behind a table, helping a young girl, when she heard them yell. She froze momentarily with excitement.

"Hi, Ha'," Stephen said, looking over at her.

Sister Eleanor stopped the boys before they reached him and told them to wait. "What have we here, and in such a pretty dress?" Sister Eleanor could see the look of despair on the child.

"Found her naked on the bank about three miles from here, Sister. She was alone. Her name is Mae," Stephen explained.

Ha' had made her way to little Mae. "I recognize the dress," Ha' stated, looking surprised.

"I stopped at your aunt's store. She gave it to Mae'."

Ha' stared at Mae', and then at her old dress. She had been about the same age when her aunt found her. Ha' coaxed little Mae out of Virgil's arms and over to a table of snacks, fruit, and rice.

"Is there any paperwork or anything, Sister?" Stephen asked.

"God, no," she said, laughing. "We will try and find out as much as we can about Mae."

"It's okay, Captain, don't worry." Ha' looked at her man's new stripes.

"I'm not a captain, really. Chief Petty Officer, they call it."

"Close enough," Sister Eleanor said.

"We brought you what we could, Sister," Stephen said.

"Then you have to join us. There is plenty. A jeep hit a goat this morning, and they brought it here! Oh, God bless them!"

Pitta looked at Gerry, and then around the courtyard. "Skip, you never told us about this place other than that it was a church."

"Just peel off the Cs," Stephen told Pitta.

Gerry and Pitta took the socks off and untied them.

"That girl is gorgeous, man," Gerry said to his skipper after sneaking a look at Ha'.

"Hey, that girl is mine, fellas. Met her last week. That was her aunt's store I went in."

"Oh, yes, Skip is working the home front," Pitta said, and they all laughed.

Pitta was rubbing his shoulder on the way back to Tan Chau; he must have thrown a thousand pitches to those kids. They all had time to hit the chapel and say a prayer. Skip stayed at the dock while Butler explored with the boys, but mostly he wanted to be alone with Ha'. The two were obviously in love.

"We gotta do something for them!" Pitta yelled as the 77 roared along.

"Like what, steal a few cases of rations?" Gerry asked sarcastically.

"No, like money. I will get them to pass the hat this weekend when my band plays," Pitta stated.

"Your band? What band?" Gerry looked confused.

The Band

Nyhan was coming from the officers' meeting quarters when he heard the men practicing in a storage area. "Hey, anything you boys need, you just tell Galligher I told you carte blanche!"

Pittman and his new band were taken aback a bit. "Who's on the mic?" Pittman asked, stepping forward.

"I want my boys to have a good time, son. Get what you need for a good show," Nyhan said.

Gerry finished wiring the last set of speakers. "Pitta, this shit's gonna thump like a mortar, man! What are you playing first?"

Gerry was into the same music, and the two were off comparing licks. It was twenty-six miles to Long Xuyen, and it might as well had been two thousand. Stephen was only thinking of one thing, and it wasn't music.

The deck of the Hilton was lined with speakers, and Pittman and Gerry were able to scrounge a bunch of channel-marking lights. Strung from the blades of the Seawolf, it looked like a space age Christmas tree.

The MC that night was a Lieutenant Ash, a real piece of work. He kissed more ass than a toilet seat. He wormed his way into the job by some overqualification.

Nyhan was proud of his sailors, but he loved his airmen, and this party was especially for them. He knew the dangers and appreciated the fact that each man volunteered for the brown-water navy. His way of thanks was to let them have some fun.

The Navy invited the locals after they were cleared to board, and they had some of them help prepare food and local dishes. It was mid-October, and a lull in enemy movement allowed for this perfect opportunity. The stage was set and the sailors and airmen were lined up to enter. Nyhan extended the offer to the SVA, who were always interested in joining in on a celebration.

Pittman didn't miss the chance to enthusiastically welcome their comrades with a little sarcasm. "All the way from the DMZ, it's the SVA feeling uneasy!"

The boys let to rip, starting with a little "Run through the Jungle." The Hilton was rocking, and before the night ended, Pittman made an announcement. "Listen up, you river rats! Now I'm going to get serious before I get loose!"

The crowd was still buzzing from their last song, "Born to Be Wild."

"Okay! I want you to thank Commander Nyhan for funding this bash!" The whole deck went wild. "We couldn't have done this without the help of his right-hand man, Lieutenant Galligher!"

The boys were whistling and carrying on, while Ken Pittman was letting it build. "There is someone else we have to thank, but she isn't here right now."

One seaman yelled out, "Yeah, your mother!" which set the crowd off laughing.

Pitman continued, "We needed help finding a sound system, and Sister Eleanor from the Saint Mary's orphanage loaned us theirs!"

A dull "Yeah" and buzz were all he received.

"Hey, I can't hear you, river rats, and neither can the good sister!"

The boys stepped it up a bit more.

"Okay, okay, well, if you won't shout it, shove it! I'm passing the ammo box for the orphanage at Saint Mary's. Don't be cheap, fellas. You may need the indulgence!"

The crowd erupted with laughter.

"So dig deep, boys. This could truly be your ticket to ride." And Pitta closed.

Stephen and Monreal took two .50-cal ammo cans and worked the crowd. Ken had the band start the last set, starting with the number one hit in Vietnam, the Animals.

"We gotta get out of this place," Stephen mumbled.

The band played the first chords over and over as the cans were starting to overflow. The two skippers worked the boxes to the front of the stage. They were overflowing when Kenny started low, "In this dirty old part of the city, where the sun refused to shine, people tell me there ain't no use in trying!"

The ship erupted in cheers. When they hit the chorus, Ken turned the mic to the crowd. "Yeah, yeah, yeah, we gotta get out of this place if it's the last thing we ever do!" Even the SVA soldiers joined in. "Girl, there's a better life for me and you!" Truer words were never spoken on that night.

Stephen was touched. He had no idea, for one, that Ken was a good singer. Second, as nice a guy, trying to help out the orphanage.

Not everyone shared the joy. Private Do was there, and he took note of their choice of charities. He had no faith, and he behaved like it. His crew might have enjoyed the band and the free food, but they were eyeballing both Stephen and Pittman throughout the night.

"Virgil!" Monreal yelled. He was buzzing and smiling from ear to ear. "Hey, your friends are here!" he said while laughing hysterically. Jones and TJ were following him and obviously ripped up as well.

"Virgil, you want us to kick that rice bowl in the ass?" Monreal went on.

Stephen had to laugh; he had more backup there than he could count.

"Look at him, that miserable little fuck! He probably likes his ass beat." TJ was locked on.

Kenny was still singing, but he saw the boys staging below and signaled to the MPs. They began circling Nagi Do and his crew, turning him and moving him to the ramp. Do was going to get his revenge, but in classic bully fashion, he would find someone weak to exact it on.

Retribution

Mark Lavenger pulled into the marina. The crunch of the crushed-coral parking area under his tires gave away his arrival. His secretary was outside, around the corner, smoking. When she heard his Chevelle, she crushed out her butt and headed in. "Hi, Mr. L," she said as she scurried back to her desk. It was January of 1970, and there was a cold front moving down from the plains. The open door brought welcomed cool air into the office.

"Where's the fire?" Mark asked.

Michelle didn't like bad news, and the look on his face was not good. "It's going to be cold all weekend, and there is no heat in my apartment."

"What about that sailor fella I saw you with? Doesn't his parents have a house nearby?" Mark inquired.

Michelle looked away, and Mark decided not to press her.

"Michelle, you can bring a few things you need here. Use the marina to shower. I won't be back till Tuesday. Maybe things will have warmed up for you."

"Thanks, Mr. L. I will check with a few of my friends. If they can't accommodate me, I will take you up on that," Michelle gratefully accepted.

"Okay, great. Now let's go over the proposals you typed out. I've got to deliver them to the senator tomorrow."

Senator Cole began every weekday at the gym, promptly arriving at 5:00 a.m. Walter Cronkite was retiring from reading the news. "Good," Joe said out loud when he heard the news anchor on one

296

of the gym televisions as he was leaving. "He was a pain in my ass, especially about the war," the senator said to himself.

Cole wanted nothing more than to win and leave Southeast Asia for good, but he could not convince Congress of how. "In order to win Vietnam, we have to stop the supply chain coming in from Cambodia," he had told his peers. They voted against Nixon, and Cambodia was now off-limits.

"Makes about as much sense as complaining about the cold when you won't shut the window!" were his last words on the floor before he walked off. Times were changing. The peace movement was gaining traction, and a new era of political correctness had begun, the war being its catalyst.

Cole and a handful of Republican senators were labeled chicken hawks, warmongers, and baby killers by the media. Every curse word imaginable spewed from the mouths of a privileged few as they protested against the war. It was at one of these rallies that happened to catch the world off guard when shots were fired at Kent State.

Cole was on his way to his office when a band of cardboard warriors surrounded him and began calling him a murderer and a warmonger. Cole stopped halfway up the stairs and looked at his watch. In his worn briefcase was the current condition of White Feather, the Marine's best sniper. Cole was trying to figure out the best way to preserve that strain when the already-superhero soldier was severely burned.

Carlos Hathcock had burns on 90 percent of his body by the time he pulled the ninth man from the blaze. Cole had detailed files on the young Marine and was in awe of his abilities. To think these ignorant kids would spit on that.

"Do any of you know why we entered the war in Vietnam? Here is your chance to convince me you are worth another second of my time," Senator Cole said confidently.

"For Dow Chemical and McDonald Douglas!" one girl yelled.

Cole was surrounded in a semicircle of a dozen or so peace queers in their full array: beads, long hair, headbands, and bell-bottom jeans. He knew who supplied the war effort, and they weren't even in the bottom fifty.

"Is that it?" he asked the hippies.

"The spread of communism, is that what you're going to tell us?" a young man asked.

Senator Cole looked at the hippie, who was glaring at him with hatred. "I was not going to tell you anything, son," Cole said sternly. "I see your sign reads 'In the name of God, stop this war now!' So I ask all of you, if the United States pulls out, will the war end?"

"It doesn't matter, as long as we end the draft!" another young man said.

"So this is more about you not serving than the lives of those who are?" Joe asked.

The group respectively calmed themselves, realizing Cole did not have to engage them in the first place and he could have easily walked away.

"Does God approve of those who can help but refuse to? Does not God say, 'I am the good shepherd, I lay down my life for my sheep'?" Cole asked the protesters.

"Don't preach to us," one boy said.

"Come on, guys, have you ever met the people of South Vietnam? Honestly, they are the sheep, okay? They need our help from being slaughtered." Joe struck a nerve with a few, and he knew it. He continued, "You may have more in common with them than you do with your parents or neighbors—you both smoke the same shit!"

He was looking for some levity and got them to laugh a little.

"Their culture is one of peace and freedom of religion. I don't expect everyone to understand why we are in Southeast Asia. I just want to know, When should America get involved?" Joe beckoned.

"Never," a young woman said.

"Well, miss, we hesitated to get involved in World War II and a lot of innocent people died. Plenty of businesses prospered from that supply chain then. Do you protest against them too?" the senator inquired some more.

"You don't care about our soldiers, you just want money for your campaign!" another boy yelled.

Joe realized that he obviously could not convince them just how deeply he cared. "You wouldn't know what I am carrying in my briefcase, nor should you."

Cole stopped and opened up his leather case and pulled from it White Feather's file. He opened it to a photo of burns to the body of the hero. "Here." He held out the photo. "Take a good look at this and tell me I don't care!"

They refused to stare at it. The skin on his hands and arms were burnt to the bone.

"This boy ran into a burning truck that had run over a mine. He single-handedly pulled nine boys to safety! Nine, out of that truck! The Congressional Medal of Honor, Silver Star, and the Purple Hearts he had already received meant nothing to Carlos, or White Feather, as he will be forever known, I'm going to make sure of that!" Cole slid the photo into his folder and closed the case.

"This soldier was the slayer of butchers, real evil. Do some research on who the Apache woman was." Cole did not want to give them any reason to hate the soldier; he was just trying to get them to understand it was more about love than hate, love of country and of their fellow man.

"You have freedom of religion, freedom to assemble, freedom of speech. So do the South Vietnamese, and all they want is what they have. They are not expanding their borders, forcing others to adopt their way of life. Imagine, if it were you, whom would you turn to and who would offer you a hand?"

The group looked at one another. They were outgunned, just like those who challenged Hathcock. Fortunately for them, the senator only fired words.

Tag Team Terror

Stephen headed down the ramp to the 77 with his river rat wing-man Marsalla off toward the 113. They had their mission orders and location, but what they did not have was permission to cross into Cambodia.

The mission at hand was to extract a member of Murder Incorporated, which, of course, meant the area was red hot. The extraction was 0200 hours up some tributary, six miles in enemy territory. The Seawolf would be on standby, with the estimated arrival time to the border approximately six minutes, plus four to the extract.

Murder Incorporated was what they called themselves after being trained in Da Nang by the great White Feather. They had no bounty like Carlos Hathcock; just the same, if they were caught, they would surely be tortured. To date, the enemy had killed fifty-nine in action.

Munro and Marsalla took their PBRs into Cambodia using night vision on the forward crew, scanning for Skull Cracker's signal. Every weapon was hot, and each crewman was scanning.

Skull Cracker keyed his mic twice, signaling he could not speak. Gerry knew not to respond and was hoping the RTO of the 113 did the same. The riverine PBR crewman had no idea how big a treat. A small platoon of NVA soldiers were sweeping the forest after the two-man team hunted down and exploded their leader while he addressed his troops.

Marsalla was staring through his Starlight scope when his rear gunner knocked over an empty can of .50 he was resting his foot on. The noise echoed across the slow-moving canal into the emerald jungle. Everyone's heart stopped, along with every creature in earshot. That was when they heard them, lots of them. What the NVA thought might be their assassins turned out to be two US riverboat gunships.

Stephen grabbed the mic and signaled the 113. "I'm still a go, fight or flight!"

Marsalla was pissed. He had a company of who knew how many heading toward his position on the bank, and now the radio call helped zero them in. The NVA converged on the hillside. They could see the muddy water, but Marsalla had the 113 tucked into the bank. Each one of his crewman had aligned with their own target but held until their skip gave the word.

"Open up!" he screamed like a tiger roars. Hitting the ignition, he pinned the throttles forward, kicking up a huge mud-foam wake. The rear gunner was responsible for the stern line tied off the bank. The 113 sprang back toward the back, spraying its jet wash. White traces were poured through.

"Cut the line! Cut the line!" Marsalla screamed over the two straining Detroits. His gunners were lighting up the jungle.

Mario, their RTO, began chopping at the cleat with a machete. When it broke, the 113 slingshot off the back, flipping Mario over and leaving him dangling off the stern.

Paul, the rear gunner, stopped firing once the rope broke. He ran to the stern to pull in Mario.

Marsalla turned back to see the two crewmen on the deck and thought the worst. Soon as the tracers stopped, he eased down the throttles, asking, "Everyone in one piece?"

Paul and Mario pulled themselves up. Marsalla called out to each one, "Paul! What the fuck? You could have gotten us killed, son! Mario, get back to the radio! We're staging here, and if the 77 starts taking fire, we are heading right back in."

The 113 drifted slowly. Listening, they were hoping the NVA would follow them away from the extraction point, and they did. Animals started making warning noises throughout the surrounding jungle as they ran through the dark undergrowth.

Marsalla called his bow gunner Cousin Johnny, but the way he said it, it sounded more like Tony, so half the guys called him Tony, the others Johnny. "Cousin Johnny, talk to me. You got anything?"

Johnny was on the Minigun, scanning with his goggles. "Cap, I got something, three o'clock."

Marsalla peered through his scope and saw three NVA soldiers setting up their mortar along the bank. He told Paul to take the helm as he cocked the stern .50. "Give me a count of five when I start shooting!" he called out.

Marsalla put his target in his iron sight. The night vision only showed a dark mark two hundred yards out. He began firing low, skipping rounds off the water, walking the vicious rounds all over the bank.

Paul was at four when he saw the first small-arms fire coming in over the gunnel, and at five, he punched it. Marsalla held on and continued to fire into the tracer's rounds that were screeching by. Paul pushed the 113 a half mile down the river and eased off when he approached an eddy.

"Bring her around and let's stage up again," Marsalla said, hoping it wouldn't be necessary.

When the NVA fired on the 113, Skull Cracker moved toward the bank. They were not convinced they were alone, and unfortunately, they were right.

Cas and Clayton had joined the Marines together. They made it through sniper school and White Feather training at Hill 55. They were sent out with intel on an infamous general who enjoyed mutilating the native women after raping them. For three days, they heard various screams and tried desperately to circle his encampment but never even saw their target until they assembled for a formal inspection.

Cas steadied his rifle on his target while Clayton read off the yardage. They were 325 yards downhill with no crosswind, which was a gift. Cas watched him stand there, as austere a figure as you could muster under five feet. His 8-power scope brought his face into recognition. Cas let his shallow breath go and squeezed one off.

When his scope settled back down, he saw panic under a pink mist. In that instant they felt naked, but they knew they had to slip over the ridge behind them and beat feat to the extract. Like striking a wasp nest and killing its queen, the two Midwestern boys caused a deadly swarm.

"Cas, let's move." And Clayton led the sniper down the slope. They needed to put some distance between the mortar rounds that were now randomly falling through the canopy.

For fourteen hours they avoided and evaded patrols along the river. Skull Cracker arrived at the extract at the same time the NVA did. Slipping under a root ball, the enemy passed them by. When the shooting started again, the two herded several more off to join in the fight.

"Don't move, shhhh," Cas whispered. He could feel someone creeping up close to them. His sigh revealed a small pig that had been orphaned. It was wandering aimlessly along the jungle floor.

"Make the call," said Cas. The radio popped, and Gerry got word, a pink flashing light confirming the signal.

Gerry called the 113. "We're checking the nets. Be advised."

Rich pulled the bowline and cut her off the bank, while Stephen and Pittman poled the 77 toward the two men. As Cas stepped onto the deck, an NVA spotted them.

The SKS was cracking copper-jacketed rounds all over the 77. Clayton caught a ricochet as he jumped from the bank and was bleeding from his face. Rich opened up with the Minigun, and at four thousand rounds per minute, he cut the jungle in two. Stephen swung the 77 out from the bank and started to run a gauntlet of starboard-side fire. Marsalla in the 113 came in hot, passing between the 77 and the bank, dangerously close to colliding.

Rich used the short pause he had to cool his barrels. Stephen swung the 77 out, giving his rear gunner a wider kill zone. Cas was lying on top of his spotter, whose injury looked worse than it was.

"You two get it done?" Stephen was asking for not just the US Marine Corps but for Ha' Chu', who had lost family to the general.

"Saw his skull split at three hundred yards. I watched it hit him. No way he lived," Clayton bellowed, trying to get up.

"Stay down until I tell you," Stephen demanded. He hammered the 77 and swung back around, waiting for the 113.

Suddenly, he heard the roar of the enemy boat and saw the phosphorus tracers bouncing off his hull. Stephen turned into the wake of the 113, and Pittman hammered the bank as they both sped away.

"Welcome home, boys!" Munro said joyfully. They had just reentered Vietnam.

"Our home is Kansas, sir." Cas was busy patching his buddy's face.

"Both of you?" Stephen asked.

"Yes, sir."

"You guys hunt whitetail?"

Stephen and Skull Cracker talked whitetail hunting all the way back to the flotilla. They, of course, invited each other to hunt their home stands once they were back in the States, but the difference was, Stephen was definitely going to take them up on it.

Home Sweet Home

Ha' placed some fresh-cooked beef and rice on the low bamboo table. Stephen sat with his legs crossed, waiting for his girl to bring their beverages over, two warm Cokes.

Ha' was very quiet. Her man's tour was ending in six weeks, and it was all she could think of.

"You know I put the paperwork in, Ha'. We have to wait and see, okay?" Stephen liked their little place near the river. It was a miniature version of his parents' home. He wrote his mother about Ha but couldn't read her through the letters on how she felt. In six weeks, he would know for sure.

Back at the flotilla, the crew of the 77 were getting ready to join their captain on two days' leave. Stephen invited Monreal, but he was on maneuvers. Gerry and Pittman were heading to the Ming Dynasty, a local watering hole. Rich met up with some friends who washed out of BUDS, and they hung out on the 77, drinking bears and reminiscing.

Stephen had the sweetest woman on the Mekong River, and he knew it. He slipped away to see her any chance he could and used his gunboat to pull up to his backyard to have Ha' feed the boys. He avoided his nemesis, Do, hoping he wouldn't expose Ha' to him and his men. It was only a matter of time when they found out, and Do was on the clock.

Do wasn't the only one who was curious where Stephen Munro went. Marsalla, his wingman, heard his men talk about his mamasan. How she fed them and took care of their skip.

Munro invited Marsalla several times, but something always came up. For whatever reason, Marsalla went looking for their hootch that night, walking a village road out of Tan Chau.

Do had been waiting for Munro. He had learned where Ha' lived and had one of his men watch their home. He waited for two more of his men to arrive before they concocted their plan.

Stephen kept his .45 on his hip, and Ha' playfully pulled it out, pretending she was a shooter. At that moment, a village dog started barking. *Boom!* The door exploded open, and four SVA soldiers wearing face masks rushed in, all wheeling dry bamboo staffs. Ha pointed the .45 at the door and screamed, "Go away! You not take my Virgil!"

Ha' was so scared when the door burst open she squeezed the trigger hard enough to hammer a round. The .45 jumped out of her hand. The shot froze Do and his men momentarily. Stephen reached for the first pole, and when he pulled it out of his attacker's hands, his elbow caught one of the intruders directly in the eye, shattering his socket.

Marsalla heard the single shot and knew it was a .45. He took off toward the small house, where the sounds of a woman screaming could be heard. Stephen was getting beaten by the men. One soldier was holding Ha' down, and Stephen managed to break the staff, hitting him in the side of the face. Marsalla, all 250 pounds of him, flung the first soldier he saw on his back and drove his fist into his sternum.

Stephen managed to get his .45 from behind Ha' and headed for the door. He slammed the door shut and stood there with the gun pointing at who he thought was Do. "Take your mask off," he demanded.

Marsalla had one soldier facedown on the ground, and next to him, one gasping for breath. Ha' was huddled in the corner, fearfully watching.

Stephen looked at Marsalla. "Take the mask off that prick right there."

Marsalla was standing on his staff and short-footed him, knocking him out cold. Stephen had big problems; all he wanted to do was kill these four SVA soldiers.

"These the fucks the villagers complain about?" Marsalla asked tactlessly.

"Yeah," Stephen said, still breathing heavily. "Ha', go, please. You can't see this."

Stephen wasn't sure if he was seriously thinking of killing the four or just scaring them. Ha' didn't want to leave; she ran to hug her man, but he was not the least bit affectionate.

"Ha', leave now!" Stephen opened the door while keeping his gun on the soldiers, who were conscious.

"Let's tie 'em up and take 'em for a boat ride." Marsalla was serious.

"You know, if I don't kill Do, he will keep harassing Ha'," Stephen confided.

The two soldiers on the ground began pleading with Stephen, earning them each a smack with their own staffs.

"You two fucks are going for a ride," he decided.

"I'll get the 113. Let's tie them up," Marsalla agreed.

Stephen and Marsalla beat and hogtied the men. Stephen dragged each one out of his house and into his backyard, booting them when they tried to call through their gags. He heard the 113 and wondered if he was alone.

Marsalla pulled the nose into the bank and hopped out. The two skippers carried the men to the gunnel and flopped them on deck.

"We going to sink 'em?" Marsalla asked.

"Fuck no! We're going to take 'em upriver and drop 'em off in Cambodia!"

The rumors were flying, and Stephen, of course, was a suspect, but when they found the four weapons and uniforms stashed along the road north of the FOB, they assumed they deserted and crossed into Cambodia.

"How did you get those weapons so far from your place while getting those gooks on the bank that fast?" Marsalla asked, sounding impressed.

"I didn't. Ha' found their shit in the bushes and humped it down the road," Stephen said.

"That's a good woman you have there. She got any sisters?" Marsalla was serious.

"No, but she has a friend, Kim. I will try and hook it up."

Stephen and Marsalla worked the SEAL teams in and out of the jungle. With his tour running down, Nyhan offered Stephen a two-week stint on a dredge, but he refused.

"No, thank you, sir. I'm going to see it through," he said respectfully.

The two gunboats had perfected their tactics, and Stephen knew that the best chance of survival for everyone was to stick together.

Ten days out and Gerry heard a call while scanning the radio. The two PBRs were on patrol protecting the flanks of a mine sweep when the air waves lit up with "Tango, Tango, I'm going in."

Captain Miller, flying his OH-6 Scout Coptor, was a legend. He had already survived eleven crashes and was one of a few Scout pilots who literally fought shoulder to shoulder with the troops on the ground. The size and agility of the Scout, combined with its armament, door gun, and a pilot Minigun, made a lethal first punch in battle. Mills was the Muhammad Ali of the jungle.

Everyone knew of Mills and what the enemy would do to him if he was captured. It wasn't long before Marsalla received the call; they were on point and now the closest to him.

The Seawolf was en route and pushing their bird hard. Stephen dropped back and passed the sweeper port side. He followed the 113, both of the boats pushing 30 knots.

Mills had gone down in a firefight. His gunner was killed upon impact. Mills, miraculously, was untouched. He hardly had time to gather his M16 and a few extra mags when the enemy caught up to him.

The ground troops he was protecting were cut off, and Mills had no choice but to run. He knew the river was less than a mile away, and he was on the radio with the Seawolf, who were adjusting their fire as he moved.

The two PBRs could see the rockets being fired from the sky platform. TJ was literally hanging out the door, pounding anything that looked Asian. Mills was running to the river, with the two Seawolfs protecting his 6. Within two hours of being shot down, Mills was on board Marsalla's 113 and heading downriver with the two Seawolf boats flanking him.

Before he left the flotilla, Stephen named Pittman to succeed him, but of course, that was ultimately up to Nyhan. He had been consumed with getting Ha' out of Vietnam but so far hadn't received the news either of them hoped for. There were a backlog of Vietnamese trying to flee Southeast Asia, and even if they were married, it would have hardly made a difference. Munro knew whom to ask but realized he needed to go home to do it.

Commander Nyhan greeted Munro at the transport. "It was a hell of a year, Munro. Sure you want to go stateside?"

"No, I'm not, sir, so keep my boat warmed up. I have to try to reach out to Senator Cole, sir. He is a friend of the family. Will you take me back if I can work it out, sir?"

"I will give you the boat of your choice, son, but don't wait too long," Nyhan responded.

Emily got up from the table and walked out into the cold to collect herself. Frank knew not to follow her. "Give her a minute," he said, looking at his two boys. Stephen was still red from the last conversation.

"Why can't you just admit we have no business in Vietnam, Steve?" Matt shouted.

"Look, I can never expect you to understand, Matt. You live safe and secure every day. The only danger you are in is when you take your balls out of the mason jar they're in," Stephen fired back.

"Hey, hey, that's enough," Emily said as she walked back in. She couldn't hide her disappointment. "Here I have in front of me my two sons, whom I love, one willing to die fighting for his country, the other against it!" Emily wasn't finished. "I only wish your wife were here, Matthew, so I could tell her the same thing. We love you, but you were born and raised and fed by a man who is an American war hero! He never pushed any of that on you! Do you see a wall of ribbons or pictures of him in combat? No! He is humble about his service…humble! Not in-your-face like you and your wife, Matt! The roads you drive, the buses you ride, the medical treatment you receive, all of it! All of it can be traced back to some military war or intervention! Open your eyes, Matthew! I did not raise an ignorant son!"

Emily was emotional but held firm her gaze, and Stephen, wisely, did not say a thing. Frank also sat impressed at how straight Emily shot. He was leaning back in his chair with his hands behind his head, twitching his biceps.

"Mom, can I say something, please?" Stephen had been biting at the bit.

Emily exhaled and leaned back.

"Matt, sorry I said I couldn't tell you from your wife from behind, okay?" Stephen said. He was the only one laughing at his joke about his brother's long hair.

"Okay, okay, come on, you two," Frank intervened, sitting up. "I want to tell you boys something."

Frank didn't reveal his emotions under normal circumstances, and that night wasn't any different. He spoke matter-of-factly. "Boys, my name—well, my family name—dates back to early Scotland. Its meaning, 'where three rivers meet,' refers to a place up in the high-lands somewhere. The meaning behind the Munro crest is 'Dread God.' The meaning to me is still unclear, but regardless, the clan had many leaders, warriors, and soldiers just like most clans, but none more important than our great-great-great-great-great-grand-father, Jonathan. He faced his destiny when he crossed the line and fired on the British at Lexington in Concord, igniting the war of independence. That action is recognized in our family's tree. You, Matthew, you are from a lineage in Ireland, Fitzgerald, son of Gerald, second most powerful family in all of Ireland. Your ancestors were stubborn, smart, brave, and strong. Their crest, a knight, symbolized inner strength."

Frank looked up at Emily and continued.

"Strong. We come from the Scottish clan famous for their courage in the Hundred Years' War and the battle against the Roman Britain Army. Their crest was a knight also."

Frank had their attention, and he looked from Matthew to Emily. "I believe we carry a part of that lineage in us, just like a dog that instinctively knows how to retrieve or point. I think there is an imprint, something you cannot understand or explain, yet it exists. Matty, remember your black dog? Did you teach him to fetch, or did he teach you? I know it's more complicated than that, but listen, you two, your instincts should not be to war against each other. You were once close friends! You, Stevie, lay off the hippie jokes." Frank wasn't kidding. "Didn't that badass Andrew Jackson have a ponytail?"

The boys laughed a little.

"Matty, you better figure out what side you're on here. America is not the enemy. Neither are the veterans or soldiers, okay? If you don't like a law or the draft, then follow the rules and change it! It's just like how you couldn't scold your dog for pointing or retrieving. You can't condemn the man who is driven to protect and fight!" Frank looked at the two boys, who were once so close. "You two used to fish side by side. Think about it. And you, Matty, you and your wife, don't bring up our grandson to despise this country, okay? Don't just teach him just about our wrongs. We've done some good too."

Frank got up and exhaled a long breath. His boys watched him as he walked around the table. Resting his hands on Emily's shoulders, he began again. "It's important, boys, to consider dishonoring your family's name before speaking. Neither of you knows what they had to do to survive."

Frank felt a bit emotional. Feeling his wife's sorrow through her shoulders, he reacted. "God knows how many names and generations I personally ended. Every action will have its consequences."

"Like Vietnam?" Matt asked.

"Yes, and doing nothing is still an action!" Steve snapped back.

"Well, if you two boys can't hash it out, don't come for the fourth," Emily said.

Matthew got up and headed toward the door.

"Wait, Matt," Steve said. "I'm not going to be here, Matt, so don't not come on my account."

Matt continued out the door.

Second Tour

Stephen Munro stepped out of the open door of the Huey and right into the path of Ranger Rick. Hill 55 Sniper School was something Stephen worked out with during his re-enlistment. His crew was short of manpower back at Chan Tau, and he had already set Ha' up in an apartment in Da Nang.

"I'm telling you, Rick, this guy Butler could be your twin, man."

Rick wasn't convinced. All he knew was his father died in combat and his mother never remarried. He didn't have any brothers, so he figured maybe Butler's father was somehow his father too. *No way! That would be impossible*, Rick thought. *He was killed in action in Okinawa.*

"Hey, whatever happened to that dude Ski Patrol?" Rick asked Stephen.

"Oh, you mean Dave Fogg? Yeah, Lucky Dave! He chose the name Ski Patrol because he said that if he lived through that fire mission, he was going on ski patrol in Germany for the rest of his tour," Stephen reminisced.

"That's so cool. You can't make that shit up!"

"You got that right! Now, when am I going to meet Gesundheit?" Rick joked.

"Real funny, Rickie. I see the word's already out!"

"Are you kidding, Stevie? I heard you were coming here last week!"

Steve and Rick paired up immediately and spent countless times on the range together. It was three days before their first mission outside the wire, and their CO gave them a two-day pass.

"We're going to my place, Rickie. Ha' has prepared some local natural foods for us. We're going to indulge before we hang the wire!"

Rickie replied sarcastically, "Anything you say, Stevie."

Rick leaned back from the floor table on some pillows. "Tomorrow you two go to market, learn about things, okay?"

Stephen had asked Ha' to find a market and a local who could teach him about local plants and vegetation. The two Rangers had more than a few odd plants to worry about.

Hill 55 was pumping out two-man sniper teams responsible for killing hundreds of high-ranking enemy officers. They were stepping up their patrols and countersniper squads.

The sniper was a precision killer, and the training was far different from the earlier training these two recruits had received. One of the men capable of maximum firepower downrange, Rickie, was impressed with the extra preparation and began to realize the gravity of the situation.

"Stevie, you're not going to ever surrender, right?"

"Not a chance in hell, brother! You know they consider every one of us to be children of Hathcock and would torture us for sure!"

Ha' got up and scurried from the room.

"Hey, sorry, Stevie," Rick apologized for disturbing Ha'.

"No worries. She is a worrier. Rickie, no shit now. When we go out, we either both come back or neither of us."

Rickie followed Stephen and Ha' as they mingled through the market. Ha' had a lot of knowledge about healing plants and chose a few from different market vendors. When she stopped at a cart with strange-looking roots, Rickie was no longer there with them. The two looked around. With his blond hair, he was not hard to spot, and the Vietnamese made that obvious.

Stephen watched where the locals were staring and headed that way. Rick was at a fisherman's cart, but it wasn't the white fish on his mind, or in his line of sight. He was focused on the fisherman's beautiful young daughter, Lan. Before Stephen saw the girl, he called out to Rick, who held his one finger back toward the sound.

Rickie let Lan know that he would be back, but she did not understand English and Rickie's Vietnamese was limited. Rick signaled Stephen over and asked him to get Ha'.

The four of them surrounded the cart but were quickly swooshed away by the girl's father, who was trying to display his goods. They stepped aside respectfully as he busily arranged his fish. The man continued to peddle fish but still made sure his daughter was close to the cart.

After acquaintances were made, Ha' asked the father's permission if Lan could join them, and after an uncomfortable silence, he reluctantly agreed. Stephen purchased four fish to ensure peace with the man and overpaid handsomely. Finally, the transaction revealed the father's subtle smile, and he nodded his approval to his daughter. Rickie parted the crowd as they walked along, not wanting anyone near the two women.

Ha' had arranged a meeting with volunteers from Our Lady of La Vang-Da Nang, and they were more than happy to meet the two soldiers. Their chapel was small but welcoming, its door open to the dirt road.

Rickie was raised Catholic and, upon entering, immediately dipped his finger in the holy water in the vestibule. Lan and Ha' also blessed themselves with holy water, and the two proceeded to the altar, kneeling and beginning to pray at the front of the chapel.

Rick looked over at Stephen, who was staring at the stained glass. He knelt as he passed the altar, catching the attention of Lan, who was doing more chatting with Ha' than praying. He stood before the statue of the Blessed Mother and began to light candles, four in all. He then placed two dollars into a small metal black box below the candelabra and knelt to pray.

Stephen was about to join Rick when a sister of the parish came in. The light from the door filled the dimly lit church, and her black shoes tapped as she walked behind the praying soldiers. Kneeling and blessing herself at the altar, the woman walked over to Ha' and Lan.

Sister More was Albanian and was doing volunteer work in Vietnam. Without a moment of hesitation, she asked Ha' to follow her and directed the others to come too. Sister More wanted to introduce her guests to a few local villagers. Ha' had expressed to the sister earlier that week that the soldiers were interested in the art of living off the land in South Vietnam.

After introductions were made, Ha' and Lan left to accompany Sister More to a larger parish, while Stephen and Rick talked to the locals. They would learn about the edible plants in the area, venomous snakes to look out for, and other survival skills.

The villagers were old and chattered in their own language constantly. The men hadn't gone ten feet into the jungle when one pointed at Rick and mimicked drinking water. Next, he pointed at a banana tree clump growing out of a side of a bank. He then pointed at the base and made a chopping motion with his hand, not at an angle, but straight across.

The second old-timer pulled out a machete and, after four swings at the trunk, pushed the tree over. While he was chopping, the first man cut a three-inch piece of bamboo and cut the end of flat. He began mushing the inside of the banana tree trunk with the blunt bamboo and then carved out the pulp. They repeated this several times until a five-inch hole was visible.

A purplish liquid began seeping out, and the four of them watched as the banana roots pumped groundwater to the surface. After skimming the loose pulp off the top, each man bent over and sipped from the trunk. The water was sweet, and each nodded and agreed.

The two Vietnamese men then moved on to the second most popular way to find water, which was within the bamboo tree itself. The old man with the machete felt through some bamboo, looking for the moistest sapling. He chose a ten-inch-around bamboo tree and cut it just above a ring. Water began seeping around his blade, and they continued to show Rick and Steve what ones would be holding water just by sight.

Each time they saw an insect, they either trapped it or shooed it away, demonstrating which ones you could touch and which ones you could not. The nature trail they took was heavily traveled, but it did not matter. The jungle was like a tide waiting to return to the shore, except it moved much slower, eating everything in its wake.

They learned what plants were edible and about ones you could rub on your skin to keep the mosquitos away.

Hours seemed like minutes, and the four men climbed and crawled around the jungle floor. Stephen and Rick didn't remember the names of half the things they learned, but that wasn't important.

When they returned to the chapel, they found Ha' and Lan, who were able to translate the soldier's appreciation. Rickie handed one of them a yellow-handled pocketknife he had brought from home, and Steve handed over a twenty-dollar bill and a cigarette lighter. The two men accepted gratefully and told Ha' to tell them they were welcome to visit their village anytime. She thanked them, and the two old villagers walked away with purpose.

"That was so cool," Munro said, and Rickie agreed, smiling at his new friend.

Ha' informed the men that Lan needed to return to help her father but she would be coming to dinner tonight. The four returned to town, and Rickie offered to help Lan. Steve immediately agreed, knowing he and Ha' would have a chance to be alone.

"Tell her I want to help her dad and see the boat," Rick said to Ha'. She proceeded to translate to Lan, and the two went off.

Ha' smiled at Stephen, and the two ran back to their apartment.

"Wipe that smirk off your face, Pasakarnis. This isn't your Boy Scout sleepover. You two sticks are going out for three days. No radio contact till 03:00 two days from now, so listen up!" Captain Jennings said to Rick and Stephen.

He was a rigid leader, and for good reason, having literally ordered men to their death on missions similar to this one. He wanted the two to grasp the importance of the mission.

"Look, you two, I'm not going to be the one behind the trigger—I'm the one pushing the papers. And I don't look forward to sending letters to your mothers! You two do have mothers, don't you?" the captain said harshly.

"Yes, sir!" they said simultaneously.

"This is not some chump lieutenant we're talking about here. This animal likes little girls, and we want him dead!"

Stephen and Rick pored over the information. They were going to a camp just over the Vietnam border in Laos. Intel had this lieutenant working the villages in that area, and local girls were turning up mutilated.

They chose to be deployed at night. The two sat side by side as the H-6 skirted the treetops, entering Laos. The pilot saw a clearing, and instead of using ropes, he signaled a touch-and-go and the two gave their thumbs-up. The H-6 pilot dropped down like a coconut from a palm tree and powered up just before impact. Rick and Stephen hopped out and were in firing position before the skids left the tall grass. Two days from radio contact unless absolutely necessary.

With night vision and scopes, they began picking their way toward Thit Con, which translated to "child butcher." The two packed light and had convinced their commanding officer that they would survive off the land.

Safe in the borders of Laos, or so they thought, was a small regiment mix of NVA and PAVN soldiers. They would use the trails and tunnels to move in and out of the war zones, attacking squads and platoons who crossed their path. Anything and everything was fair game with this crew, and Thit Con was making a name for himself as being extraordinarily brutal.

They did not have a photo but were given the green light to tap any officer in that vicinity. Both Rangers decided they wanted Thit Con and were going to kill the right man. They nested in and took turns sleeping in four-hour shifts. Both of them tried their best not to break a branch or twig, and especially not to alarm the birds nesting above.

Stitching fresh ferns and grass in their gear and webbing, the Rangers began their morning looking for a trail or troop movement from their nest. When they decided to move, they did so quietly. Changing fresh vegetation to replicate the forest floor, the two moved like mist on the water, silent and slow.

Rick was out front when he held his fist up to stop. Heading toward them was a sizable enemy squad. Rick backed up and whispered, "Follow me." He darted to the right under the banana leaves, and Stephen followed. There was a rocky cliff ahead, and Rick made a snap judgment to hang beneath it to avoid detection.

Unaware of what they had just sprinted from, Stephen stopped and waited, searching through his 8-power scope back toward the trail. He tried focusing on possible ambush positions. His heart was pounding, causing his scope to move with its rhythm.

Gripping his rifle, he focused on his breathing. Stephen had learned to lower his heart rate years ago as a bow hunter, and he quickly regained composure. He began to study the forest. He could hear men talking, but in the distance, and the sounds were not gaining but fading, coming from the trail.

Steve signaled for Rick to climb up, and he worked into a high enough position to spot the group's leader. Searching the thick jungle for those gold bars with two stars, he could see tassels and a hat with a red rim. He focused on a spot where the forest opened, but taking a shot at that moment would be suicide, and he knew it.

When their leader entered his line of sight, Stephen had a subtle feeling in his gut, something he learned to pay attention to. He focused on his face and then his shoulders. It was a lieutenant, but he still would not shoot. He studied every face he could and tried counting how many men walked by in how many seconds, estimating a twenty- to twenty-five-man squad, one two-star and two one-star lieutenants. He also thought he saw at least four officer cadets.

Stephen signaled to Rick, trying to get him to come closer. Rick was looking down the scope of his M18, his finger near the trigger and his eyes scanning the men.

"Hey, they have no clue we're here, okay?" Stephen said.

Rick smiled. "I know. This would be an awesome ambush if we had ropes with us and if we could use our mines. They would race back."

Steve thought for a second. "Look, Rickie, maybe we can track these fuckers and find out what they are doing, maybe call in some hate. I got a good look at him, at his face. I got a feeling it's him."

"What do you mean a feeling?" Rick asked.

Stephen just looked at him. "An 'I was going to squeeze one off' kind of feeling, okay? I don't know, I think it's him."

319

"Okay, I like that idea. Plus we don't have enough rope."

The two Rangers caught up with the squad as they moved freely through the forest back toward Vietnam and, according to Rick, right to Hill 140.

"We've got sixteen hours before they are expecting contact, Rick. Let's keep going till they hold up or are close enough to bomb."

Rick knew that they had to be under two miles of the border, or whatever side of a stream or creek they declared their border, before they could release heavy artillery. They were just about two hours into tracking when Stephen and Rick heard the first scream.

"Shit, that sounded like a woman!" Stephen said.

The two hustled closer. They had about three hours until it became dark, and they needed to move without attracting attention.

Stephen held back when he saw a grass roof ahead in the trees. He could hear some arguing, but nothing like the piercing screams he had heard earlier. "We need to move around toward the east to get on top of them. That way, if we need to take a shot in the morning, we can."

Rick agreed. They were five hundred meters behind the hut, working their way east, when they stopped to listen.

"What are you thinking, Rick?"

"I think they are holding up here for the night. Think they must use this as a base, because it's about three clicks from the border."

"Exactly. I think if this is our guy, he won't be butchering anyone here, plus I saw what looked like cadet insignias for sure," Stephen remarked.

"Okay, let's get ready for the morning. We can make our call at 03:00."

"Rick, we are way out on a hunch, man, but I want this guy. Set all your claymores, and let's take these guys out."

They stopped one more time to study their map. While they tried to determine what their best shooting position would be, a scream of a woman froze them. It turned out to be only a pig, and the troop was partaking with the villagers, getting ready to roast it.

The two Rangers moved below the village and crossed the main trail leading to fields yielding pineapples and other fruits. Rick moved first, and Stephen followed. There was a knoll across from the main house, and the two set up their post. Before dark, they were able to count fourteen villagers, including the children.

As nighttime fell, Stephen and Rick relaxed and adapted to the jungle. They could speak with less caution.

"Rich, it's party time over there."

"I smell that pig cooking," Rick said.

"You want to go crash their party?" asked Stephen, half-joking.

"Yes, let's take a closer look," Rick decided.

The two men felt safe under the cover of night. The village had no watchdogs that they could see or hear, and unless there were roving sentries, they felt like they could move with ease.

As they crept closer, they could see the blue smoke from the roasting pig. It was cooking on a piece of grated metal fence under a worn old pit.

Stephen crept within a yard of the jungle's edge. He studied the faces as best as he could, aware his night vision goggles could possibly reflect light in the darkness.

Moving back to Rick, he whispered, "Move east around the first hut."

Rick took a wide path, but Stephen crept in close. Hearing a voice, he thought he understood it say, "He has come for my daughter."

Stephen paused, wanting to clear his head. Between all the sounds of the jungle and the chatter, he needed to focus. Deciding to move closer, he could clearly hear a man speaking, and he sounded angry.

Creeping even closer, Stephen could see a villager talking to one of the soldiers. He watched and listened, noticing a few more villagers surround the man. One said meekly, "Help us." He watched as two more came and pulled the others away.

Rick was waiting on the east side of the camp. He couldn't see his companion but was giving him time before he moved. He could hear what he thought was weeping close by.

Stephen was a few meters from the hut and could now clearly hear a woman crying. She was most likely being offered up by her father. *This could have been Ha',* he thought. He took a few slow breaths and allowed the sounds of the jungle to reenter his mind, realizing he had to connect with Rick and draw up a plan.

"Rick, let's get this right. Once I say 'Hound Dog, we have a puppy,' we'll be committed to move, agreed?"

"Anything you say, Stevie." And they both laughed nervously.

"Hey, I'm serious, Rick. I know we can just kill them all, but the villagers, man," Stephen said.

"They were joking and feeding this asshole, Stevie. Fuck them!"

Both took a moment to themselves, knowing very well that it could be one of their last.

"Look, let's think about this, okay? I don't care if this is Thit Con or not. If this guy wants to rape those little girls, I am going to kill the motherfucker," Stephen said, gravely serious.

"Got it. How you plan on doing it?" Rick asked.

Stephen laid out his plan. Rick was to lay a series of claymores along their escape route, and he was going to either shoot or stab Thit Con.

Stephen had only practiced hand-to-hand combat training, but he headed toward his target with fierce determination. Twice Rick had to tug on his pant leg, telling him to slow down.

Stephen paused. "Okay," he whispered, "okay, there's a single guard on this hut. I will give you three minutes to get ready."

He was approaching the mission as if he were back at home, hunting whitetail. He looked back, and after Rick gave him the thumbs-up, he slithered back into the ferns.

Rick prepared for the worst. He understood that once he heard the .45, if Stephen wasn't back in thirty seconds, it was up to him to smoke the place out and call in the hate.

Stephen collected himself, and after doing a final check, he slid open his .45 and saw the brass. Placing it back in the holster, he then took out his Ka-Bar and began moving toward his unsuspecting prey.

While inching closer, Stephen clearly heard a moan and then some sobbing, followed by what sounded like slapping, coming from the hut. The guard stayed put through all the noise, his back against the wall, which ended up being his final mistake.

Stephen walked up behind the NVA soldier standing guard, covering his mouth while simultaneously stabbing his liver, then immediately slitting his throat. With haste he dragged his quivering, desperate body into the jungle.

Moving quickly now, Stephen ran back to the hut and burst through the door. He startled the lieutenant so badly that the man only had time to put his hand up in a stopping gesture before Stephen drove his blade deep into the soldier's shallow ribs, and then again through his heart.

Thit Con lunged in final desperation. Looking back at the Vietnamese girl trembling in the corner, Stephen grabbed the forehead of the rapist and began sawing off his head. His blade sliced Con's windpipe, causing a hollow, gargled scream. Cutting around, he struck his spine with the blade and it popped off with pressure.

Stephen closed his eyes momentarily, realizing what he had just done. His left hand was still gripping the scalp of Thit Con, or whoever he had just murdered. What brought him back to the moment was the sound of what he thought was gushing blood hitting the floor when, in fact, it was the young girl urinating from fear.

Stephen grabbed a blanket, wrapped up the severed head, and sprinted out the door. He had the .45 and was ready to fire, but there were no targets, no one in pursuit.

Rick was staring through his scope, trying to determine what was running toward him.

Steve stopped to check for anyone who might be trailing him, but his heart was pounding so loudly he couldn't hear anything else. He tried to breathe deep, but there was too much adrenaline pumping through his body. He needed to get back to Rick.

"What the fuck is in the bag, Stevie?" Rick screamed once he finally recognized it was his comrade coming toward him.

"Well, we need to identify this scumbag, so here ya go!" Stephen yelled back.

"Couldn't you just take a picture?" Rick bellowed sarcastically.

"If you want to photo him now, motherfucker, and leave it here on a fucking stick, that's fine with me!" Stephen said harshly, distraught from his ordeal.

"No, no, we'll hump it back!" Rick said.

Stephen and Rick waited by the river's edge for extraction. At 03:00, they had broken the silence and called it in. Nyhan sent two Swifts for extraction, and they put on quite a show for the boys, coming in at high speed with a lot of evasive maneuvers.

The two finally had a chance to talk while heading back to the flotilla. Rick began joking around, trying to make light of the scene they had just left. Stephen was only thinking of Ha'.

"Rickie," Stephen said seriously, "we've got to get out of this place, man. I'm taking Ha', and I'm getting the fuck out!"

"We've still got six months to go, Stevie."

"Yeah, well, I can't be sneaking up and cutting off dudes' fucking heads anymore, okay? That ain't me. I want to get back on these boats, man. These are our homes. This is so fucked up."

Stephen put his head between his knees as they roared down the canal. Rick just hung his hand on his shoulder.

"Stevie, let's go take the girls out fishing on Lan's father's boat. I'll set it up, man. We'll kill 'em!"

"Sounds good, and after that, I'm going to ask Nyhan if we can get a PBR or Swifty patrol. I want to stay out of the jungle, man. Fuck the jungle!" Stephen replied.

Rick knew his friend was serious, but also knew that a transfer now would be difficult.

Almost Famous

Stephen pulled his head out from under the Detroit Diesel. In his hand were chunks of bone and flesh, a piece of a skull with some hair still attached to it. "That was what was clogging one of the bilge pumps," he said out loud.

Munro's spine stiffened when he first grabbed the clog, his mind instantly returning to Thit Con's skull. Knowing he cut the head off the beast did not help in him lying low. Word had been out, and people were calling him King David.

The 24 had been shot up, and it needed a week or more in dry dock, but instead, Stephen had a mere four days to get her combat ready. Nyhan pulled a few strings, and out of an actualized desperation for crewmen late in the war, he was able to call a few men back for a large strike force scheduled later this month. Every Navy boat with a motor had become vital.

After the murder of Thit Con, Stephen never had to return back to his company. Rick had gone back to collect their personals and say their goodbyes. Their comrades had asked about Thit Con and the growingly infamous King David, but Rick simply said, "Thit Con lost his head, and Munro, he just lost his love for the jungle."

Nyhan sent the 24 to two crewmen returning from rehabilitation in Saigon. Scotty Brailey and Shedrick Jones. Shedrick had been a big brother from Saint Thomas but had gotten caught up in the war for political reasons. Somehow, he ended up becoming a citizen to join the service.

During combat, he had taken a round through his upper back, but he was naturally built so thick and strong it hardly slowed him down. Shed's platoon had been ambushed outside a tiny village near

Sambour on the Mekong River. Mortar fire began raining down, and half of the platoon was split. Shedrick had found himself in a group of seven men, four of them wounded. They luckily had a radio and were told to move to the river for extraction at Delta 6.

Shedrick fought his way back to the Mekong while carrying two of his fellow Marines. As big of a target as he was, he had managed to stay small while fighting, but not when he was carrying two wounded soldiers. While humping the two back to a waiting Swift Boat, he was shot in the back. The bullet lodged in his right pectoral. Bleeding from his side and in shock, he went back for the last Marine and pulled himself into the Swift Boat. He received a Purple Heart and a Silver Star and a special gift from CUF.

Ready Your Guns

The Mekong Delta was buzzing with American activity, and it was obvious to the enemy there was something brewing.

Stephen inspected a few of the newer PBRs and revised his side rails for RPGs. "It looks like we could use the porcelain tiles tied into our cargo net camo," he told Shed.

Shed had the motors tuned for power and took over sewing the net. "Scotty, get me some more tiles, boy."

"Who you calling *boy*? You see a boy around here, you kick him in the ass!" Rick replied. "And my name ain't Scotty, it's Rick."

Shed didn't know what to think. He thought Scotty was attempting to make a very unfunny joke. "Scotty, don't fuck with me right now. I'm in no mood."

"Who is Scotty, and who the fuck are you?" Rick said, growing angry.

Rick dropped his bag and squared off. Shedrick stood up and stepped toward Rick. "You sure you want to dance, boy?"

Scotty was returning from the supply room with more tiles when he saw himself on the deck of the 24. Bewildered, he yelled out, "Hey, Shed!"

Shedrick looked over to see who he thought was Scotty heading toward the 24 with a box full of tiles. Both Shed and Rick looked at Scott and back at each other.

"What the fuck, man! Dat boy could be your twin brada, your twin brada!" Shed said, shocked.

Rick just stood there staring at Scotty.

Scott placed the crate down and stuck his hand out. "Hey, man, I think we must be related or something."

Rick didn't say a word at first. As the ideas flowed in, he began, "Scott, when is your birthday?"

"August 23, '48," Scott answered.

Rick continued, "Mine is July 14, 1947. Where did your father grow up?"

"Near Redding, California," Scotty said.

"Where is he now?" Rick asked.

"He was killed in action in the Pacific. I never met him," Scotty replied.

Rick sat down on the starboard torpedo tube. "Okay, so we definitely look alike but grew up in two different parts of the country, are born a year apart, and both have fathers who were killed in action."

"Weird," they both said in unison.

"No. What's weird is the fact that you two look just like that dude Butler. Rick, I told you about him. Talk to anyone in my old crew and they would swear you were both Butler. You guys either have some crazy dominant ancestral gene or you are fucking aliens," Stephen said.

"Hey, I don't care if you are long-lost brothas. Maybe your mama only wanted one and one of you and the other two were adopted out. I don't care either way. You guys better fix the nets and tie in these tiles. We are heading in for something awful, man. I can feel it," Shed said.

Things were too hectic for them to care why Rick, Butler, and now Scotty looked like they could be triplets. Stephen could see the issue of the three's resemblance was bothering Rick. In an attempt to differentiate himself, he came back from supply with freshly dyed purple hair, having popped a smoke can in a barrel and mixed it with a little water and soap.

"Purple, Rick? Really? What the fuck is Nyhan going to think if one of his guys has purple hair?" Stephen was pissed; all he wanted was this tour to be over and he could be with Ha'.

Lan and Ha' waited patiently for word from their boys. Stephen had every intention of marrying Ha' and taking her home. His thoughts of cutting the heads off the enemy were overpowered by his visions of Ha'. He would often sit with his eyes closed tightly, trying to squeeze her image to the foreground. He was constantly opening his wallet and pulling out her picture. He'd look at it briefly, slip it back in, and repeat every few hours.

The four worked hard to ready the 24 and gather the sea trial before the convoy left.

Shed called the men together. "Look, man, respectfully. This means you too, Captain." He pulled out an evenly rolled joint and fired it up. Shed took two slow pulls and sniffed up the trailings. Passing it to Rick, he exhaled and continued, "Captain, man, we're going upriver and I need to know if you plan on coming back."

Rick looked over at Stephen and passed the joint. He then looked over at Scotty, trying to reassure him. "Shedrick, what's the problem? It's your captain, Virgil Munro, and Richie P. We're killers, Shed, killers."

Shed replied, sounding grave, "This boat has not been tested. We have not been tested."

Stephen passed Shed his joint. "Shed, I get it," he said, holding in his last hit, "but I plan on making it through, okay? No man left behind." Stephen leaned in and pulled his crew in tight. "Look, guys, I'm okay. I will gladly cut my enemy in half with the .50 or that fucking Mini. Yes, I still think about that creep I killed, but not as much. Man, I tell you, I pray constantly for the memory of it to pass, okay? No worries." He spoke in a mocking fashion.

"Look, boys," Scotty said. "We're going to be fine as long as we stay cool, okay? We're not going to be on the tip of any spear."

"Shed, talk to me. Where is that smoke coming from?" Stephen asked.

Shedrick emerged from belowdecks. "Cap, we just got to burn the grease and oil off her. How's her temp?"

"Ah, 185 to 87," Stephen answered his crewman.

"Okay, let's put it down now." Stephen took his PBR along the practice route and let his crew squeeze of their rounds accordingly. He went over the approach in finite detail and made sure his crew was ready to engage. He drove the 24 nose first at 40 knots, fishtailing toward the bank. At two hundred yards out, Scotty opened up on the twin .50s. Stephen wanted a solid four count, and as he mentally hit three, he began to turn hard, starboard.

Rick lit everything up he could see with his Mini, and as Stephen hit another three, he pulled down and handed over the wheel, holding another .90. Shedrick opened up on the rear .50, and Stephen was able to start the mortar rounds before Shed finished. He grabbed two motors and moved behind the tube. "Five hundred! Five hundred yards!" Stephen yelled, and Shed started walking mortars all over the shore, making precise adjustments at 35 knots.

Stephen didn't know there were eyes on him, and before he finished his second pass, Colonel Duck Harris had already made up his mind about his crew. "Get me that captain. Who is this hot shot?"

Nyhan didn't know what to say. He was about to change the subject when Nyhan's aide said, "Oh, that's King David," causing Harris to look excitedly at Nyhan.

"We could use his experience for our boys up front. Plus, the boy's almost famous," the colonel stated.

Nyhan was stuck between a rock and a hard place, but he had hundreds of kids to protect. "I'll have him bring her in, sir." Nyhan rolled his cigar and bit down hard on it. *Kid better not screw his shot up,* he thought to himself.

Tip of the Spear
Call Me Virgil!

"Look, you assholes, you're not helping matters by egging Charlie on." Nyhan seldom addressed his men in pleasantries. "Truth is, I like the name King David, the nickname Munro has acquired, but we don't need to advertise, so refer to him as Virgil, got it?"

Nyhan stepped back as the briefing officer took over. The eyes were shifting from Stephen and his crew to the officer laying out the broad view, brining the fight to the enemy, push through the mud, etc. Stephen knew his crew was in for it, and he was determined to prove them wrong.

Nyhan finished up. "Okay, men, your captain's meeting will be at 04:00, so don't sleep in!"

Lieutenant Boswel, a soldier with below-average intelligence from the naval academy, laid out the attack-and-deployment plan. His redundant circling of the landing areas was causing Stephen to grit his teeth, and he even let out a low growl.

Boswel stopped midsentence. "Something wrong, Captain?"

Stephen lightly shook his head and spoke steadily. "I wouldn't know where to begin." And the room erupted in laughter.

"Some objection to the plan, gentlemen?" Boswel asked.

Captain Bishop of the 32 spoke up. "No disrespect, Lieutenant, but I see a problem, sir."

Bishop went on to explain how deploying in a bottleneck could expose them to a devastating attack. Stephen chimed in, explaining an approach they had used where they leapfrogged up and back, covering more possible attack routes, with two PBRs and a Swift for the leap.

"Lieutenant, I'm taking ten men upriver ahead of the main invasion, then I can run motor and gunfire, covering them as they land. That's a three-boat minimum, Lieutenant!" Stephen finished.

Bishop looked over and nodded. "I'll take the 15. Shit, they stuck me in the rear because my gunner dropped acid last week and dived naked off the bow. Otherwise, I'd be in the front wave."

Lieutenant Boswel knew they were correct, and felt the rest of the men in the room were in their favor. "Okay, you guys, you three figure out your approach, but know this: we're hitting that shoreline at 18:00 and we cannot come upriver after you until it's over."

Wright, Bishop, and Munro studied the river through aerial photos.

"Okay, listen up, I'm not going hells bells in and risking these guys. I figure we leapfrog up, stage, and then I'll head up slowly with you two at my 6 a half-click back," Stephen stated. "I will run through the light fire and continue to target at, say, 10 to 12 knots."

Bishop and Wright looked at Stephen and nodded. Boswel looked over at the three as he was going over the main invasion.

"Lieutenant, we're out! See you, gentlemen, this evening, and don't forget the dope and beer!" Munro never looked back. He stopped at the end of the gangplank that connected the mulberry. "Okay, guys, I want to thank you back there. I seriously appreciate it."

"No problem, Virgil," Bishop said.

"Yeah, same here," Wright added. "I've got to collect my packages but will meet you at marker 6."

Bishop signaled with his red light, and Wright took the lead.

The jungle was quiet, and the clear late-night sky began to give way to dawn. Huddled below the 24 was a six-man observation squad who all could be CIA mercs for all they knew. They wore no badges, nothing to determine them from any branch of service. Three of them had converted Stonners, and one a pump .40-millimeter.

"That's the biggest fucking shotgun I ever saw!" Rick yelled to Shed.

"These guys give me the creeps, Captain," Shed said over the motors.

"I hear that, my man. The sooner we get these guys off the 24, the better," Stephen commented.

"Deuce Four, Deuce Four...," the radio crackled. "Deuce Four, this is Two Step. I repeat, this is Two Step."

Shed was already heading to the mic. "Two Step, Two Step, copy, over."

Two Step was a rover, a hit squad who operated in total radio silence unless absolutely necessary.

"We could use some dope," the Two Step crewman said again.

"Roger!" Shed said, chuckling. He called the 32 and relayed the message.

Bishop took over, and the 15 hopped ahead. He eased his 32 analog side along dark bank. He was relieved that he was working with guys who knew their stuff. The two who helped unload the 32 treated the crew like lepers; they didn't want any stink on them but then thanked them exceedingly when they finished.

"You cats be safe now. We're out of ammo 'cause Charlie has been busy. Watch your 6 up there," one of them said.

Stephen eased the 24 along the overhang and nosed her into the steep bank.

"Nice knowing ya," Rick said as the men jumped past his gun. Scotty's .50s were useless, so he was behind the Captain's 12-gauge.

The six men disappeared into the cover, and Stephen gave them an uneasy five minutes to clear the zone before he eased the 24 from the bank. Before he could hit the throttles, he heard small-arms fire downriver.

"The 15 is in it, boys!" Rick yelled.

The crew was already running on adrenaline, and when they hit the bend, Scotty saw the tracers and bumped another ounce. He opened up with his twin .50s and was spot-on. By the time Rick fired up his Mini, Shed had launched his first motor, and as he was readjusting, he heard his captain yell, "Smoke! Pop some, smoke, Shed! Hit the bank with smoke!"

Stephen saw the 15 dead in the water and thought the worst. "Rickie, get in the 15 and I'll block for you!" He sped the 24's nose toward the 15 and then swung broadside. When he pounded reverse, Rick did not hesitate. He jumped off the port side and slipped on a pool of blood, disappearing briefly.

Scotty was reloading the .50s, and Shed was now on his own gun with a case of HE motor rounds ready. Rick took a quick look around before he hit the throttle, and it didn't look good. Captain Wright was slumped below, and his gunner's head was lying beside him. Two men were on the deck, both holding their wounds.

"We gotta go, Stevie!" And Rick punched it.

They called the 32 and told them their situation. "We're rolling hot past the main body and to the med ship."

Bishop took up their 6, and they slowed to have his radioman, Jessy Drain, jump on and begin triage. When the three hit the Mekong, they were at 32 knots each in a staggered formation.

"We've got wounded. We're not staying!" was all Munro said when he called his radio signal at the invasion forward command.

Trailing the force was a med ship with what they called killer corpsmen on board. The USS *Kirk 1087* was a destroyer that was later converted to a freight class for the invasion. They flew the red cross, and their gunners could only return fire, so they were among the best. They outfitted her with a twenty-millimeter rapid-fire cannon.

The *Kirk* had a horizontal dock they lowered with forward stern winches. It was designed to operate while at minimum steering speed, 5-plus knots. It wasn't the ship itself that made them special, although they designed it to serve as a forward medical rescue ship with some innovative features.

On board were a team of field corpsman, first turned surgeons, then turned soldiers, and now they were a special medical insurgency outfit. Getting closer to the action and closer to their patients, between the helicopters and the high-speed rescue ships, soldiers were being treated at record time.

Rick swung the starboard side of the 15 along the *Kirk*'s portable dock. He timed its speed but was having trouble with the wake. The *Kirk* was traveling at over 8 knots, but slowing. Two Navy men were being lowered in a basket, both with their feet hanging over, the flexible dock ten feet below.

"Bowline!" yelled the corpsman as he jumped on the dock. Rick threw him the line and went back to the wheel. Jason from the 32 threw him the stern and immediately addressed the corpsman.

Rick kept the 15 consistent with the *Kirk* while they transported the captain and crew onto the dock, now pushing water just under 5 knots. He and Jessy thanked the two who were busy hoisting the captain on board.

Jessy helped with the fallen soldiers, untied the stern, and headed for the bowline when he was tossed by the wake and was nearly pinned between the dock and the 15. "Damn, man, we've got to get off this bitch before she kills us too."

Rick was ordered to bring the 15 back into action. The 24 was down one man but had nothing to complain about. Jessy was trying to get the blood, which was now dry, off the gun action. Rick was attempting to clean off the rear deck, blasting his raw water pump while steering for the convoy. He readied his station.

"How's that .50, Jessy?"

"I think I'm good, Cap!" he replied. "We're coming up on that Swift, blown in two at the channel. Crack a few when we pass!"

Three hundred yards out, a rusty Swift Boat was now being used as a river marker. Four years earlier, she was blown in two by a mine. Jessy opened up on the .50, thumping the hull, which made a slapping noise as rounds smashed into the water. "Okay, take the helm, I got to try my .50."

Jessy sped away from the wreck, and Rick opened up with a 10 Shot Spirit. He could hear the *slap slap slap* and felt good about his weapon. He cleared it and asked, "Jessy, you got any smoke?"

Rick and the 15 joined the Amphibious Ready Group's Special Landing Force, and with them, a Marine Medium Helicopter Squad equipped with twenty-four UH34s and its crew. This mobile strike force was lethal, and combined with aerial and naval bombardment, their fearless enemy could only get smaller in their holes until it was over.

Rick staged on the right shoreline flank of the fleet, heading straight to Da Nang Bay, Stephen and the 24 a quarter mile to his east. The show of force kept the enemy under cover. They were no match for the strike force guns, and drawing the enemy in was their objective.

The landing was uneventful as the small armrest staged in what they considered a secure area. Their radios were tuned to jungle chatter, and they could hear sporadic gunfire.

At 08:00, the first call came out. "Deliver a surgeon." Sergeant Huxley was hit by a mortar round just below his vest. The corpsmen could not stop but slowed the bleeding. The 24 eased their PBR into the soft bank. "We're down one."

Stephen swung the 24 port side to the *Kirk*, where Dr. Terry Flynn was waiting, M16 and all. As soon as his feet hit the deck, the 24 powered upriver. Staring upriver, he was shouting over the engines his instructions to the crew. To Scotty he shouted, "Better sharpen the spear," and Scotty smiled back.

Shed was checking his engines and emerged slowly before Flynn. "This big guy going in with me?"

Like a pile of ice melted by fire, Stephen's spine twisted when he realized Rick was not on board, but he had to join Dr. Flynn in the action. Grabbing the 12-gauge, he headed below and emerged with a jungle camo shirt and face paint. "Scotty, Shed, your call. Move her off the bank if you think it's too hot!"

Stephen hit the trail loaded for war, with Flynn crouched several yards ahead. Stephen's brain was used to washing out the white noise of the engines, but on the trail the alarm calls from the canopy birds seemed amplified. Flynn moved his hands forward, and the two jumped off. Shed kept the 24 on the shore while Scotty scanned the river.

Five minutes hadn't gone by when all hell broke loose. Mortar rounds began raining down on the 24. Shed hit the throttles and blew a mud wake on the jungle's edge. Scotty, looking back, could see rounds exploding on his captain's estimated position. Shed was on the mic, calling, "Two Step, Two Step, come in, over!" Fortunately, they all had their ears on.

Shed told them he needed them as soon as possible, adding, "Kill, kill." Shed raced the 24 back to the rendezvous shore, scanning for Two Step. Red smoke popped at their stern, and Shed hit reverse and jumped his own wake.

After radioing in command, he was minutes ahead of their right decision. Two Step was a seven-man hit squad who used speed and stealth to battle and harass their enemy. When they pulled each other from the brown-foamed water, Scotty looked each one over. He moved some forward and helped stow their gear.

"They got Doc Flynn?" one asked.

"No. Well, I hope not," Shed replied.

"They were getting pounded," another said.

"How many?" Shed asked the soldier.

"Two. Virgil, captain of the 24, and the doc," he replied.

Shed pulled out and powered up the 24. The extra 1,600 pounds barely made a difference, and he felt proud to be taking her back into the fight.

"Who's your gunner?" one of the men asked.

Shed pointed at Scotty. "That's Scotty."

"Is he cool?"

"Yeah, man, he's cool," Shed replied.

Stephen and Doc Flynn slipped through the jungle and away from the sound of the mortar rounds, heading in the direction of Hill 227 and the wounded. When they came upon the river, Stephen was back on the radio.

"Big Deuce, Big Deuce, this is Band-Aid," Stephen said.

Shed tuned in his radio and slowed to 5 knots. "Band-Aid, you whole?" he asked in his hard accent.

"Yeah, we're five miles out," Stephen said over the radio.

"I am sending in Two Step. Repeat, look for Two Step," Shed said.

Stephen rubbed the back of his hand. He was sure he and the doc could get to the extraction without help. "That's a negative. Repeat, no room to dance."

Shed looked at the four men huddled below, hanging on every word.

"Hey, Shed!" Scotty yelled. "Let's take these boys for a bone cruise. Virgil knows what the fuck he's doing."

"Yeah, man, we aren't safe here for sure," Shed replied.

Stephen and Flynn reached the checkpoint and the wounded. Doc dived in to help, and Stephen took a defensive position above the wounded and scanned the hillside.

"That's twice," Munro yelled, "ahead in the grass, one hundred or more yards out. Do you have an SVA in your squad wearing coolies?"

Stephen was now shouldering his M16 and looking to fire. The first round buzzed by his right ear, dropping him to a kneeling position. Following their tracers, Stephen began firing his bursts into the jungle. The doc was yelling to keep the rounds off him and the wounded when two of the captain's men were cut down. The NVA dropped down in their initial attack and set up their MKP, training it on the checkpoint.

"Doc, cover me!" Stephen slung his M16 and pulled out his pump. The front-grip knurls felt familiar through his beating fingertips.

The doc moved into a firing position, and Stephen waited for him to crack a round. Looking over his shoulder, he moved through the grass to flank them. When Doc Flynn opened up, the MKP was now joined by an MHG heavy machine gun.

Doc looked back at the captain and his lieutenant, who were struggling to call in a strike. His forces were spred out and half-pinned down. Doc peered over the berm, keeping him from heaven. He saw Stephen make the tree line. Doc knew it was suicide, but he felt a surge run through his body, and he tried to hold back the explosion. Like a cannon, he shot from the berm, firing and running.

As if perfectly timed, Stephen was within twenty yards of both guns and had three rounds stuffed in his mouth. When they shifted fire, he charged the emplacement. Blessed and bewildered, Stephen's first shot with the 00 buck killed the gunner and the loader. He then killed the two riflemen with two more blasts and pumped two rounds on the crew of the MGH who were taking cover. Doc started pouring on the fire and was joined in by the lieutenant.

Stephen spit his rounds in his hand and loaded, screaming, "Doc, I'm gonna kill those fuckers!" He was moving and loading.

"Hold your fire!" yelled Doc.

Two rifle shots rang out away from Doc's position. He could hear some NVA calling out an order, and then one grenade after the other began raining down, all thrown from Stephen. When the third one went off, he sprang toward the gun, blasting the alive, wounded, and dead indiscriminately. What the grenades didn't kill, he did.

Slumped over his gun was a lieutenant with his guts blown out. Stephen grabbed his thick black hair and pulled his head up, blood and drool bubbling from mouth. Stephen threw him over violently and reloaded his 12-gauge.

"Doc, you good?"

"Yeah, Virgil, we're good."

Stephen was running back through the grass. He dived over the berm and rolled into the lieutenant. "Doc, you've got to get some guys on your left flank, or you're going to be overrun."

"Already on it, Captain." Doc arranged two-litter barrels and secured his patients. "Virgil, lead the way."

Scotty rolled up two joints and lit them both at once. Passing them in two directions, he pulled himself over the awning and dropped on the deck. "Shed, I'm breaking out some mortars. Which one of you guys has M2 training?"

The crew from the 24 ran through the armament and put together a makeshift crew. Shed was on his radio, trying to raise the 38. Rick used his charm to convince the commanding officer that he'd be able to assist with the new crew.

The two boats merged out into the delta.

"Hey, flick me dat bone, mon," Rick said, his best imperson-ation of Shed.

The new guys laughed as they tied the 38 starboard side, until Rick pulled up closer. Like a fan at a tennis match, all seven of the men scanned Rick and then turned to Scotty.

"What the fuck?" one of them said, looking a bit more freaked out than he should.

"No, we're not brothers," Rick said sharply.

The men stared at Rick for a moment before one of them spoke, but as he began, a wave crashed between the two PBRs, splashing them all. Wiping his face, he looked back at Rick. "It's not that you look alike, it's that you both look just like our commanding officer!"

Rick looked at Scotty, who must have felt as confused as the rest of them, then changed the subject entirely. "Okay, listen up. You guys know what you're good at. Split up, three with Scotty and Jessy on the 38, the rest with me." Pulling away, Rick nodded over to Scotty, who was moving to the forward gun.

The two best point men were known as Heckle and Jeckle; one had an M14 and the other a Winchester Model 70.

"Going deer hunting, troop?" Rick said over the roar of his diesels.

Heckle looked over. "You going to light up that stick or keep telling jokes?"

Doc followed Stephen downhill to the river. Weasels and B-58 Hustlers tore up the sky while scorching the earth with napalm and five-hundred-pounders. Stephen signaled Doc to take position at the edge and pop smoke, while he headed back to cover the rear. Doc popped his smoke, and the 38 swooped in. The soldiers who carried their lieutenant to safety looked over the crew of the 38 and thanked them.

Stephen worked his way back to the 38 and swung himself on board. "Get straight back to your checkpoint, boys," he said, taking over the helm for Rick.

Doc was setting up plasma as the boys of Two Step took orders to ready the stern for the wounded transfer to the *Kirk*. After the heavy bombing, the main push was halted.

Rick was trying to raise the Seawolf. "TJ, TJ, come in, over."

"What's up, Rick?"

"We are," he replied. "Come pick me up."

Richie and TJ had become good friends while serving. TJ had the best Thai stick connection but needed Rick to sweet-talk the villagers into docking their vessel.

"They want a pig this time, Rick," TJ proclaimed.

"Damn." Rick started scrambling.

"Deuce Four, Deuce Four," Shed was saying over the mic.

"Shed, you see the bank all tore up just east of you?"

"What you mean 'tore up,' man? Da whole hillside is roasted!"

"No, not from war, from pigs," Rick replied.

"Pigs?" Shed asked, confused.

Scotty overheard the conversation. "If we need a pig, then we need a pig!"

"Roger, 38. We'll take a look." And Shed got off the radio.

The remaining four men of Two Step knew the men of the 24 were looking to barter, and one of them, with a heavy Midwestern accent, spoke up. "Y'all want a pig? Half a click from where you grabbed us, there's a whole herd of them."

"You boys think you can get a pig for our man Rick?" Shed asked.

The four just smiled and said simultaneously, "Guaranteed!" before they all broke out in laughter.

"Okay, we'll go, but no joking around!" Shed said.

Shed raced the 24 back near the extraction point downriver.

"Okay, let those two off here and we will set up just up there," the Midwesterner said, pointing to a small peninsula.

Shed did what he was told and took the 24 around the point.

"Shut her off and wait."

"Wait for what?" Shed had no sooner asked than he heard a pig squeal, and it was heading their way.

"They've got to get them out on that point."

Shed then heard three shots and a lot of squealing, and out of the bush emerged the four men and three dead pigs. He was more than impressed and immediately got in touch with Rick.

"We eating good tonight, man," Shed said.

"Hey, they're not for us," Rick replied.

"Yeah, man, one for you and two for me!"

All the guys on the boat broke out in laughter.

"Awesome," Rich said, and he started calling out a rally point.

He had the pig in a body bag when TJ brought the Seawolf over to meet him. They lowered the basket like they were rescuing a soldier. Rick flipped the hog off his shoulder and followed it into the basket.

"Every guy wanted them to dredge, Rick," Shed was pleading with the pilot.

"What about the pig?" the pilot responded.

"We've got it wrapped in a body bag, man."

With that, the pilot gained speed but lost altitude, causing the basket to hit and start plowing water. Rick was being dredged like an oyster. The crewmen of the 38 and 24 were both hysterical as Rick managed to collect himself, intent on flipping them all off.

After gaining his composure, Rick immediately started dressing the pig. As the Wolf dropped over the rise, he said, "Tell the pilot to drop just behind that hill."

"He knows," TJ said. "Just be cool, Rick, be cool."

Rick jumped out of the plane and ran to the village elder. He had a few cans of rations and revealed the pig last. Smiles broke out on all the villagers' faces, and the elder signaled for his courier. She was a wiry Vietnamese girl with long legs and wearing a bulging native bag. She handed the bag to her elder and returned to the hut, the smell of marijuana permeating behind her.

The elder sniffed the bag and smiled proudly, then handed it to Rick. For a fleeting moment, Rick nervously wondered if there were explosives in the satchel, but it was dry bud, nothing more. He opened the bag and, without showing disrespect, dug his hand in slowly and removed an enormous bud.

As he ran back to the aircraft, TJ was waiting in the doorway. "We good, Rick?"

Rick handed him the satchel. "You tell me!"

TJ wasted no time stuffing a pipe. He offered up a hit to the pilot, but he refused. "I'll catch you later!" he yelled, waving his hand low and no.

Rick took a few deep pulls and enjoyed the short ride back to the 24. They had a plan to meet later and move some, but with the apparent victory on Hill 217, there was a party to be had.

Rick was on the horn while Shed and Scotty we're making arrangements for their celebration. Nyhan ordered his boats back to the flotilla, and the plans were set. That day, there were four killed in action and twelve wounded. Didn't seem like a victory, but in a four-hundred-man assault squad, they were impressive numbers.

That evening, the pigs were almost finished. The crews were all gathered on the deck, awaiting word from Commander Nyhan. When he emerged, there was a sharp salute given.

Nyhan paused on the top step, and grabbing the railing, he leaned forward. "Men, you performed brilliantly today. Under the watchful eye of our commanders, you performed above and beyond, and because of that, I won't ask you where you got the pigs!"

Laughter broke out among all the crewmen.

"I want to thank you personally for that. I am particularly interested in hearing about our surgeon immersion and how it went. Word is that two of my boys will be receiving the Silver Star."

Chatter and some grumbling broke out as to who it could be. Stephen didn't even consider what he had done to be heroic, just something that needed to be done, and Doc Flynn felt the same.

That was not so for one of Flynn's counterparts, Dr. James Smalls. Dr. Smalls put the *C* in *cocky*, and he rubbed a lot of guys the wrong way. When Nyhan bypassed him to get to Doc Flynn, more than a few guys noticed and laughed as they lighted up for chow.

"Tell me something, Doc. That all true what happened?" Commander Nyhan asked.

"I swear, he never hesitated. Virgil acted like it was nothing. Damn, I don't think I killed one commander, but Virgil moved like a deer, seriously, like a fucking deer."

Nyhan chuckled and grabbed the doctor's shoulder. "We appreciate what you guys are doing, and so do they." He paused, looking out on the chow line of crewmen. Nyhan then roared, "Captain Munro, front and center!"

Ha' greeted Stephen with her usual smile, instantly noticing his Silver Star. "This I want you to keep here for me," she said, placing her hand over his heart, being her playful self.

"Ha', I wrote my mother about you. About you going there before I am finished with this tour." Stephen had a plan to get Ha' back to the States, but it would require him to marry her first.

They would both like to be married in the church at her home, but logistically, that would not be possible. Instead, Stephen organized a small wedding and asked the chaplain to do the honors. Nyhan intervened and performed the ceremony himself, on the *Kirk*.

The news reached home, and soon the paperwork arrived. Emily was not unfamiliar with the red tape, and she plowed through efficiently.

"Frank, will you come with me to the airport to pick up Ha'?" she asked her husband.

"You know I will, dear. Lizzy too," he replied.

The Munros were excited as they waited in Cincinnati. Lizzy was talking to every soldier she saw, asking them if they knew her brother, a captain.

Emily stared at the gate door, wondering what exactly she was thinking taking home a strange Vietnamese girl. She thought of those three dogs in a box and would rather have those crazy hounds to the unknown, but she did know her son, and he would never marry a woman if he did not think it was the right thing.

As soon as Emily finished her thought, the first passenger emerged, his legs obviously stiff from the flight from LAX. Ha' had left Southeast Asia thirty-six hours prior, and she would be exhausted, Emily thought. After half the plane passed, Emily noticed a young girl helping an older man with his bag, her elbow trying to keep him upright.

"Frank," Emily said softly, looking over at the two.

Frank immediately saw he needed help, and Lizzy was right on his heel.

"Excuse me, are you Ha'?" Frank grabbed the bag he was trying to wrestle from Ha'.

Emily came over, shook her hand, and welcomed her. Frank suggested they head to the luggage carousel, and the five of them walked at a snail's pace to the escalator. Lizzy did not mind; she was walking in circles, asking Ha' all types of questions. Emily was surprised at how calm Ha' was and how she answered almost every question.

"You must be exhausted, Ha'. After we collect your luggage, we should reach our home in just over an hour. Of course if you're hungry, we planned on stopping," Emily said to her new daughter-in-law.

Ha' smiled and bowed her head. "Thank you, Mrs. Munro."

"Please, Ha', call me Emily. That's Frank, and of course, Lizzy!"

Frank carried the luggage to their car and had Ha' sit in the back with Emily. "Lizzy, you're shotgun." Frank decided to keep Lizzy away from the girl so he could get a word in. "So, Ha', how's our boy—I mean, our man doing over there?"

"Oh, Stephen, he is wonderful. He is a captain, as you know, very brave. He tells me not to worry, just to pray," she said.

Frank looked in the rearview mirror as he pushed the Chevy hard down the highway.

"Are you in a rush, soldier?" Emily said jokingly. "Was that your stomach, or do we need a new transmission? Hold on, Lizzy. Your dad is craving the meat loaf at the Blue Bell!"

Frank parked in front of the diner. He immediately opened the door for Ha', who was looking back at the statue in the square and then back at the diner.

"Come on, it's freezing out here," Lizzy said, standing at the door.

Frank held the door for his girls. The diner was quiet, with only two farmers at the counter and a family of four at a back table. Frank motioned for Emily to sit in a booth. He pointed to Ha' to do the same and sat right next to her. Lizzy looked disappointed, but Frank immediately asked her if she was having blueberry pie with whipped cream for dessert.

Frank wanted Ha' to know he would protect her, without using words, that she would be welcomed and safe in his presence. Ha' saw her husband in his father and felt at ease.

"What type of work did you do in Vietnam, Ha'?" Emily asked.

Ha' was looking at the menu, perplexed. "I think I will like a hamburger and fries," she said.

"Oh, you're just like my brother. I am getting the meat loaf and gravy," Lizzy stated.

Ha' looked at Emily. "My aunt owned a shop, a dress shop, but mostly I taught at the orphanage where I grew up."

Emily was fascinated with different cultures and wanted to know their similarities. One thing she learned quickly was that Ha' was willing to work. Frank kept on butting in, asking about his son's missions and any other action he had told her about.

Ha' was not sure what to say. "One time, when four men came to hurt me, Virgil—I mean your Stephen—he saved me. He could have killed them, but he took them to Cambodia instead."

"What? Cambodia? What men?" Frank asked sharply.

"SVA soldiers. They beat and rape my friend, my family. Virgil, he took them away."

"Oh, I knew it! Our kid is a crazy bastard, Emily. I told you he would find trouble."

"No, Virgil in no trouble. Everyone loves him much, he famous," Ha' said reassuringly.

Emily smiled as she looked at the menu. "Famous, all right," she said under her breath. "I imagine he is a lot like his father."

Suddenly, a chubby waitress in a blue apron pushed through the shining door to the kitchen. "Hey, folks, I hope you like pie," she said joyfully as she strode toward their table, pen in hand.

Ha' watched every move, trying to study the new culture. There had been many times when she was with her Virgil that she dreamed about America. During some of their conversations, she pictured a place just like the Blue Bell.

"Why do you call my brother Virgil?" Lizzy asked Ha' before she could order.

"Lizzy, wait until she's finished ordering, please," Emily said routinely.

Lizzy sat impatiently, building small building with the cubes of sugar. Ha' looked over at Lizzy, who hadn't a care in the world. Thousands of young girls she knew would give anything to be in Ha's position. A safe place to live, loving family, considerate men, and carefree children.

"Lizzy, we call him Virgil because he says he's like a TV show," Ha' replied.

"Lizzy, honey, guys—well, soldiers—often pick nicknames. Sometimes based on appearance, where they are from, how they sound...I guess they think your brother looks like that sailor on *McCain's Navy*," Frank explained.

Emily blushed; both her Stephen and husband looked like Virgil.

"What did they call you in the war, Daddy?"

"Sergeant, mostly," Frank said with a smile, then reaching across the table with his finger and sticking it in her collarbone, making her squirm.

"You two stop that," Emily scolded. "Ha', don't mind those two. They are joined at the hip, as you will see."

Ha' smiled at them. Lizzy continued asking Ha' question after question, and both Frank and Emily just let it go. They could learn more from listening.

What they learned was that Ha' had a hard life, but she was not bitter. She accepted her situation and, with the help of the sisters, learned to carry her cross. Ha' explained that there were so many children that were so much worse off who had experienced more horror, so she was grateful.

Emily and Frank held hands as they drove home. Lizzy and Ha' were still chatting in the back seat.

"Dad, are you going to see if that big buck is in the field?" Lizzy asked as they rounded the corner at Fisher's Farm.

Frank just looked back at her in the mirror.

"Come on, Dad, we're almost there! Ha' wants to see it!" Lizzy begged.

He glanced back at Ha', who was looking back at him. "Okay, but just a quick look."

"Frank," Emily said, "we're not in that truck of yours."

Frank eased Emily's '64 Impala down the steep dirt drive. He managed not to scrape the bottom of the transition off Route 3. "Okay, it is primetime, ladies," he said with excitement. "It will be dark in a half-hour."

"Look, Dad!" Lizzy had spotted two does feeding opposite each other in the field near the Fishers' barn.

Frank drove slowly as the rolling field of barley dipped out of sight. "Where the two hills meet is where he will come from," he said, pointing, and he continued driving.

Several does and a few young bucks were out in the back field, chasing one another like it was already rut.

"Should be any week now, Emily, and rut will be on," Frank commented, watching the deer.

"Oh, I am ready to be a tree-stand widow again if you just don't obsess over this one deer," she said playfully.

"Aww, you know me, Em. I will get us a nice one!"

Frank found a flat spot to turn the car around. As he did, he noticed that all the bucks ran from the rear hay field. "Okay, watch the wood line, girls." He shut the car off, and they all stared at the wood line some three hundred yards out.

Sure as Christmas, a massive whitetail buck stepped out into a dark low spot by a thick honeysuckle vine. Frank felt his heart beat stronger and commented, "Now that's a buck!" He had estimated that the male deer was about seven years old, 14 points typical, and well over 250 points in today's standards of measurement.

"Dad, you think Mr. Fisher will let us hunt here this year?" Lizzy asked her father.

"God, I hope so," Frank said humbly.

They all watched as the buck began to rub its huge antlers on an alder bush.

"No way he is leaving here, what with all the does we have seen recently. We've got to ask him eventually, right, Lizzy?" said Frank.

"Yeah, or just sneak in," Lizzy said.

"Frank, see what you teach your daughter? God, I swear, you two! Sometimes I think I have four kids!"

Frank started the Chevy, and the four of them drove quietly out of the farm. Frank shifted through the gears and beeped as he drove past the house, just in case someone was watching them.

"Maybe if I can get your mother to make some of her famous peach cobbler, Lizzy, we can go see Mr. Fisher tomorrow," Frank said with a smirk.

Short

Stephen relaxed in the shade of the 24's canopy. It was late in the day when he began drifting in and out of his fantasies. He was lost in the smell of the locals burning brush, mostly palm fronds.

What he did not know was that back at the Dominican Sisters of Peace Mission, Sister Aiyana Limgo of Cebu City in the Philippines was lighting incense before the altar and began to pray. She had always been close with her younger brother, but this was especially true while he was fighting the Japanese. She remembered the name Munro from his letters and asked the sisters about him. The mother told her what she needed, and through mail back home, she began putting the pieces together. That afternoon, she prayed in earnest.

It was at 15:00, the hour of the Divine Mercy, when Stephen reached for the rosary beads hanging from a clip. His crew had gone to mess, so Stephen grabbed the beads, knelt down under the gunnel, and began to pray. The sisters had taught him their prayers, and since they were rhythmical, he began thumbing the beads and making the sign of the cross.

He began, "Eternal Father, I offer you the body and blood, soul and divinity of your dearly beloved Son, our Lord, Jesus Christ, in atonement for our sins and those of the whole world." Moving his fingers from each of the ten consecutive beads, he prayed, "For the sake of His sorrowful passion, have mercy on us and on the whole world."

Stephen thought hard about every soul he had met and perished. From Charlie T to the guy he and Doc humped off Hill 227. He was near the end of his prayers when, looking up, he began to see the sky transfix into a transparent cell of moving creatures. Each looked like translucent bamboo, and between each ring, other beings resembled nutcracker soldiers.

Stephen watched as these figures marched in rhythm. As he stared at this vast ocean of soldiers, he couldn't help but notice the stern look on their faces, each staring in the direction of where Cambodia lay. Quietly kneeling at the foot of these giants, Stephen allowed his mind to ask humbly, "Are you angry at me?"

As this thought had just finished formulating in his brain, one of the soldiers stuck his head through the tubelike cell, filling a quarter of the sky. It looked Stephen straight in the eye and winked at him, its huge face scrunched up, revealing a giant smile.

Stephen felt a rush of inspiration like he had never felt before. The sky turned to a brilliant blue once again as he absentmindedly crushed the rosary beads. "Holy God, holy mighty one, holy immortal one, have mercy on us and on the whole world," he finished.

No sooner had Stephen rose to his feet than commotion erupted next to the Vietnamese Hilton. One of the fisherman was trying to pull his daughter's hand free from a blocky man named Chow Toe. Toe was not a local; rather, a Mong who would wander into villages, taking young girls and turning them into prostitutes. He had established quite an unsavory reputation for himself and seldom took no for an answer. Like any pimp, he prayed on the weak, which made any man with a soul despise him.

Stephen raced down the dock past the guard on duty and leaped over the gate. Heading down the road to the Hilton was a jeep with two lieutenants and a captain from the *Kirk*. They could see the panic as they pulled up. Toe was pulling the young girl as if she were a dead dog.

Stephen quickly stepped around a fish cart behind Toe and slapped the side of his head with his closed hand. Instantly Toe released his prey.

The men in the jeep watched wide-eyed as Stephen proceeded to twist Toe up in a half nelson, slamming him face-first in the compacted dirt. Running almost horizontally, he screwed Toe's face into the ground, causing the three men to head in his direction.

Stephen had managed to blow out Toe's eardrum, bestowing excruciating pain on the predator. "You piece of shit, Toe, I heard about you!" he bellowed as he continued to grind his face into the dirt. "I should break your fucking neck, you maggot!" Stephen said slowly as he strained Toe's neck with his own hair.

"You want us to call the Military Police, or are you going to ride him out of town?" the captain asked.

Stephen looked up at the three men watching. Several fishermen had gathered around him as well.

"I'm serious, Sailor," the captain now said.

Stephen didn't let Toe go, but he did stop grinding in his face. He squinted and, for the first time, noticed that the man speaking was a captain. "Sir, this pimp piece of shit has been taking young girls and turning them out. These people count on us to protect them!" Stephen was breathing heavily and was still willing to snap Toe's neck.

The whole market had gathered around the two men on the ground. The girl who had been dragged was clinging to her father and weeping.

"Give me that jeep for twenty minutes, and I will get rid of him, sir," Stephen said.

The captain looked around; he was all too familiar with guys like Toe. He was not here for hearts and minds; he was there for his soldiers. It was his third tour, and he had just been assigned to the Hilton along with two new surgeons.

The driver of the jeep ran down to tell them that the MPs were on their way.

"Did you call them, you prick?" Munro asked over Toe's weeping and moaning.

"No, I swear, Virgil!"

"Virgil? So you're the guy I'm here to replace," the captain then said.

Stephen continued holding Toe until the MPs arrived. They were all swarmed by chattering South Vietnamese men and women who were defending Stephen, and one MP even recognized Toe.

"Mr. Toe," he said with authority. Stephen pulled him up and faced him at the soldier. "You look like you fell down!" The men began to chuckle, as did the villagers, after some translation.

Stephen pushed Toe at the MP and was prepared to face the music. His heart began pounding as his rage-filled adrenaline began subsiding. "God," he said to himself in disappointment, "I just felt the most joy I could ever imagine just moments ago. I'm sorry."

A soft woman's voice seemed to come from above his head. "Heaven, Stephen, is never-ending joy."

Stephen was so wrapped up in his recent rapture, and then his anger in wanting to kill Toe, that it didn't register that he had a replacement coming for him. He was seventeen days short, and Nyhan wanted him on his hip until then.

"So, Virgil, you mind I call you Virgil?" the captain asked.

"Nope," Stephen replied.

"Where's your crew? I would like this to go smooth." Captain Robert Cabbrol handed Stephen his marching orders. "Nyhan told me he would give you some time, but he wanted you in that jeep by 18:00. We've got just over two hours."

Stephen gathered his gear and made a sweep of the ship. He stopped in to say goodbye to Doc Flynn and even managed to say a few kind words to the cocky Doc Smalls.

Everything was happening too fast. His crew wasn't back yet, and he began to see it was not by chance.

"TJ, my brother, make sure you tell the boys I love them. Don't be a fuck and not look me up when you get home, man." Stephen gave TJ a big hug and headed for the jeep.

"Virgil, the crew of the Seawolf just got a call to fly their commanding officer to the *Kirk*! Fuck that jeep," TJ said. "You're going with us!"

Stephen took his last look at the Hilton as the Wolf banked east. The *Kirk* was twenty-five miles out, cruising in safe water. The twenty-eight miles upriver from the Hilton was a twenty-minute ride.

When they hit the beach, Stephen looked back at Vietnam. The huge delta, flooded with activity, faded rapidly. TJ signaled Stephen that he had smoke for him and smiled from ear to ear.

Stephen stepped from the quarters he was sharing with a young seaman ensign. He was fresh from Virginia and green as a cucumber. The boys of the *Kirk* all knew Stephen as a likable guy and he was admired for his courage. He had shared some of his stash with a few of the gunners his first night on the *Kirk*. Since then, his 6 had a lot of action.

Stephen wasn't going to try to smuggle any of his Thai stick back to the States. He had already decided to sell what he had, and he spent a few hours rolling up joints. He hid his stash in the toolroom, where they stored the Hue batteries among other things. Armor boxes were watertight, so he filled two boxes with his stash.

In his first week on the *Kirk*, he made $1,200 and still had one container to go. Four days out, Stephen was down to two rows, equating to about sixty joints. He thought about what he could barter the rest for. He had lost his AK-47 and had always wanted to take one home. There were slim pickings on the *Kirk*, but he did manage to trade a corpsman for a SKS.

The *Kirk* departed the waters of the South China Sea and headed for Honolulu. Stephen was glad the SKS only cost him fifteen joints, about seventy-five dollars, and so was the rest of the crew who would go out and toke in places where the breeze was prevailing. Nyhan knew his crew smoked; he just never knew how much or how often.

Their trip back to the States was relaxing. The crew was a mix of short-timers and fresh meat. Stephen spent a lot of free time hanging with the veterans. Nyhan had a few light duties for him, mostly classroom stuff, training the men in brown-water navy tactics. Most guys who volunteered and spent time in combat were worn-out by their second year.

Stephen had yet to share his intense vision with anyone; however, in that moment, as he was kneeling by his gunnel, Stephen had been changed forever. It had eliminated any doubt in his mind whether or not God was real. He felt blessed not to just be alive but for God not being angry with him. The vision he saw gave him an internal smile.

Stephen had spent the last fourteen days thinking of that sky and the ethereal woman's voice comfortably telling him that "heaven is never-ending joy." He was even happy when Nyhan told him that Chow Toe, the predator, was shot while trying to escape. Having the clarity that there are absolutes set a fire to his conviction.

Stephen spoke freely to Nyhan. They were twenty miles out, and there were volcanic mountains on the horizon. "I want to thank you for looking out for me, Commander. I know it must be difficult for you to lose your men, sir."

Nyhan shared some personal stories about the men he had lost and missed the most.

"Sir, they are all fine now. I am certain," Stephen disclosed. "Everyone is where they are supposed to be. I've learned that firsthand."

Both men looked at each other, understanding what it was like to have been in battle.

"Kinda makes my job a bit insignificant, doesn't it?" Nyhan said.

"Not at all, sir. I don't believe it's destiny that guides us," Stephen said. "I believe it is our faith in our beliefs that guides us."

Nyhan thought briefly. "Faith like at church or in prayer?"

"No. Faith in our skills to perform. In our abilities, our equipment, and our leaders." Stephen paused, then said, "I am not staying in the Navy or Marines, sir." He swallowed hard. "But if you ever need me, if anything happens where you need a good boat driver, sir—"

"No, Virgil, we are getting out of South Vietnam, and that whole place will suffer."

Both men stood silently, imagining life beyond their tours in Vietnam.

Home for the Hunt

Stephen stepped off the Californian flight 220 plane onto the frozen tarmac. Winter had come early to Southeast Ohio, and the Greater Cincinnati Kentucky Airport was not ready for it. The cold felt good on his face as he walked into the airport wearing his dress blues. No one saluted him, and barely anyone had even made eye contact with him on his flight home, but Stephen paid no mind. He knew that he had more joy waiting for him at home than could fit in that 767.

Stephen was heading for the carasal when he heard a familiar voice yell, "Virgil!" He looked up just in time and saw his beautiful wife, Ha', holding hands with Lizzy as they ran to greet him.

Frank had stayed in the Chevy while Emily went in to see her son. He would never fully know the worry or fear a mother experienced when her child was at war. The relief she felt in that moment as she stared at her son was overwhelming. Holding his wife and sister's hands, Stephen quickly moved toward his mother, and when they embraced, Emily broke down. No words were spoken; she just needed to feel her son breathe in her arms.

"Ma, I'm fine! Ma, come on, let's get out of here. I'm starving!" he said, smiling at his tearful mother.

Frank pulled the '64 up to the curb and proudly told the attendant, "I'm picking up a war hero!" Frank popped and opened the trunk. He could see his family coming toward the car through the glass. He couldn't help but notice the look of bliss on Emily's face as she smiled and wiped away her tears. Frank stuck out his hand, but his son walked right into his arms instead.

"Dad, I missed you," Stephen said, squeezing him tight like he had a million times before. Frank immediately began to well up. "Oh, not you too, Dad," Stephen said, patting his father on the back.

Stephen hadn't had a chance to properly kiss his wife, so he opened the door for his mother and Lizzy and then held up Ha' on the curb so she was closer to his height. She looked stunning in a short polyester dress and hoop earrings. Stephen grabbed his woman with one arm, dipped her, and kissed her passionately.

"Let's go, you lovebirds," Frank called out.

"Dad, are we going to stop at the Blue Bell? I've been craving their meat loaf as soon as I smelled those burgers at the airport," Lizzy asked.

Frank just looked in the rearview mirror and smiled.

The Animals were playing in the background. "Dad, can you turn this up?" Steve asked. As he held his woman in his arms, they sang along to the chorus.

Stephen and Ha' took over a small farm overlooking the Muskingum River in Beverly, Ohio, near Coal Run. The slow-moving brown water reminded Ha' of her home in Vietnam.

It was the summer of 1976. Elton John was the top rock star of the day, and the country was celebrating its 250th year of independence from her tyrannical cousins, the British. The war in Vietnam had been over for almost a year, and the smash new TV show *Charlie's Angels* had made its debut.

Steve drove through McConnelsville on his way to Marietta to see his folks. His green 1969 GMC was clean as a whistle and gleamed in the day's sunlight. His father had helped him with the engine swap from a straight 6 to a 327, 300-horsepower V8. The truck sounded so good to Stephen he hardly ever tuned in to the radio, but on this July 1, he was glad he did.

WIBA in Maddison was running a commercial for a huge firework display in Wheeling, West Virginia. Wheeling was about seventy miles up the Ohio River.

New Chris-Craft 53-ft. Constellation. Choose from twin or triple engines or twin or triple Diesels to 800 h.p. speeds to 29 m.p.h. A magnificent ocean-going beauty, with everything you could ask for in yachting luxury.

Stephen had intended to arrive at his family's house to help with their July 4 celebrations, but now, he was about to throw a monkey wrench in the plan.

The cobble under his wheels made him smile as he sat up in the seat, peering around the boathouse. Instantly their black Lab, Molly, waddled up from the marina. "Hey, you fat girl, you!" Stephen said as he bent over to pet her.

Molly was a full-breed Lab whom he jokingly referred to as a crumb hound, one time eating the cane out of the sweet corn in Emily's garden. She was so lovable that every customer on the river would bring her a treat.

"Hey, Dad."

Frank was grinding a mooring ball when Stephen pulled up. "Hey, Steve." Frank put down his grinder and walked to meet his son.

"Your dog is way too fat, Dad."

"Did you drive all the way here just to tell me that?" Frank was smiling, his face speckled with rust.

"Dad, I heard they were having a huge Fourth of July celebration in Wheeling, and I think we should get your boat ready for a family trip, instead of the usual family backyard barbecue. What do you think?" Stephen suggested.

Frank did not have to think long. He was almost finished with his project boat, a gorgeous '55 Chris Craft Constellation he bought at an auction over a year ago. It had suffered a small fire in the galley, but it didn't ruin the main panel.

It would require the whole family to pitch in, and Frank brought it up to Emily and Lizzy at dinner. Lizzy, now a beautiful young woman, was waiting to ask if her boyfriend, Cas, could come for the Fourth.

"Before you two get us all going in five different directions, I invited Matt and his family this year," Emily stated. The table was quiet. No one commented on her news.

Finally, Lizzy changed the subject. "So we are going to fix Dad's boat for the trip up the Ohio?" She smiled at her brother for making the suggestion in admiration.

Frank let Stephen take the lead on finishing the wiring of the helm and the new electronics. He had Ha' come down and stay until the Fourth, promising her he would run back and forth to the farm to feed the cows and chickens.

Ha' had learned to sew from her aunt and was better than most. Frank had acquired a heavy-duty sewing machine years back and spent a few hours readying her up. Frank and Ha looked over the cushions that were smoke-stained and water-damaged.

Frank had his yacht running with hot wires, and he was confident in her structure, glad he was able to acquire the vessel in the winter auction. Frank and Stephen replaced what had been damaged in the fire on their days off, and now there were only a few finishing touches needed.

Emily pulled up and told Ha' that she needed to come with her, and they took off up the driveway in Emily's Chevelle. The triple-black '71 Chevelle had a factory 396 four-speed, and Emily would try hard not to throw gravel when she eased off the clutch. Ha' loved Emily; she was a strong woman with a fun side.

Emily saw the material her husband picked up at a rug shop in Zanesville, and it was awful. "Ha', we're going to pick up some material for our boat. They have half a day of wiring in front of them, and we don't want them in our way," she said, laughing as she ran through the gears of her Chevy. "Oh, and I told Frank to have Stevie put that sewing machine in the salon, where we will be working when they are finished."

Ha' just smiled and said, "Okay, thank you, Emily."

Emily stopped at several dress shops and upholstery places in Marietta. During their errands, Ha' asked her what they called their yacht. "Virgil says you have to name it after a woman. Why is there no name on it?"

Emily was told they removed it at the auction because it was offensive. The previous owners from Delaware named her *Peace Queer*. "Let's try and come up with a name for her while we are out," Emily suggested as they stopped for lunch at Kreskie's. "We used to have a boat called the *Annabelle Rose*, a real riverboat. I told Frank to name it after her, but he said he wanted it to be special."

"I like *Emily Rose*," Ha' said as she sipped her tea.

"Stevie told me that you are working at his friend's drive-through store?" Emily asked.

"Yes, and I like it. I've met so many nice people," Ha' said, looking down momentarily.

"Heidi and her husband are very nice. I have met them several times," Emily said, reassuring her and sharing in her joy.

Ha' told funny stories about some of her customers and how she would like the Maxwells to come on the trip to Wheeling.

Emily knew they had a large family, but her boat could hold eighteen people comfortably. "I think we should go to your store and ask them right now," Emily suggested while getting up to pay the bill.

"Please, Ms. Emily, may I please pay for lunch?" Ha' asked.

Emily knew that Ha' was proud she had a job and her own money. "Why, thank you, Ha'. That's sweet. I will go pull up the car."

Fireworks

The Munro marina was hoping that Fourth of July. Besides the obvious holiday boating, it was a Sunday after 10:30 a.m., and the church had let out. Most of the activity was within the Munro family.

Matt and his family had arrived late Saturday night while most of the house was asleep. Rachel was a spoiled brat from the east whose liberal ideology had been ingrained in her since she was a small child. Her elitist attitude was shared by her friends, resulting in their participation in the peace movement. Most of them were now teachers at universities, where their zeal for dominating sheep was tempered.

During those days of glory, a handful of the affluent took advantage of the masses who gathered to protest the war. Easily led and singularly issued, they manipulated, experimented, and praised their philosophies about a more perfect world.

Not everything was antiwar. They were also passionate about the assault on the environment, and Frank and Stephen respected and appreciated that aspect of their movement.

Rachel was awakened by Molly, who always barked when Frank first let her out in the morning. She was letting the world know that she was on duty. Rachel looked out the second-floor window to see her father-in-law walking toward the maritime flag post. He stood there, pausing with his folded flag. He remembered the first time he raised the flag at Camp La'gune. He also thought of his first sergeant and the friends he lost in battle.

Rachel couldn't see the tears form in Frank's eyes or how they twitched as they welled. She only saw him raise the flag stand and watch it in the still morning air. Rachel felt a brief surge of emotion. "That was strange," she thought out loud. She had seen hundreds of flags flying all over the country but hadn't ever actually seen one raised.

Frank was walking back when he noticed Rachel in the window and waved at her. Sheepishly she raised her right hand chest high and waved back. She felt as if she was spying on him. "God, this is awful," she said quietly as she sat on the corner of the bed, her husband, Matt, still fast asleep. "I'm always so anxious here," again, she said out loud to herself.

Rachel went in and checked on her son, Thomas, who was sleeping soundly. She was thinking about going back to bed until someone else woke up when the photographs crammed on the hallway wall caught her eye. Hanging were pictures dating back to the late 1800s of the Strongs, the river house, and their riverboat. She saw the coal barge crew's soot-stained faces, but what mostly stood out were their smiles. Decades of history in a few choice photos. Rachel noticed how impressively it was all laid out. She noticed the ribbon and metal frames of the decorated Strong men at the hall's end. Frank Munro's was presented in the center and full of color.

"Rachel," Emily said in a whisper, calling up the stairs. Rachel did not hesitate to proceed downstairs toward her. "I heard someone up. You know how these old floors are," Emily said with a smile. "They both sleeping?"

Rachel was trying to ease to the bottom of the stairs. "Yes," she said, and she began to follow Emily to the kitchen.

"Does he take after his father?" Emily asked as she poured Rachel a cup of coffee.

"In what way?" Rachel asked politely.

Emily handed her the cup. "Are they both cement heads in the morning?"

Rachel almost spit out her first sip as unexpected laughter overtook her. She tried wiping it before Emily saw. "Oh my god, I swear a train could roll through the bedroom and they would think it was just a breeze!"

"Yes, that's my Matty, all right! It is not such a bad thing, you know. Frank out there sleeps on eggshells, and if he hears the slightest noise, he is up and looking about."

"Is that because of the war?" Rachel asked.

"Oh, hell no! I met his family. They are all light sleepers. Frank, he would go on and on to tell me how difficult it was to sneak out of his parents' home to join his friends and smoke cigarettes."

Rachel felt at ease with Emily. It was probably because she was a confident woman who could cut right through the bullshit. "Can I help you with breakfast?" Rachel said in earnest.

"Yes, of course. I know Matty told me he is craving my blueberry muffins. Here." Emily handed Rachel a metal bowl and pointed in the direction of the blueberry bushes. "Over to the right before the boathouse, you will see them. We will need a whole bowl. I will start the mix."

Rachel was not the least bit a country girl. The only blueberries she had ever seen were in a green cardboard container with plastic wrap on them.

"Oh, Rachel, here." And Emily handed her a fresh cup of coffee. "Frank is near there somewhere. I usually bring him out his cup."

Frank was sitting on a bench overlooking the river. He was making his checklist for the trip to Wheeling. He and Stephen had taken the boat out for two hard runs, and it seemed as though they had her tuned and ready for the trip. The 671 twin-diesel riverboat was at the top of her class in '55, and what Emily and Ha' accomplished in a mere day and a half made her worthy of her former crown. Now Frank was just being his cautious self, making sure he had everything.

When Rachel handed him his coffee, without looking up, he said, "Thank you, dear," and when there was no reply, Frank was immediately taken aback by Rachel innocently standing before him. "Sorry, Rachel, I was..."

"It's perfectly fine, Mr. Munro—I'm sorry, Frank." Rachel was always nervous around Frank, even though he was a lighthearted man.

"Sorry? I'm the one who should apologize," he said, smiling. "Sit down, Rachel." And Frank moved over. "Where's Matt? Sleeping?" Frank asked her.

"Yes. He had a long drive. I was able to sleep some too," she responded.

"That kid, he could sleep through a bomb, I swear. Hardest kid to get to go to sleep, hardest kid to wake!"

Rachel laughed lightly.

"Little Tommy just like him?" Frank asked next.

Rachel smiled to herself at the similarities of her in-laws. "Yes, he is pretty much the same."

"Well, the heavy head is not a bad thing for you and Matty, if you know what I mean!" Frank nudged his shoulder into hers. "I see you have the dreaded blueberry bowl," he said sorrowfully. "Make sure it's full. I'm sure you were told," he said quietly and laughed, causing Rachel to laugh nervously. "Come on, I will help you. The quicker we pick them, the sooner we can eat!"

Frank showed Rachel his technique of finding a big clump of mostly ripe berries and pulling them into his palm. "Emily hates when I do it like this, and my dad is the same way. They pick each berry, takes forever, just make sure there are no greenies mixed in. Those are the unripened berries."

Frank walked along and explained how he had dug the bushes from his parents' home in Massachusetts twenty years ago and how there were two different types, early and late berries. They were picking the early berries, and he showed her the difference.

Rachel was still in her pajamas as the two rummaged through the bushes. Frank heard the sound of his son's truck and said, "Let's get these washed off, Rachel. Here, I have to meet Stevie in the driveway."

Rachel looked over at the empty driveway and then back at Frank. Suddenly, she heard the gravel and a low roar and then saw the green Chevy rolling down the drive. "I will, Frank, and thank you," she said as she climbed the steps.

"Hey, Dad, was that Rachel?" Stephen asked as his father approached.

"Yeah. We were just picking berries."

"Oh, nice. Mom making muffins?"

"Never mind. Do you have the plaque?" Frank asked.

Earlier, Stephen had names engraved and gold-leafed by the Coroza Sign Shop in Malta. "Mom's gonna love it, I swear!"

"Well, let's hope she does, or no muffins for us!" Frank joked.

The cookout began at noon, and several friends and family members were invited. Frank checked the river current twice before noon to make sure it was calm enough for them to take off. "Ah, 1.5 knots!" he said enthusiastically.

He planned to travel at 20 knots and expected their trip to take about three hours and twenty minutes one way. The fireworks would begin at nine thirty, so if they left at four, they would have no problem reaching Wheeling in time to see them.

Frank had the charcoal burning when his first guests arrived, a few folks who had boats of their own at the marina. Frank had one thing on his mind, getting Emily to the dock for the ceremony at three o'clock. With all the commotion going on at the party, she had forgotten the ship had yet to be named.

When the Maxwells arrived, Heidi was immediately met by Ha', who was happy her boss had arrived. She was eager to show her around, but first she helped with their food. Emily also saw them drive in and was heading out to greet them. Frank stopped her husband, Claud, and the two of them went off to the boathouse, only to emerge with a brand-new, handcrafted picnic table.

Everyone helped set out the food and shared in the cooking. Frank did not drink himself but did not mind if the others partook. The crowd was now well over fifty people, and Frank was now hoping that they all wouldn't want to come for the firework cruise.

Christening the Ship

Frank was not at all comfortable at speaking to a crowd, so he had Lizzy make the announcement. "Lizzy, let's try and make this as fair as possible, okay? It's only an hour or so drive by car—well, faster if your mother's driving—but an hour away by car and a four-hour drive upriver by boat are obviously two different things. Since a few of these people are going to drive up anyway, let's give them the choice to go one way and drive the other. I am comfortable with taking twenty-four, so let's see if the kids can go first, and then, well, the adults can cruise back."

Lizzy thought it over. "Okay, so when are we naming the boat?"

Frank just smiled. "We are having the naming ceremony at three o'clock, remember?"

"Yeah, Dad, so after, right?"

"Lizzy, just make everyone feel welcome. I'm going to get the new placard for our boat."

"What did you end up naming her, Dad?"

"You will see at three, Liz," Frank said, waving his hand and walking away.

He had covered the new placard with a picnic table cloth to disguise it from Emily. He called for Stephen but saw that he and Matt were fishing side by side on the far dock. Claud was close by, so he volunteered, and both he and Frank carried the sign down the grassy hill to the marina. Emily saw them and thought it was just another table.

Claud jumped on board where he and Frank had installed hooks for the placard. The two men reached over the stern and hooked up the eight-foot name. *Emily Rose* was outlined in gold and highlighted in red, the flat back engravings making it pop, and Frank couldn't be more pleased.

"Now I hope the pastor arrives soon," Frank said, looking at his watch. It was now two o'clock.

Suddenly, commotion could be heard. Stephen had hooked a big river catfish, and he and Matt were fighting to keep it from wrapping upon the piling. Matt saw a gaf in a boat still in its slip and jumped on board to retrieve it. He helped fend the line off the pier until it was time to gaf it. The brown water was swirling below the two as they laughed and carried on.

"Don't miss, Matt!" people in the crowd cheered. All the focus was on the two men fighting the fish.

"Now, Matt, now!" Stephen screamed.

Matt reached the half-hook into the thrashing water, and pressing the wooden handle, he felt the fish and pulled it up in a short, deliberate motion. "Got him!" he yelled.

Emily was now watching as her two boys wrestled the fish up onto the dock.

"My Virgil catch a fish?" Ha' said with a smile, then she headed down to see for herself.

Rachel and Emily were also smiling as the two boys carried the thirty-five-pound catfish to the cleaning table. Ha' gathered some spices and olive oil and headed for the pile of corn.

"What are you doing, Ha'?" Lizzy asked.

"Oh, Virgil will make everyone fish on the grill."

"Ugh, I hate fish!" Lizzy said while making a face.

"No, you see. Virgil knows how." Ha' took the fresh sweet corn on the table and began shucking. "Lizzy, we need twenty or so pieces just like this," she said, showing her a fresh leaf of husk.

Both of them pulled them apart carefully. Ha' walked over to her husband and whispered that she had the corn husks and spices for him. Stephen cut the fish into finger-thick strips.

"Okay, everyone, you're in for a real treat! My wife, Ha', has a special recipe she is going to share! Let's go over to the grill!" Stephen carried the tray of fillets over to the grill. Ha' had the corn husks laid out, and they both began laying the fish on top of them. Next came the olive oil, and then several spices. It took all only about a minute to prepare, and by this time everyone was watching.

Ha' began laying the husks on the grill, and each one immediately closed up, wrapping the fish in the oily spice. "Okay, five minutes, okay?" Ha' said as she moved each piece into place.

Emily was not a big fan of catfish, but it was fresh and it was her daughter-in-law's recipe. Stephen took the fish off the grill and put it onto plates. Lizzy and Ha' went around with plastic forks, giving everyone who was willing a sample. Frank took two for himself and sheepishly walked away.

Ten minutes before three, the local pastor arrived at the marina. "Hello, Emily," he said in a deep voice. Pastor Reynolds was serving in Marietta for just a few months and hardly knew a soul. He was invited to several celebrations for the Fourth but was most interested in stopping at the marina.

"I smell something familiar," he said as Lizzy passed by with her tray of fish.

"That's some fresh catfish my boys caught," Frank said, sticking out his hand.

"Here, Pastor." Lizzy handed him a plate and fork.

Frank looked at his watch; it was important for him for the ceremony to begin at three o'clock, so before Pastor Reynolds could have a second plate, he reminded him of their scheduled trip upriver. "Pastor, you're welcome to stay as long as you like. I would just like to get the ceremony underway now if we could."

The pastor was a few years younger than Frank, and he respected his tone. He started moving toward the boat.

"Everybody, please, if you could come down to the dock!" Lizzy yelled out.

Emily had a bottle of champagne on the porch and rushed in to get it. Still not even considering what the name on the boat might be, she gathered herself briefly and headed out back.

Lizzy was on the top deck of the vessel, overlooking the crowd. "My family wants to thank each and every one of you for coming today. My father, brother, mother, and sister-in-law worked hard these last few days getting this boat ready for today. My father is going to take her to Wheeling for the fireworks, as you have heard. Some of you are going by car, but my family would like to extend an invitation to twenty-four of you to accompany us. If some of you would like to split the ride, then more of us can share the experience."

Frank was proudly looking up at Lizzy as she continued with her speech.

"Now, years ago, my parents had my grandfather's old riverboat, the *Annabelle Rose*, right here in this spot, so my dad thought it would be sweet to name her the *Emily Rose*, after my mom."

Applause broke out as Lizzy called out her mother's name. Emily, looking up, saw the name on the stern for the first time as she walked to the bow. She held the champagne bottle tight, took a strong swing from it, and called out, "I christen thee *Emily Rose*," before exploding the bottle on her hull. More applause erupted from their family and friends as Emily was called onboard by her daughter.

Frank handed the pastor a bottle of holy oil. "Pastor, this oil is special. If you could bless my boat with this, especially the helm," he asked, and Pastor Reynolds was happy to do so. He and Frank made it to the upper deck, where he openly announced a blessing for their newly named yacht. Frank then escorted him to each and every room, asking him to bless them all while making the sign of the cross in oil over each door.

Pastor Reynolds did not see Frank in Mass but appreciated his faith in tradition. "Frank, did I taste Vietnamese spice in that fish?"

Suddenly, Ha' was standing in the doorway to the helm. "Yes, my daughter-in-law, Ha', cooked it," Frank replied.

Pastor Reynolds began talking with Ha' as Frank began showing off his boat to his guests. He gathered the party for the ride up and was explaining in detail how long it would take and what the plan was.

Most of the people there had never been on the Ohio River, let alone on a four-hour cruise, but the *Emily Rose* was a luxury liner for her time, and comfort wasn't an issue. Frank also took preparations for his crew. Of course, his sons were going, but he had been prepping Lizzy and two of her friends for the trip, Jenna and Melissa.

Ha' saw Emily shed a tear as she walked past her, trying to look busy. "Emily," she said with her soft voice, "I have something to tell you."

Emily stopped dead in her tracks, thinking for some reason that it was something awful.

"Virgil and me, we're having a baby," Ha' said.

Emily turned and held Ha', starting to cry through her smile.

Ha' continued, "We wanted to wait until everything here was—"

Emily did not want to hear why. "Oh, Ha', how could you keep this from me?" she said lovingly, then hesitated. "Okay, I won't tell anyone until after this day is over. God, I did not think it could be any better. Thank you, Ha'." Emily hugged her again tightly. "You know, Frank is up to something, I just know it. I have been trying to put my finger on it. Did he tell you he was naming her after me?"

Ha', surprised, looked at Emily. "No, not at all. Virgil said it was a secret, so I only asked him twice," she said, and they both laughed.

"I'm sure he has been busy with something. Maybe it has to do with Lizzy," Emily said, walking toward her daughter.

"Where are you three going?" she asked the girls as she approached.

"In to change for the trip, Ma'," Lizzy said and kept moving toward the house.

Still, Emily had no idea what they were up to but was now distracted by her new grandchild.

Frank, always the hard worker, was not ever without dreams of his own. A test run for his Pittsburg "booze cruise" was just the thing to keep hope alive, and Lizzy and her friends would help him seal the deal.

Upriver

Frank headed out with five crew members and twenty-four passengers north to Wheeling, West Virginia. With no rain in the Midwest for over a week, the debris and hazards were to a minimum as the Ohio washed down the lap streak planks. On deck, Frank had designed a portable bar by using a horse trough, full of ice, and a variety of beer porcupining out.

Stephen was busy running back and forth from the engine room for a quick visual to their stateroom, which was now doubling for beer and food storage. On deck and in the salon, the girls traded stations as their friends and customers enjoyed the ride upriver. Cas kept on volunteering to help, but Lizzy was shunning him. Frank noticed and had Stephen take him around and show him the main functions and safety measures.

Frank was a proud captain, and he kept his *Emily Rose* between wakes and coal barges as he pushed upriver, checking his wake behind him. Ha', Emily, and Rachel stayed behind but were going to meet their men in Wheeling. Matt also stayed to help clean up and was going to join the girls on the ride home.

Frank had his son take the wheel. He wanted to mill about and see how his plan was progressing. He told no one about this; he only told Lizzy he wanted to pay her and two friends to crew the boat for the trip. Now his gears were turning when he saw the boat at its capacity and how he could improve on his plan before telling Emily.

Steve gripped the wheel and steered for the center channel, avoiding a pressing tug's wash. The feel of the wooden wheel and the smell of the diesel were more than enough to stir up memories of Vietnam.

Claud walked into the wheelhouse and peered out of the window overlooking the bow. "Nice view, Stevie," he said sharply.

Stephen looked over.

"Why's your wife call you Virgil?"

Stephen and Claud chatted about the military. He was like Frank, a Korean War veteran, but spent most of his time assembling radio towers on the many ridges and islands east and west of the Korean Peninsula. They both had amazing experiences avoiding danger, living on the razor's edge. Claud was a good hunter, and the two men spent the next hours talking about deer hunting rather than war.

Frank eased the *Emily Rose* up to the fuel dock at Stimer's. They closed at 7:00 p.m., and it was 7:40 when they left the channel. Frank was barking orders to Stephen and Lizzy, who were putting out their bumpers. Frank eased her alongside the dock, and Stephen jumped onto it, securing the stern line on a cleat. Lizzy threw him the bowline as the momentum and tight stern pinched her in.

"Looks like you have done that before," a voice said from behind the pump shack as Stephen cleated the bowline.

He looked to see if he recognized the man, but he did not. "Steve Munro," Stephen said, walking toward him with his hand out.

"Jerry, Jerry Johnson," the man said, shaking his hand with a crooked grip. "You know they're closed," he said, referring to the fuel dock.

"Yes, we know. We're here for the firework display," Stephen said enthusiastically. He looked over to see a row of chairs that were set up perfectly to see the barge across the river where the display was to begin.

"Well, Jerry," Stephen said, "tonight, you and your guests are welcome on board the *Emily Rose*. My dad did secure this spot from Mr. Stimer, but I do see you were here first."

Jerry looked at him sideways.

"What's wrong, Mr. Johnson?"

"I don't think my wife and friends would like it very much, considering the activity on the upper deck."

"Well, there is plenty of room on the bow. Here, let me bring your chairs on board." And Stephen walked over to move the chairs.

"Wait now, my wife..." Jerry was in midsentence when Claud stepped off the boat and onto the dock.

"Hey, old Jerry, you giving Stevie a hard time?" Claud asked.

"Claud, now, don't you start with me!" Jerry said harshly.

Claud once had a run-in with Jerry down in McConellsville over a missing beer.

"What's going on down there?" Frank shouted from the flybridge.

"Nothing, Dad," Stephen said.

"This guy was just leaving!" Claud yelled up to Frank.

Stephen looked at the two of them and thought there was going to be a fight. Jerry was about sixty, and Claud fifty-five, but Jerry was weathered and no physical match for Claud.

Just then, Emily and the girls arrived. Heidi was with them and could see Jerry as soon as she stepped on the dock. "Claud, is that who I think it is?"

Jerry was now surrounded by the five women, all staring at him. Frank looked over the starboard side again to see his family below surrounding this old guy. "Hey, what the hell is going on?" Frank yelled down, breaking everyone's stare.

"This guy had his chairs set up here!" Heidi yelled.

"Hey," Frank said, "I had this set up with Mr. Stimer days ago!" Then, pointing at the bow, he said, "You want to watch, watch from there." And everyone but Heidi turned to see where Frank pointed.

Jerry walked over to his chairs and angrily folded one after the other, four in total. Claud took two and immediately walked up the ramp to the parking lot above. The lot was getting full, both with cars, trucks, and pedestrians. He could see Jerry struggling with the remaining chairs and helped him up the ramp. "Here, set them up here." He pointed near the railing. Claud was back on board in no time, escorting his wife up the steps.

"What was that all about?" Emily asked Heidi as they all made their way to the upper deck.

"Oh, that guy tried to beat us for a beer."

"Me too," Ha' said. "He argued with me one time, said 'You only give me five, only five.' I told him, I check his truck, he drove away swearing at me."

"That's the guy you were telling me about?" Stephen asked, passing his wife. "Well, I invited him on board. Glad now he refused!"

After the argument, Emily and Ha' took their places at the port side of the boat, overlooking the river and city skyline. The *Emily Rose* was elegantly lit, making it perfect for night viewing.

Stephen was talking to his mother when the first fireworks ignited off a barge, causing him to tighten briefly as if cognitively reinforced. With the skin raised on his neck, he turned to see the first of several hundred explosions.

Emily was holding her husband's hand but turned to check on her son and saw his hair still raised. Emily felt shame and sorrow simultaneously. How many men's deaths had she aided in? How many were now wounded or dead because of women like her? She tried to rationalize it as the fireworks burst in the air.

Emily watched as her two sons held their wives. Although her husband and son were warriors, they were still very good men, caring and loving in their own manner. It wasn't until the grand finale when the tugboat horns erupted and applause sounded that Emily snapped out of her funk.

What am I doing? she thought to herself. *I did what I thought was best, and I did what I knew was best for my country. Not with guns and knives, but with honor nonetheless.* Emily thought of the soldiers like her son, her husband, and her friends. *We all have our crosses to bear,* she thought to herself, closing her mind.

Looking at the delight of those on board, she turned to her husband. "Frank, that was wonderful!" Emily said as she kissed her man. Frank hit the horn on the *Emily Rose* like he was a teenager. "Okay, let's take her home!"

Into the Eighties

Senator Cole was a senior senator who remained in position to assist the defense department. With control of budgetary spending, he made sure CUF was appropriately funded. He also kept close records on the soldiers who survived the fields of Vietnam and was amazed at his very own sperm soldiers' accolades both in and out of battle.

As soldiers, they were courageous, and in treatment they were steadfast. On average, they were 70–80 percent less likely to have what was known at the time as the thousand-yard stare—shell shock, battle fatigue, or as it's now known, posttraumatic stress disorder.

Joe looked into the soldiers' lives as best as he could. He was successful at supplying several sperm banks with black and Latin sperm, but there again he was amazed at how many parents wanted blond hair and blue eyes. This, of course, was not always the case, and Senator Cole appropriated research money into the scientific research in human DNA, specifically the X and Y chromosomes.

Research was promising, and scientists discovered the different strands of DNA and what that could mean to the human condition. Cloning was all the rage in Europe as the Italians cloned the first sheep they named Dolly. Not the progression Senator Cole expected, but it was a new field, and exploration seemed necessary, if not eminent.

Melissa walked into Joe's office with a few papers for him to review. With her tight white blouse and even tighter navy-blue skirt, Joe's concentration was blown when her silhouette broke the doorway.

"Senator, if you could," she asked.

"Oh, yes, I'm sure of it," he said aloud, laughing.

"Did I miss something, sir?" she asked.

"No, but let me read this first, okay?" he said to her while looking over his reading glasses.

Melissa was in her early thirties, not married, and apparently not looking, although she must have enjoyed the attention she received on the train to DC every morning.

"Looks good, Melissa, as usual." Joe signed the papers and handed them back to her. "Melissa, now if you could, I need to reach Mr. Lavenger. I put in a call earlier. Please, if he calls, send someone for me." And he walked out with the freshly signed documents.

Lisa put the paper down and looked over at Mark, who was stripping the line off a fishing reel in the living room. "Hey, hun, have you heard from the Coles at all? Joe was supposed to call." Lisa held her stare until her husband looked at her.

"What?" he finally asked.

"You have to do that up here in the living room?" Lisa inquired.

"Well, I am still living, baby," he said wisely.

"Mark, Mark, Mark, always the smart-ass."

"You know what they say about that, don't ya, Lise?"

"Yes, Mark," she replied, and then they said together, "Nobody likes a smart-ass, but everyone likes a nice one!" Mark laughed, and Lisa went back to reading the paper.

"We're going to head to the Keys for a few days, you know, Lise."

"Thought you said you hadn't talked to Joe," Lisa said.

"I didn't. I'm telling him we're going. I rented us a place above the marina on Marathon Key. Fishing should be good, Lise."

Lisa always marveled at the excitement Mark had for fishing. "Mark, you know it's going to be hotter than hell down there, so make sure your little spot has air-conditioning."

"Yes, dear," he said sarcastically, then immediately laughed and apologized. Not a minute later, the phone rang. "Saved by the bell," he said, getting up for the phone.

"Hey, Joe, we were just talking about you," Mark said into the receiver, and the two went on and on about their fishing trip. "You know we got to meet that one guy, then we are free and clear," Mark said, referring to a Navy contract with Zodiac.

"Yes, good idea scheduling it for the Keys, Mark," said Joe on the other end.

"Well, no matter the weather, we can run her inside or out," Mark said happily. "Okay, see you Thursday." And Mark hung up the phone.

Lisa, too late, said, "Oh, tell Joe and Robin hello for me."

"Oops, sorry, hun," Mark said, walking toward her.

Lisa was ten years younger than Mark and, at fifty-five, still had quite a nice shape. Walking the steep five-hundred-foot driveway for the paper every day helped keep her that way.

Mark was no slouch, although he decided last year for the first time to have the firewood split and delivered. He opted to cancel the order this year because he had gained ten pounds. Now a few weeks into wood detail, he was just starting to get into shape.

"I can't wait to get you with the top down, Lise," he said lovingly to his wife.

"Why wait?" Lisa said sharply as she raised her glass of wine and smiled seductively.

Mark looked at the pile of fishing line coiled on the floor, bassinet, and couch.

"Looks like a huge pile of pubic hair," Mark said aloud, causing Lisa to start laughing.

"Not mine," she said between breaths.

"Lise, I never should have stripped these reels up here," Mark said, surrendering.

"Well, don't take too long," she said, walking toward the bedroom.

"Lise, wait, throw me a knife or something!"

Graduation

The summer of 1994 was one of change for the Munros. The youngest to enter the armed service was leaving for the naval academy in Pensacola. The USNA had a special squadron known as the Naval Academy Training Squadron, or VT-NA. It was a professional training organization at the United States Naval Academy dedicated to the cultivation and training of our nation's future naval aviators.

This would give midshipmen the opportunity to be selected to fly jets, a must first step in becoming a fighter pilot. On board, they would learn every aspect of a mission, from aircraft and readiness to air traffic control. Some four hundred would be selected out of ten thousand, so to shine one needed to have a diverse background.

Max Munro stood before his fellow graduates, his shoe-bristle flattop shining in the sun, as was his smile. Ha' was proud of her son but, as a mother, worried to death. Frank and Emily were there and stood tall during the ceremony.

Midshipman Max Munro was entering the training academy at eighteen years old. His two years in the NJROTC program elevated his entry rank, and his experience on the water was evident to his superiors immediately. Max had one thing going for him over the other cadets: he had the highest score on the college admission test that year.

"Midshipman, what are you, like, sixteen?" said a cadet who was sitting next to Max at mess. "Well?"

"Okay, hotshot," Max said, putting down his bowl of cereal, "let's go. First one to box a compass owes fifty pushups."

Most everyone in the mess hall heard fifty and wanted in. There are thirty-two points to a compass that needed to be called in order.

"Okay, you first," Seaman Riley said aloud.

Max stood up and ripped off all thirty-two in exact order, no mistakes, and got twenty-two the second time. Riley shook his red head in disbelief and walked out. Max was a quick thinker and daring like his father, but built more like his mother. At five foot six, he weighed 156 pounds, but all gristle. Gristle that, in the weeks to come, will be tested.

About the Author

Evets Ornum was born in Brockton, Massachusetts, into a loving, hardworking family. He was fortunate to have parents who put family first, he and his brothers and sisters had no reason not to repeat what they learned. His mother, a singer for fifty years, took him with her to work as a young child. She sang for funerals and weddings in the city they grew up in. His father owned a bakery, where he provided bread and rolls to the school system and several local restaurants. Blessed to have such a hardworking father, he and his siblings enjoyed their summers in Kingston Bay, where the author learned to fish.

CPSIA information can be obtained
at www.ICGtesting.com
Printed in the USA
LVHW022302020820
662216LV00001B/42